MISSOURI
Brides

Hope is Renewed in Three Historical Romances

Mildred Colvin

BARBOUR
PUBLISHING

Cover Image: Anne Rippy/Stone/Getty Images

Published by Barbour Publishing, Inc., P.O. Box 719, Uhrichsville, Ohio 44683, www.barbourbooks.com

Our mission is to publish and distribute inspirational products offering exceptional value and biblical encouragement to the masses.

 Member of the
Evangelical Christian
Publishers Association

Printed in the United States of America.

Dear Reader,

Thank you for selecting *Missouri Brides* to read. I hope you enjoy these three stories based on the early pioneers who settled near Cedar Creek in Missouri. In fact, Cora's life is based on the stories my mother told of her great-grandmother. As I thought about my great-great-grandmother's family moving to the wilderness of southern Missouri, Cora Jackson and her family began to develop.

When I write, I can never stick to the original story, so only bits and pieces of Cora's story are remotely true. For instance, there is an account of someone actually taking shelter during a storm in a hollow tree located somewhere near the Cedar Creek area, and the pioneers did purchase land in Cedar County, Missouri, for $1.25 per acre and started building their homes there in 1832.

A visit to the historical society and museum in Springfield, Missouri, helped me create a setting for my book that closely resembled the small town of Springfield that existed in 1836, where Eliza made her home.

While the tiny village of Ivy that Deborah visited with Dane is the product of my imagination, there was at one time a settlement in the same area by that name.

I believe at some point in their lives, my ancestors, like Cora, came to the realization that being good is not enough. Cora fought against the gentle call of her Savior until her eyes were opened to her very personal need of salvation, and she put her faith and trust in Jesus. As one life touched another, so God's grace moved through Cora's family and neighbors. My prayer is that as you read *Missouri Brides*, you too will turn your life over to Jesus and let Him be Lord over all, as you touch other lives for His glory.

Mildred Colvin

CORA

Dedication

To the memory of my mother, Odie Evelyn Conner.
"Favor is deceitful, and beauty is vain: but a woman that feareth the Lord,
she shall be praised." "Her children arise up, and call her blessed;
her husband also, and he praiseth her." Proverbs 31:30 and 28.
Mom's great-grandparents settled in what would become
Cedar County, Missouri, in 1832.
These early pioneers were the inspiration for Cora and her family.

Chapter 1

Autumn 1833

Cora stood in brown, rippling prairie grass up to her waist. The afternoon sun sat low on the horizon. She looked from the ribbon of water on her right to the distant forest on her left. Her gaze swept past the autumn beauty, seeking some indication of human habitation. Her heart sank. There was none.

She watched her family unload necessary supplies out of the wagons that had brought them from their home in St. Louis. She waded through the grass to her father. "This isn't your land, is it?"

Orval Jackson's light hazel eyes shone with the pride of ownership, and he nodded. "This is it."

"But, Father, there's nothing here." She grabbed a handful of grass and broke it off. "Look at this. It's so thick you can't see the ground. We can't live like this. We need a house. And a yard. There are no streets. No town. No people." Her voice faded as she fought tears.

Her father frowned. "I know it isn't St. Louis, Cora. It's our dream. Over a hundred acres of Jackson land. We'll make a home here." He spread his arms wide, taking a deep breath. "Smell the fresh air. Fill your lungs with it. Isn't this better than that stuffy candle shop? Than St. Louis?"

Cora shook her head. "I miss home."

He patted her shoulder. "This is new country, Cora. Soon others will come. One day you'll have your town. We'll set up camp now and build a shelter tomorrow. You'll get used to country life."

But she wouldn't. Not without George. All her life he had been next door. Always ready to play and, when they were older, eager to plan the day they would marry.

"Here." Her younger sister, Eliza, shoved a pile of bedding into her arms. "If you're just going to stand around watching the rest of us work, the least you can do is make up your own bed."

Cora made a face at her sister's back. She looked at her family. Her older sister, Vickie, and her husband, John, were eager to farm their own land, and they already had one young son, Nicholas. To Cora's brother, Ben, just one year older than she, the move was an adventure. Eliza, her precocious sister, always agreed with their parents, so her opinion didn't count. Their younger brother, Lenny, was too young to have an opinion. That left Cora in the middle, and she wanted very much to go home.

Cora barely avoided colliding with her little brother and nephew as they ran past. She dropped the quilts on the ground near the other bedrolls and straightened as a cold gust of wind crossing the creek blew against her face. Winter was coming and they had no home. George had promised to come for her at Christmas, but right now George and Christmas seemed far away. She walked with dragging steps to see what else she could do to help.

❦

For three days the men cut trees and worked to build a temporary shelter scarcely twelve feet square. A blanket covered the south-facing door. Foot traffic flattened the prairie grass floor. Mother's wooden rocker filled one corner. Her old cast-iron cookstove took up the other corner with a small wooden table beside it. One bed had been set up for the girls. The rest slept in the wagons. The ceiling was made of cedar branches lying across pole rafters.

On the fourth day, when Ben made preparations to go hunting, Cora followed him to the door.

"Ben, I'm going with you."

"Cordella Jackson! You'll do no such thing." Her mother's shocked voice stopped Cora's progress.

"Why not?"

"Young ladies do not go traipsing off into the woods to hunt."

"Why would you want to?" Eliza looked at her sister as if she'd lost her mind.

"I want to spend some time with Ben. And I'd like to see the countryside. Maybe I can find some nuts." She turned to her father, knowing his weakness. "Didn't you say pecan trees grow around here?"

His eyes twinkled. He always understood her better than anyone else did. "Yes, you might find pecans on the ground now."

"But a young lady—" Emma tried again.

Ben cut into their mother's objection. "Hey, don't I have a say? I'm the one who'll have to take care of her."

Cora stiffened. "I can take care of myself."

"Now that's questionable." Ben grinned. "But a pecan pie would taste pretty good."

As Orval rubbed his stomach, Emma sighed. "I still don't think a young lady should go on a hunting trip."

"Please, Mother, this isn't Boston where you grew up. It isn't even St. Louis. Surely, you can see it's different here. If we're going to survive in this wilderness, we'll have to go out and look for food. It isn't as if the neighbors will see me."

Cora tried to keep the sarcasm from her voice. "Please let me go with Ben."

Emma sighed and shook her head. "Stay close to Ben and be home before dark. As cloudy as it is, you won't be able to tell the time, so come back early."

Cora hugged her mother. "Thank you, and don't worry."

As Cora ran to find a basket for the nuts, her heart felt lighter than it had since before they'd left St. Louis. She enjoyed Ben's company and knew the walk through the woods with him would be fun. She lifted her eyes to the line of trees at the edge of the woods. What exciting secrets did they hold? She smiled in anticipation.

"You'll have to be quiet if you want any meat for supper," Ben warned.

Cora nodded.

"There might be some pecans over that way." He pointed. "They like water. The creek is just beyond."

Again she nodded. Ben's voice followed her. "Don't get out of my sight. Make sure you can always see me."

She waved and continued through the thick bed of dried leaves until she was several yards from her brother. At the sharp report of his rifle, she turned quickly. Had he already shot something? She hoped not. She didn't want to go back to camp yet. A sigh of relief escaped when she saw him look her way and shake his head. He must have missed. She laughed. The freedom she felt was a welcome relief from the burden she had carried since they'd started this horrible move. There was no duty calling, just an exciting afternoon of adventure.

She thought of George, wishing he were with her. Most of their outings in the last year had been to the courthouse. Every trial or hearing open to the public found George there, an absorbed spectator. Just weeks before they left St. Louis, he had become a junior clerk with Gosset and Smith, two of the best attorneys in Missouri, according to George.

A low branch brought Cora up short. She dodged it, then looked for her brother. It was a moment before she saw him standing beside a large tree some distance away. With a sigh of relief, she checked out her own surroundings. She could see nothing but trees. With neither she nor her brother moving, the silence was a living thing, heavy and pressing against her ears. Then sounds of the forest crept in with chirping, scratching, and rustling noises until she wondered how she could have thought the forest was quiet.

A puff of air winding its way through the trees circled her before moving on. She shivered, tucking her bare hands into her coat pockets, letting the basket handle slide up her arm. She stomped her feet to warm her toes as she looked around. Satisfied there were no pecan trees in sight, she moved on.

When it seemed she had walked forever, with only an occasional shot from Ben's gun, Cora spotted a small grove of pecan trees by the edge of the creek. She sank to the ground and began filling her basket. When she picked up every pecan within reach, she scooted over and started again. Father would be glad to see her full basket. Even if Ben didn't get any meat, they would have pecans.

Cora worked until she heard a twig snap. She turned to see Ben walking toward her. "Did you shoot anything?" She smiled a welcome.

He shook his head. "I shot at several, but nothing stood still long enough. I'm still a little slow reloading. The animals watch me and then disappear about the time I'm ready for them."

Cora laughed. "Smart animals."

"At least you found some nuts."

"Yes, they don't run."

Ben knelt beside her and tossed some pecans into the basket. "I think we ought to start back. It's starting to snow."

A large snowflake fell on her dark woolen skirt. It slowly melted, but was followed by others landing several inches apart. She looked up at Ben. "I think you're right. We'd better get back. I hope you know the way."

He shrugged. "I think we came in a fairly straight line. If we go back the same way, we should come out of the woods about where we came in."

Cora scrambled to her feet, brushing leaves from her skirt and coat. She clutched the full basket. "You lead the way."

Snow fell until the air danced with the cold, white flakes. Cora turned her face from them. She followed Ben as he trudged ahead of her, his gun slung over his shoulder. Fluffs of white now clung to tree limbs, and the leaf-covered ground looked like a white patched carpet. Surely they would soon be at the edge of the forest.

Cora envisioned the log shelter. It wasn't a real house, but it would at least block the wind. More important, there would be a fire in Mother's stove sending out rays of warmth into each corner. As her hands ached from the cold and her feet grew numb, she longed for shelter and warmth.

The wind that had been gentle grew in intensity, sending swirls of snow toward them. As they wound their way around trees and over fallen logs, Cora tried to keep her back to the wind, but it was no use. Either the wind changed directions or they did.

She stumbled as she lifted one foot after the other. The wind lashed out in fury, slanting the cold, wet curtain of white almost horizontal. Only an occasional leaf stuck its point above the snow-covered ground.

Ben and Cora bent against the driving snow.

Even while she thought of freezing to death, Cora realized her feet were not as cold as they had been. Faint warmth settled in them. As she concentrated on her feet, drowsiness stole over her. She thought longingly of the mattress waiting at home.

In a haze, she saw Ben turn. His lips moved, but no words reached her ears.

She yelled at him, telling him she could not hear. She was sleepy. Why didn't he stop?

She tried to take one more step, but something tripped her, throwing her toward a wide, bark-covered wall. Her hand flew out in a futile attempt to break her fall. There was nothing there. As if a door opened in the huge tree, she fell inside.

In an instant Ben shook her. "Cora, get up. Your feet are out in the snow."

She fought against the hands tugging on her coat, pulling her into a sitting position. Why wouldn't he let her sleep? Her eyes opened and she pulled her feet under her. There were chunks of ice touching her upper legs. Quickly, she straightened. More awake now, she tried to see the dark interior of their shelter. "It's warm in here. And dry."

"The rotting wood gives off heat. And we're out of the wind, too." She felt Ben relax beside her. "What about your feet? Are they all right?"

"I don't know. I can't feel them."

"Take your shoes and stockings off."

Cora was unprepared for the pain as he took her bare foot in his hands and rubbed it. "What are you doing?" She tried to jerk her foot away, but he held it fast, rubbing until the color returned. "Now give me the other foot."

"No."

"Do you want frostbite? If we don't get the blood back, you could lose your foot."

Cora had heard of frostbite and knew he told the truth. As soon as he finished wrapping her tingling foot in his neck scarf, she stuck the other one out. "What about your feet?"

"Just a little cold. My boots are waterproof."

When he finished wrapping the second foot in her woolen scarf, she tucked both feet under her long, heavy skirt. The warmth surrounding them felt wonderful. "Now what do we do?"

Ben shifted close beside her. "I guess we wait the storm out."

"Mother will worry."

"I know. But, it's better she worry a few hours than the alternative."

A shiver moved down Cora's spine. Maybe the danger wasn't over yet. Maybe the storm would go on for days and they would freeze to death. Her stomach growled. If they didn't die of starvation first.

Her pecans. She looked toward the open doorway of their small shelter. There, covered with snow, were her precious pecans. Beside them lay the crumpled basket. She shifted to a kneeling position and reached through the opening. As her hand closed over the wet snow-covered basket handle, she felt Ben's arm brush hers.

"Let me. You'll freeze your hands." He scooped up several pecans.

When he had picked up all he could see in the rapidly fading light, they returned to their shelter. Cora smiled. "I'm glad we didn't lose them all. Father would have been so disappointed."

"Yes, I guess so." Ben's voice sounded strange.

A sob caught in Cora's throat. "You don't think we'll get back, do you? Ben, I'm scared. We're going to die." Tears choked her voice as a new thought came to her. If she died, she would never see George again.

Ben pulled her close and her tears erupted in a torrent. As she thought of her own death, fear settled in her heart. She prayed that God would spare her life and Ben's. When her tears ran out, she took one more shuddering breath. As she lifted her head from Ben's shoulder, a sharp crack ricocheted through the small enclosure.

"Here. Supper's ready." She felt a pecan pressed into her hand. "It's a little dark to see how to pick it out, but you'll know if you bite into a shell."

The storm raged while they ate the pecans that Ben cracked by squeezing two together in his hand. Cora lost all sense of time as the light outside dimmed. The drone of the wind whipping past the small opening in their tree lulled her to sleep.

There was no room to stretch out, so they huddled together, sharing what little space and warmth they had. Ben leaned against the inside wall of the tree while Cora curled into a ball with her cheek against his coat. The wind calmed, and a wintry silence descended on the hollow sycamore tree.

❊

Cora shifted position. Her body ached beyond belief. As the haze of sleep lifted, her memory returned. She and Ben had taken refuge in a tree. They hadn't frozen to death during the night.

"Good morning." A narrow ray of sunshine lit Ben's smiling face. "The storm's over."

Cora sat up, popping stiff joints with each movement. Ben straightened, rolling his head from side to side. "We'd better try to find our way home."

"I need to put my shoes and stockings back on."

Ben nodded. "While you're doing that, I'll step outside."

Cora reached for her shoes while Ben started through the small opening. Immediately he jerked back as a sharp twang above his head splintered a branch. Small pieces of bark flew in all directions.

"Someone shot at me!" Disbelief edged his voice.

Chapter 2

Cora froze. "Why would anyone shoot at us?" Her heart jumped before racing in fear. It was Indians. George had told her they hunted here. Every atrocity she had ever heard relating to Indians filled her memory. "I don't think they know we're here. I'm going out."

"No!" Cora grabbed Ben's coat as he started for the opening. "They'll kill you!"

Just then another shot rang out, going through the tree several feet above their heads. A shower of dislodged rot fell. Cora ducked and covered her ears with her hands.

"I'm going now before he has time to reload." Ben scrambled through the opening, yelling as he went. "Stop! Don't shoot!"

Cora grabbed her stocking and pulled it on as quickly as her trembling fingers would allow. She heard Ben's footsteps crunching through the snow. He was going away from the tree. Ben thought it was just a hunter who didn't know they were there, but what if it were an Indian or maybe an outlaw who did know? What if they took Ben captive?

Her fingers fumbled with her shoes. She peeked outside. She couldn't hear anything. On hands and knees, Cora pressed her face close to the edge of the opening and peered out. She could see nothing. Ever so slowly, she stuck her head out farther. And stopped.

There, just inches from her own, were a pair of the bluest eyes she had ever seen.

"Hi." His wide grin revealed white teeth. "You Ben's sister? He said you was in the old, holler sycamore."

A slow flush moved over Cora's face. She brushed disheveled hair from her eyes. What a sight she must be!

She took his offered hand, allowing him to help her stand. The young man looked to be near her age. She had thought George's eyes were blue, but she couldn't remember them ever being as blue as the ones looking at her now.

"I'm real sorry about shootin' at ya." A wide grin complemented his twinkling eyes. "Honest, we didn't know you was in the tree."

"We?" Cora tore her gaze away from him. Were there others in this forsaken land?

"Sure, me and my brother. He's there with yourn." He pointed to the two

13

young men deep in conversation. "I'd druther tell you Aaron was the one shoo-tin' at you, but I'll have to 'fess up." He pointed at the tree. "There was a squirrel sittin' right there on that branch. Never did hit the rascal. I'm, most of the time, tolerable good at gettin' squirrels, too."

He launched into a tale of a successful hunting experience, but she scarcely listened.

"Where do you live? Are there more in your family? What about other families?" She interrupted, eager for answers.

He grinned at her. "Ya want me to quit babblin', do ya?" As her face flushed, he laughed. "Don't worry, none. Ivy says I talk too much."

"Who's Ivy?"

"My baby sister. Worse spoiled brat you'll ever meet. She was a puny baby. Got used to bein' pampered. She takes after Aaron. They're always puttin' on airs. Only trouble is we got mighty slim pickin's most the time at our place."

"Baby sister? How old is she?"

"Seventeen come February."

Just a year younger than Cora. Maybe she wasn't as spoiled as he made her sound. She could certainly use a friend.

"Then there's Ma and Pa, too." Again his grin flashed as he stuck out his hand. She took it and he pumped furiously. "I'm Ralph Walter Stark." He bowed slightly. "I'm real proud to meet y'all, Miss. . ."

"Cora Jackson. We just got here from St. Louis."

As Cora shuffled her feet, she felt something hard and round under her shoe. It was a pecan. She bent and plucked it from the packed snow of her footprint.

"Well, I never knowed sycamores to grow pecans before." Ralph knelt beside her and brushed the snow aside, uncovering another.

"I dropped them last night." She reached into the tree for her battered basket. "Maybe I can find enough to take to my father."

Together they sifted through the snow.

"You must've had a rough night out here in the woods, Miss Cora." Ralph's grin was infectious.

Cora smiled at him. "I'm sure it could have been worse."

"Ralph, you ready to go?" The deep voice came from above them.

"Sure 'nuff, soon as we get Cora's pecans picked up."

"We better git goin'. Ben says he knows the way home now. I promised Pa we'd be back shortly. He needs help with the fence."

Ralph stood and dropped two more pecans into Cora's basket. He grinned at her, but spoke to his brother. "You're the boss."

Cora straightened to see a taller, older version of Ralph. Yet there were dif-ferences. His face was more slender, his jaw firmer. He would be better-looking than Ralph if he weren't so stern and solemn. But she didn't care. She was glad there were others living nearby, especially another girl.

Following Aaron's directions, Ben led Cora back to camp. She could see the two wagons and the shelter as soon as they came out of the woods. A thin spiral of smoke rose from the shelter as a beckoning welcome.

With flying steps, they crossed the distance to their waiting family only to find that their father and John were out looking for them.

Emma said, "They went out when the first snowflakes fell. But the storm came so quickly, they were forced back." She lay her hand on Ben's arm. "He said you would find shelter. He trusted you to know what to do."

Ben grinned at Cora. "We did find shelter, even if it was accidental."

"They promised to check in by noon." A frown touched Emma's forehead. "I hate the thought of them out looking when there's no need."

"We must have missed them somehow." Ben looked toward the woods. "I'll go see if I can find them."

"Oh, Ben. What if you get lost again?"

"Don't worry, Mother. Our footprints are easy to follow in the snow."

While Ben replenished his supply of powder and lead shot before leaving, the women returned to the lean-to. Cora looked with sinking heart at the large piece of oilcloth spread over the bed.

Sunlight came through the cracks of the walls, making a striped pattern on the room. Melting snow on top of each log ran down the inside walls to the ground. A drop of water landed with a splat on Cora's head. She looked up, appalled to see snow melting through the thick layers of cedar branches.

"Mother, everything's getting soaked." Cora turned anxiously toward her mother.

"I know." Emma sighed. "There's nothing we can do about it. The bed is covered. Everything else will dry."

"But—"

A look from Emma stopped Cora's complaint. "Remember, Cora, a lady does the best she can with what she has. It does no good to whine about the things we don't like."

Cora shut out the depressing sight before her and told her mother and sisters about the neighbors. "Ralph's so friendly. You'll like him. He's a little taller than Ben and has a really nice smile." She thought of Ralph's slaughter of the English language and wondered what George would think of him.

"Sounds like you're the one who likes him." Eliza's brown eyes twinkled above her grin.

"I do not." Cora blushed in spite of her efforts to remain nonchalant. Ralph was good-looking. And he seemed pleasant. Even when his older brother had been unfriendly, he made light of it. But she could never care for anyone but George.

"Please, tell us about the rest of the family." Emma's voice cut into Cora's thoughts.

"You said there were five of them." Vickie sat on the bed. "I assume two of the five are his parents?"

Cora nodded. "Yes, and that's all I know about them. Ralph's older brother looks a lot like him. Ralph said they have a sister named Ivy. She's almost seventeen. Ralph said she's spoiled rotten, but I'm hoping she'll become a good friend."

A faint smile touched Emma's lips. "It will be nice having neighbors. Do you know where they live?"

Cora shook her head. "No, but I think it's on the other side of the woods. They turned that way when they left."

❧

An hour later, Ben burst through the blanket-covered doorway. "There won't be any lack of meat around here for awhile! Come and see."

John and Orval stepped back from the wagon, where a large buck hung by its back legs.

Ben's eyes shone. "Father shot it right through the heart! We'll have to let it hang overnight and cut it up tomorrow."

Large brown eyes, vacant of expression, stared at Cora. She stood, frozen in place while the details etched into her mind. Drops of pink foam oozed from the mouth past its lolling tongue before dripping to the white snow below. The deer had been slit down the front from the throat to the back legs.

Cora's stomach churned. She didn't understand how Father could kill such a beautiful animal. She didn't understand how her family could stand to look at it.

The next morning as the sun touched the eastern horizon with its glow, the men skinned and butchered the deer while Emma and the girls fixed breakfast. When Cora stepped outside to call them to eat, she saw its skin lying on the ground. Strips of meat lay in piles ready to be cooked and eaten. Relief that she wouldn't have to put up with this long swept over her. When George took her home, life would be civilized again.

Orval came through the doorway, followed by Ben and John. "We need to smoke the meat so it'll keep."

Emma stood by the table. "But we have no smokehouse."

"Don't need one." Orval grinned. "When I was a boy, my pa used a hollow log for a smokehouse. It's not as fancy, but it'll work just as well."

He turned to John. "You feel like a trip to the woods this morning?"

John nodded. "Sure."

"We'll get a load of logs for the house while we're at it." He sat at the end of the table and grinned at his wife. "This looks good."

After breakfast the men headed for the woods, axes slung over their shoulders.

They took one of the huge workhorses with them to drag logs out of the woods.

Emma kept her daughters busy through the morning trying to make the shelter more livable. Cora did as she was told, although she thought it was useless. How her mother thought she could make a home out of this hovel was more than she could understand.

"When will Father begin on a house?" she asked.

Vickie smoothed the quilt over the corner of the girls' bed and sat on it. "I'm sure Father will build a house right away. John says we'll stay and help until you're settled—maybe even through the winter—and then we need to move to our own land."

Emma glanced at her oldest daughter. "What do you mean 'move'?"

"John wants his own land, Mother."

"We have a hundred acres right here. Your father expects you to have part of it."

Long brown lashes swept down, hooding Vickie's eyes. Her finger traced the star on the quilt. "Yes, I know."

"Where does John plan to settle?"

Vickie looked up, her eyes dark with feeling. "He wants to look around before he decides. Try to understand, Mother. It's important to John—to me, even—that we have our own land. Land that we buy with our own money." She rose and placed her hand on her mother's shoulder. "I know Father means well. I know you want me with you always, but I'm married now. I have my own family."

Emma sighed. "Of course, Vickie, I understand. But you didn't answer my question. Where does John plan to settle?"

"I don't know." Vickie returned to the bed. "At a dollar and a quarter an acre, we can't afford to buy much now. He wants to get where he can add more later."

"You can do that right here."

Vickie smiled. "I know, Mother. But John's a proud man. He wants to take care of us by himself."

Before Emma could say more, Lenny and Nicholas ran through the doorway. "Mans come here." Nicholas grabbed Vickie's hand, then tugged on her arm as he lunged for the doorway.

Lenny was equally excited as he ran to his mother. "They've got long guns like Father's."

Cora's heart raced with fear as she ran to the door. Men who came with guns wouldn't likely have good intentions.

Chapter 3

Cora watched the three figures grow larger. Each man had a gun over his shoulder. But something seemed familiar.

"It's all right, Mother. It's Ralph Stark and his brother. The other man must be their father." She stepped outside.

Ralph raised his hand in greeting. "I see ya'll made it home."

Cora glanced at the shelter and made a face. "Yes, if you can call it that." She smiled at Ralph. "I'd like for you to meet my mother and sisters."

After she introduced her family, Ralph pointed with his thumb. "You already met Aaron, and this here's my pa, Walter Stark."

Cora looked at the older man. His lined face had been browned by weather. On top of his thick, graying hair sat a dirty hat. He pulled it from his head and nodded toward the women. "I'm right proud to meet you folks."

Emma accepted his offered hand. "I'm pleased to meet you. We've been here almost a week and have met no one. My husband isn't home. He'll be sorry he missed you."

"No, he won't," Eliza said. "Here they come now."

Cora saw her father, John, and Ben coming with the horses.

Everyone moved toward the men. As Cora followed the others, Ralph's older brother, Aaron, fell into step with her.

"Iffen you don't mind, I'd like a word."

Cora looked up. As quickly as their eyes met, he looked away. Was he shy? How could brothers look so much alike and be so different?

She stopped, letting the others go ahead. "Of course. My brother and I really appreciate the help you gave us yesterday."

He shrugged. "We didn't do nothin' on-common." He shuffled his feet. "I didn't mean ta be short with ya. I mean about the pecans."

He pushed a white flour sack toward her. "Here."

Cora stared at the bulging sack in her hands. She could feel the small, hard bumps through the fabric and knew there were far more pecans in it than she had lost. It must weigh at least ten pounds. She looked up to voice her appreciation, but he had already moved away. All she could do was call her thanks after him.

He answered over his shoulder. "That's all right. I'm jist proud I could replace 'em." His long strides carried him across the yard to where the men were standing a hollow log upright.

Cora watched him join the others before setting her pecans in the shelter. Aaron was an interesting young man.

Ralph and Aaron helped Ben unchain the logs from the horses. Aaron worked quietly while Ralph kept up a steady chatter with Ben and Eliza. Cora smiled at Eliza's expression as she stood to the side and watched Ralph. Little Eliza was developing quite a liking for this fellow she had just met.

The Starks stayed until after lunch. While the younger men hauled more logs from the woods, the rest fashioned a peaked roof of short boards split from a log to set over the top of the hollow tree and cut a small door in one side near the bottom. Small sticks were driven through holes drilled in the sides of the tree near the top. From these, the men hung the pieces of meat that had been salted early that morning. They built a fire with green hickory chips inside the log. Cora watched thick smoke curl around the little roof and blow away in the breeze. Memory of the slaughtered deer faded as she thought of delicious venison.

Just before the visitors left, Mr. Stark looked at their shelter and shook his head. "You're gonna need somethin' better'n that afore winter sets in. Reckon ya could git enough logs cut in a week or so fer a cabin? Me and the boys'd be proud ta help put 'er up, iffen you'd like."

Orval nodded. "We'd appreciate any help."

"Jist give us a holler. There's a couple others nearby would likely come help, too. We'll git word to 'em soon as you're ready."

"I reckon I could help git the logs in." Aaron looked at his father.

Mr. Stark nodded. "Me and Ralph can take care of things fer a spell."

Aaron offered Orval his hand. "I'll be here early Monday mornin' iffen you can use me."

As Orval shook his hand, he smiled. "You bet we can."

Cora groaned at his next words. "I know we made the right decision coming here. A man's got to have good neighbors to get along in this world. You can't imagine how much I appreciate all you've done for us already. Soon as that venison's ready, there'll be a piece with your name on it."

❦

"We jist come in to say howdy," Mr. Stark's friendly voice boomed out two weeks later. "Looks like a good day fer a house raisin', don't it? Me and the boys'll step back out and git some of those bottom boards laid out for ya." He left with the men, leaving Ralph, Mrs. Stark, and Ivy behind.

"Sure couldn't say 'cat' in here without gettin' hair in yore mouth, could ya?"

Cora looked up into Ralph's laughing blue eyes. "I'm sorry. What did you say?"

"I said, you sure couldn't—"

"She heard you. Now say it proper-like so's she can understand," the girl scolded.

"Ain't nothin' wrong with the way I talk." Ralph looked at his sister.

Ivy Stark frowned. "Not if you don't never plan to better yerself." She turned toward Cora. "He meant it's crowded in here."

"I see." Cora wasn't sure what to make of Ralph's sister. She was a feminine version of her brothers. Her long, thick black hair had been done up in two braids, then coiled together at the back of her head. A creamy complexion covered perfect features on her unsmiling face. Sooty, long lashes framed large eyes as remarkably blue as her brothers'.

Cora smiled at her. "I'm Cora Jackson, and you are Ralph's sister?"

"Afraid so."

Cora forced herself to continue smiling. "I hope we can be friends."

Ivy smiled then, though her smile looked anything but friendly. "I'm sure we will be. We don't have much choice, do we?"

"Aw, don't mind Ivy." Ralph grinned at Cora. "She jist got her back up 'cause there ain't no one much around these parts."

"Oh, hush up, Ralph. You got no more ambition than a hound dog layin' by the fire on a rainy day." Ivy frowned. "You better go outside with Pa before Aaron gits all the work done."

Eliza squeezed between Cora and Ralph. "Hi." She smiled up at Ralph.

"Hi, yourself, little one." Ralph grinned as he backed away. "Guess I'll be seein' you all later. Right now, I gotta go prove I got more ambition than a hound dog."

Mrs. Stark appeared to be older than Cora's parents. Then Cora noticed her eyes. Large and brilliantly blue, they were framed by long, curling black lashes, the only clue that Jennett Stark had once been as beautiful as her daughter.

Mrs. Stark rubbed the rocking chair's smooth varnish before sitting in it. "Ya got some mighty purty things. Looky there, Ivy, if that ain't real china on that table." She pointed with an amazingly graceful, slender finger. She clucked her tongue. "Purty as it is, won't be long afore it's nothin' but chips and scratches. Tin's what ya need. Somethin' that'll last."

Emma smiled. "I'm sure you are right. Would you care for anything to eat, Mrs. Stark?"

"Aw, jist call me Jennett and I'll call you Emma. 'Tain't much need to stand on ceremony round these parts." Her snaggletoothed grin was wide and friendly. "Thank ya kindly, but me and Ivy's full as a tick from our breakfast."

Cora was glad when another family arrived. She followed her mother outside to welcome the new arrivals and found a man and woman with a wagon full of children.

"Hello," Mother said, holding her hand out to the woman who stepped down. "I'm Emma Jackson. It's so nice of you to come and help."

Cora watched the woman give her mother a quick hug. "You don't know how glad we are to have close neighbors. I'm Agnes Newkirk and this is my brood." They hopped one by one from the wagon and ran toward Lenny and Nicholas, who were playing nearby. She called out the names of the younger children, pointing as each ran past her. "That's Gilbert, Margaret, Arthur, Gerard, and Joan," she said. Then she called after the departing children, "Stay away from the workers! Margaret, keep an eye on Joan."

At the back of the wagon, a girl in her teens climbed down and lifted her hands to her baby sister. The small girl fell into her arms. Mrs. Newkirk smiled as she took the baby, kissed her on the cheek, and said, "This is Ellen, our youngest." She turned toward the wagon where the teen had gone back to help yet another girl with a large box. "That was Grace. And that's Esther, our oldest," she said, indicating the girl in the wagon.

Cora only half listened. She couldn't help staring at Esther, who appeared to be about her age. If an angel came to earth and took on human form, she would look like Esther. Her hair, the color of ripe wheat, shone in the sunlight. A gentle wave dipped across her forehead from a low side part. Her hair fell loose and full around her face, while a braid at the back of her neck held it in place.

"Here, let me get that box." Cora shifted her gaze to her older brother as he stepped to the wagon. He lifted his hands toward Esther. "May I help you down?"

Esther placed her hands lightly on his shoulders and smiled. "Thank you." Her voice had a soft Southern accent.

Ben lifted her carefully from the wagon. Cora saw the look on his face and knew he was smitten with Esther Newkirk.

He finally turned to the box, lifting it and carrying it around the wagon. "Mother, where do you want this?"

"Take it into the shelter, Ben. Vickie will show you where to put it." Emma turned back to her new neighbor. "How thoughtful of you to bring something for the meal."

Mrs. Newkirk laughed. "Anywhere I go with my bunch, I always carry extra. I wouldn't dream of expecting you to provide for all of us."

Emma looked toward the building site where the men had already started work. "I'd cook all day and all night, too, if I had to for a real house."

"I know what you mean, but about now you're probably running short on supplies." Mrs. Newkirk looked at the small shelter. "We didn't even have that good a place when we first came last year. We arrived in the spring and camped outdoors."

Cora rounded the corner of the wagon with Eliza and Ivy following her. She smiled at Esther. "Hi, I'm Cora Jackson." She turned briefly, indicating the two girls behind her. "This is my little sister, Eliza, and our neighbor, Ivy Stark."

"I'm so glad to meet you," Esther said. "I'm Esther Newkirk and this is my little sister, Grace. We've met Ivy but don't get to visit often." She turned to Ivy. "It's nice seeing you again."

Ivy didn't respond. She turned away to face the men who were already working.

"I hope you will like it here." Esther smiled at Cora, then looked at the cedar trees and the creek in the distance. "It's beautiful country."

"Beautiful!" Ivy swung around. "You can't live on beauty. You can't eat it. You can't wear it or keep warm by it." She looked back at the men and tossed her head. "The first chance I git, I'm gittin' married, but it won't be to jist anybody." Her eyes shifted to Ben. "The man I marry will have money, and he'll take me away from here. Then I won't have to work like a horse 'til I'm old and ugly."

"I know life is hard here," Esther said. "That's when I remember what Paul said in the Bible, 'I have learned, in whatsoever state I am, therewith to be content.' That always helps me."

Cora saw the bitterness and anger on Ivy's face rob her of the beauty she guarded so jealously. As Cora watched her turn and walk away, she thought of her own unhappiness in moving to the wilderness and felt ashamed.

The women kept busy while the men worked outside. Cora and Esther peeled and sliced potatoes until Cora would have liked to throw her paring knife out with the peelings. Eliza and Grace made a game of chopping onions for soup. Ivy stirred a pot of pudding on the stove and ignored the other girls.

Emma picked up the large kettle as Esther sliced the last potato into it. "You girls have been a big help. How would you like to get a count of how many we'll be feeding?"

Outside, Cora clasped Esther's arm. "I'm so glad your family came today. I was hoping there would be more girls my age nearby besides Ivy. She doesn't seem very friendly."

Esther smiled. "I'm glad we came, too. I hope we'll be good friends." Her smile faded and she looked thoughtful. "I don't think Ivy is so bad, though."

Cora shrugged, her attention shifting to the men. They had started laying the thick board walls on the rock foundation. The boards had gaps between them. Except for being larger, this house was no better than the shelter.

"Would you like for me to count the children while you count the men?" Esther asked.

Cora nodded. "All right."

She stepped closer to the building. She stared at the gaps and didn't notice Aaron until he spoke. "What do ya think?"

She glanced up at him. "It doesn't look like it will be very warm."

"Why not?"

"There are cracks between every board. The wind will go right between them."

A smile tugged the corners of his mouth. "I'd reckon your father'll chink the cracks."

"Chink the cracks?"

"Yup. Fill 'em in with clay."

"Oh." She thought about this new information. "Won't the clay fall out when it dries?"

He grinned. "Not iffen he backs 'em up with clapboards."

She laughed. "All right, I'll believe you even though I don't know what a clapboard is."

"Hey, what are you doin' layin' off work, talkin' to a pretty girl?" Ralph started over, but Aaron stepped back and grabbed one of the heavy boards.

"Take hold of that end and let's git this up."

Ralph grinned at Cora. "Guess the boss ain't gonna let me dawdle." He picked up his end of the board while Cora walked around the building.

The Starks, Newkirks, and Jacksons, plus one man she had not seen before, made a total of nine adults. She found Esther, and together they returned to the shelter.

"Twenty-six people?" Emma looked thoughtful. "I think we can seat that many outside. Cora, get some tablecloths and you girls can fix up the tables."

The girls soon had the long, makeshift board tables covered and set with all the dishes they could find. Then the women started carrying out food. When the men saw food coming, tools and boards fell to the ground and everyone found a place to sit.

As Esther slid onto the bench, Ben stepped over it. "Mind if I sit here?" His friendly grin brought a touch of color to Esther's cheeks.

"I don't mind at all."

Cora took her place on the other side of Esther at the end of the bench. The other girls filed in across the table from them with Ivy across from Cora. When Cora smiled at Ivy, she met a glare.

Father held his hand up for silence. "I'd like to say before we eat just how much I appreciate all our new neighbors and friends. The house is going up solid and it's going up fast thanks to all you men. And look at this." His hands swept out in a gesture that took in both tables. "The ladies have been as busy as we have. I know we're all going to appreciate their efforts." He turned to Mr. Newkirk. "Henry, I'd be honored if you'd say the blessing for us."

Cora bowed her head as Esther's father talked to God as if He were standing right there at the table. A hum rose as soon as Mr. Newkirk sat down. Cora ate in silence while Ben monopolized Esther. She tried to talk to Ivy but soon gave up.

Eliza, sitting between Grace and Ralph, kept the talk lively on their side of the table. Cora looked at her younger sister, amused by the obvious fascination she had with Ralph. What could she possibly see in him? He might be good-looking, but he was so crude.

With no one to talk to, Cora glanced down the long table and noticed her parents talking to the man she didn't know. She couldn't hear everything they said but learned his name was Bill Reid and that his wife and son had died of a fever in Boston.

Cora's attention came back to her table when Ivy leaned forward and asked, "Ben, have you tasted the pudding yet?"

Ben looked up with a blank expression. He turned to Esther. "I ate some pudding, didn't I?"

Esther nodded. "Remember, you said it tasted just like some your older sister made once."

Ivy's smile faded and an ugly scowl settled in its place just before her hand shot out, knocking her glass of water across the table. Cora jumped out of the way seconds before Esther's lap was drenched.

Chapter 4

An hour before sunset a few days later, the two-story cabin stood, complete with puncheon floor. Cora marveled at the workmanship evident in the floor's smooth split logs, then turned to rejoin her family and neighbors. Just outside the new house, on a cleared patch of ground, the three families gathered while Bill Reid brought out his fiddle.

Cora stood by Esther. "You know Ivy will try to get Ben to dance with her."

"I know."

"I don't know how you can be so nice to her after she dumped water in your lap."

Esther shrugged. "Maybe it was an accident."

Cora laughed. "Accidentally on purpose." Then she sobered. "You like Ben, don't you?"

Color mounted in Esther's cheeks. "I do and I shouldn't. I don't even know if he's a believer."

"A believer? You mean of the Bible? We've attended church all our lives. Of course, he is. We all are." Cora laughed. "He's hardly taken his eyes off you the last two days."

Again Esther blushed.

The lively sound of a resin-covered bow dancing on fiddle strings filled the air. Mr. Stark stomped one foot and clapped his hands in time to the music. "Grab you a partner, come on let's go." He began to chant as he kept time.

The married couples formed one square. Ben and Ralph stepped in front of Cora and Esther. Ben smiled at Esther. "Would you help me start a second set?"

Esther took his hand.

"How about you bein' my partner?" Ralph asked, grinning at Cora.

For a reason she couldn't explain, Cora's gaze shifted to Aaron where he leaned against the house, his arms folded. She glanced at Eliza, then back at Ralph. "Please do me a favor and ask Eliza."

"Your sister?"

"Yes."

"But she's just a—"

"Please ask her."

❧

Aaron watched his brother talk to Cora. Couldn't Ralph see he wasn't good enough for a girl like that? Ever since she'd crawled from that old holler tree, she'd been on his mind. He'd thought a heap about her, but he knew he shouldn't.

He watched Ralph shrug and move toward Eliza. Then, Cora looked at him. As their eyes met and held, his resolve weakened. Keeping her face before him, he pushed away from the house until he stood in front of her. He held out his hand and she took it.

Aaron felt Cora's arm against his sleeve as his father called out, "All to your places, and straighten up your faces, all join hands and circle eight. Ladies face out and gents face in, and hold your holts and gone again."

Aaron's heart, thudding with the vigorous exercise, beat even harder when he looked down at Cora. She stepped forward, hooking her arm in his as they swung around. Then she hooked arms with Gilbert and then Ralph. He felt a pang in his innards when Ralph grinned at her and asked, "Havin' fun?"

She barely had time to nod before Ben swung her around and she was with Aaron again.

Aaron relished each time Cora was his partner. Then came the final call. "Promenade and put her on a shelf. If you want any more you can call it yourself."

Aaron clasped her right hand and reached for her left with his left hand. As they skipped around the circle, he watched the smile on her face and realized she was having fun. Even getting stuck with him hadn't put a damper on her smile.

Cora's breath came fast as the fiddle sang the final bars of the song and then stopped as if it, too, could take no more. Bill Reid stood to the side, grinning broadly at the adults crowded around him complimenting him on his music.

The Newkirks left before the second set. Cora walked with Esther to their wagon. "I wish you didn't have to leave. I've enjoyed the last two days so much. When do you think we'll get to see each other again?"

Esther smiled. "We're bound to get plenty of snow before winter's over. You've got a wonderful hill for sledding. The first good snow we have, I'll come with some sleds." Esther laughed. "And probably Grace, Gilbert, and Margaret, too."

Cora hugged Esther, feeling bereft as her new friend left. She looked up at the star-spangled sky and wondered how long it would be before they'd have snow deep enough for sledding. She hoped soon.

As the Newkirk wagon rolled out of sight, lively music from Mr. Reid's fiddle called to Cora. A cool breeze swept her hair away from her face, and she ran to join the others. Another dance with Aaron would soon have her warm again.

"How'd you like to be my partner this time?" Ralph stepped forward to meet her.

Before she could answer, Aaron took her hand. "You got a partner already, Ralph."

26

Aaron's look stirred a deep response in Cora, and it bothered her. She didn't want to feel this way. Not now and not in this place. Especially not toward this tall, handsome backwoodsman. Yet, in spite of her inward protests, she found herself smiling up at him.

The first call rang out, "Swing those ladies to the center and back."

Aaron's hand felt warm in hers as he led her to the center of the circle and then back. A wonderful feeling filled her heart. She smiled at him.

Mr. Stark kept a steady rhythm, beating out the time to Mr. Reid's racing fiddle. They danced until everyone was worn out.

Just before the Starks left, Cora told them of Esther's sledding idea, and they promised to come after the first good snow. Then they walked across the grass into the black woods that swallowed their lantern light, leaving the night dark and lonely.

In the loft room she would share with Eliza, Cora slipped on her nightgown before climbing into bed beside her younger sister.

"Cora, did you have fun tonight?"

Cora thought of Aaron's dark hair and blue eyes. She'd had more fun than she cared to admit. "I suppose it was all right. Did you?"

"Oh yes. More than ever before." Eliza's brown eyes sparkled in the candlelight. "How would you like to do something Grace told me about?"

"I don't know. Do we have to do it now?"

"Yes, before we go to sleep. When you move into a new house, you name each corner of the room after a different boy. The corner you see first in the morning is the boy you'll marry."

"All right. I'll name them all George."

"You can't do that. That would be cheating."

Cora smiled at her sister's foolishness. Then, as she thought of four names, a feeling of anticipation stirred. It might be fun just to see how it came out. "All right, starting in that corner, I'll name them George, Aaron, Ralph, and Joshua."

"Joshua! Do you mean Joshua Smith in St. Louis? He's shorter than I am." Eliza laughed. "Oh, Cora, what if you see his corner first?"

"Well, I'm not going to marry him if I do. It's just a game."

"Yes, a game that might come true." Eliza pointed to each corner as she named them. "Mine are Henry, Bob, Aaron, and Ralph."

"Henry and Bob? And you think Joshua is a bad choice. Besides that, why did you say Aaron?"

"What difference does that make to you? I didn't say George and you did say Ralph. You'd better not see Ralph's corner, either."

"Don't worry, I'll turn this way." Cora turned her back to Eliza, leaving Ralph's and Joshua's corners behind.

Eliza blew out the light, then lay down facing Ralph's corner. "I think Ralph is the best-looking boy I've ever seen and the most fun, too. Good night, Cora."

"Good night, Eliza."

❊

The first thing Cora saw the next morning was Eliza sitting on the floor beside the bed staring at her.

"You're not supposed to look at me!"

Cora laughed at Eliza's crestfallen face. "If you don't want me to look at you, why are you sitting in front of me?"

"I wanted to see which corner you saw first. Oh, Cora, now we'll never know who you're going to marry."

"You really are a ninny, Eliza." Cora stretched and yawned. "You'll know well enough when I marry George."

"Well, I hope you don't marry him."

"Why not?" Cora threw the covers back and crawled from bed. "Brr. It's cold in here."

"I thought you liked Aaron."

Cora slipped from her flannel gown and pulled her dress over her head. She spoke from the security of its cover. "I like him well enough, but it's George I'm marrying."

As the dress fell into place, Cora met Eliza's disapproving gaze. "Are you honestly and truly in love with that. . .that. . . ? Oh, I don't know how you can even stand to be around him. All he wants to do is talk like a book and make everyone think he's the biggest toad in the puddle."

"Eliza!" Cora didn't know whether to be outraged with her little sister or laugh. She was so serious. She shrugged her shoulders. "Oh well, we'll live in St. Louis."

"That's another reason I don't want you marrying him."

Cora looked in surprise at her sister's bowed head. Eliza would miss her if she left with George. Love spread through Cora's heart. She sat on the bed, putting her arm across Eliza's shoulders. "Don't feel bad, Eliza. It isn't as if we'll never see each other again. George will bring me back to visit."

Eliza made an unladylike noise. "Sure he will—if he wants to."

Deep in her heart, Cora knew that was true, but to agree would be disloyal to George. "John is his brother. He will want to see him."

Cora stood and crossed the small room to the opening that led below. "Tell me which corner you saw."

A saucy grin lit Eliza's face. "Ralph's, of course."

❊

By midmorning, slow, steady rain drove cold deep into Cora's bones. And with the dreary cold came a feeling of depression. As she had expected, the gaps between the logs kept the inside temperature almost as cold as outside. She moved through her morning chores, thinking of St. Louis.

Orval came inside, dripping rain from his oilskin coat. With help from Ben and John, he started the slow task of paneling the walls. They used an auger to drill matching holes through the boards and log walls. Then they drove a locust peg into each hole until it was flush with the smooth board.

Cora ran her hand down the wall, admiring her father's handiwork. The side of each board had been beveled so that the one above and below it interleaved, creating a weatherproof seal.

"When we get the logs chinked, you won't feel the cold north wind at all," Father said.

Cora turned and looked at him. "So this is what Aaron meant by clapboards. But how will you chink them?"

"There's some sticky red clay down on the creek bank that's just what we need." A twinkle flashed from his eyes. "If you want to run down and get some, we'll let you work on the outside while we get the inside ready for you."

"I don't think so." Cora laughed and moved away.

"That's a woman for you. Afraid of a little dirt."

The rain slowed to a drizzle by late afternoon while the men worked their way along the west wall. Three days later, the drizzling rain changed to snow as the men finished paneling the house.

"Now that ought to keep out the cold." Orval stood in the middle of the kitchen admiring his work while Emma served hot cocoa to everyone.

John folded his arms across his chest and nodded. "Yep, I'd say we did a pretty good job."

Cora looked at her family and felt warmed by the love and happiness that radiated from them. She tucked the memory of the moment away to bring out later when she was in St. Louis with George.

That night Cora lay under a mountain of covers, thinking of the snow outside and her excitement grew. Would this storm bring enough snow for sledding? She hoped so. She went to sleep with a smile.

The snow continued the next day until late evening. When Ben came in from his chores, he grinned at Cora. "If it doesn't start snowing again, we should have good sledding weather tomorrow."

"Great!" Cora was tired of staying in the dark house. A romp in the snow sounded wonderful. Now, if only the Starks and Newkirks came.

Cora woke the next morning and reached for a candle.

Eliza stopped her. "Oh no you don't. I got dressed without light and so can you. Father said to conserve our candles because they have to last until spring, when he and John go back to St. Louis."

"When are they going back?"

"As soon as they can travel. Father said they'll probably be gone a month."

Cora wondered how Eliza knew everything before she did. She dressed and went downstairs. At midmorning, she heard the jingle of harness bells.

She grabbed her coat, struggling into it as she ran to the door.

"Better button that up good before you come out." Ben flashed a grin as he brushed past, hurriedly buttoning his own coat. He went outside, closing the heavy door behind him.

Eliza slipped into her coat and reached for her long, woolen scarf. Cora buttoned her coat and followed Ben, sweeping past her little sister.

Cora saw Ben help Esther climb out of a wagon bed set on runners. "Oh, how wonderful. You have a sleigh just like Saint Nicholas."

Esther laughed. "Probably not exactly like his. My father made this one from an old wagon. Is everyone here?"

"No, but here they come now," Eliza said.

Three dark figures emerged from the white-covered forest. Esther spoke in a near whisper. "They'll be frozen by the time they get here. Isn't there something we could do inside until they warm up?"

"Mother has hot cocoa. We could play a game or something," Ben suggested.

Then the Starks arrived, and Eliza smiled up at Ralph. "Hi. We didn't know you had a sled."

"Didn't till the other day." Ralph grinned at her. "Aaron studied on it all the way home from your dance, and this is what he came up with."

"You made this?" Red tinged Aaron's cheeks at the awe in Cora's voice.

"I wish I'd made one." Ben frowned. "I never even thought, but we could have used it." He looked from the sled to Aaron. "Looks like a nice one, too."

Aaron grinned. "Thanks."

As the others moved toward the house, Aaron held back. "Cora."

She stopped in surprise. That was the first time she'd heard him say her name, and she liked the sound.

He raised his head. "I was jist wonderin' if maybe you'd ride with me?"

Cora's eyebrows lifted. She hadn't taken Ralph's nonsense seriously, but Aaron was different. Yet, how could a simple sled ride hurt? She smiled. "That sounds like fun."

While Ivy stretched her feet out to the warm stove, the others gathered around the table. Ben brought out a book. "How would you like to read? I have an exciting adventure story here that I know you'll like." He held it up for them to see. "*Swiss Family Robinson*. Have you read it?"

Cora noticed the look that passed between Ralph and Aaron. Ralph grinned, leaning back in his chair. "Nope. Cain't rightly say we read that one, Ben. Why don't you read it to us?"

Ben took a swallow of hot cocoa and sat down. "Back home we used to have readings. You know, we'd each take a turn reading a page or two from a book. Why don't we do that now? By the time we've made a round, we ought to be warm enough to go outside."

Ben began reading. " 'For many days we had been tempest-tossed. Six times had the darkness closed over a wild and terrific scene. . . .' " He read the first two pages, then handed the book to John.

Cora watched the Stark brothers as the book made its way around the table. They seemed to be spellbound until Aaron stood. "Excuse me." He joined Ivy at the stove.

Ralph took the book next and passed it to Esther. "Cain't get blood from a turnip." He grinned broadly. "Y'all gotta excuse me and my brother. We ain't never had no book learnin'."

Esther nodded. "I haven't had much schooling, either. But if you'll put up with me, I'll try to read."

Cora listened to the next two pages and realized reading was not easy for Esther. As Esther paused to sound out a word, Cora looked at Aaron. He stood with his back to them, his arms folded. Cora's heart went out to him. It wasn't his fault he couldn't read.

Esther finished, and Cora took the book. For the first time in her life, she felt self-conscious as she read. Without realizing it, she read faster than normal.

"Well, that was interesting." Vickie's eyebrows rose. "I hope we all understood it."

"This is ridiculous." Cora slammed the book closed on the table. "Can't we go outside now?"

Chapter 5

The cold air felt good against Aaron's flushed face. His muscles flexed as he helped Ben lift the sleds from the Newkirks' wagon.

"Who's going to ride first?" Ben looked at everyone, but his smile was for Esther.

Aaron watched Esther's full pink lips spread and curve, while her blue eyes spoke of her feelings for Ben. "There's room for three or four on each sled."

"Ah yes." Ben grinned. "But only if they are small children. When I get on a sled, there'll be room for only one more."

Esther's cheeks flushed, and her gaze fell beneath Ben's bold scrutiny.

It didn't take a city boy with a passel of education to figure out what was going on between those two. There was no doubt that Esther was beautiful, and she was as nice as anything. A cold, hard knot formed in Aaron's chest as his gaze shifted to Cora. It sure was funny how the heart had a mind of its own.

Cora's laughter sounded like music as she grabbed her little nephew's hand. "Nicholas and I want to ride."

"Good." Ben grinned at his sister. "You can go on the second trip."

Aaron leaned against the wagon bed, his arms folded across his chest. He'd felt like a fool when everyone but he and Ralph and Ivy read. A dummy like he was wouldn't ever stand a chance with a girl like Cora. He shouldn't have asked her to ride with him.

"You can talk about it all day if you want to." John grabbed the lead rope of one sled. "But as your chaperone, I'd better take the first ride. You know. To make sure it's safe. We wouldn't want anyone getting hurt."

Vickie playfully hit his arm. "Oh sure. You just can't wait to hop on one of those sleds."

His twinkling eyes betrayed his forced frown. "Please don't undermine my authority as the oldest child here."

Aaron watched the others move away laughing and joking with each other. The rough wood of the wagon rubbed his back through his threadbare coat as he pushed away to follow them. Life wasn't fair. The Newkirks had a wagon for good weather and a sleigh for when it snowed, not to mention the two fine-looking horses pulling it. And look at all the things the Jacksons owned. His family owned nothing but their cabin and one old ox.

"Come on, Aaron." Cora waited for him. His heart thumped hard in reaction to her smile. "You can guide one of those sleds, can't you?"

He nodded. "Never tried it before, but I reckon so."

"You mean you built that fine sled, but you didn't ride on it?" She fell into step with him. Her nephew clung to her hand.

He felt self-conscious with her walking so close beside him. With an effort, he tried to change his speech pattern to fit hers. "I just got it finished this morning. There wasn't no. . ." He paused, knowing that hadn't sounded right, but unsure how to correct it. He felt his face flush as he finished his sentence. "No time to try it out."

"Oh, I'm sure it will ride beautifully. I don't know how you managed to make it so fast. You must be really good with your hands."

If his heart had been thumping before, now it was hammering. He was totally aware of the girl beside him. She was so small, even wrapped in that heavy fur coat. He felt big and awkward. Before he could think of anything to say, she went on.

"Nicholas wants to ride with me. I'm glad I'll have you to help us. The first ride's already taken. Ben's taking Esther on one, John and Vickie will go on another, and I think Eliza has Ralph talked into taking your sled. It's the one I want when we ride." She stopped suddenly and looked up at him, her light brown eyes searching his face. "You don't mind, do you? I mean about Nicholas."

Mind? He was proud she wanted to ride with him. Knowing his eyes probably revealed every beat of his heart, but unable to look away, he memorized each detail of her face. "No, I don't mind. I like the little feller."

They stood at the top of the hill watching the three couples take off. Sure enough, Eliza had talked Ralph into riding with her. Aaron felt sorry for Eliza. He knew Ralph wasn't ready to think of any girl seriously. Besides, Ralph thought Eliza was just a child. It was a wonder he hadn't tried to get Cora to ride with him.

The squeals and laughter coming from the younger children as they played in the snow while they waited for a ride caught Aaron's attention. Grace stepped to Cora's side and they started talking.

Aaron scooped a handful of snow and patted it into a snowball. It packed real good. He wondered if the girls and little kids would like to build a snowman while they waited. At least it would keep them warmer than just standing around.

He squatted, balancing on the heel of one foot. "Nicholas, look at this."

The little boy turned, his eyes large and dark in contrast to the whiteness of winter.

Aaron grinned at the child while observing his aunt's reaction. A slow smile lifted the corners of Cora's mouth. "It's going to be a snowman, Nicholas." Her warm, brown eyes met Aaron's. "May we help?"

"Sure, can you catch?"

Before Cora had time to answer, Aaron tossed the snowball. Her reaction was delayed as she reached for it, and it hit the front of her coat with a *splat*. She looked up, laughing at the expression of shock on Aaron's face. She grinned mischievously at Grace and Ivy standing to the side watching. "Are we going to let him get away with that?"

"Not on your life." Grace knelt in the snow and began forming snowballs as fast as she could. Ivy simply frowned and looked back down the hill at the three rapidly moving sleds.

Margaret left the younger children to help Grace. Her childish laughter rang in the cold air. "Come on, Cora. We'll get him real good."

Cora stood for only a few seconds, her gaze locked with Aaron's. In that brief moment, an obscure message flickered between them. "All right, Margaret." Cora reached for a handful of snow. "Let's make lots of snowballs."

"Hey, Nicholas. You ain't gonna let those girls whip me, are you?" Aaron worked frantically, trying to match the girls' growing arsenal. "Us men gotta stay together."

Nicholas ran to Aaron's side without hesitation. "Nickus help." He squatted and, scooping up a handful of snow, flung it toward the girls.

Aaron laughed. "That's the spirit."

"How dare you turn my nephew against me!" Cora grabbed a snowball in each hand. The first whizzed past Aaron's head, but the second grazed his shoulder. Grace and Margaret followed her lead and the fight began.

Lenny and Gilbert ran to Aaron's side. They each grabbed a snowball from his small supply and threw it. Gilbert's snowball went over the girls' heads, and they scrambled to retrieve it. Lenny's volley fell short.

Aaron held a brief consultation with his teammates. When they broke from their huddle, Lenny set to work making snowballs for the older boys to throw. Nicholas, unhampered by restriction, continued his own form of snowball fighting. Aaron chuckled at Nicholas's vain attempts. He sure was a cute little guy. He'd grab snow in his small mitten-covered hand and, before packing it, fling it in a spraying arch shorter than Aaron's arm.

Just then a blur of white sailed past Aaron's head. He didn't bother to dodge. The way the girls threw, they weren't likely to hit anything smaller than a barn. He worked fast, scooping, packing, and throwing in one smooth motion. He left Lenny's snowballs for Gilbert to throw. His opponents had long since run out of their supply, and they hadn't figured out they could make them as they threw them. He grinned as another landed in front of him. He reached for it, and snow suddenly splattered on his forehead. His face stung with a wet cold that dripped into his eyes so he couldn't see who had fired the wild shot that finally made contact.

He cleared his eyes of snow to find all three girls laughing hysterically. A grin touched his lips as he saw Cora lift her hand to throw another frozen missile.

Cora stared in disbelief as Aaron found his mark, knocking her snowball from her hand. Surely that was a lucky throw. She looked at Aaron's smug face. "I'm sure you can't do that again."

"Try me."

"All right, I will." Cora formed another snowball and lifted it, only to have it meet with the same fate.

"How did you do that?"

"Like this." Again Aaron demonstrated his accurate aim by knocking a snowball from Grace's hand.

"All right, girls, let's quit." Cora held her arms out to the side in front of the other girls. "As far as I'm concerned, the boys win. Next time I want to be on Aaron's side."

Cora brushed snow from her hair and coat. She crossed the distance to Aaron just as the first sled riders came trudging up the hill. "I didn't know anyone could throw like that." The admiration in her voice seemed to fluster him.

Aaron looked aside, a pleased expression covering his face. "Aw, that wasn't nothin' on-common. It jist takes lots of practicin', and I've had a passel of that." He touched his forehead. "You ain't so bad yourself."

Cora smiled. "That was more accident than skill."

"So it was you!"

Still smiling, Cora nodded, then turned as she heard Ralph's voice.

"Now that's what I call a hill. Sled works fine, too." Ralph came toward them with a wide grin. "Goin' down sure beats hoofin' it back up through all this snow, though." He looked at Cora. "You ready to give 'er a try?"

"Yes, Aaron promised to take Nicholas and me." Cora smiled at Aaron before taking her nephew's hand and turning away.

Ralph said, "I don't think she likes me." His lowered voice carried too well, making Cora feel awkward.

"Then leave her alone."

"Aw, I was jist bein' friendly."

Cora walked away from the brothers. She heard their conversation but couldn't very well let them know. She was sorry Ralph thought she didn't like him. How could anyone not like him? But as much as she liked his fun-loving nature, she couldn't imagine becoming serious about a man who wanted to play all the time.

Vickie picked up Nicholas as Cora climbed on the sled. She held him close, giving him a motherly kiss before helping him settle on Cora's lap. "Watch out for him and don't let him fall."

"Don't worry. I won't let anything happen to my favorite nephew." Cora wrapped her arms around him, pulling him close.

The little fellow laughed, his arms waving excitedly as he strained forward against her hold. Aaron climbed on behind Cora, spreading his legs on either side. He reached around her, taking the rope handle in his hands.

Nicholas leaned forward, then fell back against Cora. The unexpected weight pushed Cora against Aaron's chest. Her temple brushed his jaw before she jerked upright, her face flaming.

"Nicholas, sit still. You'll push us off backward."

Aaron's deep voice vibrated near her ear. "Don't worry. I won't let you fall."

Then someone pushed them and they were off. The wind rushed past, lifting Cora's hair and cooling her face. Nicholas squealed in delight. Cora felt as if she were in a dream world, racing across the snow. She felt safe with Aaron's arms surrounding her. She wished they could go on and on, but almost before it had started, the ride was over.

Cora laughed as she scrambled from the sled. "That was wonderful. I wish there were twice as many sleds so we wouldn't have to take turns."

Aaron smiled at her enthusiasm. He set Nicholas on the sled so he could ride the return trip, then picked up the rope. Cora fell into step beside him. They walked in silence, their feet crunching in the snow.

He grinned at her. "How about me givin' you and Nicholas another ride?"

"We'd like that, wouldn't we, Nicholas?" She turned to smile at her nephew. He clapped his hands in answer.

"Hang on, Nicholas." Aaron grabbed Cora's hand. "Come on, let's run to the top."

Cora's breath came in puffs by the time they reached the others. Vickie took Nicholas from the sled and looked into Cora's eyes. "Looks like you are having fun."

Cora glanced quickly at Aaron, who was standing by John. "I am. I didn't realize sledding could be so much fun."

"Are you sure it's just the sledding?"

Cora's gaze flew to her sister's teasing face. "What else? You know George and I plan to marry."

"I know." Vickie grew serious. "Mother doesn't want John and me to move even a few miles away. Just think what she'll do when you announce that you're moving back to St. Louis." She smiled then. "You'd better find someone right here unless you think you can talk George into settling down in this wilderness."

A sick feeling gripped Cora's stomach. Although she hadn't told Mother and Father of her plans, she hadn't realized they would object. Mother had always said the Merrills were good, respectable people. She'd been happy enough to welcome John into their family. Cora assumed John's younger brother would be welcome, too.

Vickie laughed. "Don't look so scared, Cora. It isn't as if you're planning to get married next week. Give her time. Maybe by the time you and George marry, Mother will have changed."

Cora watched her sister walk away with Nicholas to the sled where John waited. She did plan to marry George right away. Her mind whirled and she didn't see Aaron until he stood in front of her.

"Cora?"

Cora forced her eyes to focus on his face. His dark hair was a wind-curled mass. The dimple in his chin drew her attention, and an overwhelming desire to touch it shocked her.

"I made you something." Aaron reached inside his coat and pulled out a white, cloth-wrapped package. A bright red ribbon held it together. He handed the package to her. "It's almost Christmas. I reckoned this might be my only chance to see you afore then. Anyhow, this is for you."

She took it and looked up at him. "Can I open it now?"

He nodded.

Cora untied the ribbon and stuck it in her coat pocket. As the cloth wrapping fell away, she held a small cedar box with leather hinges. It had been sanded smooth and polished to a high shine. An intricate design of carved scrollwork decorated the top.

She opened the box and smelled the cedar wood. Inside, two flat partitions of cedar had been driven into carefully chiseled slots, dividing the box into three small sections.

She closed the lid and ran her hand across the carving. "Aaron, I love it. I'll keep it always. Thank you so much."

Aaron's wide grin and pleased expression tugged at her heart. "I'm real proud you like it. I thought you might have somethin' special to keep in it."

"Oh, I do. I have some necklaces that will fit perfectly."

Cora began wondering what she could make for him. The rest of the day she thought of little else, discarding one idea after another, until finally she decided to ask her mother if she could shorten the white linen tablecloth. It was much too large for the small table they now had, and it would make wonderful hand-embroidered handkerchiefs.

Chapter 6

For the next week, Cora's needle flew through the linen squares that would be Aaron's gift. She sat on her bed putting the finishing touches on the third handkerchief when Eliza's head appeared above the opening to their room.

"What are you doing?" Eliza climbed the rest of the way up the ladder and crossed the room to sit beside her sister.

Cora carefully folded the handkerchief into fourths and placed it on top of the others. She pressed them down with her hand. "I'm not doing anything now. I just finished a gift for Aaron."

"Why?" Eliza picked up the handkerchiefs to rub her finger over the embroidered initials. "I wish I could embroider like this."

"You probably could if you'd try."

"I have tried." Eliza sighed. "You know needlework is difficult for me. Why did you make something for Aaron?"

"Because he gave me something."

Eliza's eyes lit up. "He did?"

"Yes, he did." Cora grabbed the handkerchiefs from her younger sister. "Did you come up here for a reason?"

"No, but I have a reason now. I want to see what Aaron gave you."

Without a word, Cora flopped across the bed and, reaching into the gap between the mattress and wall, pulled the cedar box out. Her voice softened. "It's beautiful, isn't it?"

Eliza opened the box and sniffed inside. "I love the smell of cedar."

Cora grabbed it from her. "At least your nose works. Aaron did a wonderful job making it. Can't you appreciate the time he put into it?"

Eliza grinned. "Maybe we'll marry brothers yet."

"Oh, Eliza." Cora stretched back across the bed to return her box. When she sat up, the grin was gone from Eliza's face.

"I really like Ralph, Cora. I want him to like me, but I don't think he does." She looked at the handkerchiefs again. "Maybe if I could give him something like this, he'd like me better. But I can't sew like you can."

Something in her younger sister's manner pulled at Cora's heart. She should tell Eliza to do her own sewing, but somehow she found herself offering to help.

"All right. What do you want me to do?"

"Just make the same thing except put R W S in the corner."

"What's the W for?"

"Walter. He was named after his father." Eliza grinned. "You don't know Aaron's middle name, do you?"

"No, and I don't care. How do you always know everything, anyway?"

"It's James. Aaron James Stark. He'll be twenty-two on April 28." Eliza's smug expression grated on Cora's nerves.

She jumped off the mattress, grabbing the handkerchiefs. "I told you I don't care. I'm going to go wrap these. I think Mother saved the paper she had around her best dishes."

Cora walked quickly to the ladder and started down. As her face came to just above the bedroom floor, Eliza called after her. "About Ralph's hankies. You don't mind if I tell him I made them, do you?"

Cora stopped. "That would be a lie."

Eliza shrugged. "Not if I hem them and all you do are the initials."

"What do you mean 'all'? That's the hardest part." Cora had a feeling she was being taken advantage of. She sighed. "Oh, don't worry. I won't tell your secret."

"Thanks." Eliza smiled.

Cora worked until two days before Christmas when all her gifts were finished. She went to bed later than usual that night but woke in the wee hours of Christmas Eve to a dark, quiet house. She lay staring into the thick blackness, thinking of George. Would he come today or tomorrow? Since her talk with Vickie the day of the sledding party, she had come to a decision. If Mother would not let her leave with George, she and George could elope. She had started packing an empty flour sack with clothing and special things she couldn't bear leaving behind.

She turned to her side, her hand reaching to the space between the mattress and wall. She stretched until she felt the cedar box Aaron had given her. It was so pretty she hadn't had the heart to bury it out of sight in the sack.

With the box clutched firmly in her hands, she rolled off the mattress and landed on the cold wood floor. She felt her way carefully to the corner where Father had driven pegs into the wall for their clothing. There, hiding behind her best dress, hung the flour sack. She slid her hand to the drawstring at the top. There was barely room to push the box in.

Cora slid back into the still warm bed beside Eliza. No sooner had she closed her eyes, it seemed, until Eliza shook her.

"Cora, you had better get up if you plan on going with us to deliver gifts."

The two girls ate hurriedly and rushed through the cabin door as Ben brought one of Father's large workhorses to the front yard.

"It's about time you two came out." Ben grinned at his sisters. "Climb aboard and let's go."

Ben helped Eliza and Cora mount, then he hoisted himself in front of them. He picked up the reins, spoke to the horse, and they began a slow plodding ride west to the natural ford in the creek.

As Bill Reid's homestead came into view, Cora wondered why a man living alone would build such a large house. It was every bit as big as their own—and there were nine of them. His barn was even bigger. With a large section in the center and a shed on either side, it dominated the settlement.

Mr. Reid came from the barn as Ben stopped near the house. He lifted his hand in a welcoming salute. "Hello, there. I was just thinking how nice it would be to have company and here you are." He set a bucket down near the back door. "Come on in. I think there's some coffee left over from breakfast."

Ben jumped down and lifted his arms for first Cora and then Eliza. He turned to Mr. Reid. "We were just admiring your barn as we came up. It looks big enough for a dance."

Mr. Reid laughed. "I guess it is at that. Maybe one of these days we'll have a party here."

Cora glanced around Mr. Reid's clean, neat house before handing him the gift her mother had wrapped. "We had some pecans that Mother put into candy. She thought you might like some for Christmas."

As he took the package, his hand touched hers for a moment. She would have thought nothing of it except for the look in his eyes. She had seen that look before in boys her own age, but never in a man so old. She jerked her hand back.

"Thank you so much. I know I'll enjoy these. Don't forget to thank your mother for me. I have a gift for your family, as well." Mr. Reid moved to a bookcase against the end wall.

"This is a collection of poetry from some of the world's most renowned poets. I know your mother will enjoy it, and I'm sure the rest of you will, too."

Ben took the book and thanked Mr. Reid. Cora covertly watched the older man as he talked with Ben about some of the poems. She was glad to climb on the big horse and head back across the creek to the Newkirks'.

As soon as Cora saw the Newkirks' cabin, she knew it could belong to no one else. Even in the well-tracked snow, there was an air of order about the place. The house was smaller than Mr. Reid's, and a large shed stood several yards away with a rail fence built out from one side.

Gilbert met them at the door, and they followed him inside, where Mrs. Newkirk stooped over a large pot suspended above the flames in the fireplace. She stirred the contents carefully, then hung the long-handled metal spoon to the side of the mantel. As she straightened, she smiled. "You will stay and eat, won't you?"

Cora looked at Ben expectantly. She knew he'd like nothing better than to prolong their visit. Eliza, too, seemed to be holding her breath as she waited for his answer.

With just the slightest glance Esther's way, Ben smiled. "Ma'am, I certainly appreciate your hospitality. We'd be honored to stay."

"Good, then it's settled. Grace, will you please set the table? Esther, the bread is ready to take up."

Cora asked. "Is there anything I can do?" Eliza was already helping Grace with the table.

Mrs. Newkirk paused long enough to nod toward the fireplace. "The stew could use another stirring if you don't mind."

While Ben visited with Mr. Newkirk, the women worked together getting the table ready.

"Cora, sit by me." Margaret scooted over and patted the bench.

Cora smiled at the little girl. "All right."

As soon as everyone had settled around the table, Mr. Newkirk bowed his head to pray. Then Mrs. Newkirk stood and dished up the stew. A gentle hum rose and fell as several conversations went on at the same time.

Margaret turned to Cora. "Do you have a tree for Christmas?"

"No, not yet. My father and John took Lenny and Nicholas down to the creek this morning to cut one, though. They may have it up by now."

"Won't you help decorate it?" Margaret's eyes widened with concern.

"Oh yes, I'm sure they'll wait for us."

"I guess that means you wouldn't want to help us decorate ours." Margaret's expression grew serious. "It's outside. We're going to put it up this afternoon."

"I would love to, but I can't. We have one more stop to make, and Mother made us promise to be home well before dark." Cora laughed. "She still hasn't gotten over the night Ben and I stayed in a tree."

"You stayed all night in a tree?" Margaret parroted. "Why'd you do that?"

Cora laughed as she and Ben told of their experience.

When they finished, Mrs. Newkirk dabbed her eyes with her napkin. "God must surely have had His hand on you. How else could you have found that tree?"

Mr. Newkirk nodded. "Sounds like a miracle. It makes me wonder if God doesn't have a work for you to do. Maybe you two young 'uns will be mighty soul-winners for Him one of these days."

As soon as the last spoonful of stew was consumed, Mr. Newkirk reached for his Bible. Cora watched him with wide eyes. Surely he wouldn't preach to them.

He cleared his throat as he opened the well-worn book and ran his hand lovingly over the pages. Then he looked across the table at Ben. "Would you mind reading for us today?"

Cora thought Ben looked as uncomfortable as she felt. He took the Bible and nodded. "I'd be glad to."

"Good." Mr. Newkirk smiled. "Why don't you read from Isaiah 49? It's Christmas Eve. Let's read about Jesus from the Old Testament."

" 'The Lord hath called me from the womb; from the bowels of my mother hath he made mention of my name. And he hath made my mouth like a sharp sword. . . . ' "

Cora looked around the table. Did Ben have the right place? Even the youngest children sat quietly, with Mr. Newkirk listening intently. She shrugged.

Ben continued. " 'I will also give thee for a light to the Gentiles, that thou mayest be my salvation unto the end of the earth.' "

On and on Ben's voice droned as Cora tried in vain to pay attention. " 'Sing, O heavens; and be joyful, O earth; and break forth into singing, O mountains: for the Lord hath comforted his people, and will have mercy upon his afflicted.' "

"Amen!" Mr. Newkirk's hearty voice interrupted. "Our God is, without fail, wonderful." A broad smile lit his face. "If you don't mind, just look on over to chapter fifty. It'll tell us what Jesus came to this old, sinful world to do."

Cora looked at Esther's father. He knew where he wanted Ben to read without looking. Or was he making it up? So far, she hadn't gotten much sense from all this reading. Then something caught her attention.

" 'I gave my back to the smiters, and my cheeks to them that plucked off the hair: I hid not my face from shame and spitting.' "

Ben really was reading about Jesus. Suddenly, the scriptures took on life in her mind, and she saw Jesus surrounded by Roman soldiers. Jesus came to earth to be punished and die. But why? Why would the Son of God suffer unimaginable torture when He didn't have to?

Cora's eyes burned with tears that she refused to release. She forced the image of Jesus from her mind, concentrating instead on Ben's face.

Ben looked up as soon as he finished the chapter. "I've never read this before. I thought the Old Testament was about a time before Jesus was born, but this is talking about Him, isn't it?"

Mr. Newkirk nodded, leaning forward in his eagerness. "Yes, and this isn't the only place that tells us about Him. You can find scriptures as early as Genesis that give us the promise of His coming."

Cora looked at Eliza and was shocked to see the interested light in her eyes. What was going on? They had come to give gifts, not go to church. She watched for a break in the conversation.

"I don't mean to interrupt, but we haven't given our gifts and we have a long way to go yet." She glanced toward Mrs. Newkirk at the other end of the table. "Eliza and I need to help with the dishes."

"No." Esther's mother jumped up and reached for the nearest plate. "I've got plenty of girls to help without putting our company to work."

Ben stood, handing the Bible to Mr. Newkirk. "Maybe we can talk some more later. We do need to go."

Cora slipped out the door and back in with the package of candy and aprons. She handed the candy to Mrs. Newkirk. Eliza took one apron from her for Grace, and Cora gave Esther one. "This is from Eliza and me. We both worked on it. I hope you'll like it."

Esther held the apron up. "I do. Very much. Thank you." She hugged Cora, exclaiming over the fine work she had done. "I have something for you, too."

She hurried to the ladder in the corner of the room and climbed out of sight. She was soon back. She reached for Cora's hand, turning it palm up, then held her closed fist over it. She opened her fingers and a delicate golden beaded necklace fell into Cora's hand.

Cora let it dangle from her fingers. A tiny rosette of red beads had been worked into one spot on the gold. She whispered, "It's beautiful." She looked up at her friend's smiling face. "Did you make this?"

Esther nodded. "I like working with beads. I'm glad you like it."

"I do." Cora flung her arms around Esther. "Try to come see me soon."

Esther nodded. "I will. Maybe for your birthday. It's soon, isn't it?"

Cora smiled. "Yes, January ninth." She would be nineteen then and married. There would be no reason for Esther to come, yet she could say nothing.

As they left, Mrs. Newkirk handed Ben a large package of cookies to take home. With everyone calling out their thanks and good-byes all at the same time, Ben helped his sisters on the horse. Cora's heart filled with gladness as she waved to her friends. Ben headed the large workhorse back east toward the Starks' place.

Chapter 7

A skinny hound greeted them as they rode into the Starks' yard. He ran alongside, jumping at the horse as it carefully picked its way around various odd-shaped bumps in the snow.

The sturdy cabin appeared smaller than the Jacksons' house. It had no loft. Instead, two shedlike rooms projected from either side of the main cabin.

The dog continued to accentuate each bark with a jump at their feet. When the door flew open, two more dogs ran out, adding their voices to the din. Ralph stood framed in the doorway, a huge grin on his face. He yelled over the dogs' barks. "Hey, come on in and make yourselves to home."

Cora sat high on the horse thinking she knew how a treed raccoon felt. Eliza's grip on her arm tightened.

Ivy came to the door. "Ralph, don't you have no manners at all? Call them dogs off so's they can git down."

"Why? They's jist friendly. It ain't like they're gonna bite nobody." Ralph grinned up at the two girls.

"Old Blue!" A deep, commanding voice brought instant silence. Aaron walked around the corner of the cabin, grabbed the largest dog by the short rope on its neck, and led it around the cabin. The others followed with tails tucked.

Ben dismounted and helped his sisters down. Cora glanced at the corner where Aaron had disappeared with the dogs. She followed her brother inside, hoping Aaron would return soon.

"Howdy." Mr. Stark raised himself to a sitting position on a braided rug before the fireplace. "Git ya a chur."

He motioned toward five stumps arranged around a pole with a board on top. Cora had never seen anything like it, but she realized it was the dining table. The center pole, driven into the dirt floor, looked as if it had grown there. A hewn board pegged to the top of the pole served as tabletop and the five stumps were the chairs.

Before she sat down, she slipped the small package containing Aaron's handkerchiefs into the full gathered material of her sleeve and hoped no one noticed.

"Don't speck to see no more warm days now afore spring," Mr. Stark spoke.

"No, I don't suppose so," Ben said. "What sort of crops do you grow here?"

Ralph chuckled. "Ain't nothin' much but corn'll give you any cash. Corn liquor that is."

Mr. Stark nodded. "Yep, that's the cheapest way they is to make a livin' off'n corn. Hit'd take a whole wagon train to take as much to Springfield as we transport on our one ox's back."

"I see." Ben looked uncomfortable. "Well, we came by to wish you a merry Christmas and deliver a gift." He turned to Cora. "You've got it, haven't you?"

"Yes." She stepped across the dirt floor to Mrs. Stark. "This is from all of us to all of you. We hope you'll enjoy it."

"Well, if that ain't nice. You be sure and thank yore ma fer us." Mrs. Stark's rough, work-worn hand gently touched the white paper, then moved to the green ribbon holding it. When she looked up, Cora was struck by the beauty of her large blue eyes. An inner light seemed to radiate from the woman's soul as though she had been denied beauty for so long, she had forgotten she even missed it.

"Ain't ya gonna open it, woman? Cain't git no good outta that fancy paper."

Cora turned at Mr. Stark's rough voice, and suddenly she understood why Ivy was so desperate to marry well. She didn't want to end up like her mother, working herself into an early grave. Poor Ivy. Cora felt deep sympathy for her. How could she escape a life of drudgery except through marriage?

"All right. I'm a-takin' it off." Even as she spoke, Mrs. Stark carefully slid the ribbon to one side and lifted the paper. When she set them safely aside, she exclaimed, "Why, looky there. It's some kinda fancy candy."

"They're pecan pralines." Cora took a step toward the door. Poverty, hard work, and hopelessness fed on women like Mrs. Stark and Ivy. Slowly the life-blood was sucked from their souls, leaving them old, tired, and ugly. Sympathy for them and fear for herself rose as gall in her mouth. She wanted very much to go home.

Cora took another step backward and bumped into something. She turned, feeling foolish in her clumsiness.

"Ya didn't hurt a thing. That's my spinning wheel." Mrs. Stark's voice held a note of pride.

Cora reached a tentative hand toward the gleaming cherry wood of the head assembly. She had never seen a spinning wheel quite like this one. Especially the wheel post. An intricately carved wreath of rose leaves circled each end of the post while a single rose bloomed just below the peg holding the wheel. How odd something of such beauty would find a home in these humble surroundings. Where had the Starks gotten it?

As if to answer her unspoken question, Mrs. Stark said, "Purty, ain't it? My boy done made it fer me. Took a tolerable long time fer him to git all that foolishness on there, but it pleasures him to whittle."

"He's very good at it." Cora thought of the box Aaron had made her.

"He certainly is." Eliza brushed against Cora as she crowded close to look.

"Was your ma able to bring her spinning wheel when ya moved?" Mrs. Stark asked.

"She doesn't own one."

"Don't own one?" Mrs. Stark's eyes were wide. "You cain't make cloth without a spinning wheel and a loom. Ya got one o' them?" She nodded toward her unassembled loom leaning against the wall.

Cora shook her head and took another step toward the door. "No, Mother always had a seamstress make our clothes."

Mrs. Stark made a snorting sound and shook her head.

Ivy moved close to the spinning wheel. "Since it's a fer piece to a seamstress from here, you'll have to come over sometime and let me learn you to spin." Cora didn't miss the condescending tone in Ivy's voice.

"Thank you. Maybe I will." Cora looked at Ben and lifted her eyebrows slightly. "Right now it's getting late and we need to go home."

As Ben and Eliza moved toward the door, Cora breathed a sigh of relief.

When Ben lifted Cora to the horse's back, she felt the paper covering Aaron's gift crackle. A strange feeling of loss stole over her heart, intensifying when she heard Ralph's exclamation.

"Hey, looky here what I got. These is the fanciest rags I ever did see. That's right nice needlework in the corner there."

Eliza's cheeks flamed as she smiled up at the handsome young man. "Those are your initials." She took the handkerchiefs. "See, this is R and it stands for Ralph. The W is for Walter and the S is for Stark."

"Well, ain't that fancy?" Ralph looked impressed. He grinned at Eliza, taking her hand and giving it a little shake. "Thank ya much. I'm real put out I ain't got nothin' to give you." A cocky grin spread across his lips. "Maybe I could come callin' sometime."

The look on her little sister's face was enough to bring a smile to Cora's. Eliza nodded. "Yes, that would be nice. Please, do come."

Ben had just settled Eliza on the horse when Mr. Stark came outside. "Ma says fer me to send this home with y'all to your ma." He handed a package to Ben.

Ben looked up from the package as Mr. Stark explained. "Hit's souse meat."

"Oh, well, thank you. I'll tell Mother."

Ralph laughed. "Hit's real good eatin' iffen you like hog's head. Jist cut ya off a piece to eat cold or heat it up on that fancy stove y'all got."

"Hog's head?" Ben's voice cracked.

"Yup, like I said, it's real good eatin'."

❃

When Aaron rounded the corner of the house to see what was stirring up Old Blue, the last thing he expected to find was Cora. She was sitting up there so pretty wearing that fancy fur coat on that big fine horse with her brother and sister.

Aaron kicked at a rock sticking above the snow. He tied the dogs and left. He knew it was the coward's way, but he was too embarrassed to stay and watch her see the way they lived.

He stepped over a log, not knowing where he was going. He just wanted to get away and stay away until they were gone. Instinctively, he headed toward the hollow tree where he'd seen Cora that first time. He remembered how scared she'd looked when she crawled from the tree that morning. That was when he'd fallen in love with her.

He bent and looked inside the old sycamore before he crawled in. It was warm inside and dry. He leaned back against the wall and closed his eyes. Cora likely thought dirt floors were for animals. With self-imposed torture, he thought of Cora and the differences in their lives.

Cora was used to nice things. Things folks didn't have to have. All his family had were the necessities.

He could build a fancy cabin like her pa's and put a wood floor in it, too. He could even make some real pretty furniture. But it took money to get one of those fine cookstoves like her ma had. And what of the dishes they ate off of? Dishes like that took money and lots of it.

With a quick movement, he straightened his back and squared his shoulders. No sense pining away over something he could never have. *What am I doin', anyway, hidin' away from a little slip of a girl? I better git back home.* There was plenty of work waiting, and work was a good way to get a man's mind off a girl.

He dropped forward to crawl through the opening but stopped short of sticking his head through. A horse was coming. With his heart in his throat, he watched them. Ben sat in front, then Cora and Eliza.

He breathed a sigh of relief. They'd pass right by the tree without recognizing it. How could they remember a tree they'd only seen once even if it had sheltered them for the night? Then, in the next second, his heart raced.

"There it is, Ben." Cora pointed at the large sycamore. Aaron melted back out of sight, hoping he hadn't been seen.

They stopped scarcely five paces away. "Yep, that's it. Do you want to get down and look at it again?"

"Oh yes, let's do." Eliza bounced in her eagerness. "I've never been inside a tree. I don't see how you could have enough room to sit up, let alone sleep in there."

Aaron heard Cora's laughter, and pain shot through his heart.

"You have to realize, Eliza dear, we slept sitting up." Cora's tone sobered. "Come on, Ben, let's get home. I'm cold and it's getting late. Mother may be worried about us. Eliza can see the tree some other time."

"Sure, blame it on Mother when it's really because you think George will be there." Eliza sounded angry.

"George?" Ben asked. "He isn't coming, is he?"

"Yes, he is." Eliza spoke before Cora could. "He's coming to take Cora back to St. Louis. They're getting married, you know."

"No, I didn't know," Ben said. "Why would you do a dumb thing like that?"

"I don't see where this is your business—either of you," Cora said. "Please, Ben, let's go home. It's getting late and I'm cold and hungry."

"Might as well get it over with. If he's there, he'll stay for awhile," Ben answered.

Aaron watched them ride away until they disappeared into the trees. Then he crawled out of the tree.

So Cora was promised to a fellow named George. He sighed as he turned from the tree. He'd have to stay away from Cora. A leaden lump sat where his heart should have been as he made his way back home.

❧

George hadn't come. Cora was disappointed, but not worried. She was sure he would come the next day. It would be Christmas then. But George didn't come on Christmas Day, either.

The first day of 1834 came and left without an appearance from George. Each day Cora watched for him. Each night she felt the bag with her belongings still hanging behind her best dress.

Then, on January 9, Cora awoke the happiest she'd been in two weeks. Maybe George would surprise her and come for her birthday. She hummed to herself as she dressed.

"I hope this means you're going to stop brooding over that conceited show-off." Eliza propped herself up in bed, watching her older sister.

Cora looked up from the buttons on her dress. "Brooding? Have I been?"

"Oh, I don't know." Eliza's voice dripped sarcasm. "You've just been dragging yourself around, sighing every few minutes when you aren't looking out the door. What would you call it?"

Cora's eyes grew wide. "Have I really been that obvious? Do you think Mother has noticed?"

"No, Mother is too busy trying to make a civilized home here. She has more on her mind than your moods. Besides, I don't think she feels well."

"What do you mean?"

Eliza threw back the covers and reached for her dress. "I don't know. She acts tired."

"Maybe that's because of all the work there is to do," Cora said. "In case you haven't noticed, there isn't any hired help here."

Eliza shook her head. "No, it's more than that. We all help more than we ever did in St. Louis."

"Vickie hasn't been doing so much."

"That's true." A musing expression settled on Eliza's face. "I don't think she feels well, either."

Cora shrugged. "Maybe they just haven't gotten used to all of this yet." Her arm swept out including the cabin and all that lay beyond. "You'll have to admit, it isn't exactly like home."

"I know." Eliza grinned at her sister. "You've probably even forgotten that today's your birthday."

"Oh no I haven't." Cora smiled. "I also haven't forgotten that Esther promised to come over today."

"Well, just so George doesn't show up." Eliza's skirt twirled out as she turned quickly and flung her leg over the ladder. She dodged a pillow that sailed past her head, through the opening, to the floor below.

Both girls giggled as their father's voice drifted up. "You know, I was just sitting here trying to decide if a nineteen-year-old girl is too big for a spanking on her birthday. Then, a pillow flew right out of nowhere and hit me on the head. Cora, maybe you'd better come and get it. It might come in handy in case I decide nineteen isn't as old as I thought."

Cora followed Eliza downstairs to join the gaiety of her family as they celebrated her special day. Vickie baked her a cake, putting a ring of pecan halves along the edge. When Cora saw the pecans, her first thought was of the handsome backwoodsman who had given them to her, and warmth spread through her heart.

"Hey, Cora." Ben brushed snowflakes from his dark, wool coat. "We won't have company today. Looks like this snow's coming down to stay."

"Esther's not coming?"

"I doubt it." Ben's face showed his own disappointment. "Her father would never let them start out with it snowing. I was going to ride out to meet them, but there's no use now."

Cora threw on her coat and ran outside. Snow stung her face as she looked up at the gray sky. Ben was right. No one would be coming today. Not Esther. And not George.

A full foot of snow with drifts over three feet deep fell before it stopped. January passed and February came in before it began to melt. Then, just as Cora thought winter would finally step aside long enough for George to come, the temperature dropped, turning the outdoors into a world of ice.

As the days went by, Cora stopped looking for George. Then, one night in late February, as she and Eliza were getting ready for bed, Eliza said, "I know what's wrong with Mother."

Cora turned quickly toward her sister. "What do you mean?" She had forgotten about their mother and Vickie.

Eliza's light brown eyes sparkled in the candlelight. "Would you like to be a big sister—again?"

"Do you mean that Mother is. . .that there's going to be. . . . Oh, Eliza, are you sure?"

"Yes, I heard her and Vickie talking." Eliza squealed as Cora fell across the bed, taking her with her.

"When? When will she be born?"

"What makes you think it's a she?"

"I just want it to be."

"Oh?" Eliza raised her eyebrows. "I didn't know you liked little sisters."

Cora punched Eliza's arm. "Of course I do." She grinned. "At least part of the time."

"What about nieces?"

Cora laughed. "Ralph hasn't proposed yet, has he?"

Eliza blushed. "Not me. I mean Vickie."

"I know. I already figured that out." Cora fell back on her side of the bed. It had been six years since the fever took their youngest sister, Abigail. It would be wonderful to have another sister. She turned toward Eliza. "Are you sure you know what you're talking about?"

"Of course." Eliza sounded injured. "I heard Mother say that John can't go back home with Father because they are worried about Vickie. Then Vickie said, 'But, Mother, what of you?' and Mother said, 'I've given birth to six children and never had a sick day with any of them.' "

❧

With the advent of March, the sun returned and melted the snow. As preparations for the trip began in earnest, Cora found a sheet of paper and a pen.

She dipped her pen in ink and wrote furiously for close to an hour. She poured out her heart, emphasizing her love for George and exaggerating the loneliness of living in a land with so few people of common interests. Finally, she ended her letter; "I love and miss you so much. Each night when I go to sleep, my heart cries my longing to see your beloved face. Each morning I arise with the hope that this day will be the one when you come to take me away from this hateful wilderness. I remain forever yours, Cora."

She folded her letter and sealed it with wax from her candle. Then, she found Ben and took him aside. "I know you don't like George but—"

"No, Cora, I don't like him. I never have, but for you, I'll see if I can find out what's happened."

Cora threw her arms around Ben's neck. "I knew you'd understand. Thank you." She stepped back, handing him the letter. "Will you see that he gets this, too?"

Ben took the letter, stuffing it in his shirt pocket. "All right. I'll make sure he gets it if I can find him."

Cora smiled. "I don't think anything bad has happened. I just want to know what kept him from coming."

"Well, you'll soon know. We should be back in a couple of months."

"Are you going to see Esther before you leave?"

A light radiated from Ben's eyes at the mention of Esther. He nodded. "I wouldn't go away without seeing her first. We're leaving first light Monday morning, so I plan to go over Sunday afternoon."

Ben looked into her eyes. "Can you keep a secret?"

"Of course."

"All right, just don't tell anyone until after I ask her."

Cora grabbed his arm. "Are you serious?"

"I've never been more serious in my life." Ben grinned. "I'll never love anyone as much as I do Esther. If she can return my love, we'll be married as soon as I can get us a place to live."

❧

Late Sunday afternoon when Ben came home, a huge smile covered his face. As soon as Cora saw him, she said, "Oh, Ben, I'm so happy for you. You couldn't have picked a better sister for me."

"You may be sure that wasn't my purpose." Ben grinned.

Cora watched him go outside. It must be wonderful to have the future decided. She thought of George and shook her head in frustration. Right now, she didn't know what she'd do if he walked through the door. Would she fall into his arms or turn her back on him?

That evening just before bedtime, Mr. Reid stopped by. He said, "I hope I'm not interrupting anything. I noticed your wagons outside the front door."

Father motioned for him to sit down and then sat across from him. "My son and I are starting back to St. Louis in the morning for the remainder of our things."

"Well, I won't stay long. If I may visit with you and your wife for just a moment, I'll be on my way."

Cora nudged Eliza toward the loft. When the girls entered their room, Eliza removed her shoes, then without a sound dropped to the floor.

"What are you doing?" Cora's whisper sounded loud in the quiet room.

"Shh." Eliza put a finger to her lips. "If you talk I won't be able to hear." She crept as close to the ladder as she could without being seen from below.

"Eliza, I can't believe you're doing that. Come away from there."

"Don't you want to know what's going on?"

"No, I want to go to bed." Cora wanted nothing to do with Mr. Reid, and she didn't want to know his business. "Eliza, if you don't get up and go to bed, I'll call Father."

"You wouldn't dare." Eliza, still on her hands and knees, stared at her older sister.

Cora opened her mouth as if to call, and Eliza scrambled to her feet.

"All right. I won't listen and it'll be something important. Then you'll be sorry."

Chapter 8

B en pulled Cora close in a brotherly hug. She held him tight, missing him already. When it was her father's turn, he asked, "Can't you find a smile for this old man to take with him?"

Cora forced a smile. She knew it wasn't what he wanted, but he grinned and hugged her close. "That's better. Now I have a pretty memory of my little girl to take with me." As quickly as it came, the grin was gone. "Maybe 'little girl' isn't right. When I get back we'll have a talk about some important things. All right?"

Cora nodded, though she didn't understand. She watched her parents embrace before Orval climbed onto the wagon seat and the big workhorses strained against the harness. A faint red glow touched the eastern horizon as the wagons pulled out. Cora watched the wagons become small black silhouettes against a rising red ball until they were too small to see.

※

A week later, Cora thought of the handkerchiefs she had made for Aaron. Christmas was three months past, and she still hadn't given them to him. Her restless spirit stirred her to grab the wrinkled package and confront her mother.

"Mother, if you don't need me this afternoon, I'd like to take a walk."

"Where do you plan to go?"

"Just into the woods a ways." Cora noticed Eliza watching.

When her mother hesitated, she said, "The sun is shining. I'm sure there's no danger." Cora felt as if she'd burst if she had to stay cooped up in the house another afternoon. She stopped with her hand against the rough wood of the door. "Eliza, would you like to come, too?"

Eliza shrugged. "I suppose."

Together they walked toward the woods. John called to them as they passed the field where he worked. "Where are you two going?"

"For a walk in the woods."

He nodded. "Keep an eye out for bears, then."

"Bears?" Cora hadn't thought of that possibility.

"Sure, they ought to be coming out of hibernation right about now."

Cora noticed his grin and decided he was teasing. "I don't think we'll have a problem with bears. We won't go far and we'll stay on the path."

John nodded, and they went on. New growth appeared on the ground and in the tiny green leaves above.

Sunshine, finding entrance through the sparsely leafed trees, left a dappled pattern on the forest floor. A squirrel scampered to the top of a nearby tree and scolded at their invasion. Cora laughed at him.

Eliza, trailing behind, hadn't spoken since they left the house. Cora had almost forgotten she was following until she said, "Will you take me to the hollow tree you and Ben stayed in?"

Cora looked over her shoulder. "That's at least a mile. I told Mother we wouldn't be gone long."

"We'd be back within an hour. She wouldn't expect us before then, anyway. Please, Cora, I'd really like to see it."

Although she wouldn't admit it to Eliza, Cora hoped to see Aaron, even if she had to go to the Starks' cabin. She nodded. "All right, but if I can't find it right away, we'll come back."

They walked for some time, when Cora stopped to inspect the trees near them. "We should be getting close. You remember coming through here at Christmas, don't you? Does anything look familiar?"

Eliza shook her head. "One tree looks pretty much like another to me."

At the sharp snap of a twig breaking, both girls jumped. Eliza grabbed Cora's arm. "What was that?"

"I don't know." Cora stood rooted to the ground as she searched frantically through the trees for any sign of life.

"Was it a bear?" Eliza's question echoed Cora's thoughts.

Cora saw a dark figure disappear behind the large hollow tree they had been looking for.

"Cora, I'm scared." Eliza's whispered admission stirred Cora to action.

"Let's go back. Fast." Cora's heart thudded in her chest.

"All right." Eliza wasted no time.

Walking quietly in a forest was not easy. Cora was sure they made more noise going back than they had coming. A couple of yards farther on, she heard the sound of something large coming after them. It made no effort to be quiet.

"Run, Eliza!" Cora yelled and gave her sister a push forward. She ran with all her might, her heart beating a rapid staccato.

"Hey, wait!" The deep voice calling them was not a bear's. "Cora, wait up!" When he called again, reason returned to Cora.

She turned to see Aaron. His dark blue shirt stretched as he lifted an arm in greeting.

Eliza said, "We thought you were a bear."

"Eliza!"

Aaron grinned. "Well, I'm glad I ain't no bear. They can be mighty unfriendly this time of year. What're y'all doin' by yourselves in the woods, anyhow?"

"We were looking for the hollow tree Cora and Ben stayed in," Eliza answered.

"It's over there." Cora pointed to her right.

"You knew all the time?" Eliza raised her voice. "You said you didn't know if you could find it."

"I didn't until I saw. . ."

"Saw what?" Eliza would never let it rest.

"Aaron." Cora looked down at the ground. "He went behind the tree."

Eliza seemed to be puzzling through a problem. "If you saw Aaron, why did you tell me to run?"

Cora's cheeks flamed as Aaron burst out laughing.

"What's so funny?" Eliza demanded.

"I didn't get a good look." Cora's head came up as she challenged Aaron. "You moved so fast all I saw was a dark blur. How was I supposed to know it was you?"

"I'm sorry." Aaron looked truly repentant, and Cora would have believed him if she hadn't seen the twinkle in his eyes. Then he became serious. "Runnin' ain't the best way to git away from a bear."

"Why not?" Eliza asked.

"They run faster'n you." He grinned at Cora. "Course you scampered out of here awful fast awhile ago."

"I'll remember that the next time I see a bear." Cora stuck her nose up, her arms crossed. "I'll stand still and let him do whatever bears do."

"Sometimes playin' dead works. I knowed a feller once that lived to tell it after he met up with a bear jist 'cause he played dead." Aaron stepped back. "You still wanna see that tree?"

❧

When he'd stepped from behind the hollow tree and saw Cora and Eliza, Aaron thought he was imagining them. Now, with Cora so near, he longed to reach out and touch her. But he knew he didn't have that right and never would.

He led the girls to the hollow tree. He watched Cora's expressive eyes as she bent to look inside. The wind caught and pulled free a tendril of brown hair from the bun at the back of her neck. Aaron, watching it fly free, longed to capture and wrap it around his finger.

His hand was more than halfway there before he realized where his thoughts were leading. He jerked back and cleared his throat. "If you seen enough, I'll walk you home."

"What are these?" Eliza picked up a small bundle of twigs.

Aaron took them. "They're for Ma. It helps her headaches."

"What does?" Cora asked.

Aaron held out the twigs. "These." At their looks of confusion, he explained. "It's willow twigs. There's a willow tree over yonder by the spring. I jist gathered a new batch for Ma."

"How does it help her?" Cora asked.

"She chews on one and her headache goes away. There's healin' inside."

Cora looked at Aaron. She looked again at the twigs.

"You wanna see the tree? It's jist a skip and a holler over that way."

"Yes." Eliza spoke for them both. "I don't think I've ever seen a tree that cures headaches."

Aaron led them to a clearing. "Oh, you probably seen plenty. You jist never knowed it."

He stepped onto a large, flat rock angling up out of the ground. As Cora joined him, she stopped in wonder. Never had she seen a more beautiful sight. The rock seemed to be suspended in air, for below it was a drop of several feet. Water bubbled from a source somewhere under the rock, spreading out into a clear, trickling stream that meandered slowly through a beautiful green meadow as far as she could see. She stood drinking in the scene before her, allowing it to wash over her in soothing waves.

"Where's the tree?" Eliza's voice seemed at odds with her mood.

"Right there." Aaron pointed to the large, drooping tree that stood sentinel over the spring below them. Its long, delicate limbs bowed before the life-giving water at its feet. Thin leaves hung the entire length of each slender branch.

"How did you get down there to get those twigs?" Eliza asked.

"Yonder there's a slope. . .goes down." Aaron pointed south. "We're on sort of a hill here. You probably didn't know you was climbin' a hill when you come through the woods. It's real gradual-like."

As Eliza inspected the slope, Aaron stepped closer to Cora, his shoulder brushing hers. "You ready to head back now?"

She nodded, reluctantly turning from the meadow. "I think I could stay here forever."

"I know." Aaron's voice was hushed. "I come here real often. It sort of quietens my insides."

"Aaron." Although she knew she must hurry while Eliza was otherwise occupied, shyness made her hesitate when he turned his full attention to her. "I haven't been able to give you your Christmas gift yet."

She pulled the package from her sleeve and handed it to him, then tried to read the expression on his face.

He untied the ribbon, removed the paper, and held the handkerchiefs in his hand, looking at them carefully. She took the paper from him, and he didn't seem to notice.

He rubbed his finger across the raised letters in the corner of the top handkerchief. "Those are letters for your—"

He nodded. "I know, my name. This one's for Stark, but what's that other one? Does it stand for Aaron?"

Cora was surprised and pleased at his knowledge. "Yes, it's an A."

He looked up at her and grinned. "I don't know how you made them letters look so pretty. Thank you. I'll keep 'em for special."

When they reached the edge of the woods, Aaron bent and dug with a stick around the base of a large tree. He pulled a knife from the sheath on his side and cut something in the ground.

Cora leaned over to see better. It looked like a root. "What is that?"

"Sassafras." He held some up to her. "Smell it."

She took it and held it to her nose. A pleasant, sweet aroma filled her nostrils. She handed it to Eliza, then looked down at Aaron, still squatting by the tree. He smiled up at her, his heavy brows relaxed, his bright blue gaze tender. "Take it home and make some tea. It's real good."

"Thank you." She watched as he turned to cut another length. He put the second piece in his pocket and stood, ready to continue the walk home.

Though both Cora and Eliza invited him, Aaron stopped at the edge of the woods saying he had to get home. He promised to tell Ivy and Ralph he had seen the two girls and they'd sent greetings.

❈

The restless feeling was gone when Cora followed Eliza through the door of their cabin. In its place was a feeling of contentment she hadn't known since leaving St. Louis. The peaceful beauty of the meadow spring she already called hers filled her mind as she looked around the room. Lenny and Nicholas played quietly on the floor in front of the fireplace.

"Where are Mother and Vickie?" Eliza asked.

"Vickie's in bed and Mother went upstairs." Lenny scarcely acknowledged the girls' presence.

"Upstairs?" Cora repeated. She looked toward the steep ladder against the wall. Mother was in no condition to be climbing. What was so important that she would risk a fall, especially with Father gone? She headed for the ladder with Eliza close behind.

The first thing she saw was the flour sack that she had kept hidden for three months in a crumpled heap at her mother's feet. Her best dress was spread on the bed, her prized possessions dumped beside it.

"Cordella Elizabeth Jackson, what is the meaning of this?"

A strangled sob escaped Cora's lips.

Eliza stirred as the silence lengthened. "Don't worry, Mother. It doesn't matter. George isn't coming, anyway."

Cora whirled to her sister. Eliza's hand flew to her mouth with a sharp intake of breath. "I'm sorry, Cora. I didn't mean. . ." Eliza's eyes filled with tears. "I'm sorry."

"Eliza, this is between your sister and me. Will you please wait downstairs?"

Emma's voice was soft.

As Eliza left, Cora waited on trembling legs. She watched her sister descend the ladder before she turned to face her mother.

"Were you planning an elopement with George Merrill?" Emma's question was direct—unavoidable.

Cora nodded, still unable to speak.

"When is he coming?"

"Christmas." The word was barely audible.

"Christmas?"

"Three months ago."

Emma visibly relaxed. "Well, I guess we don't have to worry about that anymore." She picked up the flour sack. "I want you to put all these things away. When you pack for your wedding, we will do it together."

Cora dropped onto the bed.

Emma gathered the dress out from under Cora's legs. "Oh, do be careful. This will have to do for your wedding dress. I looked it over and it's in good repair. I didn't think to tell Father to bring fabric for a new one, which is just as well. We wouldn't have time to make it, anyway. That's one of the disadvantages of living on the frontier."

Cora stared at her mother in confusion. "We wouldn't have time? Mother, I don't understand."

Emma met Cora's gaze. "Cora, I know you've been friends with George since you were small. But you must realize by now that George is not coming. I know you want to marry and that's only right. You are nineteen now. Plenty old enough for marriage."

Cora stared at her mother.

"Of course, there isn't a long line of suitors at our door. And won't likely be. Not in this wilderness. That's why I was so pleased when Mr. Reid came calling the night before your father left."

Cora stared at her mother in disbelief. "Mr. Reid? Mother, I am not marrying Mr. Reid."

"Now, Cora, don't be difficult. Mr. Reid is a very nice man."

"He's old and I don't want to marry him." Cora shook her head. "How could you even consider such a thing?"

Emma turned from Cora's questioning gaze. "Mr. Reid came the night before your father and Ben left."

Cora nodded. "I know."

Emma smiled. "He's such a gentleman. He's from a very good family in Boston. I knew his grandfather. Mr. Reid is settled here on a large acreage with a good start in livestock. He has a nice house and barn." She reached out and covered Cora's hand with her own. "He would make a fine husband."

Cora jerked her hand away from her mother's and stood. "I'd rather be a spinster."

Emma stood, too. "I'm sorry you feel that way. I imagine you will change your mind once you think about it." She stepped toward the ladder and smiled. "After all, there aren't many fine gentlemen here, are there? Your father agrees with me that a union with Mr. Reid would be the best thing for you."

"Father?" Cora looked at her mother in disbelief. "Father wants me to marry an old man?"

"Mr. Reid is not old."

"He's almost as old as Father."

Emma waved her arguments aside. "Age is irrelevant, Cora. Many women marry older men and have wonderful marriages."

"Mother, I don't even know him."

"Now, Cora, we have visited with Mr. Reid on several occasions." Emma's voice was dismissive. "He is a very nice man with an excellent background and a substantial inheritance. He would like to call on you after your father returns. If you think about it, you will realize what a fortunate young lady you are."

As Emma started down the ladder, she turned to Cora with a tender smile. "I'd be so glad for you to live nearby. I love you very much." She placed a hand on her growing abdomen while a shadow crossed her face. "I can't bear the thought of losing any more of my children."

Fear and anger warred with guilt as Cora watched her mother go carefully down the ladder. She should never have climbed up to the loft in her condition, but she had obviously done so out of love. An interfering, possessive love to be sure; nevertheless, Cora knew that it was love.

Cora fell across her dress and moaned. What would she do now? She didn't want to hurt her mother, but she refused to marry Mr. Reid. Only anger toward George for putting her in this position kept her from crying.

Chapter 9

A month later, early in May, Lenny yelled, "Father and Ben's coming! Me and Nick saw 'em."

"Come on, Cora, let's go meet Father." Vickie, careful in her condition, pushed back from the table where she and Cora had been making bread. "You can finish later."

Vickie stood waiting, her hand on the small of her back, while Cora wiped dough from her hands.

Cora had to slow her steps for Vickie, but they hadn't gone far before she saw the two wagons coming from the east, following the creek bank. Would Ben have good news? At the thought, Cora became even more anxious.

She pointed to their right. "Here comes John. If you don't mind, I'll let you walk with him."

"Sure, go ahead." Vickie waved her on.

Cora quickened her steps, following the narrow trail made by her family. By the time she got there they were all talking at the same time while Nicholas jumped from one returned traveler to the other. Lenny had Ben gripped around the waist and wouldn't let go.

"Lenny, let me have a turn at Ben." Cora peeled the little boy from his hero. "Go give Father a hug."

Cora threw her arms around her big brother's neck. "You don't know how I've missed you. I'm so glad you're finally home."

"Me, too." Ben's wide grin left as he looked into Cora's eyes. "I have a lot to tell you."

"About George?" Ben's serious expression scared Cora. "Please, Ben, is he all right?"

"He's fine." Ben gently squeezed Cora's shoulders. "Let me get this wagon the rest of the way home and tend the horses, then I'll tell you all about it."

"Did you give him my letter?" Cora had waited long enough for answers.

"He wasn't there, Cora. He's back east. In law school. I mailed your letter to him."

"When is he coming?" She couldn't comprehend what Ben was saying.

"Cora, his mother mentioned another girl."

Cora felt numb. How could George do this to her? They had been inseparable as long as she could remember.

Another girl. George had forsaken her for someone else. She'd told him all the terrible things about her new home, hoping compassion would bring him to her rescue. But George wouldn't come now. He would just laugh and the girl would laugh with him.

Humiliation. Rejection. Fear. Pain. Emotions raged within Cora as the roar of a whirlwind that filled her heart and mind. She turned her back to Ben, then lifted leaden feet to carry her away from the source of her pain.

With dry eyes, she started walking, then running and stumbling in her grief. Somewhere in the far recesses of her mind, she heard Father call her name.

Cora ran past Vickie and John, not heeding their calls of concern. A sharp pain ripped through her heart. Ben's words had cut out the part of her that belonged to George. George no longer loved her. George didn't want to marry her.

She ran blindly. Grass whipped against her ankles. She stumbled over a rock. A tree limb hit her in the face, leaving a burning streak in its wake, yet the pain in her heart was far worse. Her toe caught on something and she felt herself floating through the air moments before she sprawled against the ground. She heard rather than felt a sharp crack above her ear and then a cloud descended and she sank into black oblivion.

※

"Cora." Her father's voice pulled her from the darkness. "Cora, wake up, honey."

Sounds began to enter the cocoon of darkness, and she fought against them. There was quiet peacefulness in the semi-awareness she didn't want to leave. It would be easier to return to the black sleep.

"She's not going to wake up." Sobs shook her mother's voice. "Look at her. She doesn't want to."

"Nonsense." Her father sounded angry. "Of course she does."

"Maybe not." That was Eliza. "If she wakes up, she'll have to marry Mr. Reid."

Cora's eyelids fluttered. The darkness retreated, and she saw her father turn to look at Eliza.

"Marry Mr. Reid?" Orval raised his voice. "Where would she get a fool idea like that?" Then he stopped, his expression clearing. His eyes met those of his wife's.

"Emma, what have you done?"

She dabbed at her eyes with a hanky. "I only pointed out the benefits of her marrying Mr. Reid."

Orval allowed an expletive to escape as he ran a hand over his face. He sank to the bed beside Cora and, realizing she was awake, grinned. "Well now, that's better."

"My head hurts."

"I know, honey. Keep that cold towel against it. You knocked yourself out against a rock when you fell." He repositioned the cool cloth against her temple with gentle fingers.

She reached for him and was enfolded in his strong, loving embrace.

"I'm sorry, Father, I shouldn't have run." She felt so sleepy. Her eyelids drooped.

"That's all right," Father whispered in her ear, "just don't ever forget how much I love you."

Cora nodded and her eyes closed.

Emma spoke. "Cora, I didn't mean to hurt you." Her voice broke. "I thought I was losing you."

"You pretty near did." Orval's voice sounded hard.

Cora couldn't remember Father ever speaking to Mother that way. She knew she should stay awake, but she was so tired.

"I know." Her mother's sharp intake of breath roused Cora. "Orval, she's trying to sleep again."

"Oh no you don't, Cora." Orval pushed her to an upright position, and her eyes flew open. "That's it. You'd better stay awake for awhile."

They propped her up and gave her something cold to drink. Each member of the family took turns talking to her, asking her questions and making her answer. She grew angry with them, but they refused to let her sleep. Then she got sick. She ran outside and leaned over the end of the porch until her stomach emptied. Finally, she gave up trying to sleep and gradually the drowsiness eased.

"All right, you can leave me alone now." She leaned back against the chair. "My head hurts so bad I couldn't sleep if I tried."

Emma pushed the hair back from Cora's forehead with a cool hand. "I'm so sorry, Cora. I never meant to hurt you. When I saw you had packed, I felt as if I'd lost you."

"Mother, that's not why I ran away from Ben."

Emma didn't seem to be listening. "If you and George want to be married, you have my blessing." Before Cora could protest further, Mother turned to her oldest daughter.

"I realize now I can't hold any of you. You have your own lives to live. Vickie, I'll understand if you and John move to your own land."

Vickie looked at John, their eyes meeting for a moment before John spoke. "We're going to wait two or three more months before we make any decision about that—unless you mind having us in your way?"

"You're welcome to stay as long as you want," Orval said.

John nodded. "Thank you, sir. There's some land up the creek not too far from here that looks pretty good. When Vickie's able, we're thinking about taking a good look at it. You may be stuck with us for neighbors, yet."

As the family voiced their approval, Cora realized they didn't need to know about George. She sought Ben's attention.

He smiled, then came to her side and whispered, "Maybe I shouldn't tell you the rest."

Cora shook her head. "I promise I won't run again. I'm fine now."

"All right. I'll tell you what I found out as soon as we have some privacy."

Cora watched Ben turn away. What did he mean by the rest? What more could there be?

❦

Ben rode Flash, a new saddle horse he'd brought back from St. Louis, to the Newkirks' right after noon the following day. Cora understood he was eager to see Esther, but still a knot formed in her stomach. She would have to wait until he returned to hear about George.

Two hours later, Cora saw Ben coming and started to meet him when she heard a call from the opposite direction. Ralph Stark walked across the pasture, his arm raised in greeting. Her heart sank. In the last month and a half, Ralph had been to supper at least three times. Eliza was the only one who looked forward to his visits.

She appeared by Cora's side now, her voice breathless. "Cora, Ralph's coming." She clutched her sister's arm.

"So is Ben." The reprimand went unnoticed by the younger girl.

She lifted her hand to wave at Ralph as she spoke softly to Cora. "I don't think Ben knows Ralph's been calling on me. Won't he be surprised?"

Cora couldn't help but smile. Eliza was so infatuated with the handsome young man that her happiness was contagious. "I don't know why Ben should be surprised. If there were any other young men hidden away in this wilderness, Ralph would have more competition than he could handle."

Eliza's cheeks flushed at the compliment. "I don't know about that."

"Well, I do." Cora wasn't sure why she had complimented Eliza instead of throwing out a barb as she usually did. She shrugged as Ralph and Ben reached them at the same time. Ben swung off his sweating horse, holding the bridle with his hand.

"Howdy." Ralph's quick grin swept the three young people, settling on Ben. "I ain't seen you in a coon's age. Have a good trip?"

Cora noticed a difference in Ben's smile. There was no sparkle in his eyes. He nodded to Ralph. "Yes, our trip was very successful, thank you." His smile left when he turned to Cora. "As soon as I take care of Flash, I need to talk to you. Will you wait outside for me?"

Cora nodded, and Ben turned toward the shelter that now housed the animals. Ralph took one look at Cora and whistled. "What'd you do, have a tussle with a wildcat?"

She touched her cheek where the welt from the tree limb still burned. Then her fingers found the scrape on the side of her head. She knew a purple bruise covered a good part of that side of her face. "I fell yesterday and hit my head on a rock."

"Whooee! That's some shiner!"

Eliza pulled him away, chattering all the way to the house.

"I'm sorry I've kept you waiting so long," Ben said as he came out of the shelter. "I know you're anxious to hear about George."

Cora forced a smile. She wasn't sure she wanted to hear about George. "How was Esther?"

An expression she couldn't read crossed her brother's face. "She's fine. Don't you want to hear the rest of it? About George, I mean."

"I suppose." She sighed. At the moment, she didn't care if she never heard George's name again.

They ambled toward the house while Ben talked. "I went to see the Merrills while we were in St. Louis. They send their love. They both said they miss us."

"That was nice of them." Cora kept her gaze to the ground.

Ben stopped walking and turned to face his sister. "Cora, do you remember Flanna Murphy, Mrs. Merrill's maid?"

"You mean the little, shy, redheaded girl?"

"Yes, you do remember her then."

Cora nodded. "She was always so quiet. She seemed more like part of the furnishings than a real person."

Ben jammed his hands into his pockets. An angry light shone from his eyes. "George must not have felt the same way you did."

"What do you mean?"

Immediately his angry expression changed to sympathy. "I know I shouldn't tell you this. It isn't proper, but you need to know." A sigh escaped as he looked toward the woods away from her eyes. "The Merrills have a new maid. She came in while I was there. She's an older woman. Mrs. Merrill told Father and me that she had to let Flanna go. I found out later it was because she was with child."

"I didn't know Flanna was married." Cora's interest kindled.

"She isn't."

"Then who—"

"I heard rumors—not at the Merrills', of course—but from some old friends." Ben looked away. "George's mother threatened to put Flanna out in the street to make her own way. Mr. Merrill took pity on her and sent her to his brother's family in Philadelphia. They agreed to see that she's taken care of and has a job with them after the baby's born."

Cora remembered how shy the little Irish girl had been. *Surely, Flanna wasn't a sinful girl. She wouldn't have. . .*

Then, flashes of memory told her what Ben couldn't. George following Flanna from the room. . . Flanna's fear of George, how she always seemed to avoid him. . .

At Cora's soft gasp, Ben stopped and looked at her anxiously. She searched his face with wide eyes. Her heart seemed to freeze inside her breast. Was he saying it was George's baby? Could George be so wicked?

She looked away, her voice low. "Does this have anything to do with why George didn't come here?"

"According to some of my friends, his mother insisted his father send him to law school back east." Ben turned anguished eyes on Cora. "I didn't know all this when I sent your letter on to him. Believe me, Cora, if I'd known, I wouldn't have sent it."

Cora shrugged. "Oh well, it doesn't really matter." But it did matter. It bothered her that George would read her words of love. She looked around them at the distant woods, the cedar-lined creek, the green crops growing in the fields, and the simple log house. Her heart filled with gratitude that she had been spared a life with George.

When she didn't speak, Ben looked closely at her. "Are you all right?"

She smiled at him. "Of course I am." *To be honest, I feel numb.* She certainly hadn't expected such news, but she refused to cry about it. She started walking again. "Tell me about your visit with Esther."

His expression grew hard. "There's not much to tell. Just that she's decided to go back on her word." A muscle twitched in his jaw.

Cora stared at her brother. "You mean she broke your engagement? Why?"

Ben's laugh was short and bitter. His eyes filled with pain. "That's the interesting part. I haven't the faintest idea."

"Surely she said something."

"Oh, she said plenty. It seems I'm not good enough for her."

"You are so."

"No, I'm not." Ben's voice sounded angry. "I have to confess my sins. I have to fall down before God and ask Him to forgive me for every wrong I've ever done. Then I might be good enough."

"She said that?" How could anyone think her brother was anything but perfect? And she had thought Esther was so wonderful.

"More or less. She also told me to read John and Romans in the Bible."

"Why?" Cora couldn't believe what she was hearing.

Ben shrugged. "How should I know?"

"Are you going to?"

"Going to what?"

"Read what she told you to."

Ben started walking again, and Cora fell into step with him. She had decided he wasn't going to answer when he finally spoke just one word. "Maybe."

Cora looked up at the brother she had adored since infancy. He stared ahead, lost in his own thoughts. Her heart went out to him. Esther had seemed so perfect for him. She wasn't, though. She wasn't perfect at all, or she wouldn't have found fault with Ben.

"I don't think I ever want to get married." Cora broke the silence just before they reached the house.

"I know how you feel. We're a sorry pair of rejects, aren't we?" Ben's quick grin appeared to be back to normal, but Cora wasn't fooled.

Chapter 10

Cora stepped inside ahead of Ben as Orval pulled a chair back from the table and sat down. He picked his grandson up and settled him on his lap. "People are coming into the area now the weather's warming up."

Cora looked at her father. What people? How many? Where were they settling? Questions flashed through her head even as Emma asked them.

He grinned. "Across Cedar Creek not too far from Bill Reid's place. We'll be helping put up a new cabin in a few days. Reid says a family moved in a couple of weeks ago. Been camping there ever since."

"We got new neighbors just a hoot and a holler from us, too," Ralph spoke up from across the room. "Folks is sure crowdin' in."

Cora smiled. A few months ago, she had hated the isolation of the wilderness. Now it was her home. She loved the waving prairie grass that stretched out from their log home. She loved their house, built by labor from their generous neighbors. She loved the proud cedar trees lining the banks of the creek down the hill from the house. She loved the quiet sanctuary of the woods, and she especially loved her beautiful spring meadow near the hollow tree.

Cora could scarcely believe her eyes the next afternoon when Esther drove into the yard. Her normally light complexion was even more pale than usual with dark circles under her eyes. When she spoke, her voice sounded sad. "Ben told me you got hurt. I came to see how you are."

Cora nodded. "I'm fine. Would you like to come inside?"

Esther glanced toward the house. "Can we stay out here where we can talk?"

Cora shrugged. "Sure. Why don't we walk down by the creek?" She knew the men were working on the other side of the house in the fields, and Ben wouldn't likely see them.

The two girls walked in silence until they reached the creek bank. Cora stopped under a large cedar tree, her arms folded. "What do you want?"

Esther bowed her head. When she looked up at Cora, her eyes were a blue pool of tears. "Ben said that you were hurt really bad."

Cora turned her head. "As you can see, it's just superficial."

"I didn't know. I was so worried, Cora. I was afraid you might die and I hadn't told you about Jesus."

Cora stared at the beautiful girl before her. "I know about Jesus."

"You told me you all are believers, Cora. But I found out yesterday that Ben has never been born again. Please let me tell you how you can be saved."

Cora felt as if Esther had slapped her. "I'm not a bad person."

"I know you aren't." Esther hastened to explain. "But even good people have to come to God and confess their sins."

Now Cora understood. She was surprised she hadn't seen it before. Esther had a superior attitude. Ben was better off without her.

"I'm sure you're right, Esther." Cora forced a smile. "If you'll excuse me, I need to get back to the house before my mother worries. I don't think she saw us leave."

Cora walked away without a backward glance. Esther left, but her words remained. Cora thought of little else the rest of the day. She had lost both George and Esther, and it hurt more than she cared to acknowledge. She went to bed, where she slept fitfully as images she couldn't remember the next morning robbed her rest.

Midmorning, as Cora shook out the rug, she saw Aaron walking between Ralph and Ivy as they made their way out of the woods. A wooden crate hung between the two young men.

Cora took the rug inside and announced the arrival of their guests. Eliza looked up from the oven. "Ralph usually comes in the evening."

Cora laughed. "I didn't say it was only Ralph. I said Aaron, Ralph, and Ivy are coming."

Eliza jerked off her apron and ran to the loft.

"Where are you going?" Emma called to her youngest daughter's skirts as they swished up the ladder.

"I can't let Ralph see me this way. I have flour all over me!"

Cora laughed with her mother and older sister, then smoothed her hair and went to the door.

Ivy was alone. "You look as bad as Ralph said." Ivy's greeting brought heat to Cora's cheeks.

Eliza peeked out the door. "Hello, Ivy. Where are your brothers?"

"You're right real taken with Ralph, ain't you?" Ivy asked.

"Taken?"

"Sure. Taken." When Eliza didn't answer, she went on. "I don't rightly see how a body could be, but I reckon we all have a right to hanker after whoever we fancy."

"Ralph's very good-looking," Eliza answered softly.

Ivy smiled. "Ralph and Aaron are round back with your menfolk. They brung a pig for y'all."

She turned toward Cora. "I think Aaron jist wanted to see for hisself that you're all right. He'll be around in a little when he gets the pig settled."

❧

Aaron and Ralph didn't come to the house until they were ready to head for home. Ben was with them, and Ivy's lashes fluttered when she looked at him.

She stepped outside as he held the door for her. Cora and Eliza followed. Ivy clutched Ben's arm. "Ben, why don't you walk back a ways with us? I was thinkin' maybe you could tell us how that story ended. You recollect? The one we was readin' last winter jist afore we went sleddin'?"

"You mean *Swiss Family Robinson*?" Ben looked at Ivy as if he'd never heard of Esther Newkirk.

"That's the one." Ivy smiled at the two girls. "Maybe Cora and Eliza would like to walk along with us."

"Now that's the best idea I've heard in a coon's age." Ralph grinned at Eliza and took her hand.

Cora knew what Ivy had in mind, and Ben seemed to be willing. Then Cora saw Aaron. The look in his eyes set her heart racing. She found herself nodding. "I'll go ask if Mother can spare us for a bit."

❦

Ralph and Eliza managed to get several yards ahead of the others. They seemed lost in their own world, their hands clasped in a familiar way. Ivy held to Ben's arm as if she were afraid she'd lose him. By the time they reached the woods, Ben and Ivy were holding hands.

Cora matched her gait to Aaron's, keeping the injured side of her face away from him. "I guess you're stuck with me."

He walked with his hands in his pockets. "There's no one I'd druther be with."

They walked in silence several yards. Cora's palms began to itch as she wondered what it would be like to hold Aaron's hand.

To get her mind off holding hands, she said, "You know a lot about the woods, don't you?"

Aaron grinned, his deep blue eyes glinting mischievously. "I don't rightly know, but I reckon I could tell you the difference between a oak and a cedar."

Cora laughed. "I think even I could do that. I was thinking about the herbs you gathered for your mother. Did they help her headache?"

His grin disappeared as he looked away. "They help some, but there ain't nothin' that's gonna take them away, I reckon."

"I'm sorry. I didn't know." Cora, looking up at his firm, serious profile, realized how much he cared for his mother and she admired him for it.

"Ralph said you got a headache the other day. Reckon I should've give you some willow to take home."

Cora's cheeks burned. She touched the bruise on her face but kept her gaze to the ground. Their feet crunched twigs with each step. Cora could smell the pungent fragrance of the grove of cedar trees to their left when they passed near the creek.

"Are you all right now?" Aaron pressed for an answer. "Ralph said you 'most didn't wake up."

"I'm fine." Cora looked up and saw a play of emotions cross Aaron's handsome face. Did he think she was ugly with the scrapes and bruises covering half her face? Was that why he frowned? She added, "Except for my looks."

"Ain't nothin' wrong with your looks." Such a tender expression had never come her way before. Her breath caught in her throat. Her heart beat rapidly against her ribs. Her shaky smile brought an answering one from Aaron.

❧

The month of May moved into June with warm days full of sunshine and an outward calm. One day Cora found Ben sitting on the ground behind the old shelter reading a Bible. He looked up at her and said, " 'Except a man be born of water and of the Spirit, he cannot enter into the kingdom of God.' "

"What?"

"That's what Jesus told a man named Nicodemus. I don't think Nicodemus understood it any better than I do. I guess it has something to do with believing in Jesus."

"I believe in Jesus," Cora defended.

"But is just believing enough?" Ben frowned. "This says you have to 'be born of water and of the Spirit.' Maybe water means being born as a baby. But what is born of the Spirit?"

"I don't know."

"Is there a special time for that birth like there was the other?"

"I don't know, Ben." Cora felt uncomfortable and was glad when Ben snapped his Bible shut.

He stood and shrugged. "I don't know, either. I'm going for a ride."

"Where?"

He lifted an eyebrow at her question. "Not that it's your business, but I'm going to see Ivy. Tell Mother I'll be back in a couple hours."

She watched him saddle Flash and ride away. He'd been to see Ivy a couple times after their walk through the woods. Cora wondered what was going on between them. One thing was certain, Ivy wouldn't tell Ben he was a sinner who needed to read the Bible.

❧

A few days later, Cora took the water jug to the field where the men were working. She relished the freedom of going barefoot through the knee-high grass. Clouds drifted lazily across the blue sky, and honeybees buzzed from one wildflower to the next. When she reached the plowed ground, her feet stirred little puffs of dust. She paused to wiggle her toes into an especially soft mound, reveling in the sensation.

Her father's laugh boomed out and she looked up. "We're going to make a farm girl of you yet, Cora. Get that water out here. We're ready for a break."

She smiled and ran the remaining few feet. A bothersome bee buzzed around her head, and she slapped it away. She handed the jug to her father. "Those things are all over the place. I could hear them in the grass."

"You'd better watch where you step, then." Ben grinned at her before he took a swallow of water.

About that time, another bee flew past. This one seemed intent on its purpose as it headed straight for the forest. Orval watched it only a second before he said, "Come on, boys. I think that one's going home. Let's get us some honey."

"Yahoo! Let's go." Ben took off after his father.

John drained the last of the water. He handed the empty jug back to Cora and grinned. "What do you want to bet that bee gives them a merry chase?"

Cora watched her father and Ben run and jump over soft ground and growing crops, chasing a tiny bobbing speck. In all truth, they were a comical-looking pair. She turned back to John and met his laughing eyes. "Why are they chasing a bee?"

John laughed. "Some folks say you can follow a homing bee to its tree where the honey is stored. I've never seen it done, so I don't know. I sure don't intend to go off chasing one across the country to see if it works." He turned back to the waiting team. A grin lifted the corners of his mouth. "It's a good thing they've got me to work. Of course, if they happen to find that tree, I won't be against helping haul in the honey."

Cora watched her step as she went back to the house. The thought of the sweetener her father might bring home brightened her eyes. Already the ten-pound cone of sugar they'd brought back from St. Louis had a large gouge in its side.

That night at supper John laughed again as Orval and Ben told of chasing the bee through the woods. Cora was amazed they'd kept the tiny insect in sight as long as they had.

Orval looked around the kitchen as he picked up a slice of bread. "Where's the sugar, Emma?"

"In the cabinet where I always keep it." She frowned. "Is something wrong with your food?"

"I want sugar for bait." He waved his bread as he talked. "I remember back when I was a boy, a neighbor mixed some sugar and water and soaked a corncob in it. The bee loads up on the sweetening and then heads for home. We'll soak a cob and put it out in the morning near where we lost that bee. More than likely the honey's in a big hollow oak."

The next day when Orval sent Ben back home from the woods to get the wagon, John didn't laugh. They threw the laundry tub and a couple pails in the back of the wagon, then John climbed into the driver's seat.

Cora couldn't believe the amount of honey and honeycomb they carried out of the woods. Emma exclaimed over the harvest, praising Orval for his ingenuity.

He grinned. "There's more where this came from."

Emma stood by the wagon. She stared at the golden syrup lapping the rim of her laundry tub. "Are you going back?"

Orval laughed. "No, I've sent Ben to the Starks'. It's a big tree, Emma. There's plenty and more to share. We'll let the Starks get the rest."

"Yes, that's the thing to do." She looked pleased. "Maybe we can share some with the Newkirks, too. How much do you think we have?"

"Oh, there's a good sixty pounds here and probably half that left in the tree. It's the biggest store of honey I've ever seen. Let's have a party. We'll invite all the neighbors—the new ones moving in, too. Tell everyone to fix some food to bring, and we'll make up the sweets. Bill Reid can bring his fiddle and we'll have a barn dance." He grabbed his wife's hands and did a little jig.

Emma resisted even as she laughed at his antics. She tried to pull free. "Orval, you'll wear me out. Stop this nonsense and help me get the honey put away."

"Wear you out?" Orval laughed and pulled her into his arms for a quick embrace. "You're the one talking nonsense, Emma. You have to break free and dance before you can get worn out."

Cora noticed her mother's face tinge with pink. A smile sat on her lips as she pulled back from Father. "Yes, Orval. Now, if you're finished, I'll go get the crocks."

❧

The party was the last Saturday in June. The women spent two days baking, and by Saturday, a delectable array of sweets lined the work counter. The men cut three long planks from a straight pine to make a tabletop and benches. The new table and benches were set up in the yard and made ready for the guests who started arriving just before noon.

Cora saw the Starks emerge from the woods. Mrs. Stark rode in a small wagon just large enough for one or two people. A long rope was attached to it with a harness on the end. Aaron had slipped his arms through the leather straps to pull the wagon. Mr. Stark, Ralph, and Ivy left Aaron and Mrs. Stark even before they reached the house. As Aaron drew near, Cora recognized the small wagon as the sled he had built last winter, but now wheels turned where the wooden runners had been.

Cora's heart swelled with pride. She was sure Aaron could do anything he set his mind to. No one else would have been able to plan and build such a wonderful conveyance.

She met them with a smile. "Hello. I'm so glad you could come." She turned to Mrs. Stark. "How are you feeling? Was the ride over too hard for you?"

Mrs. Stark gave Cora a snaggletoothed grin. "This here wagon's as comfortable as my own rockin' chair."

Cora turned to Aaron. "You did this, didn't you? You turned your sled into a wagon for your mother."

He barely glanced her way as he nodded. His brows drew together in a frown. The color was high in his clean-shaven cheeks.

Cora's heart pounded. "I admire your ingenuity."

"My what?" His frown deepened.

Cora mentally kicked herself for her choice of words. "Your ability to take something simple and make something so wonderful from it."

"Wonderful?"

Aaron knew he sounded like an echo, but if his embarrassment weren't enough, his mind had gone blank at the sight of Cora. She was beautiful, all decked out in that fancy blue dress with the ribbons tied in a bow on each sleeve. There were smaller bows all around the skirt. He liked her hair, too. All piled up on her head with bouncy little curls on each side. He'd like to capture one of those curls and feel it wrap around his finger. But he knew that was foolishness. He was a poor man and ignorant. Cora knew it, too, or she wouldn't have explained herself when she used that big word.

"Yes, wonderful. You can do anything, Aaron Stark." Her eyes shone as she looked at him. "I think you are wonderful."

Aaron stood where she left him. Had he heard her right? He was harnessed to a wagon like a horse. And she thought he was wonderful?

Chapter 11

As the sun threw long shadows toward the east, Bill Reid picked up his fiddle and drew the bow across the strings. The melody, slow and haunting at first, gradually picked up speed until Cora's foot tapped in rhythm.

Thirty-four people attended the Jacksons' party. Cora knew that someday this beautiful land would be settled. Pride swelled her heart as she thought of others settling her adopted land. She looked across the crowd. The Sinclairs fit right in with their two small children playing with the youngest Newkirks. Then there was an older couple named Hanson with a grown son and daughter.

Cora's gaze met Aaron's. Would he ask her to dance? Squares were already forming. Someone brushed past, and Cora saw Ben and Ivy go by. She looked to the other side of the dancers where Esther stood close by her mother.

She had been angry with Esther. Now she felt sorry for her. Esther's blue eyes appeared huge in her pale face as they followed Ben's every move. But she had done it to herself. If she truly loved him, she would have accepted him as he was.

Cora shrugged and turned back to Aaron. He was gone! How could he have gotten away so quickly?

Her eyes swept past the dancers and those sitting or standing on the sidelines. Her breath came in a rush when she saw him lean over his mother. He hadn't gone. He was only seeing to his mother's needs.

He shook his head in answer to something she said. She seemed to be urging him to do something. Again he shook his head. Then both of them looked across the yard at Cora.

As swiftly as Aaron's gaze flew to lock with hers, she realized what mother and son had been discussing. A hot flush flooded her face. The blood pounded in her temples. He didn't want to dance with her. She hadn't been sure of her feelings toward Aaron before. Now, with George removed from her life, she knew how deeply she cared for Aaron Stark.

Tears blurred her vision as Mr. Reid's violin slowed and the Hanson girl grabbed Aaron's hand, pulling him toward the sets. Anna's thick, blond hair had been braided and coiled at the back of her head with short curls framing her face. She held a tight grip on Aaron's hand and, ignoring his protests, soon had him dancing with her.

"You wanna dance?"

Cora turned to see Anna's older brother beside her. Positive he could never be a threat to her affections, she smiled and nodded.

"Yes, I'd love to." As they moved forward, she said, "I'm sorry, but I seem to have forgotten your name."

"Axel Hanson." He bowed, smiling.

Axel was a smooth, experienced dancer. He guided Cora through the steps without mistake. Then, in the lull between songs, he pulled her away from the others.

"Come on, let's sit the next one out." He tugged her hand. "I've gotta catch my breath."

Cora glanced toward Aaron and Anna and saw that they were getting ready for the next set. She shrugged. "All right."

They walked toward the house where a few women, including her mother and older sister, sat by the front door watching the small children play. Several lanterns hung on the front side, and a large bonfire blazed on an open patch several yards to the side.

Before Cora realized what Axel had in mind, he urged her past the end of the house toward the back where there were no lights.

She stopped. "There's nothing back here."

He grinned. "I know."

"I'm not going with you." They were hidden from most of the people, and Cora didn't like the look in Axel's eyes. Her heart hammered in her chest.

Axel laughed undaunted. He slipped his arm around her waist, pulling her close to his side. "I saw how disappointed you were when my sister got to Stark first. You should be glad she got him."

Cora struggled as Axel pulled her ever closer to the dark. As they cleared the back corner of the house, she opened her mouth to scream. Suddenly, Axel jerked and stumbled forward, releasing her.

An oath flew from his mouth as he staggered to right his balance. "Somethin' hit me in the back!"

He turned to look behind him just as a fist slammed into his jaw and he hit the ground hard. Cora stood apart and watched Aaron grab Axel's shirtfront, then haul him to his feet. Although it was dark, light from the bonfire reflected off Axel's blond hair and Aaron's blue shirt.

Aaron's fist drew back. Axel shielded his face. "Don't hit me again." He took a step back, his hands held up in surrender when Aaron relaxed his grip. "I figured she was available when you ignored her."

"Ignored her?" Aaron said. "I ain't ignored her from the first time I laid eyes on her."

"Sure you did." Axel wiped a hand across his mouth, smearing blood from a small cut. "You should've seen her face when my sister came along and grabbed hold of you." Axel kept moving away. "I was just trying to cheer her up some."

Aaron stared at Axel. Finally he spoke. "You ain't fit to associate with the hogs. Git outta here." He watched Axel slink away before turning to look at Cora.

Cora stood just a few feet away, her hands clasped together under her chin. Even in the dim light, he could see the color in her face. Her eyes were wide as she looked at him.

Aaron stepped close but didn't touch her. "Did he hurt you?"

Cora shook her head. "No, I'm fine."

Aaron looked at her, his heart in his eyes. "He won't bother you no more. He's too big a coward."

A slow tear slid down her cheek, tearing at his heart. Before he thought, he reached for her, wrapping his fingers around her upper arms. He was shocked to feel her tremble. His hands slid around to enfold her. Never in his life had he felt anything so wonderful as Cora next to his heart. That she seemed to melt against him without hesitation was a wonder.

Aaron wasn't sure how long they stood together while he crooned reassurances to her, but when Cora finally stopped trembling, he knew he didn't want to let her go. He lifted her chin with the crook of his finger until he could see her eyes. They were still wet with tears—and beautiful.

He smiled tenderly at her. "We'd better git back afore someone misses you and comes lookin'."

"Aaron, how did you know?"

"That you needed help?"

At her nod, he shrugged. "It wasn't hard to figure you didn't want to go with that ornery feller. I'd've come sooner, but I couldn't git away from his sister."

Cora giggled. "Is she as bad as he is?"

His eyes sparkled mischievously in the light from the bonfire. "Yeah, but I didn't have to hit her as hard."

Cora laughed. Then her eyes narrowed. "Did you throw something at him?"

Aaron grinned. "Jist a rock. I had to git his attention so's I could knock some sense into him."

She smiled. "When I said you are wonderful, I meant every word. Thank you for rescuing me."

Aaron wondered if his heart would burst. "I reckon any decent feller would've done the same."

Cora pulled back from him. She put her hands on her hips. "But you're the one who came, and that wasn't what I was talking about, anyway."

Aaron's hands dropped to his sides.

"I like you, Aaron Stark. I like you a lot." Her eyes shone in the moonlight.

"Don't you like me, even a little?"

"It don't matter how I feel if you're already spoken fer."

"Spoken for?" Cora's eyes grew wide. "What do you mean by that?" Before he could answer, she went on. "I'm not spoken for."

"I heard there was a feller from your old home comin' to—"

"No." Cora fairly shouted the word. "George isn't coming. I'd never marry him even if he did. He isn't good and kind. He isn't a gentleman like you."

Aaron ran his hand through his hair. No one had ever called him a gentleman before. "You sure you know what you're sayin'?"

"Yes, and I know what I'm doing, too. I'm making a fool of myself."

She turned to walk away, but he grabbed her arm. "Wait."

Aaron was beginning to believe Cora was serious. He couldn't let her get away until he knew for sure.

He turned her back to face him. Taking a deep breath, he plunged into a confession that he'd rather forget. "How can you care for me? I'm nothin' but a dirt-poor farmer. That's all I know. I'm so poor I couldn't buy hay for a nightmare."

The gaze that met his warmed his heart. "There's nothing wrong with farming."

"Cora, do you think your father'd let me call on you?" Aaron held his breath as he waited for her answer.

She smiled up at him. "Ralph comes to see Eliza, doesn't he?"

A quick grin covered his face. "I'll ask him tonight afore I leave." He took Cora's small hand in his and brought it to his lips for a gentle kiss. "Sounds like another dance a-startin'. Come on afore your father catches us back here and shoots me."

He kept her hand in his as they joined the others. He had never known such joy. He could only hope she never regretted her words, because he didn't ever want to let her go.

⚜

Cora sang as she went about her work. Father had given permission and Aaron was coming to visit that evening. She dusted the corner cabinet a second time.

"Cora, what's the matter with you? You've been nervous all day." Vickie laid her knitting aside.

Cora closed the glass doors and turned toward her sister, a blush touching her cheeks. "I guess I'm being silly." She crossed to the other chair and sank into it. "Aaron said he would come by tonight."

"Oh, so that's the way it is." Vickie nodded. "That must mean you've forgotten George?"

At the mention of his name, Cora felt a flash of anger. "I know he's your brother-in-law, but, Vickie, I don't think George is—"

"Kind, considerate, gentlemanly. . .need I go on?" Vickie said and smiled.

Cora laughed. "Then you understand?"

"Yes." Vickie nodded. "I've known him as long as you have. I also know he'[s] spoiled rotten by his doting mother. It amazes me that a woman can treat he[r] two sons so differently." She looked at Cora, her expression suddenly stern. "[I] hope you're not playing with Aaron Stark's affections. From what I've seen, he'[s] a fine young man."

Again the warmth spread to Cora's cheeks. She shook her head and woul[d] have answered if Ben hadn't taken that moment to come into the house. He ha[d] been across the creek helping Harley Sinclair with his haying.

"How long until supper?" he called to his mother.

"At least half an hour," she answered.

"Where are Father and John?"

"In the south field. I think they're hoeing corn this afternoon."

He nodded and stepped back outside, leaving the door open. Cora watche[d] until she couldn't see him anymore. She felt guilty over her newfound happiness knowing that Ben was still hurting from Esther's rejection.

Then, as she lifted her eyes to the distant line of trees, she saw two figure[s] walking across the pasture. Aaron and Ralph. They would be at the house i[n] minutes. She jumped up and tore off the stained work apron she had been wearing all day. With it and the dust cloth still clutched in her hand, she ran for the ladder.

"Cora, what's wrong?" Vickie sat up straight in her chair.

"Aaron and Ralph are coming." She scrambled over the last rung of the ladder and ran into her room, throwing the apron and dust cloth into a basket of laundry. As she picked up her hairbrush, Eliza climbed into the room.

"Vickie said Ralph is coming. Look at me. I'm a mess. I don't know why he didn't say something at the party," Eliza complained as she fumbled with her dress.

Cora smoothed the hair above her braid. "He probably smelled the corn bread baking."

"Cora!" Eliza let her soiled dress fall to the floor.

Cora lifted the long braid and coiled it in a knot at the back of her head. "I thought Ralph could smell food a mile away."

Eliza made a face at her sister, then reached for her clean dress and pulled it over her head.

Aaron and Ralph didn't come to the house until the men came in for supper. Even then, they barely spoke to Cora and Eliza. Cora didn't mind, as she understood it was the way of the backwoods. Besides, more than once Aaron's tender gaze brought a flush to her cheeks.

The days were getting longer with the sun's slanted rays bathing the countryside until long after supper. While the women cleaned and straightened from the evening meal, the men sat outside on Father's new porch to visit.

Cora kept one ear turned toward the open door, where she heard snatches of talk on the weather and crops.

With Cora and Eliza both working as quickly as possible, the room was soon set to rights. Cora's heart thudded as she followed her mother and Vickie outside.

Mother and Vickie were given the only chairs, and Cora sat on the edge of the porch beside Eliza. Ralph made himself at home, leaning against a post just a few feet from Eliza. Cora looked past Eliza, Ralph, and Ben to Aaron. For just a moment, his eyes met hers and the distance between them was no barrier. She felt warmth surge through her body and knew that George had never made her feel this way.

Cora was so aware of Aaron on the other side of the porch, she had no idea what the conversation was about. She heard his deep voice talking to her father and brothers, but knowing he had come to see her made everyday things of no consequence. The hum of their voices made pleasant background music for Cora's happy mood.

As the shadow of the house loomed large on the ground in front of them and the sun's light dimmed, Vickie stood. "If you'll excuse me, I think I'll go in. It's been a long day."

John picked up a yawning Nicholas and followed his wife. Ben was next to stand. "I've got some things to do in the barn."

He stepped off the porch and reached out a hand first to Aaron and then Ralph. "Good to see you again."

"Thanks. You, too." Aaron shook his hand.

Cora was glad to hear Ben whistling as he went to the barn. He seemed happier tonight, more content. Maybe he was getting over Esther.

Orval stood and took Emma's hand in his. "Isn't it getting a little chilly out here for you, Mother?"

She looked at him, her eyes wide. "I don't—" She stopped at the almost imperceptible shake of his head. She nodded. "I don't know but what it is."

Aaron stood when she did. When Ralph didn't move, Aaron kicked his foot. Ralph jumped up and smiled at Emma. "I sure do thank ya for allowing us to come over and eat with y'all."

Emma smiled. "You are welcome."

Aaron shuffled his toe in the dirt by the porch. He looked at Emma, his expression serious. "Thank you, ma'am. You set a real good table." His gaze shifted to include Orval. "Thank you for givin' us permission to visit your daughters, sir. We won't stay long."

Cora felt a tremble of excitement course through her body as her parents took Lenny inside. The door remained open, and Eliza and Ralph were still there, but when Aaron moved to sit beside her, Cora felt as if the two of them were the only people on earth.

For long moments, he just looked at her, his gaze tender yet hesitant. Then he spoke, his voice low. "I promised your father I won't stay long."

"Yes, I know."

"Cora." She looked expectantly at him when he didn't say more. His brilliant blue eyes were searching hers. "That's ever'thing I know. Just Cora Jackson. What's the rest of your name?"

"Cordella Elizabeth. But if anyone calls me Cordella, I know I've done something wrong."

Aaron laughed, his eyes twinkling. "I'll remember that."

He pulled a handkerchief from his shirt pocket. There in the corner were the initials she had embroidered. "I reckon you don't know all my name, either."

"It's Aaron James Stark."

A light shone from his eyes. "You do know. I just figured you didn't, 'cause there's only two letters on here."

"Actually, I didn't know your full name when I embroidered them. Eliza told me later. I'm surprised you still have that."

Aaron nodded. "I don't use 'em, though. I jist carry 'em with me. They're too special to use."

Cora's heart sang. Her lashes lowered as she looked at her hands lying deceptively still in her lap. "I still have the box you made me. I keep my special things in it."

Cora didn't know how long they sat on the porch and talked, but when Aaron stood and said they had to be getting home, she knew it hadn't been long enough.

Chapter 12

Cora held to the porch post and leaned out as far as possible. She could hear Vickie moaning in the house. She walked the length of the porch and back. She hugged her upper arms with her hands and rubbed the tremble from them. What was keeping Ben? More important, what was keeping Mrs. Newkirk?

The moans ceased, and she found the silence even more terrifying. Mother was with Vickie, but would she know what to do? Vickie had been so ill during the first part of her confinement that Cora feared for her sister's life.

Then she heard a wagon, and Mrs. Newkirk was there. She hustled into the house with a quick smile toward Cora. Her husband drove back the way he had come and silence descended again.

Where was Ben? Cora walked to the end of the porch and looked toward the Newkirks'. Surely he wouldn't stay and visit. With her attention wavering between her brother's absence and her sister's moaning, she sat on the edge of the porch and hugged her knees with her head lowered against them.

Vickie had still not delivered when Ben came home. Cora met him just outside the door of the old shelter where he kept his horse. "What's going on?"

Ben laughed, and she saw the sparkle in his eyes. "How should I know? You're the one who's been here."

"I'm not talking about Vickie." Cora grinned at the smirk on his face. "You made up with Esther, didn't you?"

He laughed again. "Yep."

"Does that mean you did what Esther wanted?"

Ben sobered. He took Cora's shoulders in his hands and looked her in the eyes. "I should have said something a long time ago. I went to see Harvey Sinclair awhile back."

"I know."

"We had a talk. He prayed with me. Cora, I've accepted Jesus as my Savior, but I didn't do it for Esther. I did it for myself."

"I'm glad, Ben." Cora didn't understand. But he was happy and that was enough.

"Cora! Ben! Come on. The baby's here!" Eliza's call kept Ben from saying more.

Christopher Lee soon had the entire family wrapped around his tiny finger.

When he was not quite two months old, Vickie and John moved into their own house. The two families had lived together for so long that Cora felt the void of their absence. But they had not moved far and she could visit them often.

❁

One day in early October, Cora sat before the mirror, combing her long brown hair.

Eliza climbed the ladder into the room. "Are you going someplace?"

Cora nodded, smiling. "Yes, Aaron and I are going to Vickie's for supper."

"Oh." Eliza dropped to the bed.

When she didn't say more, Cora looked up. "Is something wrong?"

Eliza sighed. "I don't know."

"What do you mean you don't know?" Cora laughed. "Even I can tell there's something wrong. You look like you've lost your last friend."

Eliza lifted her gaze to her sister's. "Maybe I have." She jumped up and started toward the ladder. Then, as if changing her mind, she turned and sat back on the bed. "It's Ralph. About every other time Aaron comes, Ralph doesn't."

"Well, Aaron and I have a very special relationship." Cora spoke before she thought.

Eliza snorted. "I thought Ralph and I did, too." Then her expression changed, and Cora saw fear in her eyes. "Cora, do you think Ralph is getting tired of me?"

A rush of sympathy for her little sister filled Cora's heart. She shook her head. "No, of course not."

"Are you and Aaron going to get married?" Eliza's change of topic caught Cora by surprise.

"No. I mean, I don't know. He hasn't asked me."

"What would you say if he did?" Eliza leaned forward, her face eager.

Cora's cheeks grew warm as she turned back to the mirror. "Don't you think Aaron should be the first to hear my answer to that? That is, if he ever asks."

"What I think is, you'd better make up your mind beforehand so you'll know what to say." Eliza stood. "I think you should say yes."

Cora laughed. "Oh, Eliza, you're being silly. He hasn't asked and maybe he never will."

Cora was still thinking about their conversation several minutes later while she waited for Aaron. But darkness descended and he didn't come. Aaron was always punctual, if not early. Cora's concern turned to worry. When Ben volunteered to take a message to Vickie, she knew Aaron was not coming, and her heart felt as if it would break.

❁

Two days later Ralph showed up just after supper. Alone. As Orval let him in, Cora hung her dish towel to dry.

"Come on in and find a spot to sit," Orval offered.

"I ain't stayin'." Ralph held his hat, twisting it. "My pa. . ." He cleared his throat. "Pa died awhile ago. We'll be having the buryin' midmornin' tomorrow. Ma'd appreciate it iffen you'd come."

Cora heard Eliza's sharp intake of breath as Father placed his hand on Ralph's shoulder in sympathy. "I'm sorry to hear that. Was it an accident?"

Ralph nodded. His brows drew together in a way that reminded Cora of Aaron. "The still blew up a couple days ago. We knew right off he weren't gonna make it. He was jist hurt too bad. We all tried to make his passin' as easy as possible."

"I'm sure you did all you could." Orval dropped his hand. "Tell your mother we'll be there. If you'd like, Ben and I can help carry the word around."

Ralph jammed his hat on his head and turned toward the door. "Thanks, but I ain't in no hurry to go back home jist yet. Might as well make the rounds myself."

Orval nodded. "I understand. What about. . . ?" He hesitated. "What about the body?"

Ralph didn't turn around. "Mr. Hanson's takin' care of that."

"All right." Orval nodded. "If there's anything we can do, don't hesitate to let us know."

"I'll tell Ma." Ralph left without a word to anyone else.

There was silence in the room until Father closed the door. Cora's eyes filled with tears as she thought of Aaron sitting by his father's bedside knowing that at any moment he would be gone. No wonder he hadn't come the other evening. She felt ashamed of the thoughts she'd had toward him the last two days.

❋

The chilly, damp October air encircled the grave site as neighbors gathered on a small rise behind the Starks' cabin. Aaron and Ralph stayed close by their mother's side while Ivy stood with them, yet apart. Her black skirt fluttered around her ankles in the cold breeze. A veil covered her eyes. Cora looked at the proud tilt of her chin and felt sorry for her. Ivy had so little, yet wanted so much.

Cora's gaze shifted to the mother. She was even frailer than the last time she'd seen her. Her face was pale, her eyes dark hollows of sorrow.

When the last family arrived, Mrs. Newkirk stepped forward and sang a hymn in her clear soprano.

As the last note floated away, Aaron squared his shoulders and lifted his head. His voice sounded clear and strong. "My father's parents followed Mr. Daniel Boone to the backwoods of Kentucky in 1775 and lived there the rest of their lives. In 1785, my father, Walter Aaron Stark, was born to James and Martha Stark. In 1814, he met and married my mother, Jennett Alice Wilkins. They had seven children, four buried in Kentucky, and the three of us, Aaron James Stark, Ralph Walter Stark, and Ivy Jennett Stark. Walter Aaron Stark was forty-nine years, four months, and two days of age when he was killed by accident while makin' a livin' for his family."

Aaron bowed his head after giving the obituary. Cora watched him, her heart swelling with pride.

Mr. Newkirk stepped forward. "Shall we pray?" As soon as the prayer ended, the men paid their respects, then shook hands with Aaron and Ralph while the women hugged Ivy and her mother, sharing tears of sympathy with them.

When Cora stepped in front of Aaron, she lifted tear-filled eyes. "I'm so sorry. I wish I could do something to help."

He took her hand and squeezed it gently. "Thank you." His dark brows were drawn together and there was no smile. He cleared his throat and asked, "Can you stay? Maybe your father'd let me walk you home."

Cora nodded, knowing her father would stay until the last shovel of dirt covered the grave.

When each person had expressed their sorrow, several men stepped forward to lower the coffin into the ground. Cora watched as Aaron scooped the first shovel of dirt and let it drop on the box that held his father. He stepped back then, handing the shovel to Ralph. After Ralph's scoop of dirt hit the box, the other men pitched in and a small mound of fresh earth soon covered the open wound in the prairie.

Everyone but Cora had gone by the time Aaron had his mother settled in the house. Cora looked at the new grave. For most of her life, she had thought death was simply sleep. But Esther said that the soul lives on either in a place of torment or in the presence of God. What if Esther was right? Where was Mr. Stark now?

Cora was glad when Aaron came and took her hand. His voice sounded husky. "I'm gonna miss him."

Cora leaned her head against his shoulder. "Oh, Aaron, I'm so sorry this happened."

"There weren't nothin' a body could do." He stared at the grave. "I started to come to your house that evenin'. Then, somethin' went wrong at the still and it blew up. He came staggerin' in and fell in the yard. I sure didn't mean to do you thataway."

"It's all right, Aaron. I understand now."

"He was in a lot of pain. We sat with him all night long." Cora saw the fatigue on Aaron's face.

She moved away from the grave with Aaron's hand still holding hers. "What you need is rest. If you don't want to walk me home, I can go by myself."

For the first time that day, Cora saw a faint smile cross Aaron's lips. "You oughta know I wouldn't let you do that. Bein' with you is better'n rest, anyhow."

Cora's heart lifted at his loving words. They walked together hand in hand along the path to the Jacksons', talking of the trees and herbs, the birds and animals that Aaron knew and understood. She was happy in his nearness and his caring attention. She felt they had just started walking when the clearing at the end of the woods came into view.

Aaron's steps slowed, then stopped just inside the shelter of the trees. He turned to face Cora, placing his hands on her shoulders. She stood still, looking up at him. He smiled while his bright blue eyes gazed lovingly into hers.

A dried leaf dropped into her hair and he plucked it off. "Cora, can I kiss you?"

Cora's heart beat a wild staccato. She leaned closer to him and smiled. He needed no other encouragement.

She had been kissed before—by George. But never like this. It was a chaste kiss, a mere meeting of the lips for a brief moment in time, yet she felt the warmth of Aaron's love—his tenderness—and especially his respect for her, envelop and claim her heart. When he slowly lifted his head and smiled tenderly at her, she knew things would never be the same between them.

"I guess I should be getting home."

"I guess so." Aaron didn't move. "Do you think Vickie and John'd give us another chance to visit?"

Cora nodded. "I'm sure they will. Would you like to go Sunday afternoon?"

He nodded. "If it's all right with them."

"It will be."

"I guess I need to git you home." Aaron's hands were still on her shoulders.

Cora nodded, then leaned forward at the same time he bent toward her. Her heart pounded as Aaron held her close.

❉

The next week, Cora moved through her work with a song on her lips. Eliza noticed and mentioned it late one night after they were in bed. "Did you and Aaron come to an understanding?"

"What do you mean, 'an understanding'?" Cora smiled in the darkness.

"Did he ask you to marry him?"

Cora's smile disappeared. "No."

"Then why are you so happy?"

Cora thought of Aaron's strong arms around her and the touch of his lips on hers. Her smile returned. "Am I more happy than usual?"

"Yes, you know you are. I'd be happier, too, if Ralph would call more often." Eliza sighed. "He never tells me when he's coming. Every now and then he just shows up."

"Why don't you tell him you'd like to know ahead of time?"

"Because then he might never come. He's so handsome and he can be so charming. I don't want to lose him."

"Eliza," Cora whispered in the dark room, "has Ralph ever kissed you?"

"Cora!" Eliza's shocked whisper was loud in the still night. "Of course not."

Silence filled the room for several moments until Eliza whispered more quietly. "He tried a few times, but I wouldn't let him."

Cora turned her back to Eliza. In the quiet darkness, she soon grew drowsy and drifted off to sleep with the memory of Aaron's kiss filling her heart.

❀

Friday afternoon Ben again went for Mrs. Newkirk. This time his mother needed her services. The baby had still not come by the next morning. Cora stood outside the door of her parents' room, listening to her mother's groans change into muffled screams as the hours dragged by. Mr. Newkirk returned after leaving his wife all night to find that the baby had refused to be born.

Vickie and John arrived just before noon, and Vickie took charge as only the oldest daughter can. She prepared the noon meal and saw that everyone ate despite the worry that hung as a thick cloud over the house.

By midafternoon, Cora retreated to the front porch to worry in private, returning later to find Ben and Mr. Newkirk together, their heads bowed. Cora was sure they were praying.

Then, as the gray pallor of the approaching autumn night settled over the land, a tiny cry silenced the room. Cora waited with bated breath until Orval opened the bedroom door. Every eye turned to his pale, unshaven face.

He closed his eyes for a moment before saying, "We have a little girl."

"Is she all right?"

"What about Mother?"

The questions flew, demanding answers.

He sank into the nearest chair. "Seven times we've been through this and never has there been a problem." He looked up and sighed. "The baby is fine as far as we know. Mother is still alive, but she's very weak."

Just then the door to the bedroom flew open and Mrs. Newkirk called to Father. "Mr. Jackson, I need your help."

As Orval rushed from the room and the door closed behind him, Cora heard Mrs. Newkirk's hushed words. "She's bleeding too much."

Cora's eyes filled with tears as she heard Ben's soft voice pleading before the throne of God for his mother's life.

Chapter 13

When Aaron came on Sunday afternoon to take Cora to the Merrills', they stood on the front porch to talk. She told him, "Vickie is staying here for a few days so this is where we'll eat."

"Oh." His brows drew together in the way Cora found endearing.

She laughed. "I have a new baby sister. Would you like to meet her?"

Aaron shrugged. "I guess so."

Cora refused to let his indifference dampen her enthusiasm for her sister. "Don't worry. You'll love her just as soon as you see her."

Aaron smiled then. "If she's anything like her big sister, I will."

That was as close as Aaron had ever come to saying he loved her. She smiled and determined that one day soon he would say the words.

She laughed again. "If you aren't careful, you'll make me jealous of my own sister."

She led the way inside to the rocking chair, where Eliza sat holding the tiny baby. Cora took the infant, cuddling her close in her arms.

She turned to see Aaron watching her. A faint flush covered her cheeks under his scrutiny. "What are you thinking?"

The flush moved to his face. "You look downright natural holding that little one."

"I've had some experience with Lenny and Nicholas."

"Well, are you gonna introduce us?" Aaron grinned.

"Of course." Cora held the infant toward him. "This is Nora Jane Jackson. Nora, this is Aaron Stark."

When he just looked at the sleeping baby, Cora pushed her against his chest. "You're supposed to hold her now that you've been introduced."

"Hold her?" Aaron threw his hands out and stepped back. "I can't do that."

"Why not?" Cora took a step forward.

" 'Cause I'd break her. Or drop her." He took another step back.

Cora heard Eliza giggle. She ignored her and moved forward. "Here, I'll keep hold of her, and all you have to do is let her lie on your arm. Can't you do that?"

Aaron felt a thrill of fear at the thought, but he didn't move away this time when Cora lifted the tiny bundle toward him. He crooked his arm like he'd seen her do, and Cora placed the infant with her wobbly, little head against the bend of his elbow.

He looked down at the miniature features of the sleeping baby's face, and a feeling he'd never experienced before beat in his chest. He wanted to be a father. He wanted to hold his own child in his arms. His and Cora's baby.

❁

Early Monday morning, two days after Nora's birth, Emma asked Ben to invite Mrs. Newkirk back for a visit. When she arrived, she entered the bedroom and closed the door.

When she left, she smiled even as she wiped her eyes. Cora watched her go and wondered what had gone on behind the closed door. She found out that evening when the family gathered around Mother's bed.

Emma told of the rebellion she had felt from youth toward her father's strict religion and of the fear when she thought she would die at Nora's birth. "But that has all changed now. Agnes led me to Jesus. I'm a believer now. I don't have that old rebellion anymore."

Ben knelt by the bed and put his arms around his mother and baby sister. Tears ran down his cheeks as he buried his face in her shoulder. "God is answering my prayers. I was afraid to tell you, but I've been praying so hard."

Cora murmured a quick good night to her mother, dropped a kiss on her cheek, and left. In her room, snuggled under the covers in the dark, she turned her back to Eliza, pretending to sleep. But her mother's words haunted her long into the night.

As autumn moved on and winter settled in, Cora watched her mother and Ben. Emma's recovery was slow. Where before she had kept busy working about the house, now Cora often found her rocking with her Bible balanced on one arm and Nora cuddled in the other.

And Ben. In many ways he was the same Ben, but there was a new maturity about him. He spent as much time with Esther as he could, and Cora was not surprised when he confided in her that they had been talking about a wedding date.

"We hope to be married in the spring." Ben's face glowed with happiness. "Esther's father started for Springfield yesterday to post a letter to her uncle, who is a minister in Tennessee."

"Tennessee!" Cora stared at her brother. "Do you have any idea how far away that is?"

"Sure, but Esther's mother says he'll come."

"Then you'll probably be married in a few months." Cora knew she should be happy for her brother, instead a feeling of depression settled on her heart. "Where will you live?"

Ben frowned. "Father suggested we move Lenny downstairs and Esther and I stay in my room."

Cora wasn't sure she liked that idea. Her relationship with Esther had been strained for some time. What would it be like living in the same house with her?

※

Christmas, the first day of 1835, and Cora's twentieth birthday appeared on the calendar before warm weather returned. Cora welcomed spring and Aaron's frequent visits.

One evening, as they walked near the house, he plucked a worm from a leaf on one of Father's new apple trees. He threw it to the ground and stepped on it. "Ma's failin' fast."

"I'm sorry." She wasn't sure what else to say.

Aaron shrugged. "I reckon that's the way of things. A body gets born, lives awhile, and then dies. Looks like there oughta be somethin' more to life, don't it?"

Cora thought of her own mother. Nora was five months old now, and Mother had still not regained her strength. It wasn't as if she were on her deathbed, but Cora felt uneasy about her. She decided it was time to talk of something else. "Ben and Esther's wedding is just a couple weeks away."

He nodded. "I know." He reached for her hand and started walking again.

Cora laughed. "Esther's preacher uncle and his family moved in with the Newkirks yesterday. Ben says there's scarcely room to walk through their house."

Aaron smiled down at her. "What've they got, a whole passel of kids?"

"That depends on what you call a passel."

"I'd reckon eight like the Newkirks' is a passel."

"Then the answer's no, because they only have four." Cora glanced up at him. "How many children do you think a couple should have?"

Aaron smiled at her before answering. "Four'd be all right. What do you think?"

An uncharacteristic shyness came over her, and she looked up at him through her lashes. "Four would be nice." Cora hadn't intended the conversation to take this unexpected turn. Her heartbeat increased under Aaron's intense gaze.

They walked out of Father's young orchard, across the open space, toward the line of cedar trees growing by the creek. Aaron's hand felt warm in hers. The setting sun's rays cast long shadows beside them.

Aaron led her through the pungent cedar trees to the bank of the creek. They sat on a fallen log and watched the moving water below.

Aaron spoke first. "It's quiet here 'ceptin' for the creek. I like the sound of water."

"I do, too." Cora rested against his shoulder. "It reminds me of my spring."

"Your spring?" Aaron leaned forward to see her. "Where've you got a spring?"

A flush warmed her face. Only to herself had she claimed ownership of the meadow spring she'd found that day with Aaron and Eliza in the woods. "It really isn't mine."

"So, where is it?"

He could be so persistent sometimes. "Not far from the hollow tree. You probably don't remember, but you showed it to Eliza and me one day. It's the most beautiful place I've ever seen."

Aaron's arm slipped around her waist. "I remember. I like it there, too. Maybe I'll build a cabin someday up on that high spot in the meadow. You can see the spring from there."

He wasn't looking at her now. Was she part of his dream?

"Aaron?"

He brushed his cheek against hers. "Hmm?"

When she didn't say any more, Aaron pulled away and turned her to face him. His bright blue eyes traveled over Cora's face, finally resting on her lips. As his head lowered, she responded with all her love. The kiss was long and sweet.

"I love you, Aaron Stark." Cora's whisper probably couldn't have shocked him any more than it did her. It seemed they sat forever, his arms still holding her close to him. Then, Cora's humiliation turned to anger. How dare he sit there like a stone after she had bared her soul to him!

Her entire body tensed before she pulled away and jumped up. She stood in front of him, her hands on her hips. She had waited long enough. "Did you hear what I said, Aaron Stark? I said I love you."

Aaron didn't move as he stared at her, a look of disbelief on his face.

Tears welled in Cora's eyes, spilling down her cheeks. She had never been so humiliated in her life. She buried her face in her hands.

"Cora, don't cry." Aaron's strong arms surrounded her, pulling her close against his hard chest. "Please, darlin', don't. I can't bear to see you hurtin'."

"But you don't love me." Cora's voice was muffled in his shirt.

He lay his cheek against the top of her head. "You know better'n that. You're everything to me. You're the very beat of my heart. I don't know how I'll ever live without you."

Cora stood still in his arms. She could feel her heart beating and hear his against her ear. Aaron said he loved her. No, he'd said more than that. He said she was the beat of his heart. A smile spread across her lips as she lifted her head.

When their eyes met, there was no answering smile. His brows drew together in a frown.

"Aaron, what is it? We love each other." Cora knew her voice held panic, but she couldn't help it.

"You know I'm jist a uneducated backwoodsman. I'll never amount to a hill of beans. You're better'n me, Cora. You need a man who can give you all them pretty things like your ma has."

Cora jerked away. "What have you been doing for the last year? Playing with my affections? If you don't want to marry me, Aaron Stark, just say so."

Her face flamed in anger. "I can't help it that I grew up in a city where I could go to school. So what if you can't read and write and I can? You've got more talent in your one little finger than all the city boys I ever met put together. You know more about nature than anyone I know. If it's so important, you can learn to read. You're plenty smart enough. Besides that, who says I want a bunch of pretty things to dust? If you really loved me, you'd know better."

The last sentences were flung over her shoulder as she ran from the creek bank, up the gentle slope toward the house. Tears blinded her, and she wiped them away with the back of one hand. Her other hand lifted her skirt above her flying feet.

Aaron stood, watching her go. All his life he'd felt inferior. It was hard to believe education and fancy things weren't important to Cora. But she sounded like she meant it when she yelled at him. Maybe she really would rather marry him than some city fellow.

His heart pounded as he ran. He overtook her, running ahead to catch her in his arms. His voice was husky. "Cora, are you meanin' you'd marry me?"

"Of course I'd marry you, Aaron, if you'd only ask."

Aaron swallowed, still unsure she meant it. "Cora Jackson, will you marry me?"

Tears ran from Cora's eyes. She nodded. "Yes, I will marry you, Aaron, if you promise to never doubt yourself or my love again."

She looked at him through teary eyes, framed by wet lashes, and he nodded. "I'll try."

He sealed his promise with a kiss before they returned to the house to tell their news.

Later, when Aaron went home, he found that his mother had taken a turn for the worse. He and Ivy stayed up with her and were by her side when she passed away in her sleep. She was laid to rest beside her husband the following day, and Ivy became Aaron's responsibility.

❧

"Can you believe we have to go to church every night for a week just because Ben is getting married?"

"Oh, Cora, what's the matter with you?" Eliza slipped into her dress. "I think it'll be lots of fun. Everyone will be there."

"I suppose." Cora parted her hair down the middle. She'd make two braids and coil them on the sides.

"Why don't you and Aaron get married when Ben and Esther do?"

Cora sighed. "I don't think I could live in the same house with Ivy."

As the Jacksons' wagon stopped at the meeting that evening, Cora saw that a large framework of poles had been covered with a canopy of green branches creating shade from the sun that was still high in the early June sky. Slab benches had been constructed to accommodate the congregation. When the wagons continued to roll onto the Newkirks' pasture, Cora was amazed at all the new faces. She found Aaron, and together they joined the group around Ben and Esther.

After visiting awhile, Esther asked Cora, "Please, could I talk to you before the service begins?"

Cora looked at Aaron. "Don't get lost. I'll be right back."

He grinned. "Don't worry. I'll be waitin' right here for you." He gave her hand a gentle squeeze before releasing it.

Cora walked beside Esther away from the others. An uncomfortable silence vibrated between them. Finally, Esther spoke. "I want to apologize for that day when I said those things and hurt your feelings."

When Cora didn't respond, she continued. "I was so worried about you that I didn't stop to think. I blundered in trying to fix everything myself when I should have stayed home and prayed." She turned to Cora with tears in her eyes. "When I marry Ben, we'll be sisters. Please forgive me for anything I've said or done to offend you. I already love you like a sister."

Cora's anger and resentment melted under the warm rays of Esther's love. Tears filled her eyes as she smiled at her friend. "I'm the one who should apologize. I shouldn't have taken offense so quickly nor held a grudge so long."

The low, sweet notes coming from Bill Reid's violin reached them, and Esther looked at the brush arbor. "I need to hurry. The service is about to start." She turned to face Cora. "I want you to stand up with me Sunday. Please, Cora. Grace will be next to me because she's my sister, but I'd really like for you to stand up with me, too. Your friendship means so much to me."

Cora didn't answer for a moment. She couldn't. She had treated Esther shamefully, yet she offered her an honored place in her wedding. She smiled. "Thank you, Esther. I will."

Cora returned to Aaron as Timothy Donovan, a young man new to the area, started leading the congregation in a hymn. After the last song ended, Reverend Arthur Copley, a small man with a thatch of blond hair, took the service. He was a dynamic preacher. Cora was sure his voice could be heard by the cows in the Newkirks' far pasture. It took all her concentration to keep from squirming as he pointed a finger that swept the gathering, yet singled her out.

" 'All'—did you hear that? God's Word says 'all have sinned, and come short of the glory of God.' " He looked first at one and then another, his eyes piercing.

Cora sat on the rough wood bench, her hands folded in her lap while she struggled with the conviction that all was not right with her soul. As the sermon continued, Cora longed to jump from her seat and run as far away as she could.

Quoting scripture after scripture, he left the front and walked down the center aisle, beckoning from one side to the other for those who felt the call of the Holy Spirit to come to the altar of prayer.

Cora heard weeping and prayers all around her. She watched as several stepped out and went forward. She sat, her hands clasped in her lap, trembling as her eyes darted about, looking for a way out. The couple beside her got up and went forward. Aaron started to rise, giving her all the encouragement she needed. She stood quickly, grabbed his hand, and pulled him behind her until she cleared the shelter.

They walked away, hand in hand. Away from the voices raised in prayer. . . away from the lanterns and burning pine knots into the gathering dusk. . . Cora breathed deeply and sighed. She said nothing to Aaron, keeping her feelings private. She didn't want him to see her the way Reverend Copley had just made her see herself.

Night after night, Cora lived through the same experience, always managing to slip away as the altar call was given. Saturday night, the night before Ben and Esther's wedding, Esther's uncle again walked the center aisle, urging all who felt God's call on their lives to come forward for prayer.

This time, when Cora reached for his hand, Aaron said, "No, Cora." His voice was low and firm. "I'm goin' up there. Are you comin' with me?"

Cora looked up into his face and saw the resolve there. Tears filled her eyes as she shook her head. "No, but I'll wait outside for you."

Her heart broke when Aaron went one way and she went another.

That night she lay in her bed beside Eliza, reliving the look on Aaron's face when he came out of the arbor. He had never looked more handsome to her than he did at that moment. His smile was alive with joy that radiated from his sparkling eyes.

He took her hands in his as a look of wonder came over his face. He patted his chest. "I got a real light feelin' in here. I reckon sin can be mighty heavy. I wish you'd gone with me."

Cora tossed on her bed, blocking out the sound of his voice from her mind. What she should be thinking about was finding someone to take Ivy off their hands so they could get married.

Cora awoke to the sunshine coming in the window. It was early Sunday morning, June 14, 1835. Ben and Esther's wedding day. There was only one more church service left. Esther's uncle and his family would be leaving shortly after the wedding.

After church and the carry-in meal on the grounds, Esther and Cora headed toward the house to dress for the wedding ceremony. Cora saw Aaron in a huddle of men surrounding Ben. She knew Ben had asked Aaron and John to stand up with him. She was glad Aaron would be in front with her.

"Look at my hand, Cora. It's trembling." Esther held her hand out before her.

"What's that from? Nervousness or fear?"

Esther gave a short laugh. "Probably both."

Cora followed Esther up the ladder into her bedroom. "I suppose being nervous is normal. But Ben loves you with all his heart. He would never harm you."

Esther's cheeks grew rosy. "I could never be afraid of Ben. It's the future, I think, that I fear."

Esther spread a soft, white silk dress on the bed. The long, bell-shaped skirt was trimmed with a wide band of gathered lace near the bottom. The tight, fitted waist, sewn to the gathered skirt, ended in a vee in front. The sleeves were banded by matching gathered lace reaching just past the elbows and slightly shorter in front. The low rounded neckline was trimmed with wide matching lace.

Cora rubbed her hand over the soft silk. "Your dress is beautiful."

"Thank you." Esther slipped out of her church dress. "We made it from a dress Ma had. Even back in Virginia, she didn't have much cause to wear anything this fancy so it's hardly been worn. She said it's a tradition to wear something old."

"Esther, what did you mean about being afraid of the future?"

"I shouldn't have said anything." Esther lifted her wedding dress and was lost in its folds. Cora helped her, straightening the soft material and buttoning the back.

Finally, Esther spoke again. "I love your brother very much, Cora. There are so many things we agree on. One is that we want to be as close to both our families as we can. I know it may be hard moving right into the house with all of you, but I'm not sorry, because it will give me a good chance to get to know you."

"What does that have to do with the future? Doesn't Ben plan to start on your own cabin as soon as he can?"

Esther looked down at her hands clutched together in front. She shook her head. "I don't know. We both have a feeling that our lives are going to change."

Cora laughed. "Is that all? Of course your lives will change. Marriage makes a difference in a person's life."

Esther smiled. "Cora, we believe God is talking to us about a work He may have for us. We don't know what it is or where it will be, but we've agreed to pray until we know what God wants."

Cora, not knowing what to say, was glad to hear Esther's mother come in and call up the stairs, "Girls, are you up there?"

"Yes, Ma, come on up."

❧

Several minutes later, Cora led the way up the central aisle of the open-air church with Grace following. She saw Ben and John in front with Esther's uncle, but her gaze locked with Aaron's as he stood on the other side of John. His lips curved in a smile, and his expressive bright blue eyes sent messages of love to her heart. If only this could be their wedding.

As Cora and Grace took their places, Esther started down the aisle. She was beautiful. Her golden hair set off the halo of wildflowers and netting above her lovely face. Cora looked beyond Esther to the waving green prairie grass and the line of cedar trees beyond. A gentle, warm breeze ruffled Esther's veil.

Cora looked back at Ben and saw adoration in his expression as he watched Esther come to him. Cora's gaze again met Aaron's, and her heart swelled with love. Somehow they would find a way, and then it would be their wedding day.

Chapter 14

Cora went out the door and around to the back lot, careful to keep the slop bucket from sloshing on her skirt. Aaron's pig, now grown into a full-sized hog, snorted his displeasure at being kept waiting for his lunch.

"Oh, hush, you overgrown critter. You're making so much noise you couldn't hear it thunder." Slopping the hog was not her favorite chore, but she'd agreed to do it so Ben could take Esther to her parents' house for some of her things. Cora lifted the almost full bucket, balanced it on the fence, and poured it into the trough, keeping her feet and skirt well back from the splash. As the hog rushed at it, grunting his pleasure, a male voice spoke.

"Pardon my intrusion, ma'am." The voice held a strong tone of arrogance. "Would you be so kind as to direct me to the Jackson homestead?"

Cora's heart froze. The voice behind her brought a flood of memories— both good and bad. She turned slowly to face George Merrill, the filthy bucket still clutched in her hand.

He held the reins of a sleek, black horse and stared at her.

She realized she stared at him, too, but couldn't help it. A dark claw hammer coat covered his white shirt with an attached collar that framed his full cheeks. Her gaze traveled down to his gray trousers and on to his black dress boots, then back to his face. She couldn't remember him appearing so soft and pale—and so totally out of place. He looked ridiculous standing next to the pigpen in his fine, city clothes.

She was surprised to see him, but judging from the expressions of distaste, shock, and disapproval flickering across his face, not nearly as surprised as he was to see her.

"Cordella Jackson, I didn't recognize you. What are you doing? Have you been reduced to a scullery maid?"

Before she could answer, he pulled a white linen handkerchief from his pocket and held it to his nose. "Whose quaint little cabin is this and where are your shoes?"

Cora looked down and saw her toes peeking out from under the hem of her skirt. A hot flush sped to her cheeks. She pulled her foot back, hiding it under her skirt.

"You haven't answered me," George demanded. "Who lives in this. . . ," he paused before spitting out, "hovel?"

Cora lifted defiant eyes to him. "This is the house my father built when we moved here. Father and our neighbors."

"Are you telling me you live in this?" His emphasis on the last word left no doubt to his impression of the house she had come to love.

"Of course, we live here." She was amazed that George's power to intimidate her was gone.

His voice softened and he smiled. "I suppose life is rather different here than what we are used to. Even John and Vickie live in a hovel with which, for some reason, they seem quite content."

Cora felt anger at his ill-chosen words and started to turn away but his next comments stopped her. "A dinner will be held in my honor at John's this evening. Of course, you and your family are invited." He turned as if to leave. "Please, do wear shoes."

"Are you leaving without speaking to Father?" Cora ignored his latest barb.

He turned a pointed look toward the bucket still clutched in her hands. "We'll visit tonight under better circumstances."

He took several steps before turning, his handkerchief again pressed to his nose, to ask, "You do have the means of bathing here, don't you?"

Cora considered throwing the bucket at him but instead forced a smile. "Certainly, the creek is nearby if I feel the need." She turned her back on his look of disgust and went to the house.

❧

That evening at Vickie's, Cora picked at her food while George dominated the conversation. "I received honors for my class standing at law school."

Cora watched the pride on John's face and the polite look on her father's. Only Emma smiled encouragingly. When he paused for breath, she spoke up. "I'm sure your mother and father are proud of you. You seem young to be a lawyer."

"Actually, I am. I was the youngest in my class." George puffed up, and Cora remembered Eliza calling him the biggest toad in the puddle. She laughed to herself.

George smiled across the table. "Tell me, Cora, aren't you proud of your old playmate?"

"Oh, of course, George. I was under the impression, though, that you would not be going away to law school until a year later than you did. Why the hurry?"

George was silent for the first time that evening. Cora delighted in watching his throat work when he swallowed. Then he schooled his features and smiled. "It is true that my plan had been to wait another year, but the way opened for me to go. When opportunity knocks, only fools refuse to answer."

Opportunity! Ha! Cora would have liked to wipe the self-satisfied look off George's face. Instead, for the rest of the evening, she sat quietly, playing with

Nora and Christopher until it was time to go home.

Cora carried her sleeping sister out to the wagon. She started to lift Nora over the sideboard when she sensed another presence. She turned quickly, almost bumping into George in the dark.

"What are you doing out here? I thought you'd stay inside with your admirers."

"Ah, Cora, are you angry with me?" George reached for the baby. "Here, let me help you with your sister. She's just as cute as you were when you were little."

"How do you remember what I looked like? You weren't much older." Cora let him take Nora and lay her on some blankets that Emma had brought for that purpose. The baby stirred, but went back to sleep.

"The question is, how could I forget? And, of course, the answer is, I could never forget you, Cora. I still love you." George's voice was soft and caressing, yet the sound grated on Cora's nerves.

"You love me?" Cora repeated. "You've never loved anyone but yourself, George Merrill."

"You are angry with me." George reached for her. "You know I'd have come for you if I could. How can I make it up to you?"

Cora neatly stepped aside. "There's nothing to make up."

"That's my Cora. You've always been forgiving. You're still as sweet and unspoiled as I remember." This time, when he reached for her, she did not escape. He held her gently by each upper arm.

She looked toward the house.

George smiled in the moonlight. "Don't worry. They're busy talking about some Fourth of July party being held in a barn. It'll be awhile before they come outside."

Cora recognized derision in his voice. "The only barn around here big enough for a party is Bill Reid's. You might understand why they admire his barn if you saw it."

George frowned down at her. "What's come over you, Cora? First, I find you wallowing with hogs and now you're defending a barn. Surely this place hasn't changed you that much."

Cora looked at George in the dim light of the moon. At one time she thought the sun rose and set at George's command. How wrong she had been.

She smiled at him. "Yes, this place and the people in it have changed me. It's been two years, George. I'm not the same girl you once knew."

"Oh, you think not?" A wicked gleam came into his eyes. "We'll see about that."

His grip on her arms tightened, and he swiftly bent his head to capture her lips under his.

As Cora fought, George's kiss became more possessive. His arms slipped around her, crushing her against him. She wanted to scream but had no air. Her arms were pinned to her sides so she could not fight.

George released her and stepped back, an arrogant smile on his lips. "I usually get what I want, Cora. You know that. I want you and I intend to have you."

Cora considered slapping the smirk off George's face, but she knew he would hurt her in return. She wiped her mouth with the back of her hand. "I wouldn't marry you if you were the last man on earth. I'm betrothed to a wonderful man right here, and this is where I intend to stay."

George's eyes widened at Cora's news. "You must be jesting."

Cora was glad to see her family come out the door of the house. "I'm very serious. Aaron is everything you are not. I love him very much."

That night at home in her bed, silent tears fell as Cora mourned a childhood friendship that was now dead. It was not for George that she cried, but for the memory of a little boy who had been her companion and friend through many happy years. Tonight she had seen George with new eyes. No longer was she blinded to the evil streak in him. As she wiped the last tear from her cheek, she knew his hold over her was broken. Gone was the girl who bowed to his every wish. In her place was a woman strong enough to give her love to a real man—a man of honor and integrity—Aaron Stark.

❧

By July 4, when George had not come to visit, Cora was sure he thought to punish her by his absence. She was thankful she had not been forced to endure his presence and dreaded seeing him again.

Then, early that afternoon, he came with the Merrills. They were going with the Jacksons to the celebration.

George took Cora's elbow and spoke close to her ear. "In spite of our primitive surroundings, I expect to have a good time tonight. I'm riding with you."

Cora tried to pull her arm from his grasp only to have him tighten his hold. She knew further resistance would bring pain, so she relaxed. Surely she could put up with him for the short ride to Bill Reid's. He could do nothing once she was with Aaron.

In the wagon, George scooted close to Cora and, under cover of her billowing skirt, slipped his arm around her waist. She sat next to a box of food, giving her no room to get away.

"George. Please remove your hand," she whispered.

George just smiled. "Don't pretend with me. You know as well as I do that you aren't still angry. You never could hold a grudge."

"Of course, I'm not angry with you, George." She smiled sweetly at him. "How could I be angry with someone I care nothing for?"

George frowned. "Oh, you care all right." His voice turned hard. "I have proof of that."

"Proof? What proof could you possibly have?" Cora laughed at his nonsense.

A gleam entered George's pale blue eyes. "I have your undying words of love right here." He patted his chest.

"Oh, George, I said a lot of things when we were back home that have changed. For the sake of our childhood, can't we just be friends?"

"Friends!" George's whisper rose louder than he intended. He spoke again, his voice lower, but no less threatening. "Cora, I told you I get what I want. Did I also tell you I keep what is mine?"

"I belong to Aaron."

"We shall soon see about that." George settled back in silence with a smug expression on his face.

※

At each public gathering, Cora saw new faces, and this time was no exception. Mr. Reid's barnyard had been transformed for the event. Long tables standing outside the barn door were laden with every dish imaginable. Cora was sure there were already close to fifty people milling around the tables and in small groups talking, and that didn't count the innumerable children running here and there, squealing with laughter. But Aaron was not there.

"Shall we join the peasants?" George stood close to her.

Cora turned hopefully back the way they had come and saw the Hansons' wagon coming. "No, wait. Here comes Aaron."

She pointed. "Aaron is the one with the dark hair."

"Really?" George smirked. "She's not bad-looking."

Cora threw a glance his way as she started toward the wagon. "That's Aaron's sister, Ivy. She isn't just good-looking, she's beautiful."

George was only a step behind Cora. "Are you testing me with a barefoot backwoods wench? Cora, you know me better than that. I couldn't stoop low enough to keep company with these people. I want only you."

"There's nothing wrong with these people, and I'd appreciate it if you'd stop saying there is. But don't worry, I wouldn't push my worse enemy off on you." Cora ran to the wagon, stopping a few yards away.

Aaron's ready smile held a questioning look for George. He jumped to the ground and slipped his arm around Cora's waist. She lifted loving eyes to feast on the handsome young man that would one day be her husband. A lock of unruly dark hair fell across his forehead as he smiled down at her.

"I've missed you," Cora said.

Aaron's grin grew even wider. "I couldn't've been here this evenin' if I hadn't worked from sunup to sunset."

"I know." Cora turned at the sound of George's voice behind her.

"So, you must be the beauty Cora told me about."

George lifted Ivy from the wagon while Ralph and Axel left with Anna. Ivy inspected George from his slicked hair to his black leather dress slippers. She smiled up at him. "I don't recollect us bein' introduced."

"Oh, I'm sorry." Cora stepped forward. "Ivy, this is George Merrill, John's brother, and an old friend of my family's. George, this is Ivy Stark, my future sister-in-law."

Ivy smiled at George. "I'm real proud to meet you, Mr. Merrill."

George gave Cora a mocking smile before offering his arm to Ivy. "The pleasure is mine, Miss Stark. I've been here only a few days. Would you be so kind as to show me around?"

Ivy took his arm, smiling at him with wide, innocent eyes. Cora watched them go, a frown on her face. She didn't particularly like Ivy, and she'd love to see her married, but even Ivy didn't deserve George.

Aaron watched the unhappy expression on Cora's face as George walked away with Ivy, and his heart sank. As soon as she'd said the man's name, he'd recognized it. George was the one she was waiting for that first Christmas. The one she planned to marry. When he didn't come, Aaron had forgotten about him. It sure didn't look like Cora had.

"You wishin' you was in Ivy's shoes?"

"No." Cora spoke quickly and looked deeply into his eyes. "Of course not. I'm just worried about Ivy." She smiled. "I don't think he'll hurt her, though. He's probably just trying to make me jealous."

"Make you jealous?" Aaron repeated, his heart growing even heavier.

Cora nodded. "Yes, you see, George and I grew up together. He thinks he owns me. He's used to getting what he wants, but now that he's seen us together, he'll be fine."

"What do you want, Cora?" Though the words were hard to say, Aaron had to know.

"I love you, Aaron. How could I ever want anyone but you?"

She seemed sincere. Aaron smiled. "All right, but I don't know what's wrong with your thinkin'. A dandy like that could give you anything your heart desires, while I'll do good to put a roof over your head."

"Are you trying to get rid of me?" Cora looked up at him, her head cocked to one side.

Aaron reached out and pulled her close. "I don't ever want shed of you. I jist want you to have the best."

Cora leaned her head against his shoulder. "You are the best, Aaron. You and a roof over my head are all I want." She looked up with a mischievous grin. "Some walls and a floor might be all right, too."

Aaron gave her a quick kiss on the forehead and grinned. "Here we ain't even married yet and you're already demandin' a bunch of fancy stuff."

"Are you hungry?"

Aaron grinned. "You're as changeable as the weather."

Cora smiled. "I baked a pecan pie."

"You still usin' the pecans I gave you?" Aaron, his arm still around Cora, started walking toward the tables.

Cora shook her head. "No, these were some I picked last winter. Yours were gone a long time ago."

They walked around, speaking to both new and old acquaintances. Finally it was time to eat; after a short prayer by Timothy Donovan, the new minister, Cora picked up two plates and handed one to Aaron.

"Are we getting enough to eat?" George's voice cut into Cora's happiness like a dull-edged knife.

She turned, pasting a smile on her face. "Where's Ivy?"

"Oh, she's quite the charmer, Cora." His voice dripped sarcasm. "She needed to talk to—um—a fiddler, I believe. About some music for the dance tonight."

Aaron touched Cora's arm. "Let's sit down and eat."

She moved quickly, letting Aaron guide her away from George. George just smiled before turning away.

The sun moved steadily toward the horizon while the long tables were cleared of their burden of food. Finally, the women packed their respective dishes away.

Orval passed Cora and Aaron with Lenny and Nicholas by the hand. He stopped long enough to say, "Mother's getting tired so we're taking the young ones home. You come back with Ben and Esther whenever they're ready."

Cora nodded and moved with Aaron inside the barn as the music started. Lanterns, hanging around the perimeter of the barn from the rafters, added to the party atmosphere. Fresh straw had been spread on the floor for dancing.

A man called out, "Grab you a partner. Come on, let's go."

Aaron pulled her to join the others. After they danced a couple of sets, the music stopped and a break was called.

Aaron took Cora's hand. "You want anything?"

"A drink of water would be nice."

Cora lifted the dipper and took a sip just as George appeared by their side. "How about letting me dance with Cora?"

Aaron shook his head. "Naw, I don't think so." His arm slipped around her waist.

"You're not afraid of me, are you?"

Cora felt Aaron tense, then he looked down at her. "What do you wanna do?"

What did she want? She wanted to stay with Aaron. But George had been good enough to stay away from them most of the evening. Besides, he was an old family friend. Maybe she owed him this much.

"Aaron, do you mind? Just this one dance and then I'll be right back."

Aaron's brows drew together, but he shrugged. "If that's what you want."

"So, you've finally come to your senses." George's smile was self-assured as he pulled Cora away.

"Yes, I have," Cora said. "The day I said yes to Aaron I came to my senses."

"You don't mean that and you know it." George guided her across the floor to a group forming by the open back doors across the room from Aaron.

"I certainly do. Why are we coming way over here?"

"This is where I've been all evening in case you haven't noticed." George sounded surly.

Cora didn't respond. She focused her attention on keeping up with the dance. George was every bit the gentleman as he kept step to the lively calls. His smile was friendly, his touch light, reminding Cora of the boy she had known.

Then the last call rang out, and before Cora realized what he was doing, George pulled her through the open doorway into the dark night. He held her wrist and walked away from the building. She had no choice but to follow.

"George, what are you doing?" Cora finally found her voice. She stumbled in the dark, trying to stay on her feet and, at the same time, resist the pull on her hand.

"Don't worry. Your beau was across the room when we left. He doesn't even know we're gone." George pulled her to the back, where a copse of trees hid them from prying eyes.

"George, if I scream, someone will come," Cora threatened.

He laughed. "Go ahead. There's so much noise coming from that barn, no one will hear you."

Cora listened to the loud music, stomping feet, clapping hands, and laughter that poured from the open door. George was right. No one would hear her. Fear washed over her.

His hand on her wrist hurt. She struggled to get away, and he pulled her against him, holding her close. "George, please don't do this."

"You're mine, Cora."

She shook her head, pushing against him. "No, I'm not."

"Since we were children, you have belonged to me and you always will."

Cora struggled against his imprisoning arms without any success.

"I'll set up practice back in St. Louis and we can be married."

"No, George." Cora stopped struggling, and he relaxed his hold. "I love Aaron. I'm marrying him."

George laughed. "Cordella Jackson married to a poor dirt farmer who's probably never set foot inside a real town in his life. Can't we just see that?"

"You'll see it if you stay around here long enough because that's what's going to happen." Anger replaced Cora's fear. "Can't you understand me? I love Aaron. I love him more than I've ever loved anyone."

In the dim moonlight, Cora saw George's eyes become slits of anger. "Oh, you do, do you?"

Keeping a grip on her wrist with one hand, he reached into his shirt pocket and pulled out a white slip of paper. "Do you know what this is?"

"A letter."

"But not just any letter." His smile made her feel uneasy. "This is a love letter written by a desperate hand. You wrote this letter, Cora. To me. In it, you tell of your love for me in no uncertain terms. Oh yes, my darling. I believe you love me, not your friend the dirt farmer."

Waves of remorse flooded Cora's soul. How could she have been so ignorant as to write that letter? She had wanted so much to leave this wonderful land that she'd lowered herself to begging through flowery words of misplaced love. Her letter had come back to mock her foolishness.

"It's different now, George. I love Aaron. He loves me."

"How long do you think Stark's love will last once he reads this? Why don't we see? Why don't I let him see for himself how fickle your love is?" George smiled wickedly as he held the letter up.

Cora knew how Aaron had struggled to believe her love for him. If George told him about this letter, it would destroy everything. She grabbed for the letter, but George held it out of her reach.

"Aha! So you don't want him to know?"

"It would be a lie. I don't mean what I said in that letter anymore. Maybe I never did." She eyed the gleaming white paper, wishing she could reach it and tear it to shreds. "You aren't that cruel."

"Of course I'm not." George's voice turned soothing. "Tell the country bumpkin the truth and I'll burn the letter. Fight me and I'll show your lover how you really feel. I'll let him read it for himself. He can't deny what's written in black and white."

It was like George to leave no room for her to win. Then the words "read it for himself" blazoned across her mind. She had nothing to fear. Aaron couldn't read the letter, and his pride would keep him from letting George know he couldn't.

Relieved, she said, "Go ahead. Aaron loves me too much to let something like this come between us. Show him the letter, because I will never give you what you want. I'll never do anything to hurt Aaron."

George's eyes blazed in the moonlight. In one swift movement, he crushed her against him. His mouth covered hers before she had time to escape. This was no kiss of love but of power. She tried to get away but was helpless against his superior strength. He released her abruptly, and she staggered to regain her footing.

She looked into his sneering face, rubbing the wrist he had held. He spoke in a cold voice. "Don't worry. I will let Stark read this, and then, mark my words, you will be mine." With that, he turned and walked away, leaving her alone in the dark.

Cora stood trembling for several moments until she realized she had to find Aaron before George did. It was true. Aaron couldn't read the letter, but what George might say to him would do as much damage.

She smoothed her hair and straightened her dress as she ran toward the barn, slowing to a walk when she reached the back door. Music and voices raised in laughter and conversation mingled in her mind as she elbowed her way into the crowded room and began a frantic search for Aaron.

Chapter 15

Aaron couldn't find Cora. During the second set, she had disappeared. He searched every corner of the barn and decided she must have gone outside with Merrill. He headed for the front door.

As he walked around the side of the barn, a man came toward him. "Well, if it isn't Farmer Stark."

Aaron couldn't mistake the arrogant voice of George Merrill. He knew a Christian, even a new one, was supposed to love everyone, but he was having a hard time with this poor excuse for a man. He demanded, "Where's Cora?"

"Oh, I imagine about now she's fixing her hair. You know how girls are."

Aaron clenched his fists. "I asked you where she is."

"I left her out back. In that little grove of trees."

Aaron didn't realize he'd swung until his fist made contact with George's face. George sprawled on the ground, one hand holding himself out of the dirt, the other spread in front of his face. "Wait. I have something to show you."

He dug inside his pocket, pulling out a handkerchief for his bleeding nose, then a folded piece of paper. He held it toward Aaron. "Here. Take this."

Aaron shoved his hand away, reaching instead for his shirtfront. He hauled him up. "You tell me straight out if you hurt Cora."

"She's fine." He pushed against the hand holding him. "I wouldn't hurt Cora, you ignorant bumpkin. I'm in love with her. I'm taking her home with me."

Aaron's hand fell away. George's fist couldn't have hit him as hard as his words had.

George extended the paper again. "Cora and I had quite a talk about things. We decided the easiest way to break our news would be to let you read this."

"I don't believe you." Aaron's eyebrows drew together. He stood with his feet apart, his arms crossed over his chest.

"I didn't think you would. That's why I insist you read the letter."

Aaron's heart was cut in two by the razor-edged words of the educated man before him.

George took his blood-soaked handkerchief from his nose and smiled, a sneer in his voice. "Surely you wondered why I came to this forsaken land. Cora begged me to rescue her. As soon as I got her letter, I came."

George pushed the letter into Aaron's hand. In a daze, Aaron unfolded it. The full moon overhead supplied barely enough light to see the ink. He stared blankly at it. His face was an emotionless mask.

George watched him. "Aren't you going to read it?"

Aaron looked up without a word.

George laughed. "I don't believe this. How did Cora get mixed up with the likes of you? You can't read, can you?"

Aaron didn't answer as George's laugh taunted him.

"Cora was always at the top of her class. She won every spelling bee in St. Louis. She started reading when she was five. She's the only female I have ever known who was my intellectual equal. We belong together. We've planned on being married since we were children. But then her father brought her here." George flung his hand out before adding, "And look what it almost cost her."

Still Aaron stood, watching George.

George snatched the letter. "Here, let me read it to you."

Finally Aaron spoke. "Don't. I can't read, but I ain't stupid. You can give her all the things I can't. I ain't gonna stand in your way 'cause I love Cora." He turned to walk away, then stopped. "You probably don't know it, but you ain't good enough for her neither."

Aaron went around the barn to the back door. He'd look for Ivy or Ralph and tell them he was heading home.

He stepped into the brightly lit barn, letting his gaze slide over the crowd. Cora was at the front door. With George. Sharp pain sliced through him. He moved toward the musicians and Ivy.

Ivy caught his hand. "Aaron, Mr. Reid wants a word with you."

"I'm goin' home, Ivy. Can you ride back with the Hansons?"

"Yes, but first, Mr. Reid wants to talk to you." Ivy tugged on his hand.

"You wanna see me?" Aaron glanced toward the front door. They were still there. He could see Cora's back as she faced George.

"Yes." Mr. Reid cleared this throat. "I know it's proper to speak to the father, but in Ivy's case. . .well, I thought I should ask you."

"Ask me what?" Aaron stared at the back of Cora's head.

"I've asked Ivy to be my wife. She's consented if you will give us your blessing."

Aaron's eyebrows rose before lowering in a scowl. He turned to face Mr. Reid. "You what?"

"Ivy has agreed to become my wife." Ivy stepped to Mr. Reid's side and took his arm. "We would like your blessing."

Aaron looked into his sister's face. She watched him, a hesitant smile tugging her lips.

"Is that what you want, Ivy?"

She nodded, her bright blue eyes wide and shining. "Yes, very much."

"All right. If you're sure." Aaron offered his hand to the older man. As they shook hands, he nodded. "You have my blessing."

"Thank you, Aaron." Ivy gave her brother a hug and a quick kiss.

Aaron left by the back door. It was a long, lonely walk home through the moonlit night, and he spent most of it making plans.

❀

Cora had looked everywhere for Aaron, but he was nowhere to be found. She stopped at the front door and looked back the way she'd come.

"Looking for me?" She froze at the sound of George's voice.

She turned, her voice icy. "No, I wasn't."

"Don't tell me you were looking for that ignorant bumpkin."

"Aaron is anything but ignorant. He's intelligent. He's very talented and he's—"

"Gone." George finished for her.

"What?"

"I said he's gone."

Cora stared at George's smirking face. So he had told Aaron what was in the letter. She had never seen a more hateful, self-satisfied, arrogant bag of wind in her life. "George, I don't ever want to see you again." Cora spoke slowly and distinctly, then walked away. She went to Vickie's side and stayed there the rest of the evening.

❀

The next morning, Cora woke late with puffy eyes, a headache, and a vivid memory of the evening before. Aaron had walked out on her. If he didn't come by noon, she would go to him.

But before noon, Ivy came to call. She asked Cora to walk with her so they could talk.

They walked a few yards back toward the woods before either spoke. Then, Ivy turned to Cora. "Did you know Aaron's gone?"

"Gone?" Cora repeated.

"Yes, gone. He went before sunup this mornin'." She looked intently at Cora. "He didn't tell you he was goin', did he?"

Cora shook her head. "No."

"That's what I thought. You don't know why he went, neither, do you?"

"Because George Merrill lied to him."

Ivy faced Cora. "What'd that struttin' rooster say?"

"That he came for me because I sent for him."

Ivy shook her head. "That ain't the real reason he took off."

When Cora didn't say anything, she continued. "He did it for you. He don't want to get in your way. He thinks you want that rooster, all right, but he mostly thinks you need him and his money."

"What for?" Cora stared at Ivy.

"A big house with a buggy and high-steppin' horses to pull it. Fancy clothes and pretty dishes and stuff like that. He said he can't get you all them things and George Merrill can. He said Merrill was smart, like you."

Cora grasped Ivy's arm. "Ivy, I told George last night I never want to see him again. I want Aaron. Nobody but Aaron."

"I guess you lost your chance, 'cause he said he ain't never comin' back."

Ivy's blunt words hit Cora with a pain so severe she barely heard Ivy's next words.

"I sure am sorry it turned out this way. I'd like to 've been your sister-in-law. I was going to ask you to stand up with me at my weddin'. You think you might still?"

"Your wedding?" Cora stared at her. "I didn't know you were getting married."

Ivy smiled, her bright blue eyes dancing. "It happened last night. At the dance. Bill Reid asked me. Aaron give us his blessin' before he left."

"Mr. Reid?" Cora wondered if she'd heard right.

"Yes. Can you stand up with me? It'll be end of this month."

Cora had trouble taking it in. Ivy was marrying a man a good fifteen years her senior. She couldn't help but ask. "Do you really want to marry Mr. Reid?"

"Of course I do."

"But he's so old."

Anger flashed from Ivy's eyes. "He ain't old. 'Sides, it ain't none of your business what I do, Cora Jackson. Now do you wanna stand up with me or not?"

"I'm sorry, Ivy. Of course I'll stand up with you. I just wish I could ask you to return the favor."

Cora thought she'd exhausted her supply of tears the night before, but when she thought of Aaron, her eyes filled again. She wiped them away as she struggled to keep from crying.

"You really liked him, didn't you?"

"I love Aaron with all my heart." Cora pulled a handkerchief from her sleeve and blotted her eyes. "I'll never marry anyone else. Please tell him I'll wait for him the rest of my life if I have to."

Ivy shook her head. "Cora, I'm right real sorry for you and Aaron both, but I don't look to ever see him again. He said he's never comin' back."

❧

That evening when George came, Cora refused to see him. Her father climbed to her room. "Is there something you've forgotten to tell me?"

Cora looked up into her father's kind eyes and opened her heart to him. By the time she'd finished, silent tears streamed down her face.

"I love Aaron, Father, and George made him leave. I told him I never want to see him again and I meant it."

"All right." Orval stood, his face stern. "I'll get rid of George and then we'? talk."

Cora heard the mumble of voices and the door slam. She waited a few min utes before peering down from the loft. Orval stood at the foot of the ladder He smiled at her. "Come on, Cora. I think George decided he'd overstayed hi welcome. He's going back to St. Louis."

Cora sat on the floor at her mother's feet. A warm feeling spread through her heart as she looked at her family.

Orval asked, "Now, where did Aaron go?"

"I don't know."

"Was he on foot?"

Cora nodded. "He told Ralph he could have the farm."

"Then he doesn't plan to come back?" Ben spoke from across the room.

"No." Cora's voice choked with tears. "He said he's never coming back."

Orval swore under his breath. "It looks like George did his dirty work well."

"Father, why don't we go after him? He can't have gotten far." Ben straight-ened, a determined gleam in his eyes.

Orval nodded. "We'll wait until morning when we can see better."

Cora's heart lifted at their words.

❧

Sunday was the longest day Cora had ever spent. She went to church and thought of Father and Ben out on the prairie looking for Aaron. At noon, she picked at her food. The afternoon stretched on forever. Preparations were started for sup-per, and they still had not returned.

The sun sank below the horizon a full thirty minutes before Cora heard the horses. "They're back." She tore from the house.

"Father, did you find him?" she called before he dismounted.

He shook his head. "I'm sorry, Cora. We looked everywhere."

Cora slid down the porch post and crumpled in a heap at its base. With her head bowed, she cried great, wrenching sobs. Esther and Eliza helped her into the house, where she sank to the floor with her head in her mother's lap.

Forever, it seemed, she lay there, pouring out the anguish of her broken heart. Aaron was truly gone. God had failed her.

Orval and Ben came in and dropped into the nearest chairs. Esther put her head on Ben's shoulder and wept in sympathy with Cora. Orval finally lifted her in his arms and helped her up the ladder to bed.

She slept for twelve hours. When she awoke Monday morning, her head hurt, her body felt weak, and she stumbled through her morning chores, vaguely aware of Eliza's presence alongside her. If Eliza spoke, Cora didn't hear. She moved automatically through the rest of the day, falling back into bed early that evening, where she fell into another sleep of oblivion.

During the darkness of the night, she awoke to softly spoken words coming from Ben and Esther's bedroom, and she knew they were praying for her. She slept again and woke in predawn darkness.

Aaron was gone. Though her heart ached with the weight of broken love, she slipped from bed and dressed.

With the silence of a shadow, she descended to the floor below and found her way to the kitchen. By the time the summer sun touched the eastern horizon and the family began to stir, breakfast sat on the table.

Day after day, Cora looked for Aaron. Night after night, she went to sleep with a prayer that God would send him home. She took no joy in living, but always kept a watchful eye out the door. Then came Ivy's wedding.

A rough log building now stood where the brush arbor had been three months earlier. Brother Timothy Donovan waited in front with Bill Reid at his side. Harley Sinclair stood behind Mr. Reid. Cora started down the aisle, carrying a bouquet of wild roses. The primitive plank benches on either side were filled with smiling neighbors. Her heart heavy, she took her place in the front and turned to watch Ivy come down the aisle. Ralph walked beside her.

Aaron should have given Ivy away. As Ivy took her place beside Mr. Reid, anger toward Aaron rose in Cora's soul. He should have trusted in her love. Why would he choose to believe a lie when the truth was so obvious?

All through the wedding and the dinner following, Cora raged inwardly at Aaron. That night when she went to bed, she was still angry with him. The next morning, she woke early, dressed, and went downstairs to start breakfast.

The more she thought about Aaron, the angrier she became. Ivy was married now, living in the nice house she had always wanted. His only sister married, and he didn't even show his face.

She slammed the bread pan on the table. A smear of lard went into it. She reached for a bowl, a scoop of flour, lard, milk, salt, and leavening. Her spoon beat a staccato against the sides of the bowl as she stirred.

Orval came out of the bedroom, his hair tousled. "All right, you can stop the noise. I'm up now."

Cora looked up. "Oh, Father, I'm sorry. I didn't mean to wake you."

He grinned. "You didn't. I usually get up about now." He sat at the table and pulled on one of the shoes in his hand. "But we might hold down the noise for your mother. She's not feeling well."

"What's wrong?"

Orval's normally merry eyes became serious. "She didn't get much sleep last night. This might be a good time to move Nora to her own bed."

"She could sleep with Eliza and me."

Orval grinned. "Why? So you can spoil her some more?"

Cora nodded. "She's one of the few pleasures I have left."

"Is that why you were beating a hole in that bowl?"

Cora dumped the dough out and cut biscuits with a tin cup dipped in flour. "I've decided to be angry with Aaron."

"Good." Orval nodded. "That's a healthy emotion."

"He believed a lie. He had no right to listen to someone like George. He should have trusted me."

Orval smiled. "I couldn't agree with you more. He oughta be horsewhipped."

"I wouldn't go that far. . . ." Cora looked up and met the amusement in her father's eyes. She laughed with him. "Oh, Father, I'm angry with him and defending him at the same time. What's wrong with me?"

Orval stood and gave her a hug. "Nothing. There's not a thing wrong with my Cora." He headed toward the door. "I'll be outside. Let me know when those biscuits are done."

Cora had meat frying, oatmeal cooked, and was taking up the biscuits when Ben and Esther came downstairs followed by Eliza. Ben went outside and the two girls joined Cora.

"What'd you do, get up in the middle of the night?" Eliza gaped at the evidence of Cora's activity.

"I couldn't sleep." Cora set a skillet on the table. "If you want to help, there's still gravy to be made, and Mother's not well, so I think we should fix her a tray."

Cora let Esther and Eliza finish the meal while she fixed the tray for her mother. She got Lenny up and sent him outside to get the men, then she took the tray into the bedroom. She glanced briefly at Nora and saw that she was still sleeping.

Emma sat up when she saw Cora. She reached for the second pillow to prop behind her back, setting off a spasm of dry coughing.

"Mother, are you all right?" Cora set the tray on the foot of the bed and rushed to her mother's side.

"I'll be fine." Emma pressed her hand against her chest. "I've caught a chest cold. They always seem worse in the summer."

As she leaned back against the pillows, Cora picked up the tray. "I brought you some breakfast."

"Thank you, Cora. That looks good." Emma took the tray and placed it on her lap. As Cora turned to leave, she asked, "Do you have time to visit while I eat?"

"Of course." Cora sat on the end of the bed.

Emma bowed her head, praying silently, then looked up with a smile. "I haven't carried my share of the load around here lately, have I?"

Cora shook her head. "We don't want you doing anything except getting well. Esther's a hard worker and so is Eliza."

Emma smiled. "Yes, Ben's wife is a treasure among women. Just as my daughters are. I couldn't ask for better girls."

Cora's heart warmed at the praise.

"Cora, are you going to be all right—about Aaron?"

Cora looked at her hands clutched in her lap. "I don't know. Right now I guess I'm too angry to do anything." Her anger flared as she thought again of Aaron's lack of trust in her.

Emma's eyebrows rose. "Angry? What about?"

"Aaron." Cora flounced off the bed. She walked away a few steps and then back. "Oh, Mother, he had no right to leave. The least he could have done was talk to me to learn the truth. Don't you see? He believed a lie when all the time the truth was right there in front of him. All he had to do was ask."

Emma leaned her head back and closed her eyes.

"Mother, are you all right?" Cora asked.

"I'm fine," Emma said. "Cora, I'm the one you should be angry with, not Aaron." Tears slid from her closed eyes.

"You've done nothing wrong."

Emma's eyes opened, her gaze intense. "I taught you to believe a lie, Cora. I trained you to believe you are a Christian even though you have not been born again."

"I don't understand," Cora said softly.

"Don't you see? What you said about Aaron is true for you as well. You believed all the years of your childhood that we were Christians. Ben believed, too, until he discovered that Jesus said, 'Ye must be born again.' He could remember no time in his life when he had been born again."

Cora was silent, not wanting to hear her mother. A tingle of dread crept through her body.

Emma groped for her handkerchief and dried her eyes. "Please hand me my Bible."

Cora picked up the Bible lying beside the bed and handed it to her mother. Emma turned to the passage she wanted and handed it back. "Will you read? It's Ephesians 4:18. It's talking about those who don't know Jesus Christ as their Savior."

Cora took the Book and began reading. " 'Having the understanding darkened, being alienated from the life of God through the ignorance that is in them, because of the blindness of their heart.' "

She looked up. "Are you saying I'm blind to the truth?"

Emma nodded. "You have been, but I think lately you've been forced to see."

A look of pain crossed her mother's face. "I thought regular church attendance was all that was required to be a Christian. I was wrong. I'm sorry, Cora. More sorry than I can ever say. God has forgiven me. Can you?"

"Of course, Mother," Cora whispered, her head bowed.

"Can you understand what I'm trying to tell you?"

Cora nodded. "All my life I've believed a Christian is someone who goes to church and lives a good life. You're saying that isn't true. Then what is a Christian?"

"One who is born again."

Cora stood. "Mother, I have work to do and I know you're tired. You've scarcely touched your food."

She put the Bible back. "I'll think about what you've said. I'm not angry with you, though." She smiled. "I'm not even angry with Aaron anymore."

Cora did think about what her mother had said. She realized that her mother's lie had begun to crumble the day Esther told her she needed to be born again. Then Ben had discovered the truth. And her mother. Even Aaron. With each, a larger chunk fell from the lie, until now it lay as dust, leaving a vacancy in its place.

For several days, as her mother grew weaker, Cora searched the scriptures for the truth. One day she turned her Bible to John 14:6 and read: "Jesus saith unto him, 'I am the way, the truth, and the life: no man cometh unto the Father, but by me.'"

She felt as if she had reached the end of her search. At that point, a restless feeling entered her heart, and she returned to her mother's room.

"I was thinking of you, Cora." Emma's voice sounded weak.

"Mother, do you feel like talking?"

"Of course."

Cora sank to her knees beside the bed. "I've been thinking about what you said the other day. I looked in my Bible to see if I could find the truth." She paused. "I think I've found it."

Emma smiled encouragingly.

"Everything in the Bible seems to point to Jesus. He said a man cannot come to the Father, except by Him." Cora paused to watch her mother's expression. "Jesus is the Truth, isn't He? I want to know Him. I want to be born again, but I don't know how."

A light entered Emma's eyes. She seemed to regain strength as she reached a hand to stroke her daughter's hair. "I won't lie to you this time, Cora."

As her mother led her through the plan of salvation, Cora recognized the sins that had been in her life all along. Rebellion, envy, anger, and simply neglect to come to the One who had loved her enough to die in her place. Mother's hand rested on her head as she wept tears of repentance.

Finally, she looked up, smiling through her tears. "Mother, I really do understand now. I know what it means to be born again."

Her mother lay back, a smile on her lips. "I'm glad, Cora. You and Ben are safe in the fold now, and I believe the others will come in. I only wish I could see it."

"You will, Mother." Cora didn't want to believe otherwise.

"We've had enough lies, Cora." Emma's hand on Cora's arm was hot.

Cora touched her forehead. "Mother, you're burning up."

"I know." Emma closed her eyes.

From that hour on, they took turns sitting by Emma's bedside bathing her with cool cloths. Two days later, she went home to be with the Lord.

Chapter 16

Vickie and John came home with the family after the funeral. Orval sat in Emma's rocking chair with his head down, his shoulders slumped.

Vickie knelt by his side. "Father, I want to take Nora home with me." He stared vacantly at her.

"No." Eliza held her baby sister close. "We can take care of her."

Cora knew how Eliza felt. It seemed that one after another, the ones she loved were being taken from her. And now it was Nora. The sweet, innocent baby who had filled all their hearts with love. But could they hold on to her when she would be better off with Vickie?

She spoke up. "Eliza, I know it hurts, but Vickie won't take her far. We can go see her whenever we want. The important thing to consider is what's best for her."

"Cora's right, Eliza." Vickie appealed to her little sister. "It won't be permanent. Just for a few weeks until Father feels better. Nora needs to be away from the disruption that she'll feel if she stays here."

Tears welled in Eliza's eyes. "All right, but as soon as we can establish some sort of normal life again, she comes home."

She hugged her baby sister close, then let Cora take her. With Nora snuggled in her arms, Cora buried her face in the baby's soft neck and blinked away her own tears.

❊

For the next two weeks, Orval spent long hours working outdoors, going to bed long after the house was quiet. One day he came inside early.

"Esther, I want you and Ben to have the bedroom. I can't sleep there anymore." He fought to control his emotions. "If you don't want to trade with me, I'll sleep in the barn."

Esther lay her hand on his arm. "Of course we'll trade. If there's anything else we can do to help, just let me know."

"When I'm gone, the farm will be Ben's. I want you to consider the house yours now. If you don't like the way things are, just move them until they suit you. The girls will want to divide their mother's keepsakes, but we'll turn the rest over to you and Ben."

Esther gave him a kiss on the cheek and a quick hug. "Thank you, Father, but everything is fine the way it is. I'll switch the bedrooms this afternoon."

Cora looked at Eliza and lifted her eyebrows. Eliza shrugged.

The bedrooms were traded and as one month gave way to another, the house became more Esther's and less Mother's. It wasn't that Esther made changes that Cora could see, but she felt the difference. Perhaps it was Father that made it seem that way. As he played the part of a guest in Ben's house, Cora began to feel the same way. Often she caught herself asking Esther how she wanted something done.

As Christmas neared, an undercurrent of longing for her mother and for Aaron kept Cora from enjoying the holiday preparations. One cold, snowy December afternoon, while the house was quiet, she climbed the ladder to her room, hoping to find comfort in her Bible.

Muffled sobs reached her ears before she saw the crumpled heap of her sister on the bed.

"Eliza, what's the matter?" Cora sat on the edge of the bed, placing her hand on Eliza's back.

Eliza shook her head.

"Please, maybe I can help." Cora continued stroking her sister's back.

"No one can help." The words were muffled.

"Just tell me what's wrong." Cora pulled her hand back as Eliza rolled over, her face wet with tears. Damp hair clung to her cheeks. She brushed at it. "Oh, Cora, everything's wrong. I miss Mother so much."

Cora knew Eliza had been especially close to Mother. As much as she missed her, she realized Eliza likely missed her more. Her heart went out to her sister. "I know it's hard, but Mother's in heaven now and someday we'll see her again."

Eliza began talking, pouring out her troubled heart. "Every morning I wake up expecting to see her and she's not here. Father is hurting, too. It's so hard to watch him keep to himself." Her lashes lowered. "Cora, I haven't seen Ralph since the funeral, and that's been four months. When I need him most, he isn't here."

Cora had been so wrapped up in her own problems, she hadn't noticed Ralph's absence. "I don't know why Ralph hasn't been here, and I don't know why Mother had to die. But, Eliza, I know Someone who can give us comfort in our troubles."

Eliza looked at her sister, an expectant light in her eyes. "Who?"

"Jesus." Cora prayed her sister would not reject the message of salvation.

Again Eliza's lashes lowered. She sat up, her hands clasped in her lap. "I know. Mother told me before she died. I've watched you and Ben, and I do see something different."

Cora smiled. "Eliza, are you ready for a change in your life?"

Fresh tears fell as Eliza nodded. "Yes, please help me."

Cora's depression lifted as she led her sister to the Lord. Several minutes later, they sat on the bed sharing a hug.

Cora laughed while tears of joy wet her face. "We may never be sisters-in-law like you wanted, Eliza, but now we're double sisters. What more could anyone ask?"

Eliza smiled through her tears. "Nothing. Nothing at all."

Early the next morning, Cora caught Ben alone. "Isn't it wonderful about Eliza?"

He had just come out of the barn, an empty bucket in his hand. He grinned at his sister. "It sure is. That leaves Father and Vickie, and I think Father's not far from salvation."

Cora smiled. "Great." She laid a hand on his sleeve. "But there's something more Eliza needs."

At his questioning look, she told him about Eliza's concern for Ralph. "He hasn't been to see her since before Mother's funeral. Now that Ivy's married, Ralph's living alone in their cabin. You don't suppose something's happened to him, do you?"

Ben frowned. "It's possible." He nodded toward the creek. "Tell you what. As soon as I get the stock watered, I'll head over that way and see what I can find out."

Cora smiled. "Thank you, Ben. I won't tell Eliza you're going. Let's wait until we know something."

❧

Just before noon, Cora saw Ben coming back. She slipped into her coat and met him at the barn, where he unsaddled his horse.

"Well, did you find out anything?" Cora closed the door behind her. The musty smell of hay and warm animals assailed her nostrils.

Ben looked up, his brows drawn together in a frown. His jaw clenched as he jerked the saddle from the horse's back. He hung it on a nail and turned toward her.

"From what I could see, Ralph's doing fine. But he's not living alone."

"What do you mean?"

"Ralph's married."

"Married? Ralph?" Surely she hadn't heard right.

Ben sighed. "Over three months ago, he and Anna Hanson went to Brother Timothy and had a very private ceremony. They haven't told anyone. I doubt if Ivy even knows."

Cora's mind whirled. Poor Eliza. This would break her heart. "Why did he marry Anna? I thought he liked Eliza."

Ben closed his eyes for a moment. "Cora, he had to."

"He had to?" Cora repeated. Then the import of Ben's meaning became clear. Anna was carrying Ralph's child. Her heart sank. She turned toward the door. "I understand. I'll tell Eliza."

Ben's voice stopped her. "Eliza will be fine." As Cora turned away, he added, "Be sure and tell her for me, everything works together for good to those who love the Lord. Tell her I'm praying for her."

Cora nodded and opened the door. As soon as she stepped out into the cold, she began praying for her sister.

Eliza took the news better than Cora expected. Silent tears slid down her cheeks as she looked at her sister. "It's all right, Cora. If he was that kind of man, I wouldn't have wanted him, anyway." From that time on, she never mentioned him that Cora heard.

❀

In early spring as new life began to show itself across the earth, Ben and his father knelt in the plowed field while the horses stood waiting. Cora saw an immediate difference as the burden of sin and despair was lifted and Father's smile returned.

On July 5, the first anniversary of Aaron's departure, Cora felt restless. She had worked hard all morning doing laundry, while Eliza and Esther snapped green beans on the front porch. Cora wandered through the house dusting furniture that had no dust. As she reached for the rocker to straighten it with the boards on the floor, she stopped.

"What am I doing?" She spoke out loud and then laughed. "I must be losing my mind. I'm now talking to myself." Loneliness and longing for Aaron filled her heart. She slumped into the rocker. Not a day went by that she didn't think of him and pray for him. Where was he? What was he doing? Did he have enough to eat? Did he have shelter? A place to sleep? Was he still serving the Lord? Had he found someone else? There were so many questions, yet she knew she'd never have the answers.

One thing she had learned in the past year was that Jesus was sufficient. She now read her Bible with interest and, through the reading, had grown in her faith.

She jumped from the rocker, grabbing a bonnet as she went through the front door. She smiled at Esther's and Eliza's inquiring looks. "I'll be gone awhile. I'm going for a walk unless there's something you need me to do."

Esther shook her head. "No, it will do you good to get out. Don't worry about hurrying back."

As Cora walked the familiar path, she felt happier than she had for ages. The trees were full and green. The grass beneath her feet was soft. Squirrels scampered through the dry leaves, scolding as they went. Wild rabbits and other small game fled from her intrusion. The sun felt warm on her head until she entered the forest.

Swiftly her feet carried her to the hollow sycamore. She peered through the opening, letting her eyes adjust to the darkness within. It all looked familiar and dear.

She turned from the tree and walked the short distance to the large flat rock that overshadowed the spring. She stood with the bubbling water at her feet, looking over the green meadow, and her heart constricted at what she saw.

Intruders had entered her paradise. She remembered Aaron's words from a time that now seemed so long ago.

"Maybe I'll build a cabin there someday. There's a perfect place for one up in the meadow where you can still see the spring."

Someone else must have agreed, because a half-built cabin stood on her land—hers and Aaron's.

She stood on the rock staring at the unfinished cabin. From her position she could see that the walls were nearly as tall as a man. She saw movement behind the back wall. Surely the family was new to the area, or they would have asked the neighbors for help. She remembered when her father's cabin had been built and all the help they had been given. In return, they had helped others build. How could one man and one woman put a roof on a cabin alone? Her heart went out to the woman who faced such hard labor.

She turned toward the gentle slope that led down into the meadow. She would put aside her own feelings and meet the new family.

She smoothed her hair and crossed the meadow. Late-blooming wildflowers added a touch of color to the gently waving grass. Silently, she approached the cabin, noticing the care that had gone into fitting the logs together. One thing was certain. The man who was building this cabin was a craftsman.

She placed a smile on her face and turned the corner. Her smile vanished as a soft gasp escaped her lips. There, with ax in hand, one foot on a log, stood Aaron Stark.

❄

In all his wildest imaginings, Cora had never looked as lovely to Aaron as she did now. He stood frozen, staring at the realization of all his dreams.

He'd gone to Springfield a year ago intending to never return. He'd found a job in the stockyards and worked long, hard hours. He was certain Cora was married and living in a fine house in St. Louis. She'd have a housekeeper to care for her house and a cook and maid to wait on her. She would want for nothing.

But he couldn't forget Cora. As long as he had breath, he would love her. Daily, he found himself praying for her and for her happiness. He thought often of the times he had spent with Cora and realized they were the happiest of his life. He especially remembered the day she'd told him she loved him. She had also told him about her spring meadow that day. Each time he thought of it,

120

he felt drawn to the place she had loved. So, after a year, he returned to Cora's spring meadow.

He'd been here a week, camping while his cabin grew. Every waking hour he spent selecting and cutting trees, notching the logs, and erecting a cabin he could be proud of.

He'd told no one of his return, not even Ralph. Yet, here was Cora, looking at him as if he were a ghost.

"Aaron, is it really you?"

He looked beyond her, expecting to see George Merrill following her around the corner of his cabin. "Where's your husband? Are you visitin' your folks?"

"My husband?" Cora crossed the space between them until she stood at arm's length before him. "What are you talking about? I'm not married and I never will be. The only man I could ever love deserted me a year ago today. He didn't even have the consideration to tell me he was going."

Aaron's brows drew together in a familiar frown. So, Merrill had left her high and dry, had he? What kind of man was that dandy, anyhow?

"Well, don't you have anything to say to me?" Cora crossed her arms while the toe of her shoe tapped the ground.

Aaron didn't understand why she was mad at him. He hadn't done a thing. It was that dandy she should be mad at. Aaron was glad he was gone, even if there were no satisfaction in it since she said she couldn't love anyone else. What did she want him to say?

He finally spoke. "I'm mighty glad to see you, Cora."

"You're what?" she shrieked at him. "How can you stand there and say you're glad to see me after what you did to me, Aaron Stark?" Cora let out an exasperated sound and, with tears streaming down her cheeks, doubled her fists and pounded Aaron's chest. Aaron stood, taking her punishment until her hands went limp and she sobbed against him.

"Cora, don't cry." Aaron reached into his shirt pocket and pulled out a handkerchief as his other arm slipped around her shoulders. "Here, darlin', let's dry your eyes and then have us a talk. We jist ain't gettin' our meanin' to each other, it don't seem."

Cora accepted the handkerchief and wiped her face and eyes. As she handed it back, she saw the initials embroidered in the corner. She lifted her gaze to his. "It's the handkerchief I gave you."

He nodded. "I told you I always carry it over my heart. I ain't changed any, Cora."

Cora reached her hand toward him. "Could we talk?"

A slow smile warmed his face as he took her hand and helped her settle on the log. He sat beside her, keeping her hand in his. "I thought you'd be married by now and livin' in the city."

She looked up at him. "How could I be? I told you the only man I could ever love left me."

"Cora, I think we better speak plain out. What happened to that dandy, George Merrill? Why ain't he here with you?"

Cora looked at Aaron's wonderful face with the heavy brows and the dimple in the chin. The firm jaw and the unruly dark hair. And most of all, the brightest blue eyes she'd ever seen. She didn't want to waste her time talking about George. She wanted to find out where Aaron had been. What he had been doing. If he'd found someone else. A sudden pain stabbed her heart. Was that why he was building a cabin? Had he married?

She slipped her suddenly cold hand from his as a chill moved down her back. "George became a nuisance so I had Father run him off. He left the day after you did, and we haven't seen him since. Last I heard, he married a girl from back home. I think her name is Alice. I understand she's from a fine family with money and influence. It's the sort of thing George would find necessary in a wife."

"Then you don't love him?"

Cora sat looking at her hands clasped tightly in her lap. She was baring her soul, yet she knew nothing of what Aaron had been doing. Finally, she swallowed her pride and told the truth. "I never loved George. I thought I did at one time, but that was before I met you."

"You said you only loved one man and he left you. I thought you was talkin' about George."

Cora sighed indignantly. "You're the one who left me. Without a word, you just walked away. I looked all over Mr. Reid's barn for you and you weren't there. How could you do that?"

"I thought you didn't love me."

"How could you think that? What did I do to make you think that?"

"George had a letter."

Cora looked down then. "I know. A letter I wrote when we first came here. I was homesick. I—I shouldn't have written it."

"He said he come as soon as he got the letter. He was gonna take you home with him."

"George lied. He got the letter long before he came. I wouldn't have gone anywhere with him."

"You left the dance with him."

"No, he forced me to go. I couldn't get away from him. That's when he threatened me with the letter. He said he'd show it to you if I didn't go back with him."

Aaron took both her hands in his and held them. Finally, he spoke. "I should've done more than bloody his nose for him."

Cora looked up at him. "Aaron, why are you building a cabin here?"

"To live in."

"Ivy said you were never coming back."

"Did Ivy git married?"

Cora stared at him. She pulled away from him and jumped up. Her hands went on her hips. "Aaron Stark. How dare you sit there and tell me you haven't even seen your sister! She's got a little baby boy. Just born. Of course she got married! And where were you when she did? Did you know Ralph walked down the aisle with her? You were supposed to do that. You are her oldest brother. But, no, you weren't here. My mother died and I needed you, but you weren't here then, either, were you?" Tears kept her from saying more.

"Cora, darlin', I'm sorry." Aaron was beside her in an instant, pulling her into his arms. "I didn't know about your mother."

He held her close, talking softly to her. "I wouldn't hurt you for the world. I love you, Cora. With all my heart I love you. It near killed me seein' you with that dandy. I didn't figure you'd want me anymore, after seein' him again."

"Then why'd you come back?" Her voice was muffled against his shirt.

"So's I could see you standin' up there above the spring or walkin' in the woods. And hear your voice when the wind whispers through the trees. I couldn't do that in Springfield. Here's where you were livin' in my remembrances."

"Oh, Aaron, I love you."

"I love you with ever' beat of my heart, Cora. I always will." Aaron brushed his lips across the top of her head. "Will you forgive me?"

Cora nodded. "I've already forgiven you. I even forgave George for the horrible thing he did. I did that the day God forgave me."

Aaron's eyes shone as he stepped back and looked closely into hers. "Does that mean you got—"

Cora's smile lit her face as she interrupted. "Yes, I've been born again just like you and Mother and Ben."

Aaron's smile deepened. "I reckon that's one thing I can quit prayin' for, then."

"What else have you been praying for?" Cora couldn't resist asking.

"That you'd be happy."

"Well, I wasn't."

A mischievous light came into Aaron's eyes. "Maybe you been livin' in the wrong house."

Cora couldn't help the quick shift of her eyes toward Aaron's unfinished cabin. She nodded, looking back at him. "Yes, I do think that may be my problem."

All serious now, Aaron held her at arm's length. "Cora Jackson, will you marry me and live here with me in our cabin as soon as it's finished?"

"How long will that take?" Cora was just as serious.

"Will a week be too long?"

Cora nodded. "Yes, but I suppose it will have to do."

Aaron's grin covered his face. "In that case, we'll git some folks in here and have us a house raisin'."

"Did I tell you I love you, Aaron Stark?"

"Not in the last minute," Aaron mumbled as his lips touched hers.

Cora yielded to his kiss and knew she had found her home. This wild land was where she belonged. God had brought her here, had given her love's fulfillment, and, best of all, had taught her of His salvation.

❧

On July 10, 1836, after the Sunday morning services, Cora walked up the aisle of the little log church to stand beside Aaron. Together they promised to love, honor, and cherish each other as long as they both should live. When Brother Timothy pronounced them man and wife, Cora lifted her lips to Aaron's for a kiss that would seal their love for all time.

As they walked down the aisle together, Cora saw the happy faces of her family and friends who had spent the last two days finishing a home for her and Aaron. She caught her father's smile and nod of approval. Her answering smile held a touch of sadness for her mother's absence. She stepped through the door to a beautiful summer day and lifted her eyes to the blue sky above.

Aaron pulled her close. "I'm sure she knows, darlin'. Both our mothers know."

Tears misted her eyes as she looked up at him and smiled. He understood. Then, in her memory, her mother's smile warmed her heart, and Cora leaned her head against her husband. "Yes, and they're just as happy as we are."

He nodded, adding, "As happy as we always will be."

ELIZA

Dedication

To my sister Jean Norval for her untiring help with
making suggestions, solving problems, editing, and polishing.
Without her input, I would still be struggling
with stacks of unreadable manuscripts.
To my sister Pat Willis for reading *Eliza* twice—
first to voice her concerns and then to okay the changes.
Also, to my daughter Becka del Valle who delights in finding
and deleting unnecessary words.
Plotting is a joy with your input, Becka.
Thanks so much, Becka, Pat, and Jean.

Chapter 1

October 1836

D o you think Lenny will be all right?" Eliza looked back at the small frame schoolhouse as if she could see her ten-year-old brother inside.

"I wouldn't worry about Lenny." Her father slowed his steps to match hers.

The early October sun felt warm on Eliza's back as they turned down South Street toward the business square in Springfield, Missouri. "I suppose you're right. It's just that Mother always taught him."

Father laughed. "Lenny can take care of himself."

Eliza sighed. "I suppose."

Although her mother had been gone more than a year, the pain of her passing remained with Eliza. She missed her gentle ways and the love she had shown to each of her seven children. Eliza thought of Nora, her baby sister, and a smile touched her lips. Nora's birth had weakened their mother and indirectly caused her death, but the sweet baby had brought so much love and happiness into their lives as well, and Eliza missed her.

Nora lived sixty miles north in the country with their oldest sister, Vickie. Eliza longed for the day when they could return to their old home and bring Nora to Springfield. She held to Father's promise that as soon as they were settled here, they would go after Nora.

A freight wagon rumbled by. They stepped up on a low boardwalk leading past a large, two-story shop. The sign over the door read LEACH'S GENERAL STORE.

Eliza's father waved across the square to a man coming from the bank building. He smiled and nodded at two women hurrying past on their way to the general store.

Eliza said, "Springfield is smaller than Saint Louis, but after living in the wilderness it seems large."

Her father smiled and nodded. "Three hundred inhabitants and growing."

They approached a small white building sandwiched between a millinery shop on one side and a larger empty building on the corner. A sign over the door read CHANDLER SHOP, ORVAL JACKSON, PROPRIETOR.

Eliza stepped inside, and the familiar odor of tallow assailed her senses.

Father watched her sniff the air. "There's nothing like the smell of a candle shop, is there?"

Eliza wrinkled her nose. "I can think of things that smell better."

He laughed. "Wait until nearer Christmas when I start using bayberry. You girls always liked it."

Eliza thought of her sister just older than herself. "I think Cora liked it best. I wish we could send her a bayberry candle for Christmas."

Father nodded. "But with no delivery service to our old backwoods home, she'll have to do without."

"I guess." Eliza ran her hand over the shiny dark oak counter that stood along one wall. Tall, slender candles lay on one end of it, sorted by size. Other candles hung by the wick from hooks on the walls and ceiling. Shelves along one wall held sconces, candleholders, lanterns, and snuffers. In one corner was a pile of cotton yarn waiting to be made into wicks. Sitting around the room were several candle stands made of walnut, cherry, oak, and the less expensive, pine. On top of each was a candle in a tall, brass candlestick.

Her father moved about, lighting the candles on the stands until a soft, warm glow filled the dark shop.

Eliza watched her father. "I guess it's time for me to go home and clean house."

"You can stay all day if you want, but I need to get to work. I've got an order to get out for Mrs. Wingate."

"Who's that? Someone important?"

"Her husband helped finance my business. His bank's across the street."

Eliza glanced toward the window as the front door opened.

A young man stepped into the shop. "Mr. Jackson?"

"Yes, may I help you?"

The young man's gaze met Eliza's for just a moment before he turned his full attention to her father. "I'm James Hurley. Mrs. Wingate sent me. She said you were thinking of adding a cooperage and would be needing help."

"Of course." Father stepped forward, and the men shook hands. "I'm glad you stopped by." He nodded toward Eliza. "This is my daughter Eliza."

James acknowledged her presence with a slight bow. "Mrs. Wingate mentioned that you and your brother would be arriving in town soon. I'm glad to meet you."

Eliza smiled at him. "We came in last night. I was just on my way home. I'll see you later, Father. For dinner?"

Her father nodded. "I'll pick Lenny up, and we'll be at the house about noon."

"All right." Eliza closed the door behind her and started across the square toward home. So her father was already adding on and would be hiring an employee. Perhaps the challenge of starting a new business was what he needed to heal his grieving heart after her mother's death.

She turned up the path to a large, two-story house set back from the road on the outskirts of town. She knew her father had bought the house by using most of his savings from some investments he had made years ago when they lived in St. Louis. The house had come completely furnished because the woman who had lived in it couldn't tolerate the frontier existence of Springfield. Eliza smiled as she wondered what the woman would have thought of the log cabin they had just moved from. Their nearest neighbor had been almost two miles away.

She let herself in, and an hour later she had fluffy mashed potatoes, fried pork, a pan of corn bread, and a bowl of leftover brown beans sitting on the table. She stood back and studied her work. Father liked fruit with his noon meal.

She looked around the well-ordered kitchen. Was there a pantry? When they'd come the evening before, she hadn't explored the house so she didn't know what treasures it held.

She opened the back door and went through a small anteroom lined with tools and a bin of firewood to the outdoors.

A long, white wooden door lay at an angle from the ground to the upper foundation of the house. She lifted the door, leaning it against the outside of the anteroom. Musty dampness filled her nostrils as she descended the steps. She stood at the bottom to light the candle she had brought.

The back door slammed. "Eliza, where are you?"

"Down here, Father." She turned, glad to run back up the steps to the bright, sunlit yard. "I thought there might be some fruit in the cellar."

"Well, what are we waiting for? Let's see if we can find a jar of peaches."

A flurry from behind him brought Lenny to the front. "I want to go, too."

"Great, you can keep the mice and bats away." Eliza grasped each of Lenny's shoulders and held him in front of her. "How was school this morning?"

"Aw, it was all right." He swiped at a spiderweb.

"Look at this." Father's voice brought her attention back to the cellar. "Mr. Wingate said it was fully stocked, but I didn't expect to find a cellar full of food."

"Father, you've been here more than two months. Haven't you even looked down here? How have you been eating?" Eliza looked from the full shelves to her father.

In the soft light of the candle, Father's grin looked sheepish. "There's a café in town for men like me who can't feed themselves."

Eliza took a jar of peaches off the shelf. "Well, you won't need to go there anymore." She left the cellar, calling over her shoulder. "Come on, our meal is getting cold."

❦

The next morning Eliza woke to a thick blanket of clouds and drizzling rain.

The rain stopped midmorning, and by the time she had the noon dishes clean and put away, she felt she had been confined to the house long enough. About an hour after her father and brother left, she grabbed her shawl and headed out the door for town.

She hummed a hymn as her feet covered the damp ground. Not until she saw her father's shop did she slow her gait. There had been no real reason to come to town. As far as she knew, the house was well stocked. She didn't need to see her father about anything. Yet she would have to pass by his shop to reach the general store. Without a doubt he would see her and welcome the chance to tease her about neglecting her duties. She giggled. She wouldn't give him a chance. She'd tell him the clouds made it so dark inside she needed more candles.

Eliza pulled open the door and stepped inside. "Father, you wouldn't believe how dark it gets when the sun doesn't shine."

The man behind the counter was not her father. She knew it before he turned and looked at her with those clear, gray eyes that she remembered from the day before when James Hurley had first stepped into her father's shop. A slow smile lit James's face. His voice held a deep timbre, smooth and resonant. "Yes, but if the sun shone all the time, we'd sell very few candles."

Eliza glanced toward the back room. "Where is my father?"

"He stepped out for a few minutes."

"And left you here alone?" As soon as the words were out of her mouth, she wished she could call them back.

One eyebrow lifted as James pinned her with a glare. "I don't plan to steal the profits, Miss Jackson."

A flush spread over Eliza's face. "I'm sorry. I didn't mean that. I just meant it's only your second day on the job."

"Actually, it's my first." James grinned. "I'm a quick study. At least your father seems to trust me enough to leave me alone for ten minutes."

"Oh." Eliza had never found it hard to talk to anyone before. But there was something about those gray eyes looking at her and the way James smiled that made her want to leave and stay at the same time. She decided it would be best if she left when memories she had thought long buried rose in her mind.

Ralph Stark, a young man from her old home, had smiled at her in much the same way. When Ralph had looked at her with that same intense gleam in his eyes, she had felt special and pretty. She had loved him and thought he loved her. Then, during their courtship, he'd married someone else, leaving her with the pain of rejection. Strength gained through her newfound relationship with the Lord had brought her through that time, yet she wondered even now if she would ever forget her first sweetheart.

The cool, damp air felt good on her hot cheeks as she turned back toward home. Her appetite for browsing through the general store had been squelched.

❦

When Thursday morning dawned clear, Eliza decided it was time to wash clothes while she could hang them on the line. She worked hard all morning, barely finding time to fix the noon meal for her father and brother.

But she soon had stew simmering on the stove and was throwing the potato peelings into the slop bucket when she heard steps at the door. Moments later, Lenny ran into the kitchen.

"Look what I got this morning." He strutted up to her and lifted his face.

Dried blood lined one nostril. He squinted at her through his red, swollen left eye. Eliza looked toward the doorway where her father lounged against the frame.

He shrugged. "Ask him what happened."

She turned back to her little brother, her hands folded across her chest. "Well, are you going to tell me?"

"Ah, Eliza, it ain't nothin' to get upset about." Lenny looked pleased with himself. "It was just a little old fight."

Her father spoke proudly from the doorway. "If you think he looks bad, you should've seen the other fellow."

Eliza turned toward her father. How could he condone this?

He laughed. "Don't look at me that way. It was over by the time I got there."

"Lenny, why did you get into a fight?" Eliza asked.

" 'Cause I ain't no teacher's pet."

"You're not the teacher's pet," Eliza corrected.

"Right, I ain't." He touched his eye tenderly. "Cletis sure can hit hard."

"Cletis?"

Lenny nodded. "Yeah. Cletis Hall. Can he come over sometime?"

"Here? To our house?" Eliza couldn't believe him. "Why do you want him to come here? I thought you just had a fight with him."

"Your sister doesn't understand a man's way of doing things, Lenny." Father pulled out a chair. He looked at Eliza. "You see, Cletis didn't have any respect for the teacher's pet, but he's got a lot of respect for the first boy in school who was brave enough to whip him."

Eliza could hear pride in her father's voice. She looked from him to Lenny. "So you made a friend by beating him up?" She shook her head. "You're right. I don't understand it. Bring your friend here to play if you want. Just make sure he doesn't mess my house up. And there'd better not be any more fighting."

Lenny grinned and as quickly grimaced. Father stood. "Come on, Lenny. Let's take care of that eye."

Eliza watched them go and shook her head. She reached for the long-handled spoon to stir her stew. She didn't need to worry about Lenny. Obviously, he could take care of himself.

Chapter 2

Eliza tilted the coffee canister and looked inside. Less than half full. She wanted to see what Leach's General Store had in stock, and this was as good an excuse as any.

She ran upstairs to change into her afternoon visiting dress. The black-and-pink-striped silk was terribly out of date, but she had nothing better. She shrugged, reaching for the matching silk bonnet. She went downstairs and out the front door, determined to enjoy her afternoon. Only this time she would avoid the chandler shop and James Hurley.

Red and yellow leaves, blending with the green of the trees overhead, provided a colorful canopy for her walk. In the distance a dog barked and another answered. Smoke from a backyard fire wafted by, teasing her nose as she passed a house.

She reached the business square a few minutes later. She tried to hurry past her father's shop, but before she reached the door, two women came out, each clutching a package.

"Thank you, and please come again." James smiled at the women as he held the door for them.

Eliza looked up and caught his gaze on her. She smiled. "Hello, Mr. Hurley. I see my father is keeping you busy."

He grinned. "Good afternoon, Miss Jackson. Could I interest you in candles, a new cherry candle stand, or maybe a snuffer?"

"No, thank you. I'm on my way to the general store."

"Ah, Mr. Leach's gain is our loss."

She smiled as she went on. Maybe her father's new employee was just being friendly when he smiled at her.

It took a moment for her eyes to adjust to the dim interior of the store. A potbellied stove held center stage with an open cracker barrel nearby. Elderly men took from its contents while they argued politics.

The aromas of tobacco, leather, and fresh ground coffee mingled with the familiar smell of the wood-burning stove. She hesitated a moment as she looked around. Mr. Leach must have the best-stocked store in town, with not an inch of space wasted. Everything from Bibles to medicine, coal oil to calico, and school supplies to candy had its own special place. A wide assortment of hardware, household goods, and groceries filled the shelves.

Eliza's heels clicked on the wooden floor as she moved down the center aisle past the grocery counter and dry goods shelves. Mr. Leach, busy behind his high counter in the back, greeted her with a warm smile. "Good afternoon. What can I do for you?"

Eliza smiled. "I need a pound of coffee."

"Then a pound of coffee you shall have." The storekeeper nodded toward one side of the store. "Have yourself a look around while I get it. We just got in some new calico the other day."

Eliza turned and wound her way past kegs and barrels of flour, sugar, vinegar, and molasses. Close to a half hour later, oblivious to the activity around her, Eliza picked up the corner of a blue-sprigged calico and rubbed it between her fingers. How she wished she could sew decently! But no matter how often her mother or her sisters, Vickie and Cora, had tried to teach her, she could never force her fingers to take the tiny stitches needed for dressmaking.

"Are you finding anything you like?" Eliza turned to see a middle-aged woman, her plump face wreathed with a friendly smile.

Eliza sighed. "Oh, there are so many, and I like all of them." She refolded the calico and turned away. "But I came for coffee, not fabric."

"A young girl can always use a new dress." The woman eyed Eliza's outdated frock. She extended her hand. "I'm Alice Leach, the storekeeper's wife."

Eliza placed her hand in the woman's strong grasp. "I'm glad to meet you. I'm Eliza Jackson. My father recently opened the chandler shop down the street."

"Oh yes. Mr. Leach was telling me that the chandler's family had arrived. Welcome to Springfield."

Eliza nodded. "I guess I should be starting home. I'm sure your husband has my coffee ready by now."

"Come back anytime. Next time you need a new dress, let me know, and we'll find you something pretty."

Eliza took the coffee and turned to leave as another customer came in. She watched the girl breeze through the store to the high counter where Mr. Leach stood.

"Hello, Miss Vanda," Mr. Leach greeted her. "What can I do for you today?"

Eliza slipped out the door as the other girl gave her order. Vanda. What an unusual name. It was pretty, just as the girl was.

Eliza crossed the square and turned north on the road leading home. Dust swirled about her skirt as she hurried. She had spent most of the afternoon accomplishing nothing. She'd better be thinking of supper.

She set her package of coffee on the table in the kitchen and then went upstairs to change clothes. She had no sooner taken her bonnet and wraps off than a knock on the door downstairs startled her.

With her heart pounding, she ran downstairs and opened the door, surprised to see the girl from the store.

"Hello. Won't you come in?" Eliza smiled and stepped back.

Vanda stood unmoved. "Is your mother home?"

Eliza's heart constricted at the question. She shook her head. "My mother died a year ago."

"Your father isn't here, is he?" An uncertain expression crossed the girl's face.

Eliza shook her head. "No, he's at work."

"Then you are the only one home?"

"Yes, won't you come in?" Eliza repeated the invitation.

Vanda walked to the middle of the room and looked around. Her eyes rested briefly on the covered sofa with gleaming mahogany legs and two matching chairs. Her gaze swept past the fireplace, then dropped to the carpet before she turned to Eliza.

"Won't you sit down?" Eliza could scarcely believe she had company.

Vanda looked at the sofa but shook her head. "No, what I've got to say won't take long."

"Oh." Eliza wondered at the sharp tone in the girl's voice.

"You have a brother named Lenny, don't you?" Vanda's eyes bore into hers.

Eliza nodded. Surely Lenny couldn't have done anything to Vanda.

"Is he about nine or ten years old?" Vanda's hands were on her hips now.

"He's ten." Eliza was puzzled. "He's been in school all week, except at night when he's been home. We just moved in last week."

"I have a ten-year-old brother, too. Maybe you've heard of him." Vanda paused. "Cletis Von Hall."

"Cletis Von Hall?" Eliza repeated the name. She frowned, trying to remember. Lenny had said the boy he fought was Cletis Hall.

Eliza met the other girl's gaze. "Yes, Lenny told us about the fight he had with Cletis. He also said he and Cletis are now good friends."

"Good friends!" Vanda's eyes widened. "Good friends don't give each other black eyes."

"Oh, I don't think they were friends when they fought." Eliza wasn't sure she could explain what she didn't understand herself. "You see, the fight itself is what made them friends."

A sneer crossed Vanda's face. "My little brother was beaten black and blue, and you tell me he's friends with the boy who did it?"

"I know it doesn't make sense, but that's what Lenny said."

"It certainly doesn't make sense, and I don't want it to happen again." Vanda took a step forward, her forefinger lifted toward Eliza. "Either you see to it, or my father will."

Eliza watched the angry girl step to the door.

"I'm sorry Lenny hurt your brother." Eliza followed her out. "I'll speak to him about it."

Vanda paid no attention to Eliza. She stood on the porch, her hand resting on a post.

Eliza looked over her shoulder to see what had caught her attention. Coming up the road arm in arm was Lenny with another boy.

"Cletis Elliot Von Hall!" Vanda's exclamation brought the boys up short. "What on earth are you doing?"

The boy shook a heavy lock of blond hair off his forehead. "I ain't doin' nothin' wrong."

"What are you doing with. . .him?"

Cletis frowned at his sister. "Me and Lenny's buddies."

Cletis had gotten the worst of the fight. Both of his eyes were blackened. His lower lip had swelled, and a bruise marred his cheekbone.

The two boys stood in front of Vanda. Cletis looked up at her. "Ah, sis, you ain't gonna make a big thing out of that old fight, are you?"

Vanda stood, her arms crossed, looking at her brother. Finally, she spoke. "Do you mean you let some boy beat you up, and then you made friends with him?"

Cletis waved his hand at her. "Don't worry, sis. This is men stuff."

Vanda made an exasperated sound and turned to Eliza. "He got that from my older brother and my father. Every time they do something stupid, that's what they say. Sometimes I get so mad I could bite a nail."

Eliza smiled. "I had the same conversation with Lenny and my father last night. They told me I wouldn't understand."

For the first time since they met, Vanda's expression softened. "I'm sorry for the way I stormed into your house and for the things I said."

Eliza shook her head. "Don't be. You were only protecting your little brother. I'd have done the same."

Vanda held her hand out. "I'm Vanda Von Hall. I don't know your first name."

Eliza smiled and grasped her hand. "Eliza."

Vanda shook her hand. "I guess I'd better be getting home." She picked up her bundle of purchases. "I need to get supper before my father gets there."

Eliza laughed. "It sounds like you have the same job I do. My father will be home before long, too, and I haven't even decided what to fix."

She turned to Lenny. "Does Father know you came home from school without him?"

Lenny nodded. "Sure. We went by the shop, and he said it was all right."

"He was probably glad to get Cletis out of his shop."

Eliza laughed at Vanda's cryptic remark.

135

"Can I stay and play with Lenny?" Cletis looked at his sister.

"No, you'd better be home when Poppa gets there."

Cletis kicked at a rock and mumbled.

Vanda shook her head when Cletis shuffled away. "I'm so sorry. Sometimes Cletis gets out of hand, and my temper does, too. It's hard without a mother, but I guess you know that. Mine's been gone two years now."

"I'm sorry. About your mother, I mean." Eliza laid her hand on the other girl's arm. "I'm glad I got to meet you. When you have time, come back and visit. I get lonesome with just my father and brother."

"I know." Vanda smiled. "I've got to go." She walked away, calling over her shoulder, "I'll be back, I promise."

Eliza watched as Vanda grabbed her little brother's arm and pulled him down the road. When they reached the corner, they both waved. Eliza and Lenny stood on the porch waving until their new friends turned the corner and were lost to sight.

❦

Eliza woke early Sunday morning. She hurried through a breakfast of biscuits and oatmeal before getting ready for church.

Three hours later, Eliza sat at the end of the pew beside Lenny. She had hoped the Von Halls would be at church. But she saw neither Vanda nor Cletis.

As she turned her attention back to the sermon, the eerie feeling of someone staring at her crept up her backbone. She turned to meet the scrutiny of James Hurley. His gray eyes locked with her brown ones for only seconds before she turned away.

Eliza tried to pay attention to the sermon, but her mind wandered up and down the pews. There were several young people near her own age. Would they accept her? Would they become her friends?

She sighed, forcing herself to listen to the remainder of the sermon. When the last "amen" had been said, people began to stir. Eliza stood and stepped out into the aisle ahead of Lenny and Father. They made their way to the back door, nodding and speaking to everyone they saw.

Finally, they reached the minister. "We're so glad to see you again this morning, Mr. Jackson." He clasped Father's hand and gave it a hearty shake. "I haven't had the privilege of meeting your children."

As Father introduced them, Eliza saw James Hurley help a woman, who she assumed was his mother, into a farm wagon while a young girl climbed in the back.

The pastor smiled at Eliza. "We've got a good group of young people here. It won't be long until you have many friends."

"Thank you, sir." She smiled. "I hope you're right."

As he turned to Lenny, she looked back toward the road and saw James climb in beside his mother. He picked up the reins, then looked at her and smiled.

Her breath caught in her throat. With a flick of the reins, the wagon moved out. Eliza watched until he turned the corner and drove out of sight.

"Mr. and Mrs. Wingate, so good to see you." The pastor's voice brought Eliza's attention to a fashionably attired, middle-aged couple stepping out of the church.

"Good sermon, Pastor. Just what we needed this morning." Mr. Wingate put a tall-crowned, brushed-beaver hat on his head. He stepped off the porch and shook her father's hand. "How's that chandler shop, Orval?"

Eliza moved with her father and the Wingates a short distance from the church. Lenny ran off to play with some other boys.

"Considering the condition of our pocketbooks at this time, not bad." Father smiled at Mrs. Wingate. "I appreciate your business and the customers you've sent."

Mrs. Wingate, a tall, blond woman smiled. "I recognize quality when I see it. I would never go back to making my own candles."

Eliza couldn't visualize the woman before her bent over a vat of foul-smelling tallow.

"Have you thought more about adding a cooperage?" Mrs. Wingate asked.

"Actually, yes." Father nodded. "I took your advice and hired the young man you sent. We've been working on getting the building next door ready. James is a good worker."

"Excellent." Mrs. Wingate looked pleased. "I thought he would be."

She turned to Eliza. "You must be Mr. Jackson's daughter Eliza."

Eliza nodded. "I'm pleased to meet you, Mrs. Wingate." She felt dowdy compared to the well-dressed woman before her. In the country, it hadn't mattered, but here she felt keenly the difference between her dress and the clothing worn around her.

The woman linked her arm in Eliza's. "I'm so glad you've come to Springfield to live. We've enjoyed having your father here, and I know you and your brother will become dear to us as well." She didn't wait for a response but asked, "Have you met my son Charles?"

Eliza shook her head. "No, I've been here only a week and haven't met anyone." She thought of Vanda and added, "Except one girl."

"Oh? Who might that be?" A spark of interest shone from the woman's eyes as she centered her attention on Eliza.

"Her name is Vanda Von Hall. I thought she might be at church this morning, but I didn't see her."

"No, she wasn't here today." Mrs. Wingate frowned. "Her older brother,

Trennen, is our driver. I've often wondered if we should have him drive us to church on Sundays just to get him here."

She smiled then. "How do you like living in Springfield?"

"It's very nice. I love the house Father bought."

Mrs. Wingate nodded. "Yes, it is a nice place. You were very fortunate to get it." She paused a moment before saying, "It must be hard trying to keep up with that large house and an active brother, too."

"Oh no." Eliza shook her head. "I enjoy my work."

"But a young girl needs to get out and play once in awhile. Maybe your father will remarry someday, and you'll be free to pursue other interests."

Eliza had been close to her mother. She could never imagine another woman taking her place. She shook her head; her voice lowered. "No, I don't expect my father to ever marry again. I don't mind taking care of the house. He doesn't need a wife."

Eliza recognized the calculating look in Mrs. Wingate's blue eyes as she nodded. "I'm sure you do a wonderful job, dear. My husband claims my worst fault is interfering." She glanced toward her husband and smiled. "Speaking of Mr. Wingate, I believe he's ready to leave." She patted Eliza's arm. "I'm glad we got to visit. You come see me sometime, all right?"

At Eliza's nod, the older woman turned away. Eliza collected Lenny, and they left, too.

"Winter will soon be here," Father commented as they walked home.

"Yes, that's true." When the snow and cold weather moved into the area, Eliza knew she would be confined to the house. She didn't look forward to that time.

"Seems someone is having a birthday before long." Father smiled at her.

"Is that right?" Eliza fell into his joking mood. "Are you going to get that person something nice?"

Father laughed. "Sounds like you know whose birthday is coming up."

Eliza laughed with her father. She was well aware that she would soon be nineteen. Plenty old enough to run a motherless household.

Chapter 3

A week later, Father opened his cooperage in the building next to the chandler shop. Unlike the shops in St. Louis he had shared with his brother, there was no door connecting the two buildings, so he rigged a string and bell from one shop's door to the other. When either door opened, the bells would ring in both shops. It wasn't a perfect system, but it let Father and James know when they had a customer.

After working both shops for two days, Father came home exhausted. Eliza found him sprawled across the sofa after supper. Lenny lay on his stomach on the floor, reading a book.

She touched her father's shoulder. "I know it's early, but if you want to go to bed, I'll see that Lenny settles down at his bedtime."

"What would I do without you, Eliza?" Father pulled himself up. "I wouldn't be so tired except for running back and forth between those two shops."

"Can't you move them both into the same building?"

He shook his head. "No. Neither place is big enough. What I need is another person to run the candle shop until I get James trained."

"Is he having trouble learning?"

Father shook his head. "No. He's doing fine. It's just that there's so much to learn. I want him to learn the chandler trade as well. That way I can trust either shop to him if necessary."

"Father." An idea took shape in Eliza's mind. "Could I take care of the chandler shop?"

Father stared at her. Eliza's heart beat fast against her ribs. A log in the fireplace snapped, sending sparks into the room. They both rushed to step on them, crushing them out before they burned through the rug.

Father returned to the sofa. When he finally spoke, his expression was solemn. "For two weeks in the afternoon only."

"You mean I can?"

Father laughed. "You'd think I just gave you a gift." He patted the sofa. "Sit down here and let me tell you what you're getting into."

As Eliza listened to her father explain her new duties, she tingled with excitement. Finally, she would be in the hub of the town's activities. Every afternoon for two weeks she could visit with the women and girls who came into Father's shop.

Eliza's excitement continued into the next morning as she hurried through her chores. She heard a knock on the door downstairs just as she smoothed the covers on Lenny's bed.

"Oh no." She groaned. "I have little enough time without someone calling." She smoothed her hair and ran down the stairs.

She opened the door to Vanda's smile. Eliza stepped back. "Please, come in."

"I intended to come sooner, but I've been busy." Vanda's gaze swept the room. "You have such a nice house."

"Thank you. We really like it." Eliza closed the door. "Won't you sit down?"

As Vanda sat on the sofa, Eliza took the chair and leaned forward, eager to share her news. "Oh, Vanda, you'll never guess what I'm going to do this afternoon."

Vanda relaxed back into the sofa. "What?"

"I'm going to work in my father's shop." Eliza's light brown eyes sparkled.

"When do you start?"

"Right after noon."

"Oh, then I'm probably keeping you." Vanda stood.

Eliza knew she should finish her work, but she and Vanda hadn't had a chance to talk. She shook her head. "All I have left to do is prepare dinner. That shouldn't take long."

"What are you fixing?"

"I've had beans on the back of the stove since early this morning. I need to bake corn bread and fry some meat."

Vanda nodded. "How long until your father comes?"

Eliza looked at the clock sitting on the mantel. "Almost an hour."

"Let me help," Vanda pleaded. "I'll leave before he gets here. He needn't ever know I was here."

"That won't be necessary." Eliza frowned. "I mean, you don't have to help. Just stay and visit with me. Why don't you stay for dinner?"

"Oh, I couldn't do that."

"Is your father expecting you?"

Vanda shook her head. "No, Poppa's gone all this week. He's working at a sawmill east of here."

"Then there's no one to worry about you, unless your brothers. . . ?"

"No, Cletis takes his lunch, and Trennen eats at the Wingates'."

Eliza took her arm. "Good, then it's settled. Let's go to the kitchen while we talk."

She led the way, and they were soon visiting like old friends. Vanda insisted on mixing the corn bread while Eliza fried meat and set the table.

When Eliza set four plates out, Vanda looked at her. "Are you sure your father won't mind?"

Eliza laughed. "He'll be glad I've found a friend."

Vanda pulled the golden-brown corn bread from the oven just as Father stepped through the kitchen doorway. His hazel eyes twinkled. "Well, what have we here?" He turned to Lenny, who had come in behind him. "You put a woman to work outside the home, and the first thing she does is get help with her household chores."

Lenny stepped around his father. "Are you going to be our housekeeper?"

Vanda's cheeks flamed as she looked at Eliza. Eliza took Lenny's shoulder and pushed him toward the sink. "Go wash your hands. You know Cletis's sister. She's our guest."

Father ran his hand over his hair. He smiled at Vanda. "I'm sorry. I sometimes get carried away teasing my daughter. I'm glad you're here with Eliza. Please, make yourself at home."

After that they enjoyed an uneventful dinner hour until time to go back to work and school. Eliza rushed through the dishwashing with Vanda's help. As they put the last dish away, Vanda glanced toward the door leading to the parlor.

"Your father seems nice. Is he always like that?"

Eliza made a face. "Actually, he was on his best behavior. The way he acted when he first came in is more like his true self. He's terribly fond of teasing."

"That's because he loves you."

"Yes, I know." Eliza started for the door. "What's your father like? Does he like to tease, too?"

A crease formed between Vanda's eyes as she frowned and followed Eliza. "No, Poppa doesn't tease. Especially not since Momma died."

"He must have loved her very much." Eliza picked up her cape as they passed through the parlor. Father and Lenny had gone ahead so the two girls would be walking by themselves.

Vanda shrugged. "I suppose." She followed Eliza out the front door and waited while she closed it.

A touch of dampness clung to the air under a canopy of gray clouds. Eliza pulled her cape close, glad for its warmth. She glanced at her friend, realizing for the first time that Vanda's clothing was as outdated as her own.

Several minutes later the two girls stopped in front of the chandler shop. After saying good-bye to Vanda and promising they'd get together soon, Eliza went inside. She didn't see her father in the store so she looked in the back room. No sign of him there, either. She stood in the doorway and looked at the disarray that made up his workroom. He and Lenny had left the house several minutes before she and Vanda. Where was he?

❦

James glanced out the front window of the cooperage and saw Eliza go past with Vanda Von Hall. He stepped closer to the window. They stopped in front of the chandler shop and talked a moment before Vanda moved on. Eliza went into the shop, setting off the bells that were rigged to ring if either shop door opened. James ignored the ringing bell and turned back to his work. He didn't have time to stare at a girl when he had barrels to make.

The half-finished barrel he had been working on was the last of an order that needed to be delivered that afternoon. He'd better get it finished. He stepped over and around tools, metal rings, barrels, and tubs to the far wall where wood slats were stacked. He crouched down behind a large barrel to select the slats he needed from the pile on the floor.

The door opened with barely a jingle of the bell. James peered around the barrel and saw the blue of Eliza's skirt. His stomach turned somersaults as he watched her gaze sweep the large room. When she turned as if to leave, he stood up, afraid she would go and he wouldn't get to talk to her. In his haste, he bumped the large barrel in front of him, causing it to rock on its bottom. He grabbed a cloth to wipe his sweating palms and stepped out from the barrel.

Taking a couple of steps toward her, he asked, "May I help you, ma'am?"

James couldn't keep the silly grin from his face when she turned back to face him, her eyes wide and beautiful.

"I'm looking for my father."

"Do you make a habit of misplacing him?" He couldn't resist teasing her.

"Oh, honestly!" She reached for the door.

Instantly contrite, James chuckled. "I'm sorry. He isn't back from dinner yet."

"I see. Have you eaten?"

James's smile grew wider. "Not yet. I'll eat when your father gets back. I brought my lunch. Thank you for thinking of me, though."

James admired the red that tinged Eliza's cheeks as she stammered, "I didn't. . .think. . .oh, that's all right."

As she jerked the outside door open and slipped out, he reached to stop her before he realized what he was doing. Eliza Jackson was his boss's daughter. He had no business teasing her or even thinking of her in a romantic way. Again, he turned back to work.

❦

Eliza hurried toward the chandler shop and almost bumped into her father.

"Well, have you been visiting with the new apprentice?" His eyes sparkled as they searched her red face.

"Father!" Eliza welcomed the cool breeze that floated by. "I was looking for you. I thought you'd be here by now since you left the house before I did."

Her father laughed as he opened the door to the chandler shop. "I stopped by the school. Lenny said his teacher wanted to talk to me."

Eliza stepped into the store ahead of her father. She turned quickly, her embarrassment forgotten. "What did he do?"

"Nothing." He chuckled. "She wants some of the fathers to build props for the school Christmas program."

"Christmas already?" Eliza gave him a skeptical look.

Her father laughed. "Yes, Christmas already. It's not a bad idea to get started early on the construction."

❧

After supper on Saturday, Father challenged Lenny to a game of checkers. He won the first game against Lenny, so Eliza played the second and also lost to him.

She set her pieces back on the squares. "Now it's time for the losers to play, Father. You may watch this game."

Father let Lenny take his chair and grinned at Eliza. "You think I can learn something from watching you two play?"

She nodded. "Certainly. If you watch closely enough, you can learn how to lose."

It wasn't long until Lenny jumped one of Eliza's pieces. She tried to concentrate on the game, but too much was on her mind. Finally, Lenny jumped her last piece. He sprang to his feet, twirling around. "I won. I won."

"Well, don't gloat about it." Eliza picked the game up and carried it across the room to the mantel.

Father laughed as Lenny fell down against him. "Eliza was right. I did pick up some pointers from her game."

Eliza tried to make a face at them, but it soon turned to a laugh. "All right, so I'm not a good checkers player." She sat in the chair opposite the one they shared. "Do you know what today is?"

Father nodded, his voice subdued. "Yes, it's Nora's second birthday." He pulled Lenny onto his lap. "She's old enough now to come home. As soon as we can, we'll bring our little girl here to live with us. I promise."

Eliza clung to his promise. She missed her little sister so much. Vickie had taken her right after their mother's funeral to care for along with her own son, Christopher, who was just a few months older. The arrangement should have been temporary, but the first few months had been hard as Father grieved for his wife. Then, Father gave his life to the Lord one day as his oldest son, Ben, prayed with him. After that, Father decided to move to Springfield, and the time never came to bring Nora home.

Father pushed Lenny from his lap. "Run and get my Bible. It's almost bedtime."

Father read a passage of scripture and prayed. Then he stood, running his hand over his thinning hair. "I completely forgot. Lenny, your teacher said there'll be a spelling bee and social next Saturday night at the schoolhouse."

Lenny's eyes brightened. "Can we go? I bet I can outspell everyone in that school."

Father laughed. "In that case, we'll have to go and see. How about it, Eliza? Do you think you can outspell everyone in school?"

She smiled. "I don't know, but I'm willing to try if you are."

A wide grin set on Father's face. "I wouldn't miss it."

❄

Eliza saw James Hurley come in to the crowded schoolhouse with his sister and mother. He smiled and spoke to her as he passed.

"I'm glad you came." Vanda took her arm. "Would you like to meet my poppa and Trennen? They're both here."

"Of course." Eliza followed her across the crowded room.

"Poppa, I'd like you to meet my friend."

"If you'll excuse me." Mr. Von Hall nodded to the men he had been talking with. He smiled at Eliza.

"Poppa, this is Eliza Jackson. She moved here a month ago with her father and brother."

"I'm pleased to meet you. I hope you'll like our town." Mr. Von Hall was a tall man with thick blond hair and blue eyes. He appeared warm and friendly. There was something about his carefree smile that reminded her of Ralph. Eliza decided that she liked him.

She smiled. "I already like Springfield very much."

"Poppa, where's Trennen? I want to introduce him to Eliza." Vanda searched the room and jumped when a masculine voice spoke behind her.

"Who are you wanting me to meet?"

Eliza turned with Vanda to see a tall, slim, dark-haired young man with an engaging smile. His gaze shifted from Vanda to Eliza as his sister started talking.

"Trennen, I want you to meet my friend, Eliza Jackson." Vanda smiled at Eliza. "This is my big brother, Trennen."

Eliza's smile froze as she met the blue eyes of Vanda's older brother. His look swept over her before resting on her face. Her heart thumped hard. Her lashes lowered. "Pleased to meet you."

She felt his hand close around her fingers as he lifted them for a quick handshake. "And I'm pleased to meet you."

Eliza noticed the personal tone of his voice. She pulled her fingers from his grasp and turned away, glad for Miss Fraser's shrill voice demanding attention.

"We're ready to start," the schoolmarm announced. "Please, let's have order."

The room grew quiet as all eyes turned toward the raised platform where Miss Fraser stood. "The children and I welcome you to our school for our annual community spelling bee. Everyone who wishes to compete, please form a line around the room. The rest are welcome to sit at the children's desks and watch. Thank you."

Again the hum of voices filled the room as everyone shuffled around, finding their places.

Eliza squeezed Vanda's hand. "You're going to spell, aren't you? I promised Father I would."

Vanda shrugged. "I might as well, I guess. But I'm not a good speller. I'll probably be put out the first word I get."

They were in line before Eliza realized that Trennen stood behind her. He cocked his eyebrows at her and smiled. "Good luck, Miss Jackson."

"Thank you." She tried hard to ignore his presence.

Miss Fraser stood behind her desk with a sheaf of papers lying before her. She raised her hand for silence and gave the first word to a small girl. "Miriam, give us the definition for the word *good* and then spell it, please."

One by one the words were given out, and the spelldown began. When either the definition or spelling was wrong, that person had to find an empty seat in the center. Several rounds later, the words grew in difficulty as the number of spellers diminished. One after another sat down when the word *stultiloquence* was given. Eliza knew it meant foolish talk, but she wasn't sure she could spell it. Surely someone would get it right before they reached her.

Vanda made a face, whispering, "Where'd she come up with that?"

Eliza shrugged and shook her head. "I don't know, but I hope someone spells it soon."

Her father was next. Eliza held her breath when the woman in front of him sat down.

Father said, "Stultiloquence means foolish talking, which I think has been established already." A ripple of laughter swept the room before he went on to correctly spell the word.

Eliza watched James step forward.

Miss Fraser looked up from her list. "Define and spell *serry*, please."

Eliza was aware of Trennen standing behind her, making occasional comments, obviously trying to hold her attention, and she compared the two. While James was at least three inches shorter than Trennen, he had a broader, more muscular frame. Trennen sported rakish good looks with his thick dark hair and expressive blue eyes. James, with gray eyes and light brown—almost blond—hair, was not as handsome, although he was far from homely.

Now he said, "Serry means to crowd and is spelled s-e-r-r-y."

Miss Fraser looked up and smiled. "It looks like our spelling is improving." She nodded toward James. "You may take your place at the end of the line."

As James passed Eliza, their gazes met and held for several seconds. He smiled and nodded.

Vanda missed the next word, passing it on to Eliza.

Miss Fraser smiled at her. "Miss Jackson, please define and spell *pulchritude*."

Eliza took a breath to calm herself. "Pulchritude means beauty. P-u-l-c-h-r." She stopped. A vowel must come next, but was it *i* or *e*? She said the word to herself and guessed. "I-t-u-d-e."

Miss Fraser beamed at her. "That is correct. Please step to the end of the line."

Trennen stayed with her through the next round, and then left Eliza with six others, including her father and James. She listened to James define and spell *pneumonitis* without hesitation and decided Father had been right when he said James was intelligent.

One more round brought Eliza to the front with only four people behind her. She felt proud of staying in so long. Even Father had taken a seat. She felt confident when Miss Fraser smiled at her and said, "Miss Jackson, your word is *timous*."

What an easy word! Eliza smiled. "Timous means timely. T-i-m-e-o-u-s."

"Oh, I'm sorry." Miss Fraser frowned.

Eliza's face burned as she took a seat with Vanda and Trennen. "I thought you'd never come sit by me." Vanda made light of Eliza's mistake.

Eliza sank into the seat, trying to compose herself. "I can't believe I did that. There's no *e* in timous. I must have had the word *time* on my mind."

"That's what it means." Trennen smiled at Eliza.

"Yes, but I knew better."

"Hey, you stayed in longer than I did." His easy grin soon had her feeling better.

Another competitor sat down. Vanda indicated the two remaining. "I wonder who will win—James Hurley or Mr. Stenson?"

"I don't know."

Miss Fraser threw out words that Eliza had never heard, and still the two men battled.

"This could go on forever." Vanda yawned.

Eliza nodded. "It certainly looks that way."

But it didn't. Whether he was tired or he really didn't know the word, when Miss Fraser called out *repudiation*, Mr. Stenson shook his head and frowned. "Don't reckon I know the meaning of that one." He looked up at Miss Fraser. "I could spell it though, I imagine."

"I'm sorry, but the definition must come first." Miss Fraser smiled. "Mr. Stenson, you've done a wonderful job of defining and spelling. Thank you."

Mr. Stenson nodded and stepped toward a nearby seat. Eliza watched James as he took a step forward and waited until Miss Fraser repeated the word. "Repudiation means rejection. R-e-p-u-d-i-a-t-i-o-n."

"That is correct." Miss Fraser shuffled her papers and laid them neatly to one side while the room erupted in applause. She smiled at James. "Mr. Hurley,

I'm certain I speak for everyone here when I say congratulations on an excellent evening of spelling. Will you please step forward?"

Eliza watched James step on the platform beside the schoolmarm's desk. He stuck both thumbs in his pockets and waited while she spoke.

"I want to congratulate all of our participants. However, a spelling bee may have only one winner. Some of our leading citizens decided that the winner of tonight's spelling bee deserved a prize. Mr. Wingate, on behalf of his bank, donated a half eagle that I am presenting to our 1836 spelling bee winner, Mr. James Hurley."

James took his right hand from his pocket. His neck was red as he reached for the five-dollar gold coin. He cleared his throat. "Thank you, Miss Fraser." He turned to the crowded schoolroom and nodded. "Thank you."

As he started to step down, Miss Fraser stopped him. "Mr. Hurley, we want you to lead the way to the refreshments, with Mr. and Mrs. Wingate coming next." Miss Fraser's high voice cut into the rising hum of voices and shuffle of feet as people began to move about. "Reverend Appleby, will you ask the blessing, please?"

As soon as the prayer ended, Eliza turned to Vanda. "Shall we find a place in line?"

But at that moment, Cletis tugged on his sister's arm. "Come on, Vanda, Poppa wants to go."

Trennen smiled down at Eliza. "I'd be glad to escort you."

"Miss Jackson." Eliza turned at the sound of James's voice. "You did a fine job tonight."

She smiled at him. "Thank you, Mr. Hurley, but you are the one to be congratulated."

He shrugged. "Spelling was never a problem for me."

"You seem to do a great many things well. My father is very pleased with your work at the cooperage."

"I enjoy my work."

Eliza glanced at her father and saw Mrs. Wingate take him by the arm. She led him to a woman she had been talking to earlier.

"That's good. I think Father enjoys what he does, too."

"Is there something wrong?" James touched Eliza's arm to get her attention.

She lifted concerned eyes to his. "I don't know. Do you have any idea who that woman is my father is talking to?"

He looked across the room. "Do you mean Mrs. Wingate or Mrs. Hurley?"

"Mrs. Hurley?"

He smiled. "My mother."

"Your mother?" Eliza almost choked on the words. She looked again, and recognition dawned in her mind. Of course. That was the woman she had seen with James at church. Mrs. Wingate had said she was a widow. Her father could easily become attracted to such a woman. Eliza knew she attended church regularly, and for her age she was quite nice looking. Eliza watched her father's smile and easy conversation with the women and felt the noisy, crowded room close in on her.

She turned to Trennen. "I'm sorry, but I don't feel like eating. Maybe some other time. Excuse me."

She grabbed her wrap, fleeing out the door into the cold night. She leaned against the front of the building and looked up at the black, star-filled sky. She thought of her mother and the love her parents had shared. Even after a year, she missed her mother so much. It didn't seem right for Father to look at another woman when he should still be missing Mother as much as she did.

She started as the door opened. "Are you all right?" James asked.

"Of course." Eliza spoke with a sharper voice than she intended and added, "I just needed some fresh air." She brushed past him as she went back inside, leaving James watching her with a puzzled expression.

Chapter 4

The day before Eliza's birthday she went out back of the house to throw corn to the chickens. They squawked in protest, running a few steps away, only to hurry back and peck at the corn on the ground.

Eliza lifted her eyes to the fields in back of their property and beyond to a distant stand of trees. Autumn colors made a splash across the horizon. She loved fall. It was a time of harvest. A time of gathering in the bounty that God had provided. It was also her birthday.

Father was planning a surprise for her. He hadn't said anything, but she knew. She could hardly wait until tomorrow to discover what it might be.

Eliza ducked her head as she stepped into the dim interior of the small henhouse and gathered a half-dozen eggs. "Good. This is plenty for my cake."

She needed to hurry with dinner because Father wanted her at the chandler shop while he and James made a delivery.

She went in the back door, meeting Lenny in the kitchen.

"Where have you been?" Eliza set her eggs on the table and eyed her brother, dirt-streaked from his head down to his bare feet.

"None of your business."

"That's where you're wrong." Eliza's hands went to her hips. Father allowed Lenny entirely too much freedom, coming and going as he pleased. "As long as I'm the only adult in this house, your whereabouts are my business."

"You ain't no adult," Lenny sneered.

"I'll be nineteen tomorrow, and that's a whole lot more adult than any little ten-year-old boy." She took a threatening step toward him. "How'd you get so dirty?"

He shrugged. "Playin' with the guys."

"What'd you do? Roll around on the ground?"

He grinned. "Part of the time. We were playin' keep away with a wagon wheel rim. It ain't that easy to keep it a-rollin' with three or four guys trying to get it away from you."

"You'd better take a bath before we eat." Eliza pulled the washtub from the back porch. "There's some hot water on the stove. After we add cold, there'll be enough." While she talked, she filled the tub and then dipped her hand in. "This feels fine. I'll give you ten minutes to get that dirt scrubbed off, and then I've got to start cooking. Hurry and get in while I get you some clean clothes."

"Do I have to take a bath?" Lenny whined.

Eliza turned at the door. "Yes. Father wants you to go with him on a delivery this afternoon." Her voice softened at his crestfallen look. "If you stay clean, you won't have to take another bath tonight."

"Another bath?" His voice rose in panic.

Eliza laughed. "You want to be clean for church tomorrow."

When he stared at her, his eyes wide and his mouth open, she pointed toward the tub. "You'd better be in there by the time I come back, or I'll put you in myself. And don't forget your hair."

As usual, Lenny didn't tarry in the water. With his bath out of the way, Eliza had just enough time to mix a cake before she fixed the noon meal. She heard the front door open as she reached for the oven door.

A tendril of hair escaped the confining bun at the base of her head and flew into her eye just as Father came into the room. She brushed at her hair with her left hand while she wrapped her right hand in her apron and reached for the hot pan. Pain seared her finger. The pan clattered to the floor as she jerked her hand back.

"Ow!" She put her finger in her mouth. "Where's the butter?" Tears blinded her eyes.

"Cold water works best." The deep voice and gentle hands guiding her to the sink were not her father's yet were familiar.

She looked into James's gray eyes. What was he doing here?

He pushed her hand into a pan of fresh cold water. She closed her eyes, savoring the relief.

"Keep your hand in for a few minutes." He turned to her father. "Do you have any burn salve and bandages?"

"I think so." It was the first thing Father had said since he came in the door. Eliza could hear him rummaging in the cabinet. She heard someone pick up the cake pan.

"Is my cake all right?" She wiped a hand across her eyes.

"It's fine." James moved back to her side. "How's that hand coming?"

"The water takes the pain away."

He lifted her dripping hand and laid it on a towel. "Let's get your hand dry so we can wrap it."

"Here we go." Father handed James the salve.

Eliza kept her gaze away from James as he blotted her hand. She reached for the can of salve the same time he did. "I can do it."

"Are you sure?" He sounded doubtful.

"Of course. It's just a little burn."

She sighed with relief when the men moved away.

"Is your hand still hurting?" James asked when she joined them at the table.

"Not much." Eliza realized Mother would have been ashamed of her manners. "Thank you for helping me. The cool water took most of the burn out. I'll remember that if it ever happens again."

James smiled. "Let's hope it never does."

As soon as they finished eating, Eliza cleared the dishes from the table and stacked them by the sink. Lenny ran outside, calling over his shoulder that he'd be ready to go anytime.

James shoved his chair back and crossed the room to the sink.

"Do you need help? You don't want to get your hand wet."

Before she could stop him, he was at the stove, bringing the teakettle of hot water. She stepped in front of him to pump cold water into the sink. She pointed to the counter. "Just set it there. I can handle this."

"Are you sure? I don't mind helping." He hesitated. "At least let me pour the water in for you."

"No. I can do it myself." She knew her voice was sharp, but his presence so close made her jittery. It wasn't right that a man wash dishes.

"Aren't we going to get some of that cake for dessert?" Father asked.

Eliza looked at the cake James had set on the cabinet. She shook her head. "I made it for tomorrow. It isn't even frosted yet."

"That's right. Someone's having a birthday tomorrow, aren't they?"

Eliza turned toward her father in time to see the smiles that passed between the two men. So James knew what Father had planned for her birthday.

"I guess we'll have to wait, James. Eliza's quite a stickler for doing things up right."

Eliza stiffened. Had Father just invited James Hurley to her birthday party?

James went back to the table and pushed in his chair. "I've enjoyed the stimulating conversation and excellent food. Thank you. Maybe sometime you can all come out to my mother's home and share a meal with us."

Eliza heard Father's chair slide under the table. She turned to see him smile at James. "We may take you up on that one of these days."

Eliza frowned as her father and James went into the parlor. Mrs. Wingate should have minded her own business. Father didn't need a wife.

She hung up her apron, looked at the wet bandage on her index finger, and her frown deepened. Maybe she should have let James wash her dishes, after all. Her finger throbbed. She pulled off the sopping wrap and threw it away.

As she tried to wrap a clean strip of cloth around her finger, the kitchen door opened and James stuck his head in. "I thought you might need some help with the dishes. Your father is hitching up the wagon."

"They're all done." She turned her back toward him.

She sensed his presence beside her. "Here, let me do that for you."

"I can do it myself." She was ashamed of the sharp tone in her voice.

"Miss Jackson." He took the cloth from her. "I don't bite. Besides, your father wants to get started on that delivery, and you may as well ride to the shop with us."

Eliza's face burned as she submitted to his gentle ministering. As soon as the bandage was in place, she fled the room, pausing at the door long enough to say, "Thank you, Mr. Hurley."

❧

The chandler shop was quiet with no one next door in the cooperage; so, between customers, Eliza finished her current novel.

While she walked home, she thought of what to fix for supper. Father had said they might not be home until late. Maybe she could fix vegetable soup.

There was no sign of life in the house as Eliza stepped on the porch. She pushed the door open and went in.

"Happy birthday, Eliza." A chorus of voices met her.

Several matches blazed, bringing lanterns and candles to life. Father stood in the middle of the room, his arms outstretched. Eliza moved into his embrace. "Happy birthday, sweetheart." He gave her a quick hug and kissed the top of her head. "Some of our friends have come to celebrate with you a day early. You don't mind, do you?"

"Mind?" Eliza looked around the room. "Of course I don't mind."

Except for the chairs from the kitchen, there was not a stick of furniture in the parlor. Instead, the walls were lined by people, some she knew and some she didn't. Her eyes met James's briefly. He smiled at her. His sister and mother were there. Miss Fraser. The Wingates. The pastor and his family. Everyone laughed, and the hum of conversation picked up. So this was Father's surprise. She looked at him and smiled. "Someone has been busy this afternoon. Did you really make a delivery?"

He nodded. "Oh yes. Mrs. Wingate and Vanda spearheaded this renovation."

Vanda hugged her. "Happy birthday, Eliza. This is the first party I've gone to in a long time. We're going to have so much fun. My father couldn't come, but Trennen's here somewhere." She leaned close and whispered. "I think you made an impression on him at the spelling bee."

Others pressed close to speak to Eliza. One by one the older people clasped her hand, saying a few words before moving on through the open door into the kitchen. Eliza could see the table groaning under the weight of the food that had been brought in.

She turned to her father and laughed. "I was worried about getting supper ready, and look at this. There's enough to feed the entire town."

He smiled. "I think that's about how many we'll be feeding. Mrs. Wingate is in charge of serving. I'd better see if she needs anything."

"Oh, Father, shouldn't I help?"

Vanda grabbed her arm. "Not tonight. You're going to stay in here with us and play. We'll eat when the older people are finished."

More than a dozen young people and as many younger children laughed and visited in the parlor. Vanda clapped her hands together and raised her voice. "Mrs. Wingate said we couldn't eat until we've played at least two games." Amid laughter and token protests she continued. "Everyone knows 'Skip to My Lou,' so grab hands and let's go."

Trennen grabbed Eliza's hand. "I've got my partner." He smiled. "Happy Birthday, Eliza. You sure look pretty tonight."

Eliza returned his smile. "I might have fixed up if I'd known I was going to a party."

His gaze moved over her in a way that brought a flush to her face. "No need. You look perfect to me."

"Thank you." She glanced toward James. He paid no attention to her and Trennen. He was too busy talking to his partner, a girl Eliza hadn't met.

Vanda started singing with the others joining in. "Skip, skip, skip to My Lou, skip, skip, skip to My Lou, skip, skip, skip to My Lou, skip to My Lou, my darling."

Holding Trennen's hand, Eliza skipped around the circle, adding her voice to the others. She cast a side glance at Trennen. With his eyelids lowered lazily, he smiled, and her heart fluttered. After Ralph's rejection she thought she would never look at another man. Now, with Trennen smiling down at her as if she were the only girl present, she wasn't so sure.

❊

Eliza strolled toward town, her surprise birthday party of two nights ago filling her mind. She giggled as she thought of the look on Trennen's face when Joe Martin had grabbed her after "Skip to My Lou" ended. Joe lasted through the next game, then Daniel Ross stepped between them, and so on it went the entire evening. Every game had found her with a different partner. But never James Hurley. He had kept his distance, and she hated to admit, even to herself, that she was disappointed.

Then the adults had come into the parlor to join the fun. When they played "Pig in the Parlor," Eliza noticed that Father picked Mrs. Hurley for his partner.

She and Father had laughed and talked as if they'd known each other for years. Eliza didn't understand how Father could act that way toward a woman other than Mother. He behaved as though he didn't miss Mother at all. Eliza missed her, and seeing Father with another woman stirred the pain of her loss so much more. How she wished Mrs. Wingate had never interfered!

Eliza pushed through the door to Leach's General Store.

"Good morning, Miss Jackson," Mr. Leach's voice boomed from the back of the store. "How are you today?"

"Fine, thank you."

"Thought you might be feeling a bit old after that birthday party." Mr. Leach's broad face beamed at her over a stack of feed sacks.

Mrs. Leach bustled in from the back. "You had a lovely party." She smiled. "What can I do for you?"

"Father told me to buy some dress fabric as my birthday gift."

Mrs. Leach led her to the bolts of material on a counter against the wall. "That's a wonderful idea. Let's see what we've got." She picked one up, holding it next to Eliza's face. "How about this pretty blue sprig? You've just the right coloring to go with it."

The minutes slipped by while Eliza and the storekeeper's wife selected several pieces of fabric. Finally, they had the yardage cut and folded neatly in a tall stack beside her. Eliza looked at Mrs. Leach with a nervous laugh. "Do you know of a seamstress?"

"I certainly do. The Kowskis are about as reasonable as you'll find, and they're good."

A few minutes later, Eliza left the store with a large bundle in her arms and directions to the Kowskis' house. The package was heavy and cumbersome, so she decided to stop first by the chandler shop to show her father what he had given her.

She found him alone in the back room. She went in and dropped her bundle on the worktable. "What've you got there?" he asked. "It isn't dinnertime, is it?"

Eliza shook her head, smiling. "No, are you hungry?"

He rubbed his middle. "Now that you mention it. . ."

Eliza laughed. "You'll forget all about your stomach once you see what I bought."

Father wiped his hands on his big apron and moved to her side as she untied the paper, letting it fall away. "Well, I'd say you've picked out some pretty dresses. How are you going to get that all sewn up?"

"That's what I wanted to talk to you about." Eliza felt her face flush. "Mrs. Leach gave me directions to some women who do sewing for a living. She says they're very reasonable. But I didn't know if you could afford the extra expense."

Father patted her back. "I'd forgotten which one of you girls was so handy with a needle. It was Cora, wasn't it?"

Eliza nodded. "Cora and Vickie are both good. I couldn't sew a decent seam if my life depended on it."

She heard a noise and turned to see James standing in the doorway.

He nodded to her. "Hello, Miss Jackson."

"Hello." She turned away to cover her fabric, her face burning. She hoped he had not heard her last words.

While James and her father discussed an order for unusual-sized barrels, she prepared to leave. Father hadn't said if she could hire the women to sew for her, but that was all right. She'd ask again later.

She waited until a lull came in their conversation and then spoke. "Father, I've got to get home. I'll see you at noon."

James took a step toward her. "I have a few minutes to spare. I'll walk you home."

Eliza frowned. "That won't be necessary."

"It is if you're planning to take that. You'd never be able to carry it all the way to your house." He took the bundle from her before turning to her father. "This shouldn't take long and then I'll get right on that order."

Eliza turned imploring eyes on her father. "I don't need any help, Father. Maybe he should start the order now."

The twinkle in her father's eye was unmistakable. "James knows what he's doing. Getting you home is more important than any order."

Eliza stretched to her full height. "Father, I've never needed assistance finding my way before."

"But you've never had such a big package to carry." He grinned, obviously enjoying her discomfort.

Eliza turned, defeated, toward the door. Her father's words followed her. "Go ahead and hire those ladies to sew your dresses for you."

Eliza went through the shop into the autumn sunshine without a backward glance. She turned toward home, walking in a near run.

※

James followed Eliza, watching her ramrod-straight back with an amused grin. It was obvious she didn't want his company—just as obvious as it had been the night of her party. He'd been unable to get near her for all the other fellows.

Her package was heavy, but mostly it was cumbersome. Strong as he was, he felt the pull on his arms before they had gone far. Of course, it might be easier handled if he didn't have to go in a half run to keep up with her. He tried to think what he might have said to offend her but could think of nothing.

He shifted the package to his shoulder, taking the strain off his arms. How was she going to get it to the dressmakers'? He took a few running steps to overtake her as she started down the Booneville Road.

"Would you mind slowing down?"

"You may stop and rest if you're tired." Her cute little nose went into the air.

"Miss Jackson, I'd like to ask you something, and it's all I can do to keep up." Her pace slowed.

She acted like his little sister in a snit. He tried again. "Once I get started on that barrel order, I won't have much time. Have you considered how you're going to get your dress goods to the dressmakers'? Right now, I've got the time to deliver it. Wouldn't it make sense to take it there instead of your home?"

As fast as she'd been walking, James wasn't prepared for her sudden stop. He also wasn't prepared for the flashing brown eyes she turned on him. "So you did hear."

He hesitated, uncertain what was wrong. "Hear what? When we left your father said—"

"That since I can't sew, I'll have to go to the dressmakers'."

Her large brown eyes glistened. He nodded—then shook his head—confused. "No, that wasn't exactly what he said."

She shrugged, straightening her shoulders again. "He might just as well, because it's true. But I don't think you should go with me."

"Why not?"

Her eyes met his. "Because I don't want you to."

"Oh, really?" He grinned, intrigued by her show of independence. "I'll tell you what I'll do. I'll carry your fabric to the dressmakers' house, and then I'll leave. Is that a deal?"

Her eyes never left his. "Do I have a choice?"

"No." His grin grew even wider, and he was sure he saw an answering one tug at the corners of her mouth before she twirled away.

This time, as she turned back, she slowed her gait. James walked behind and to her side. He didn't want to overstep the boundaries she had put between them until he was sure where he stood with her. Somehow, Eliza Jackson had caught his fancy. As he watched the proud set of her shoulders, he determined to find a way to break down the wall she had erected against him.

❧

When they reached the dressmakers' home, Eliza took the package from James and thanked him. His cheerful whistle as he tripped down the steps toward town brought a smile to her lips. She knocked on the door of the small cabin, hoping Mrs. Leach's directions had been correct and this was the right place.

A girl near Eliza's age opened the door. A smile of recognition crossed her face. "Eliza Jackson, how nice to see you again."

Eliza looked from the friendly green eyes to a sprinkling of freckles covering the girl's alabaster skin. Her deep auburn hair was long and curly, pulled back at the nape of her neck to hang free down her back. Eliza remembered seeing her at church and at her party, but she couldn't remember her name.

"Miss Kowski?" At least Mrs. Leach had told her that much.

"Oh, please, call me Kathrene." She stretched out a small, dainty hand and grasped Eliza's arm. "Come inside. I want you to meet my mother. She didn't go to your party. She had some work to finish and couldn't take the time."

Eliza followed Kathrene into a cheerful sunlit parlor.

"Mother, this is Eliza Jackson. I went to her birthday party Saturday night, although I don't think she remembers me." An impish grin lit Kathrene's face as she looked at Eliza.

Eliza couldn't help blushing any more than she could stop the laughter that escaped at her own expense. "I'm sorry. It's just that there were so many there." She smiled at the woman sitting in a chair in front of the window. "I'm pleased to meet you, Mrs. Kowski. I'm in need of a seamstress, and Mrs. Leach recommended you."

Mrs. Kowski pushed the garment she was working on to the side and stood, stretching her back as she did. "How nice of Mrs. Leach. Here, set that package on the couch. It must be quite heavy."

Kathrene and her mother could have passed for sisters. *Almost twin sisters,* Eliza thought as she looked from one to the other.

"It is a little heavy." Eliza deposited it on the couch and untied the string.

"I love to look at new fabric." Kathrene pulled the paper back and lifted the first piece. "This is so pretty. You'll be beautiful in it."

Mrs. Kowski thrust a magazine into Eliza's hands. "This is the latest *Lady's Book.* See if you like anything."

"Won't you need a pattern?" Eliza wasn't sure, but she thought Cora had always used a muslin pattern for their dresses.

Kathrene laughed. "Don't worry, Mother will make a pattern from the sketches in the magazine."

"Oh." Eliza was impressed with a talent she knew little about. She perched on the edge of a chair and thumbed through the magazine until she found a dress that she thought would be perfect for church.

"Could you make this one from the blue print?" She held the page for Mrs. Kowski to see.

"Yes, I think the blue print is a good choice for it. Would you like to pick out the rest or wait and see how this one turns out?"

Eliza stood. "I'd like to look further, but it's time now for me to be home fixing my father's dinner. If you made your own dresses, I'm sure mine will turn out fine."

Mrs. Kowski smiled as she set the magazine aside. "Before you leave, may I take a couple of measurements so I can cut out your dress tonight?"

A few minutes later with the measurements recorded by Eliza's name and a price agreed upon, Kathrene walked out to the front gate with her. "I really enjoyed your party Saturday night."

Eliza smiled. "I'm glad you came. I'm sorry I forgot your name. We've been here just a month now, and I've met so many people I have trouble remembering everyone."

A warm smile lit Kathrene's face. "I'll just have to make myself more noticeable from now on."

"I thought you would be two older women, maybe sisters. Then when you turned out to be my age, I was a little nervous about letting you know I couldn't sew. I thought you might laugh at me." Eliza smiled.

Kathrene shook her head. "I could never laugh at someone else when there are so many things I can't do." She laughed softly. "My mother is a wonderful cook, but I think she's about despaired of ever teaching me."

Eliza took Kathrene's hand and squeezed gently. "Speaking of cooking, I've got to go. I'm really glad I got to meet you."

Kathrene nodded. "Let's make ourselves known at church, too. I've seen you each week, and now I'm ashamed I didn't introduce myself."

Eliza edged toward the road. "That's all right. I didn't do any better Saturday night." She waved as she started down the dirt road toward home. "Come over and visit me sometime."

"All right, I will." Kathrene stood by the gate to wave before turning back inside.

Eliza thought Kathrene was every bit as nice as her best friend, Grace Newkirk, from back home. Now she had two new friends, Vanda and Kathrene.

She hummed "Home, Sweet Home" until she caught sight of her father's shop. Only to herself would she admit that James had been right. She would have struggled to carry her package as far as he did. She appreciated his help but wished she wasn't so attracted to him.

Chapter 5

O h, Eliza. It looks perfect on you." Kathrene clasped her hands under her chin and sighed. "You have such beautiful coloring."

After several fittings throughout the first part of November, Mary and Kathrene had finished the first dress.

Eliza smiled. "Thank you."

Mary Kowski bustled in from the other room. "Here are some more magazines you may look at for the rest of your dresses, Eliza."

Eliza smiled at Kathrene's mother. "Thank you. I love this one."

She still found it hard to believe that Mary Kowski was old enough to be Kathrene's mother. Mary's energy seemed boundless as she rushed from one project to another.

Several minutes later, Eliza hurried home with a light step. With Mary's and Kathrene's help, she had picked out the other three dresses.

That night just before bedtime Father said, "I've been doing some thinking about Christmas."

"Christmas is more than a month away, Father." Eliza looked from her father to her brother. Lenny just shrugged his shoulders.

Father smiled. "Yes, I know. But it may take us that long to get ready. I'm just getting started on the bayberry candles. Your dresses are not finished. We should be looking for gifts. And we mustn't forget, it's a two-day trip even in good weather."

Lenny's eyes grew wide as Eliza leaned forward. "What are you talking about, Father? A two-day trip where?"

"Oh, did I forget to mention that?" The twinkle in his eyes warned Eliza that Father had something special planned.

"Yes, you did."

Lenny looked smug. "I already know."

"How could you? Father, did you tell—"

"No." Father shook his head. "I didn't tell Lenny anything."

"All right, smarty." Eliza turned to her brother. "Where are we going for Christmas?" The words had no sooner left her lips than she knew. She jumped from the chair and flung her arms around her father's neck. "Home. We're going home to see everyone for Christmas, aren't we?"

"Where else would we go that takes two days?" Lenny's look of scorn was lost on Eliza's enthusiasm.

"How can you do that? What about the shops?" Eliza asked.

Father made room for Eliza on the couch. "James can handle anything that comes, and if not, he can close up until we get back."

"Yeah, it'll probably snow, and we won't go, anyway." Lenny hid his eagerness behind a look of indifference.

"You've got a reasonable concern there, son." Father's smile disappeared for a moment. "But the weather has been unusually mild so far, and according to the almanac, it should be for awhile."

"Oh, Father, you're right. There's so much to do." Eliza began counting on her fingers. "I'll have to prepare food for the trip. I want to bake something special to take. We need to take gifts for everyone. What do you think they'd like?" Before he could answer, she smiled. "We'll see Nora and Christopher, too. I just know they've grown."

She swung toward her father as a new thought entered her mind. "Are we bringing Nora home?"

Father shook his head. "I want that more than you know, Eliza. But I don't see how we can at this time. The shops are just getting started, and I need your help much too often for you to tend an active two year old, too. But soon we will."

They talked, making plans until it grew late and Father sent them off to bed.

※

Their coming trip dominated the conversation at breakfast the next morning. Father swallowed his last bite of biscuit and pushed his chair back. "I've been thinking we ought to invite our old friends for Christmas dinner."

Lenny looked up. "I'll bet the Newkirks will come because Ben's married to Esther. But what about the Starks? Aaron will come with Cora, so that just leaves Ralph and Ivy."

At the mention of Ralph's name, Eliza's spoon dropped to the table. She hadn't thought of him. In all the excitement of seeing her family again, she had forgotten Ralph. But of course he would be there. With his wife and baby. She gathered the dishes from the table while dread crept over her soul.

"It looks like your sister's ready for us to get out of her way, Lenny." Father stood and stretched. "I'll lay aside the next batch of bayberry candles to take back for the girls. I'll be working on them today. How'd you like to come down and tend the shop this afternoon, Eliza?"

"Fine." She pulled Lenny's spoon from his hand as he shoveled in the last of the oatmeal. He swiveled around with a frown. "Hey, can't you wait until a guy finishes?"

"Good, then I'll see you later." Father guided Lenny toward the door. "Tell your sister bye and thank you for breakfast."

Lenny turned to peek under his father's arm at Eliza. He crossed his eyes and stuck out his tongue. "Good-bye, Eliza, and thank you for what I got to eat before you jerked it away."

Father's back was turned as he pushed through the kitchen door into the parlor. Eliza lifted a heavy iron skillet as if to throw it at Lenny. "I'm glad you enjoyed it, little brother. Would you like some of this, too?"

Lenny ducked under his father's arm and ran through the door. By the time Father looked at Eliza she was drying the skillet. She smiled at him. "Bye, Father. I'll see you at noon."

When the front door closed behind them, the house grew quiet, allowing memories of Ralph to beat without mercy against Eliza's heart. How could she go see the man she'd thought she would marry when he was married to another? She finished the dishes and hung the wet tea towel on a rack to dry. She put beans on the stove to simmer, yet the image of Ralph would not leave. She moved to the bedrooms, making beds, straightening, dusting, and sweeping. Still Ralph haunted her.

With sudden determination, she ran to the kitchen, shoved the beans to the back of the stove, and grabbed a heavy, woolen shawl. There was plenty of time to see Kathrene and Mary Kowski before noon.

The fresh air felt good on her face as her feet carried her to the small cabin across town. Kathrene opened the door at her knock.

"Eliza, come in." Kathrene's smile of welcome gave a sparkle to her green eyes.

"I didn't intend to come today, but I have wonderful news, and I need some adjustments made." Eliza moved into the room past Kathrene.

"What is your news?" Mary gave Eliza a warm hug.

All thoughts of Ralph faded as Eliza sat on the couch between the two women and told of her eagerness to see her family at Christmas. "I'd like my other three dresses adjusted to fit my sisters."

"Oh, Eliza, how sweet of you." Mary patted Eliza's hand.

Eliza smiled at her friend. "I want the pink for Esther. It's soft and feminine just like she is."

Mary smiled and stood. "I'll get some paper and a pen to write down the changes we'll need to make. Are the girls much different in size from you?"

Eliza frowned as she brought each to mind. "No, not really. Esther's taller and a little thinner. Cora and I always wore each other's clothes, so there shouldn't be any changes to make there. Vickie is older, but she's probably an inch shorter than Cora and me. She has two children that she says have made her fat, but she really isn't."

Mary wrote, trying to keep up with Eliza's descriptions. "Then you think Vickie might be just two or three inches larger around than you?"

Eliza nodded. "Yes, that's about right."

"All right." Mary laid the pen and paper down. "I think I have enough here Why don't you pick out the fabric you want for each sister?"

"I think Esther should have the pink, Cora the blue, and Vickie the green calico."

As she left, she touched Kathrene's arm. "Please pray for me while I'm gone."

"Of course. Mother and I both will. Besides safe travel, is there something special we should be praying about?"

With a sigh, Eliza met her friend's concerned gaze. "There was a young man." She hesitated as moisture threatened her sight. "He married someone else." She took a deep breath and brushed a hand across her eyes. "Just pray that if I see them, I won't make a fool of myself."

Kathrene gathered her into a hug. "I understand. I'll pray that God will show you He has something better for you than what you lost."

Eliza straightened and smiled. "Thank you. Now I've got to run home before Father gets there. I may have burned beans for him to eat if I don't hurry."

Kathrene laughed, calling after Eliza's retreating figure, "I burn them when I'm right there watching. Yours will be fine."

True to Kathrene's prediction, the beans had cooked down but were not scorched. Lenny and Father each had two bowls full.

At the shop that afternoon, Eliza kept busy most of the time. A customer left just as Vanda came in.

"I didn't expect to see you." Vanda smiled.

"Does that mean you wouldn't have come in if you'd known I was here?"

Vanda laughed. "Of course not. It means I'd have been here sooner so we could visit longer."

"You say all the right things, but that doesn't explain why I've scarcely seen you all this month." Eliza pretended to pout.

Vanda picked up a bayberry candle from the counter and sniffed it. "My father hasn't been working as much so I've had to stay close to home." Her smile didn't reach her eyes. "He has some old-fashioned ideas about women. He doesn't like for me to be away from home any more than necessary." She quickly changed the subject. "M-m-m. These really smell good, don't they? What are they?"

Eliza glanced toward the candle in Vanda's hand. "Bayberry. Father's making them for Christmas. I've sold several today."

A wistful sound came into Vanda's voice as she put it back. "Maybe nearer Christmas I can get one. But for now we just need the cheapest candle you have."

Eliza came around the counter. "You know, we do have a candle that costs a little more, but in the long run it's more economical because it lasts so much longer."

"Oh really?"

Encouraged by Vanda's interest, Eliza reached for the special candles and handed one to her friend. "These are made with whale blubber and burn as long as three or four tallow candles. The light is brighter, too. But they only cost about twice as much."

"H-m-m. That sounds like a good deal." Vanda smiled. "I'll take two of them."

The bell above the door rang as Eliza wrapped the candles for Vanda. She looked up, meeting James's gaze.

"Good afternoon, ladies." His presence seemed to dwarf the room.

Eliza returned to her work, her hands trembling as she tied the string. Vanda smiled at him. "Good afternoon, yourself." She turned back and tapped Eliza's arm. "I believe he was speaking to both of us."

Eliza lifted her gaze to the gray eyes watching her. A half grin sat on his lips. She felt a stirring deep inside that she didn't want to feel. "Hello, Mr. Hurley."

His lips spread into a full smile.

She felt her face flush. Why did he have to look at her like that? "Is there something you need? My father is in the back room."

He shivered violently. "B-r-r-r. We may get that first snow before Christmas, after all." He grinned, doffed an imaginary hat, and strode across the shop. He stopped, turned, and nodded with a big grin at Vanda before disappearing through the back door.

As soon as the door closed, Vanda turned to Eliza. "Why did you treat him so cold? It's obvious he likes you."

"Likes me!" Eliza's voice rose. "Where'd you get an idea like that? He was rude to me."

Vanda laughed. "He wasn't rude. He was just reacting to the way you patronized him. Just because he's your father's employee—"

"Oh, Vanda," Eliza interrupted. "I didn't mean it that way. It's just that he makes me nervous. Here are your candles. I think you'll like them very much. They are about the only kind I use at home."

Vanda reached for the bundle, a smile softening her face. "James Hurley likes you, and I think he has caught your fancy, too."

Eliza didn't answer except to tell Vanda good-bye as she left. While her friend was right about Eliza's feelings for James, Eliza couldn't allow herself to like him. Ralph's rejection still hurt too much for her to trust her heart to another.

The shop filled with customers, so she was busy when James walked back through on his way to the cooperage.

Chapter 6

Eliza could scarcely sit still when Cedar Creek and then the log cabin came into view. A wave of homesickness for her mother swept over her. She watched the closed door of the cabin coming closer, half expecting Mother to be standing there, waiting with a welcoming embrace. But Esther opened the door.

Esther laughed as she stepped out to greet them. "Father. Eliza and Lenny. Oh, Ben will be so surprised."

Father gave her a warm hug. "Where is my oldest son?"

"At the barn. We have a cow down that he's taking care of." Esther looked as beautiful as ever. Her wheat-blond hair, done up in a loose bun, fell in a soft wave across her forehead. Her lips, full and pink, curved up at the corners.

Father looked toward the building that had served as shelter when they first moved to the country. "Lenny, you can help me with the horses. We'll see what Ben's up to."

Eliza stepped through the heavy oak door ahead of Esther, allowing memories of the three happy years she had spent there to course through her mind.

"I'm so glad you came." Esther hugged Eliza. "Your sisters and Ben will be thrilled. We all talked the other night about how hard it would be to have a real Christmas with you gone. Why don't we invite everyone over to share Christmas Day with us? Grace will want to see you."

"That would be wonderful." Even as Eliza agreed, a twinge of fear struck the pit of her stomach. "Everyone" included Ralph.

"You must be worn out from your trip and probably hungry, too." Esther turned toward the kitchen. "Did you get any sleep?" Esther stirred the fire in Mother's old cookstove while Eliza stifled a yawn.

She laughed. "Some. I didn't feel tired until you started talking about it. Even now, I'm so excited I don't think I could rest."

Esther smiled. "That's good, because I expect Ben will have your sisters here before we finish eating."

"Is there anything I can help you with?"

Esther shook her head. "No, you go greet your brother."

Ben crossed the room in long strides and grabbed Eliza in a warm hug.

Father and Lenny followed him into the room. Ben turned to face them, his arm still around Eliza's shoulders. "I'm having trouble believing you're here.

We'll have a real Christmas, after all."

"Yes, if gifts are not important." Esther's soft voice brought a groan from Ben.

"Oh, I forgot. We didn't know you were coming."

"Don't worry about gifts." Father laughed. "Eliza already said the best gift she could get is coming home for Christmas."

Eliza nodded as everyone looked at her. "That's true. I just want to be with my family. What could be better than that?"

Ben smiled. "Of course you're right." His eyes, so like their father's, twinkled. "The only problem is, I saw your wagon. It's loaded to the top."

"Yes, and we need to unload." Father jammed his hat back on his head. "Come on, Ben. Show us where you want these supplies. We need to lighten the wagon for our return trip. Then someone needs to tell Cora and Vickie we're here."

As soon as Cora and Aaron arrived, Eliza ran from the cabin with her father and Lenny behind her while Ben and Esther waited on the porch.

Aaron lifted Cora from the horse's back, holding her waist until he was sure she had her footing. Cora smiled up at him. "I'm fine, Aaron, really."

Eliza pushed past her brother-in-law to catch her sister in a fierce hug. She laughed. "Are you surprised to see us?"

"Yes and very glad."

Then Lenny and their father pulled Cora away, and Eliza stepped back. It was good to be home.

"How you been doin', Eliza?"

She looked up into Aaron's bright blue eyes. How much like his brother Ralph he looked! She ignored the pounding of her heart and smiled at her brother-in-law. "Just fine. I'm so glad we could come home."

"Yeah. Ben said we'd have a big Christmas dinner. Be jist like old times, won't it?"

Her heart lurched at the thought, but she managed a weak smile. "Yes, it should be really nice." She thought of Aaron and Ralph's sister. "How's Ivy getting along?"

Aaron smiled. "She's doin' real good. That little fellow of hers ain't no bigger'n a minute, but he sure runs her a merry chase. He's already crawlin'."

Eliza laughed. She tried to imagine Aaron's sister as a mother. It was hard to see anything but the sullen girl she had been before her marriage to Mr. Reid. "Is Ivy happy?"

Aaron grinned. "Happy as a pig in the wallow."

"I'm glad she's happy. It'll be good to see her."

"You're the one I want to visit with." Cora linked her arm in Eliza's as they turned toward the house. "We've got three months of catching up to do. You're going to tell me all about that big city you live in and what you've been doing there."

"Don't worry, I will."

"Here comes Nicholas." Lenny's excited voice drew attention to the trail behind the house. Although Lenny was several years older than his nephew, the two boys had always been close.

Eliza and Cora followed the others to meet their sister Vickie and her husband John. But it was their oldest son, Nicholas, who scrambled from the wagon before it stopped and ran past them to grab Lenny.

"Let me have those babies." Father reached for Christopher and then waited while John set Nora on his other arm and then turned to help Vickie.

After a warm hug from Vickie and John, while the others visited, Eliza watched the two little ones look at Father with solemn faces. She noticed his eyes were moist as he clutched them close. Nora lifted a tiny hand to her father's cheek. "You mine papa?"

A smile lit his face. "Yes, I am."

"Me, too." Little Christopher reached up to tug on his chin.

Father smiled down at his grandson and kissed his cheek. "I'm Grandpa to you."

"Eth. Bampa." Christopher nodded his head while Nora snuggled against her father's chest.

"Well, it looks like they haven't forgotten Father," Eliza said.

"Of course not, and they haven't forgotten you, either," Vickie spoke beside her. "It seems like a lifetime, but you've only been gone a short while."

Cora pulled Eliza by the hand. "Let's see if we can get Nora away from Father."

Nora stared at Eliza with wide brown eyes. Slowly a shy smile tugged at her mouth, and she leaned forward.

It wasn't hard to talk Vickie into letting Nora spend the night. Eliza took advantage of the short time with her little sister before John came midmorning the next day to take her back home so she wouldn't be in the way of Christmas preparations. Ben and Father made the rounds of the neighbors, inviting them to Christmas dinner, while Esther and Eliza cleaned house and baked a wide assortment of pies and cakes.

That afternoon, Cora and Aaron came. They hadn't been there long before Cora took Eliza's hand and pulled her toward the door. "Grab your wrap. We haven't had that talk you promised me." She nodded toward the ladder leading to the loft. "We can't share our secrets up there anymore. Now we have to go outside where we can find some privacy."

"Don't you girls be gone long. When Vickie and John get here, we'll open gifts." Their father's eyes twinkled. "You won't want to miss that."

Cora laughed. "You're right, we won't. We'll come right in when they get here."

"So tell me what it's like in Springfield," Cora said before they stepped off the porch.

Eliza described the house and shops. She told about the church and several of the people she had met. "I've made two friends. Kathrene Kowski helps her mother as a seamstress. They are both wonderful. I know you'd love them, too."

She went on telling about the friendship that had grown between herself and Kathrene. Then she said, "I have another friend, Vanda Von Hall. Vanda reminds me of a will-o'-the-wisp. I don't know where she lives, and she doesn't come to church often. I only see her when she comes to me."

Cora shook her head. "She sounds strange."

"Oh, but she isn't. Actually, she's very nice." Eliza defended her friend. "I've met her father and brothers. They seem nice, too."

"Brothers?" Cora smiled. "And how old are they?"

"One is Lenny's age."

"And the other?"

"About twenty-one." Eliza's face felt hot in the cold air.

"So have you met any other young men, or is this the one?" Cora grinned at her sister's discomfort.

Eliza turned to face Cora. "I don't have to settle for the first man who looks my way. Father gave me a surprise birthday party, and I'll have you know I was the most sought after girl there." She interrupted as Cora started to speak. "No, I wasn't the only girl."

Cora laughed. "I'm glad to see living in the city hasn't changed you."

Eliza relaxed as she laughed with her sister. "I don't know if I've changed, but I do know it's good to be home for awhile."

"Only awhile? Does that mean you're anxious to get back?"

Eliza thought of the well-furnished, roomy house awaiting them and shrugged. "I suppose in a way I am. It's nice having my own house to care for, even though sometimes I'd like to turn all the work over to someone else."

Cora didn't speak for several moments and then said, "Have you considered that Father might marry again?"

Eliza's heart lurched as she thought of Mrs. Hurley. She turned on her sister. "How can you even think such a thing? He loved Mother too much to desecrate her memory."

"But Father is still young enough to have. . ." She paused, then added, "Feelings."

Eliza stopped near a young apple tree, its bare branches moving in the cool air. "If you don't mind, I'd rather find out about all of you. And don't tell me Vickie is going to have another baby. I already know."

Cora laughed. "You always know." She paused. "Almost everything."

"Do you mean Esther?"

"How did you know she was, too?"

Eliza shrugged. "By the way she acts, and I thought I noticed a difference in the way she looks."

Cora shook her head. "You are a wonder, but you don't know everything."

Eliza looked at her sister. What had she missed? Then she noticed the protective way Cora's hand rested on her abdomen. With a glad cry she threw her arms around her. "You, too? Oh, Cora, that's wonderful. No wonder you look so happy. I thought it was because you're so much in love with Aaron."

Cora laughed. "Well, of course, I am." She patted the slight bulge under her coat. "But I already love this little fellow, too."

The jingling of harness and rumbling of a wagon announced John and Vickie's arrival. Eliza looked toward the west as they came into view and began to laugh.

"What's so funny?" Cora touched her arm. "We promised Father we'd come right in when Vickie got here."

"But that's just it." Eliza could scarcely get her breath. "We have to open gifts now." She wiped her eyes, trying to stop laughing. "I just realized I had dresses made for each of you, and not one of you will be able to fit in them."

Cora linked her arm through Eliza's. "If you think you're going to take the dresses back, you can think again. We'll just save them until we can wear them." She smiled. "Come on, let's beat Vickie and John to the house."

Eliza enjoyed the time spent with her family as they gathered around the Christmas tree and exchanged gifts. Both Father's bayberry candles and her dresses were welcomed. She sat on the floor with Nora snuggled in her lap. She couldn't resist squeezing her little sister, knowing that their time together was short.

❦

Eliza woke the next morning to a churning stomach that could be attributed to only one thing. Before the day ended, she would see Ralph.

Esther's father and mother came early with their seven children and more than enough food for everyone. Eliza grabbed her friend Grace in a welcoming hug. "It seems like ages since I saw you last."

Grace squeezed Eliza. "What do you mean, 'seems like'? It has been ages." She pulled away and looked at her friend. "This is the lonesomest place ever with you gone. What's it like where you live? You've got to tell me all about it."

The girls wandered off arm in arm, falling into the easy friendship they had known before. Eliza spent the morning close to Grace, watching and listening for Ralph. Each step on the porch or opening of the door caused her heart to quicken, but he still had not come by midmorning.

"Is that a wagon I hear?" Vickie pulled the kitchen curtains back.

Cora looked over her shoulder. "It's Ivy and Mr. Reid." She turned to Eliza.

"They have the sweetest little boy."

Eliza saw Ivy, still seated in the wagon, hand down a blanket-clad bundle to her husband. "I can't see him. Ivy looks well, though."

"I think you'll appreciate the change in her, too." Cora laid a hand on Eliza's shoulder. "Becoming a mother made her a different person. Of course, the real change came when Ivy accepted Jesus last month."

"Oh, that's wonderful!" Eliza smiled as Ben opened the door.

Ivy's long, shiny black hair was done in a braided coil on top of her head. Her carriage rivaled that of a queen as she stepped into the house with a warm smile. "Ben, it's good to see you."

Ben nodded to Ivy and shook hands with her husband. "Good to see both of you, too. All three of you." He lifted the baby's tiny hand in his large one. "This little fellow gets bigger every time I see him."

Cora stepped forward to greet her sister-in-law with a quick hug. "Ivy, I'm so glad you came. Now Eliza can see you while she's here and get to meet my nephew."

Eliza started to shake hands with Ivy but was surprised when she received a hug instead. "You've given us all a nice Christmas gift by coming home for a visit."

"Thank you, Ivy." Eliza didn't know what to make of the changes she could already see. Ivy had always been beautiful, but now a look of radiance surrounded her.

As the Reid family mingled with the others, Eliza stole a quick glance through the window across the field to the woods.

"I think we're ready to set the table." Vickie's voice put Eliza back to work.

Several minutes later, Eliza stood at the end of the table with Grace and counted the place settings. "Will there be enough room for everyone? We squeezed in ten places here at the table. What about the others?"

"Howdy, folks." Ralph's cheerful voice rang out, sending a chill down Eliza's back. "Reckon you'uns thought we wasn't gonna make it."

"No, we knew long as there was food awaitin' you'd git here, Ralph," Aaron greeted his brother.

Eliza stood, her hands gripping the back of the chair in front of her.

"Eliza." Vickie's hand felt gentle on her shoulder. "We can eat in shifts or spread out into the other end. It's warm enough so the older children can eat outdoors."

Eliza nodded. Her senses numb, she heard the hum of conversation mingling with childish shouts. Yet through it all, Ralph's voice sent waves of warmth to her face. She turned slowly, hoping her cheeks were not as red as they felt.

He stood, as handsome as ever, talking with the other men. She almost hated him for being so good-looking. Then his eyes lifted to hers, holding her gaze for a heartbeat. She turned away. She was glad when the men moved outside.

"Do you mean you walked with the baby? I figured you'd hitch that old o: up to something." Ivy took the baby from Anna.

"Ralph broke the axle on that wagon you gave him, and he's never gotten around to fixing it." Anna shrugged. "It wasn't so bad, though. Ralph carried the baby part of the way."

"Oh!" Ivy's foot hit the floor. "Sometimes I have trouble believin' Ralph' my brother." Her voice softened as she turned back to Anna. "Mr. Reid and I will take you and the baby home."

"Thank you, Ivy." Anna's pale blue eyes looked tired. "I'm sorry we didn' bring anything. Ralph said not to. He said it'd be too hard to carry."

"He was right." Cora smiled at her sister-in-law.

Eliza kept her distance from both Ralph and Anna. In the crowded house it wasn't hard, yet their presence seemed more real to her than those with whom she visited.

The men and children came inside, and then Father prayed. The children took heaping plates to the porch, while the women relaxed in the parlor end of the large room to feed the babies, and the men sat at the table.

Eliza vied for the privilege of helping Nora. She soon found there was little she could do as Nora insisted on feeding herself.

But Ralph didn't appear to have the independence of a two year old. As Anna fed mashed potatoes to their nine-month-old son, Eliza heard him call his wife.

"Hey, woman!" His voice carried over the steady hum of voices. "Get me some coffee."

Anna set the baby on the floor and made her way to the kitchen.

Aaron looked across the table at his brother. "Why don't you get it yourself? Ain't you got legs?"

Ralph grinned. "Sure do." He nodded toward his wife. "See 'em comin'?"

Aaron's dark brows drew together. "One of these days, Ralph, somebody's gonna set you down."

Ralph grinned and took the coffee Anna handed him.

Anna had her baby cuddled in her arms, nursing him, when Ralph called again. "I'm needin' some of that pie, woman."

Ivy jumped up, handing her baby to Cora. She looked at Anna. "Doesn't he even know your name?"

Anna sighed. "It's just his way."

Ivy snorted. "You sit still. I'll take care of my lazy brother."

Eliza watched Ivy stalk to the sideboard at the far end of the kitchen. She picked up a pie and headed for Ralph. She lifted a piece of blackberry pie and slapped it upside down on Ralph's plate, juice splattering everywhere.

Her softly spoken words barely reached the women. "I know you're too lazy to scratch your own itch, Ralph, but if you bother Anna again, you'll be eatin' the rest of your food off your lap."

Ralph looked up at his sister in surprise. "What got your back up? Cain't a man eat in peace?"

"Just be sure that's what you do. And let Anna have some peace, too." Ivy rejoined the women, took her baby from Cora, and sat back down.

Anna gave her a wan smile. "Thank you, Ivy."

"I don't know why you put up with him." Ivy shook her head. "If Mr. Reid did me that way, I'd be hurt plumb through."

Anna shrugged. "I don't mind."

The women had to clean the table before they could eat and then clean again when they finished. Esther peered into the water bucket. "We're out of water for the dishes. I guess I'd better ask one of the men to get some."

"I'll go," Eliza said. A trip to the well by herself would be a welcome relief.

She picked up the empty bucket and, threading her way through men and smaller children, went outdoors. The cool air against her face felt good. She could see Lenny and Nicholas playing with the Newkirk children. Their childish laughter filled the air. She envied them their innocence.

Eliza lowered the water bucket into the well until she heard it splash and sink. She tugged on the rope to pull it up. When Ralph's voice startled her, she dropped the rope, turning to find herself less than a foot from him.

At the sound of the bucket hitting the water again, Eliza swung back and grabbed the rope.

"I said howdy, Eliza."

She fought to control the pounding of her heart.

"Ain't ya gonna say nothin'?" Ralph persisted.

Eliza set the full bucket on the rim of the well and faced him. "Hello, Ralph. It's nice to see you again."

A familiar grin spread across his face. "It's right nice seein' you, too."

Ralph was handsome, and he knew it. She stood under his spell, unable to control her heart.

"Come walk with me a ways. I'm full as a tick." He reached out.

She started to take his hand; then, as if a fog lifted, she saw him as she'd never seen him before. He needed a shave and a haircut. A bath wouldn't hurt. He had a wife, yet he asked another woman to walk with him. He was lazy and inconsiderate, with no respect for his wife.

The image of James Hurley filled her mind. He worked hard at his job. He was always clean about his person and in his speech. James was a Christian. Ralph was not. How could she have spent so much time yearning for a man who could never be faithful to anyone, not even his own wife?

She shook her head. "I don't think so, Ralph."

"Come on, Eliza. It'll be like old times." He grinned his most persuasive. "I missed you."

A sudden flash of anger struck her. "In case you hadn't realized, you're the one who up and got married."

"Now, Eliza, you know that weren't my idea."

She gave him a withering look. "I feel sorry for Anna. I wouldn't go across the yard with you, Ralph. Go back inside and get your wife if you want someone to walk with."

She pivoted away from him toward the well, shutting him once and for all out of her life. Freedom such as she hadn't experienced for almost a year released her heart.

She picked up the full bucket of water, turned around, and shoved it at him, splashing the front of his shirt. "Here, take this to the house so we can wash dishes. It'll make a good impression on your neighbors—and your wife."

Not waiting for him to talk his way out of it, Eliza went to the house. Happier than she'd been in a long time, she announced, "Ralph's bringing the water."

Ralph followed her with the bucket balanced in his right hand, a frown on his face.

Ivy laughed. "I don't know how you did that, Eliza, but you'd better tell Anna your secret."

Eliza smiled. "Oh, Anna, Ralph told me he wanted to go on a walk. Why don't you go? There's enough of us to do these dishes and watch your baby for you, too."

Anna's tired eyes shone as they met her husband's. He looked from Eliza to Anna, and a good-natured grin lit his face. "Guess I know when I'm whipped."

Anna took his hand. "Since I don't have to walk home, I'd be proud to go with you, Ralph."

Chapter 7

Winter remained mild with little snow. In the months following their brief visit, Eliza missed her family even more. Each day she longed for the time when Nora could come to Springfield where she belonged. Yet she had much to be thankful for. No longer did Ralph's image haunt her. How could she have thought she loved such a lazy, faithless oaf?

"Spring's just around the corner."

Eliza turned from the dishes at her father's voice.

"It doesn't look much like it." She glanced toward the window where the bare oak branches stood out cold and forlorn. "Of course, no more snow than we've gotten, it hasn't felt like winter, either."

"That's true." He grinned. "I ran into Miss Fraser downtown." He pulled out a chair and sat down. "Miss Fraser has decided the perfect way to raise money for the school would be a box social."

"When will it be?"

"She wasn't sure. The first month without an *r* in it, I think she said." He grinned at Eliza. "I've been thinking. You'll need a new dress to wear. Why don't you pick something nice out and take it to your seamstresses?"

"That sounds like a good idea." Eliza laughed with her father.

⚜

The box social was set for the first day of May. Eliza woke early to prepare a tempting meal. A young fryer from the chicken coop went into her skillet, and potatoes boiled in a pan on the stove. She decided to make two blackberry tarts for dessert. Once they were in the oven, the potato salad could be made.

She tied the handles of her wicker basket together with a bright red hair ribbon, then stood back to admire her work. She nodded with satisfaction as her father came into the kitchen.

"Are you ready to go? I've got the buggy hitched."

Eliza smiled. "Oh, so we're going in style today."

"Of course." Father reached for her basket. "We don't want anything to happen to this." He lifted it, pretending to almost drop it. "What have you got in here? It weighs a ton."

"Oh, Father." Eliza laughed. "I know it isn't that heavy. It's just potato salad, chicken, and tarts."

"Can we go now?" Lenny ran into the kitchen, slamming the door behind him. "I'm starving."

"Which reminds me." Father set Eliza's basket back on the table. "Did you fix enough for Lenny?"

"Of course." Eliza stepped to the cook table and picked up another box. "This is for you and Lenny. It's a good thing you said something, because I almost forgot it."

Father took the box in one arm and carried the basket in the other. As he went out the door, he grinned down at his son. "Looks like you'll have plenty, Lenny. I'll be eating some other lady's cooking today."

Eliza's heart sank as she followed him to the buggy. She thought he had lost interest in Mrs. Hurley. By the time he parked among the other wagons and buggies, she decided that if there were any way possible to keep him away from Mrs. Hurley, she would do it.

Eliza's feet slowed as she neared the table set under a tree in the middle of the yard. Mrs. Hurley stood behind the table holding a white box with a sprig of goldenrod tied on the top. Eliza watched her place it on the table and walk away.

Eliza walked around the table. She set her basket in front of Mrs. Hurley's box. Then in one quick motion, she pushed the box to the center of the table between two others. To make sure it was one of the last auctioned off, she covered it with her own basket.

"Are you guarding the food, or did you just get here?" A voice at her elbow startled Eliza.

"Oh, Kathrene. And Mary. I didn't see you come up." Eliza smiled at her friends. She held out her skirt in a curtsy. "How do you like my new dress?"

Mary straightened the collar in a motherly gesture. "I do believe you look prettiest in blue."

"Thank you." Eliza watched as her friends added their colorful boxes to the growing pile on the table. "Everyone will want to eat with you. Your boxes are so pretty and clever."

"Well, they aren't so pretty underneath. That's why we covered them with fabric scraps." Kathrene adjusted the ribbon on hers. "Of course, the food is delicious since Mother wouldn't let me help."

"I believe they're about to begin." Mary touched Kathrene's arm. "Let's move to the shade of that tree."

Eliza saw her father nearby talking to James and his mother. Her emotions churned as she watched. Then her eyes shifted to Mary. Maybe she could talk Father into buying Mary's dinner. A smile sat on Eliza's lips. It might work.

After the minister prayed, the auction began. One after another, the boxes sold, and the couples separated from the others to share the contents.

Eliza saw James and Mrs. Hurley walk away from her father. Seizing the opportunity, she stepped to his side.

Father grinned at her. "See that big box on the end? I'll bet it's got a good meal inside."

Eliza had no idea to whom it belonged, and she didn't want to take the chance. She shook her head. "No, just because it's big doesn't mean anything. Look at those two on the other side."

"In brown paper?"

"No, in calico. One is Kathrene's, and the other is her mother's. I know they'll be good."

"Your seamstresses?" The tone of his voice made it sound as if a woman couldn't do two things well.

"I'll have you know Mrs. Kowski is a good cook," Eliza announced.

"In that case, I'd better buy her box." Father was joking, but Eliza grasped his words as a lifeline.

She smiled. "Oh yes. You will, won't you? I know you won't regret it." The auctioneer picked up the one next to it and began his chant.

A frown touched Father's forehead. "Which lady is Mrs. Kowski?"

"She's standing over there by that tree with Kathrene."

He looked where she indicated, and his eyes widened. "Do you mean the two little redheaded women? I've seen them at church and thought they were sisters. Which one's the mother?"

Eliza laughed. "Mrs. Kowski is on the right."

Father turned back without a word as the auctioneer picked up one of the fabric-covered boxes. Eliza nudged him. "That's it, Father. That's Mrs. Kowski's."

"Now what am I bid for this pretty box. Why, if the food inside's half as good as the covering, it oughta be worth a dollar. How about it? Do we hear a dollar?"

Father raised his hand. "I'll bid fifty cents."

"I got fifty cents. Do I hear seventy-five?"

Eliza held her breath. If Father didn't get Mary's box, there would be nothing she could do to stop him from buying Mrs. Hurley's.

After bidding it up to one dollar and a quarter, the auctioneer stopped. "Sold to the gentleman who keeps us in light." Father claimed his meal amid laughter.

"I believe I just bought your box, ma'am." He offered his arm to Mary.

Eliza was surprised to see a faint blush touch Mary's cheeks. She smiled up at him and slipped her hand under his arm. "Perhaps we should find a place to eat, then."

Kathrene giggled as they walked away without a backward glance. "Well,

well, imagine my mother walking out with a man after all these years."

Eliza stared after the departing couple. Her victory left a bitter taste. "What do you mean, walking out? This isn't a social engagement. We're here to raise money for the school."

Kathrene's eyebrows raised. She turned back, clasping her hands. "Look, my box is next."

"Yes, and there's Charles Wingate waiting with a smug expression on his face." Eliza inclined her head toward the young, well-dressed gentleman. "We know who you'll be eating with, don't we?"

Kathrene just smiled.

"Well, looky here. If there isn't another pretty one." The auctioneer held up Kathrene's box. "Let's see if we can start this one at a dollar. How about it?"

Charles's hand shot up. "I'll bid a dollar."

"Make it one-fifty." A stranger spoke from the edge of the crowd.

"One-fifty it is. Do I hear two?"

Charles nodded.

"Two and a quarter." The stranger's dark eyes flashed a challenge.

"Two-fifty." Charles ignored the auctioneer.

Kathrene's face flushed as she watched the two men battle over her box. Eliza nudged her. "Who is he?"

Kathrene shrugged. "I've never seen him before."

"Well, he wants your box awfully bad." Eliza stared openly at the tall young man. His dark brown hair blew across his forehead in a gust of wind. Eliza could see that he was quite handsome.

Charles called out, "Five dollars."

The stranger bowed toward his opponent. "Enjoy your meal."

Charles smiled and nodded. He held out his hand to Kathrene. "Let's find a quiet place to eat."

Eliza watched Kathrene glance over her shoulder toward the stranger. He caught her gaze and smiled.

After a couple more boxes sold, the auctioneer picked up Eliza's basket. "A finer looking container than this couldn't be found today, gentlemen. I hear tell the contents are just as fine. What'll you give for a chance at this good meal?"

"A dollar." Again the voice of the stranger called out.

Eliza's heart quickened. Would her basket go as high as Kathrene's? She glanced toward James. Would he counterbid?

He stood in a group of men, his arms crossed. His eyes met hers. He grinned and shook his head. Her face flamed. The nerve of him. She hadn't asked him to bid on her basket. She turned her back to him.

"I was told you are the young lady I'm to eat with." A deep voice by her side spoke.

Eliza looked into the stranger's deep brown eyes. She'd been so busy fuming about James that she hadn't realized her basket sold. Without thinking, she asked, "How much did you pay?"

His eyes twinkled as his lips lifted in a lopsided grin. "Exactly one-fifth of my present assets."

At her blank look, he took her arm to lead her away. "This day finds me a poor man, Miss. . . ?"

"Jackson." Her heart quickened at his masculine good looks. "Eliza Jackson."

"Miss Jackson. I paid one dollar for your basket and from the weight. . ." He lifted it toward his nose and sniffed. "And the aroma, I'd say I got a bargain."

Her face grew warm as her lashes lowered. "You flatter me, Mr. . . " She looked up at him. "I don't know your name."

"Stephen Doran, Miss Jackson."

❧

Kathrene lowered her coffee cup and smiled at Eliza. "The box social yesterday was a success, wasn't it?"

Eliza stared across the kitchen table at her friend. "A success?"

Disaster would be a better word. James hadn't bid on her basket. Stephen Doran's bid was the only one she got, and then when they joined Kathrene and Charles, he scarcely noticed her. She couldn't even bring herself to think of her father and Mary.

Eliza tried to not listen as Kathrene chatted about how much her mother had enjoyed Father's company.

One thing was certain. Mary had kept Father away from Mrs. Hurley. The entire afternoon, Eliza had seen him only once when he'd told her he was giving her friend a ride home and would come back for her and Lenny.

"Don't you think so, Eliza?" Kathrene's voice cut into her angry musings.

"Think what?"

"Stephen Doran. Don't you think he is quite handsome?" Kathrene's green eyes sparkled.

Eliza stood and walked to the sink. "You know he only bought my box so he could get close to you."

"Why, Eliza!" Kathrene's eyes widened. "Have you taken a fancy to Mr. Doran?"

Eliza let out a short laugh. "How could I take a fancy to someone who spoke no more than two sentences to me? I notice he found plenty to say to you, though." She crossed her arms. "Didn't you feel sorry for Charles? I'm sure he felt as left out as I did."

"Left out!" Kathrene jumped up, setting her coffee cup on the table with a loud *thunk*. "I think you're jealous."

"Jealous?" Past hurts and frustrations boiled in Eliza, spilling over into

177

words she didn't mean. "How could I be jealous of you? I have everything I want right here." Her hand swept out. "You can have your Stephen, and Charles, and James, and every other man in town if you want them. I certainly don't."

"And you think I do?" Kathrene's eyes flashed. Her freckles stood out against her white face. "If that's what you think of me, I won't trouble you with my presence."

Kathrene wrenched the kitchen door open and stomped through the parlor. The bang of the front door echoed through Eliza's head, accusing her.

A verse from the Bible came to her mind. "For jealousy is the rage of a man: therefore he will not spare in the day of vengeance." Tears welled in her eyes. Kathrene was right. She was jealous.

Before she could move, the door opened and Kathrene peeked around the edge. "I'm sorry, Eliza. May I come back in?"

Eliza nodded, meeting her embrace.

"I shouldn't let my temper get away from me," Kathrene said.

"No, I started the whole thing because my pride was hurt by a stranger we'll probably never see again." Eliza wiped her eyes.

"Let's agree that no man will ever come between us," Kathrene said.

Eliza nodded.

❧

"We've been invited to dinner at the Kowskis' Sunday after church," Father announced that evening. His wide grin gave him a boyish look.

Sunday at the Kowskis' was all Eliza had feared it would be. Her father and Mary kept up a lively conversation about church happenings, discussing the sermon that morning and their hopes for the young man who came forward for prayer.

Lenny remained quiet throughout the meal except when he asked for more to eat. Eliza frowned at him, but he didn't notice. When he finished his second helping, she picked up her own and Lenny's plates. "I'll wash the dishes, and then we need to be getting back home, don't you think, Father?"

He groaned and patted his stomach. "I don't know if I can move. You've outdone yourself on this meal, ma'am." He smiled at Mary. "It was even better than the box social."

"Thank you." She gave him a warm smile. "I enjoy cooking."

Eliza stood and moved to the wash table. Mary's hand on her arm stopped her. "Leave the dishes to Kathrene and me. You're our guest."

Kathrene laughed. "Yes, Eliza. I may not be able to cook, but I can wash dishes."

Eliza smiled before turning to her father. "Don't you think we should be going? I'd like to rest before church tonight." She stepped toward the door.

Father pushed his chair back and stood. "Come on, Lenny. You heard your sister." He looked at Eliza with an affectionate smile. "I don't know what I'd do without my little girl. She's taken over the running of the house and Lenny and me." He patted her shoulder. "Does a real good job, too."

She looked up at him with accusing eyes. "Thank you, Father, but Mother was a good teacher."

Mary met her stony gaze with a warm smile. "Your mother must have been a wonderful woman to have raised such a beautiful daughter."

Eliza's lashes lowered. "Thank you, Mary. Yes, my mother was a wonderful woman."

But was she the only one who thought so? Father seemed to have forgotten his late wife as his interest in Mary grew. At church that evening Father sat beside Mary.

Chapter 8

Eliza watched her father's relationship with Mary develop and knew she could only blame herself. One day, toward the middle of June, he came into the chandler shop and told her Mary had agreed to become his wife.

After he left, Eliza stood in the middle of the floor while the words *He doesn't mean it* kept running through her mind.

"Did I catch you daydreaming?" James's voice penetrated her befuddled brain.

"What do you want?" Did he always have to catch her at a disadvantage?

"I have a question for your father."

"He isn't here." Eliza didn't want to be rude to James, but she couldn't seem to stop.

"It's a good thing you don't have any customers." James lounged against the counter.

Eliza turned her full gaze on him for the first time since he came into the shop. "Why?"

A slow grin spread his mouth. His eyes twinkled merrily. "Because, Miss Jackson, an old grouch like you would drive a less brave person away. What's got your back up today?"

Her hands clenched at her sides. "My father."

Sandy-colored eyebrows arched above his gray eyes. "Your father?"

"He says he's getting married."

"To Mrs. Kowski?"

She nodded. Tears filled her eyes. "Oh, James. . ." Her voice broke, and she found herself leaning against his chest. His arms encircled her as the tears fell.

After awhile she stepped back and blew her nose. "I'm sorry. I don't usually cry in public."

"No one's here but me." James smiled tenderly at her. "Are you going to be all right now?"

She tried a smile of her own. "I don't think I'll ever be all right with my father remarrying. But I'm okay now. Thank you."

"I guess I'd better get back to work then." James moved to the door. "When your father comes back, would you tell him I need to ask him something?"

She nodded.

He opened the door. "And, Eliza. . ."

She looked at him.

"If there's anything I can do, you know where to find me."

When her father returned, Eliza told him James had been looking for him. He went to the cooperage and stayed there the rest of the day.

A couple of days later Eliza came into the house from the garden with her apron full of new potatoes and green onions. Father and Lenny sat at the kitchen table.

"You mean I get to stand up in front of the church with you?"

"That's right." Father smiled at his son. "I think you're old enough to do that, don't you?"

Eliza tried to ignore them as she set the vegetables out on her work counter. Lenny didn't understand what it would do to their lives if Father remarried. Eliza picked up a potato, washed it in a pan of water, and began scrubbing the soft skin off.

"What about Eliza?" Lenny asked. "She gonna do somethin', too?"

"Of course." Eliza could feel her father looking at her, but she refused to turn around. "Mary wants Eliza and Kathrene to stand beside her to demonstrate that we'll all be one family." Father cleared his throat. "Why don't you run along so I can talk to Eliza now?"

"Okay." Lenny slammed the door on his way out.

Eliza stiffened when her father moved to her side.

"I'd like for you to be happy for us, Eliza." Father's voice was low and pleading.

A flush moved over Eliza's body. So Father knew how she felt. She sighed. She never had been good at keeping her feelings to herself. "I don't want you to marry her, Father. How can you replace Mother so easily?"

Her father flinched as if she had hit him. "I loved your mother. I still love her memory and always will. Mary is not a replacement for Mother. I will never forget your mother, Eliza. But I love Mary for herself, and I intend to marry her for that reason."

"I don't want you to marry her, Father," Eliza repeated with stubborn determination.

When her declaration met with silence, she turned toward him. The saddest look Eliza had ever seen covered his face. "I love you very much, Eliza, and I'm sorry you feel this way; but in all honesty, I have a perfect right to remarry. I'm trusting God that in time you'll accept it. In the meantime, Mary is waiting for you to pick out your dress."

Shame for her thoughts and words filled her heart. Still, she could not bring herself to accept her father's decision to remarry. "I don't need a new dress."

Father frowned. "Go to Leach's this afternoon and get some fabric to take to Mary. She's got enough to do without waiting until the last minute to make your dress."

Eliza knew she had pushed her father far enough. She nodded and turned back to her vegetables.

❧

Eliza walked to town that afternoon, kicking at every rock in her path. She crossed the square and entered Leach's General Store.

"Good afternoon, Miss Jackson," Mr. Leach greeted her. "What can I do for you?"

"I'd like to look around, if you don't mind."

"Not at all. Make yourself at home." He turned back toward the door as the bell rang again.

Eliza wove her way through the barrels and counters of merchandise toward the stacks of fabric along the far wall. She held a blue silk up to her face.

"That's very beautiful," Mrs. Wingate spoke beside her.

Eliza lifted her head in surprise. She hadn't heard anyone approach. "Yes, it is."

"I understand your father and Mary Kowski will be married in a few weeks."

Eliza shrugged. "Yes, I suppose so."

Mrs. Wingate laid a sympathetic hand on Eliza's arm. "Don't you think your father ever gets lonely?"

"He has Lenny and me. Why would he need anyone else?"

"You won't always live at home." Mrs. Wingate smiled. "Eliza, many older people who have lost their spouses remarry for companionship and to share the burden of living."

Eliza remembered her father's confession that he had eaten downtown before she and Lenny came. He loved Mary's cooking. Surely, Father's marriage would be one of convenience. When Mrs. Wingate left, Eliza turned back to the fabric with a lighter heart.

Mary finished Eliza's dress the day before the wedding. When she went to pick it up, Kathrene met her at the door. "Mother went to town with your father, but I guess you already knew that."

"No." Eliza frowned, hurt that Kathrene knew her father's whereabouts when she didn't.

Kathrene pulled her inside. "Come and see what I've got." She pointed at a small round table by the window. An assortment of wildflowers filled the vase sitting in the center.

"Where did you get those?"

Kathrene blushed. "Do you remember Mr. Doran, the young man who bought your box at the social?"

How could she forget?

"He gave them to me." Her voice dropped to a whisper. "He asked me to walk out with him."

"You didn't. . . ?"

Kathrene shook her head. "No, of course not. We know nothing about him."

"What about Charles?"

Kathrene flashed a smile. "What of Charles? He's a good friend, nothing more."

Eliza followed her into the bedroom, where her dress lay across the bed. She couldn't help noticing the sparse furnishings in the small cabin. Kathrene and her mother shared the double bed that took up most of the floor space in the small room. Her bedroom was twice the size of theirs.

Eliza scarcely noticed her dress as she looked around the small cabin. Her eyes rested on the cracked chinking in the walls, and she wondered how the women survived the cold winter winds. Mary had good reason to marry her father.

She smoothed the billowing blue silk skirt and smiled at Kathrene. "It's very lovely, as is all your work. I'll wear it proudly when I stand beside you tomorrow."

❀

"Dearly beloved, we are gathered together. . ."

It was a lie—the five of them standing up together as one family. Eliza tried to forget where she was. She did fine until the minister turned to her father.

"Wilt thou love her, comfort her, honor, and keep her, in sickness and in health; and, forsaking all others, keep thee only unto her, so long as ye both shall live?"

A hard, empty ball expanded inside her stomach. Surely she had never missed her mother more than at that moment.

As in a dream, Eliza watched her father slip a gold wedding band on Mary's finger. The minister said, "I now pronounce you man and wife. What, therefore, God hath joined together, let not man put asunder."

Eliza bowed her head with the others as the minister prayed, but she did not anticipate his words when the prayer ended.

The minister nodded to her father. "You may kiss your bride now."

Father gathered Mary into his arms. Eliza stared hard at the floor. How could he kiss her? Mercifully, the moment was over quickly.

Kathrene elbowed her. "We're supposed to follow the bride and groom outside."

"How wonderful! You two girls are sisters now." Mrs. Wingate stopped them near the back door. "Congratulations."

"Thank you, Mrs. Wingate," Kathrene answered for them both.

Charles stepped around his mother as she turned away. He smiled at Kathrene. "May I have the pleasure of your company for dinner?"

"We would be honored, wouldn't we, Eliza?"

"You go. I'll eat alone." Eliza dropped Kathrene's arm and slipped outside into the fresh air. She had never felt so alone in her life.

She crossed her arms, leaning her shoulder against a tree. A slight breeze ruffled her hair. She lifted her face to it, closed her eyes, and let it cool her cheeks.

"Eliza," James's low voice intruded.

Again he appeared at the worst possible time. She opened her eyes to look at him. "What do you want?"

He laughed. "Your use of the English language never ceases to amaze me. Are you always so stingy with words, or is it just with me?"

She sighed. "I'm sorry. It isn't you."

He grinned. "Good. I wanted to ask you to eat with me." His voice lowered. "I know you're having a hard time today. I'd like to help if I can."

Eliza gave a short laugh. "I don't think that's possible. They're already married."

"Sometimes having a friend helps."

"A friend?" Eliza hadn't thought of James as a friend before and wasn't sure she wanted to. She suddenly realized that "friend" didn't sound like enough.

At his nod, she smiled. "All right."

She looked up, saw Vanda approaching, and called to her. "I was afraid you wouldn't be here."

Vanda's laugh brightened Eliza's mood. "Me? Miss my best friend's father's wedding? Not on your life."

She looked at James.

Eliza moved away from the tree. "James is eating with us. Is that all right with you?"

Vanda shrugged. "Sure, but I think we'd better be going if we're going to get anything."

They reached the grounds set aside for the dinner just as the minister prayed. Mary and Father led the line and then sat at a special table prepared especially for them. A white cotton tablecloth covered the rough wood, giving the table an elegant look.

Vanda peered closely at her friend. "Do you think you'll like having a new mother?"

Eliza's eyes narrowed. "You mean stepmother, don't you?"

Vanda nodded. "I guess that answers my question."

"I don't mean to be so snappish. This whole thing has been a strain."

"Maybe we should get in line." James touched Eliza's arm.

Lenny and Cletis ran past. "Hey, you gonna stand there and let all the food get ate up? Come on. We'll let you get in front of us."

Vanda lifted her eyebrows. "I wonder why they're so interested in us all of a sudden."

They wound around tablecloths spread on the ground picnic style and people with their plates piled high. Lenny and Cletis stepped back for each of the stragglers until the last guest was in line.

Vanda frowned. "They must be up to something."

James laughed. "They're boys. Boys are almost always up to something."

"I suppose you know from experience?" Eliza realized she felt better. James was right; she had needed to be with friends.

"Of course." He grinned down at her, making her heart do flip-flops.

Eliza smiled but agreed with Vanda. She knew her brother. Sometimes Lenny was more than she could handle, and as much as she liked Vanda, she realized his behavior had gotten worse under Cletis's influence.

As Eliza filled her plate, she saw Lenny and Cletis scramble from under the table where Mary and Father sat. The boys ran a short distance away. They stood behind a large oak tree, their hands stifling giggles, their eyes dancing in merriment.

She kept them in sight as she ate. She was certain they had pulled a prank on Father and Mary, but she couldn't think what it might be. With her attention divided, she kept up her end of a lively conversation with James and Vanda.

Vanda glanced over the crowd. "What happened to our brothers? I forgot to watch them."

Eliza nodded toward the oak tree. "They're standing over there." Even as she spoke, the merriment went out of the boys' faces. Lenny's eyes grew wide. Cletis grabbed his arm, pulling him back.

"What on earth are they doing?" Vanda sounded as puzzled as Eliza felt.

"Maybe we'd better find out what they've already done." Eliza looked toward the table where her father sat. Father and Mary were visiting with others who had joined them. Eliza let her gaze roam over the table, trying to find something out of place.

And then she saw it. A thin wisp of smoke curled upward from the end of the table. As she watched, the smoke disappeared in a sudden burst of flames.

"Fire!" Eliza's outcry created pandemonium. Father lifted Mary from her seat. With one arm around her, he tossed his glass of water on the flame. Others followed his lead as they scrambled back from the burning cloth.

"Cletis and Lenny did that, didn't they?" Vanda searched through the excited crowd. "Where are they?"

Eliza pointed. "They just ducked behind that tree."

The two girls set off in a run to catch their brothers. As angry as Eliza was at Lenny, she was even more angry with herself. She had known he was up to something, and she hadn't stopped him.

Vanda grabbed Cletis first and held tight in spite of his squirming attempts to escape. Lenny ran a few steps before Eliza caught his arm. He turned wide, fearful eyes on her. "We didn't mean to, honest."

"That's right. We didn't make any fire." Cletis tried to wrench out of Vanda's grasp. "Ow! You're hurtin' me."

"I'll hurt you a whole lot more if you don't tell the truth." As Vanda reached for a better grip on her brother, he jerked free. He stumbled from the sudden release, then took off running. Vanda turned a troubled face toward Eliza. "I hate to think what Poppa will do to him when he finds out. I'd better catch him." She left in a run, calling over her shoulder, "I'm sorry."

Eliza watched her for a moment before turning toward the crowd gathered around the table. She looked down at Lenny. "Well, are you going to tell me what happened, or would you rather tell Father?"

He shrugged his shoulders. "I told you we didn't mean to."

Eliza closed her eyes for a moment, then looked at her brother. "Lenny, you obviously did something, even if you didn't mean to. What did you do?"

He clamped his lips shut, looking defiantly up at her.

"All right, then." Anger welled up in Eliza as she pulled him toward their father.

Chapter 9

Lenny trembled beneath Eliza's hands. Her anger turned toward Cletis. How dare he run off and leave Lenny to take the blame for what he had instigated!

"Leonard Jackson, do you know what this is?" Father held a small object between his fingers.

Lenny nodded. "It looks like an old firecracker, sir."

"It's a firecracker, all right, but it's not old, and you know it." Father pointed a finger at Lenny. "Go to the buggy and wait until we come."

Lenny jerked from Eliza's grasp and ran. Eliza looked up, meeting the gray eyes of James Hurley. "I hope your father isn't too hard on Lenny."

"Why? Don't you think he deserves to be punished?"

He shrugged. "Probably, but I doubt there's a man here that hasn't pulled a stupid trick like that at some time in their lives. It's part of growing up."

"Trying to blow up the table your father is sitting at is more than a stupid trick."

James laughed. "That little firecracker wouldn't have done much more than make a big noise."

"But it didn't make any noise. Instead it made a fire." She crossed her arms. "You know, what's bad is that Cletis Von Hall got away, and he was probably the one who did it. Lenny was just with him."

James lifted his eyebrows. "In that case we'd better hope that Vanda doesn't tell her father what happened."

"Well, I should hope she would," Eliza said. "He deserves to be punished even more than Lenny."

"I suppose, but—"

"Eliza, are you ready to go?" Her father stood with his arm around Mary's waist. "Kathrene is coming later with Charles."

Eliza looked at James. "I guess I need to go."

He nodded. "I'll see you at church tonight." He turned and walked away.

※

As soon as they entered the house, Father laid a gentle hand on Eliza's shoulder. "Would you mind going upstairs? I need to talk to your brother alone."

Eliza sat on the stairs out of sight while her father decided Lenny's punishment. When Mary suggested he not play with Cletis for two weeks, she crept upstairs to her room.

Eliza felt the strain of the day especially at supper that evening. As soon as her father laid his spoon down, she pushed her chair back, picking up her bowl "I'll wash dishes."

"No, Eliza," Father said. "The dishes can wait. Mary and I have something to say."

Father looked first at Eliza, then Lenny, and finally Kathrene, before his eyes met Mary's. She nodded slightly.

He smiled at her and began. "Mary and I have decided it would be good for us to go away for a short time."

"Where are we goin'?" Lenny asked.

"Not all of us, son." Father ran his hand over his thinning hair in a nervous gesture. "I meant just Mary and me."

Lenny frowned. "What do you wanna do that for?"

Kathrene leaned forward, a smile on her face. "I think that's a wonderful idea. When will you be leaving?"

"In the morning." Father turned to her. "I just need to speak to James tonight, we'll pack a few things, and then try to get as early a start as we can tomorrow."

"Well, don't worry about us. We'll get along just fine." Kathrene shared a smile with her mother.

Eliza shrugged when her father's gaze met hers. "Sure, we'll be fine."

Father's hazel eyes darkened. He reached across the corner of the table to clasp her hand. His voice was soft. "Eliza, we're going after Nora."

Eliza sat in stunned silence until she pulled away from her father, her chair crashing to the floor as she sprang up and ran from the room, the dishes forgotten.

Emotions she didn't understand flooded her being as she stumbled up the stairs to her room. For almost a year she had planned to go with Father when he brought her sister home. Now Mary would be the one. Mary would take over her sister, her father, and even her house. She fell across the bed to release a torrent of tears into her pillow.

❀

Sometime later, a tap on the door brought Eliza upright. "Who is it?" Her voice sounded hoarse from crying.

"Kathrene. May I come in?"

Eliza scrambled from the bed and across the room to her washbasin. She splashed cool water on her face and blotted it with a towel. She moved to the door, smoothing her wrinkled dress with her hands.

If the remains of her crying bout were still on her face, Kathrene made no notice. She stepped into the room, a gentle smile the only evidence of her concern. "They sent me to tell you it's time to get ready for church."

"You're glad, aren't you?" Eliza struggled with the hooks on her dress.

"Glad about what?" Kathrene's hands felt cool against her back as she helped.

Eliza stood still to let Kathrene unfasten her dress. "All of it. Your mother. My father."

"In a way I am. Mother has been alone so long. I'm happy she has someone to love and to love her."

Eliza felt tears burn her eyes. "What about your father? Have you forgotten him? I haven't forgotten Mother and neither has my father. He'll never forget her. He'll always love her."

"Oh, Eliza, of course I haven't forgotten my father."

Eliza turned and saw the matching tears in Kathrene's eyes. "Mother will always love him. But I should hope there's room in her heart to love your father, too."

❧

The evening service passed in a blur until James stopped her after church. Concern softened his expression. "Are you all right, Eliza?"

"Do you know how many times you've asked me that in the time you've known me?"

He smiled. "No, it does appear to be a habit I'm developing."

"I don't know if I'll ever be all right again. When my mother died, my world was turned upside down. It just seems to get worse every day."

"I'd like to help if I. . ." His voice trailed off as Eliza's father placed a hand on his shoulder.

"Mr. Hurley, you are just the person I need to talk to."

Eliza backed away. She felt betrayed and cheated as her father made arrangements to return to their wilderness home without her.

When they got home, Mary turned toward Father's bedroom, her bonnet and their Bibles clutched in her arms. Eliza stared at her as she went through the door.

"Come on, Eliza." Kathrene tugged on her arm. "There's no towel in my room. Where do you keep them? Your father said he didn't know."

Eliza followed Kathrene up the stairs.

Kathrene led her to the guest room and stepped inside. Eliza pulled the middle drawer of the chest of drawers open to reveal neat stacks of towels and washcloths. She looked at the bed where Kathrene's dress of the afternoon sprawled where it had been thrown. A petticoat lay in a circled heap on the floor as if she had just stepped out of it. Even Cora hadn't been this careless with her things.

Kathrene pulled a washcloth and towel from the drawer and turned to the washbasin, a bright smile on her face. "This room is so wonderful. I've never had a room all my own before. And this is such a big, pretty room. I love it."

Somehow the idea that Mary had married Father for their house eased Eliza's pain.

❧

Eliza pushed her bedroom curtain aside and looked out. In the early morning light she watched her father's wagon move slowly out of the yard. A movement on the seat in front caught her eye. Father waved at her. Mary, sitting beside him, looked up and waved, too.

Eliza hadn't found it in her heart to see them off like Kathrene and Lenny had. As soon as breakfast was over, she had told them good-bye and retreated to her room. She lifted her hand for a moment and then let the curtain drop back into place.

She sank to her bed, where she stayed until a knock on her door interrupted her time of self-pity. "Eliza, please, may I come in?"

"What do you want?"

There was a moment's silence, and then Kathrene said, "It's Lenny. I can't find him."

"He's probably outside playing."

"I don't think so. He was in the house reading while I washed the breakfast dishes. I went out to feed the chickens, and when I came in, he was gone."

"Those chickens are mine. Father bought them for me." Eliza pulled the door open to glare at Kathrene.

"I know they're yours, Eliza. I was just feeding them." Kathrene's voice was soft. "I thought you might want some time alone this morning."

Eliza's gaze dropped to the floor, her conscience pricked.

"I've looked everywhere, Eliza. I don't know what else to do. Your father said Lenny was not to go anywhere without our permission. Don't you think we should do something?"

Eliza shrugged and met Kathrene's worried gaze. "He's probably run off to play with Cletis. He'll come home as soon as he gets hungry."

A spark of green fire lit Kathrene's eyes. "He's disobeying his father, and I'm not going to let him get away with it. We have a responsibility to see that Lenny obeys. If we don't stop him now, he won't listen to a thing we say the entire two weeks our parents are gone."

Finally Eliza nodded. "All right. Let me get my bonnet. I'll go downtown and see what I can find out." She turned back into the room.

"Shouldn't I go, too?" Kathrene followed her. "Isn't there someplace I could look?"

Eliza tied her bonnet under her chin. "No. I think you should stay here in case he comes back."

"I suppose you're right." Kathrene looked doubtful. "But if he isn't back by dinner, I'll go with you this afternoon."

Eliza laughed off Kathrene's concern. "Oh, don't worry, he'll be here when it's time to eat."

The midmorning sun warmed her back as she tried to imagine where little boys went on summer mornings. She knew they sometimes rolled wagon rims across the square. Maybe James had seen Lenny.

Eliza went to her father's shops. James was busy with a customer, so she stepped inside and waited.

After placing his order, the man left, nodding to Eliza. James looked up with a smile. "I didn't expect the pleasure of your company today. What can I do for you?"

"I'm looking for Lenny and thought you might have seen him."

James's smile disappeared. He shook his head. "No, I haven't seen him. Is something wrong?"

She shrugged. "Probably not. He just left home without permission."

"I'll close up shop and help you look."

"No, that's not necessary." She stepped back. "I'm sure he'll come home at noon to eat."

James shrugged. "All right. I'll keep an eye out. Maybe he'll come by."

"Thank you." She turned and ran from the shop. She asked Mr. Leach and looked everywhere she could think but didn't find him.

Kathrene and Eliza ate a hurried meal at noon. Eliza expected any moment to hear the front door open and see Lenny come in demanding food. But he didn't.

"Where should we go?" Kathrene placed her plate on the counter. She turned as Eliza started to speak. "And don't tell me I have to stay home again. I won't do it. I may be just a stepsister, but I care."

"All right, we'll go together." Eliza sighed. What if Lenny wasn't with Cletis? What if something terrible had happened? She didn't know where to look for him. Surely she had exhausted every possible place that morning.

"Where will we look?" Kathrene asked again.

"I guess we could go back to town." She stood and picked up her plate. "Maybe Mr. Leach has seen him since I was there."

But Mr. Leach shook his head. "No, I haven't seen him since church last night."

"Where do we go now?" Kathrene asked.

Eliza looked across the square at the cooperage. Should she check back with James? She knew he would willingly drop whatever he was doing to help them search. While she tried to decide, she saw Vanda walking toward them.

"There's Vanda. Maybe she knows something."

The girls met in the middle of the square.

"Have you seen Lenny?"

"Have you seen Cletis?" Both spoke at once.

"That settles it." Eliza sighed. "They're together, but where are they?"

"I don't know." Vanda frowned. "Cletis slipped out early this morning after my father left. I managed to keep his stupid prank yesterday quiet, but if he doesn't get back home before long, there'll be nothing I can do."

"Have you talked to Trennen? Maybe he has seen them." Eliza felt as if she were grasping for straws.

Vanda nodded. "I just came from the Wingates'. Where have you looked?"

Eliza's hand swept out in an all-inclusive gesture. "Everywhere we could think of. Do you know of any special places they might go?"

Vanda looked thoughtful. "Have you looked at the creek?"

"I didn't know there was a creek." Eliza's eyes grew wide. Until that moment she hadn't thought that Lenny might be hurt. "You don't think they've drowned, do you?"

"No, I didn't mean that." Vanda started across the square. "There's a creek just northwest of town. It has a quiet spot where the boys like to swim. As warm as it is today, they might be there."

The girls turned down the dirt road leading west out of town. Eliza sighed, and Kathrene looked at her. "It is terribly warm, isn't it?"

She nodded. "I understand if they went swimming in this heat, but Lenny's still in trouble."

"Cletis, too. It isn't much farther." Vanda pointed to their right. "Just beyond those trees."

Before they were through the trees, Eliza heard laughter. Her temper flared, and she ran into the clearing on the bank of the creek. Lenny was there, all right. So were three other boys, including Cletis. And all were stripped to the bare skin.

"Oh, my." Kathrene's soft gasp as she came up behind Eliza stopped the boys' horseplay, and all four dove under the water.

Cletis was the first to break the surface with a ferocious scowl. "Get outta here. Go on. Beat it." He hit the water toward them.

The other boys came up for air one at a time. Guilt sat on Lenny's face even as he frowned at Eliza. "Yeah. Go away." He copied his friend.

Eliza wasn't sure what to do. The boys' clothing was scattered along the bank where they had let it fall. She knew they couldn't come out of the water as long as the girls were there, yet how could they be trusted to come if someone didn't stay and enforce it?

Vanda planted her hands on her hips. "Cletis, if you don't get out of there, I'll come in and get you." She picked up some pants from a pile of clothing, then stepped to the edge of the creek, her feet just inches from the water. "Here, put these on."

"I can't. I'll get 'em all wet. What do we gotta get out of here for, anyhow?" Cletis asked. "We ain't hurtin' no one."

"Poppa's going to be home in a couple of hours, Cletis. You know that."

The change in Cletis's expression amazed Eliza. "Guess you guys heard. We gotta go home now."

At their outcry, he shrugged. "Can't help it. That's just the way things is. We'll come back tomorrow."

Eliza thought to herself, *Oh no, you won't.* She kept her opinion quiet, though, saving it until she had a firm grip on Lenny.

"We ain't gettin' outta here with you standin' there," Cletis yelled at his sister. "Go on. I'll be along shortly."

"All right. I'll go, but you'd better follow me home. And the rest of you better go on home, too."

As she talked, Vanda tossed Cletis's pants to the side. What happened next took them all by surprise. Vanda stepped backward, landing on loose rock. Her ankle twisted under her. Her arms flew up as if to embrace the creek, and she fell full length, face forward into the water.

The boys' hoots of laughter as Vanda struggled to right herself released Eliza from her stupor. She rushed to the water's edge, shouting at them to be quiet. "Don't you know Vanda could be hurt?"

She reached her hand toward Vanda. "Here, let me help you out."

Vanda sat in waist-deep water, her clinging skirts draped about her bent knees. Her face flamed as she struggled to her feet. "I can do it."

Eliza asked, "Can you make it to my house?"

At Vanda's nod Eliza turned to the boys, still watching with smirks on their faces. "As soon as we're gone, you get out of there and go home. Do you understand me?"

"We done said we would, didn't we?" Cletis answered for them all.

She turned away, knowing she would have to trust them. Vanda needed her immediate attention, and she wouldn't worry now that she knew where Lenny was.

The three girls set out, walking quietly until they were past the grove of trees. Then a giggle came from Vanda. Eliza looked at her in surprise. Their eyes met, and the merriment in Vanda's expression was contagious.

"I must have looked ridiculous sitting in that water." She grinned.

As Eliza nodded, laughter burst from both girls. Before long all three were laughing hysterically.

As they neared town, Kathrene gained control first. She spoke between giggles, "Honestly, I'm just glad you didn't get hurt."

"So am I." Vanda looked down at her dress. She held it away from her legs as she walked. "I feel stupid. Dunking myself that way." She grew sober. "Maybe I should go on home."

Kathrene shook her head. "It'll be no trouble for you to stop by our house and change."

Eliza led the way upstairs to her room while Kathrene headed for the kitchen to wash the neglected dishes from their meal.

Eliza crossed to the bed and spread the quilt over it. "When we discovered Lenny gone this morning, our housework was forgotten." She apologized for her unmade bed in the otherwise neat room.

"Your house looks wonderful to me." Vanda stood in the middle of the floor. "I'm afraid I may drip on your rug, though."

"Don't worry about it." Eliza opened the door to her wardrobe. She reached for one of the dresses Mary had made, but Vanda stopped her.

"How about this one instead?" Vanda pulled one of Eliza's oldest dresses from the wardrobe.

"Take one of these new ones."

"If I can't wear this one, I won't borrow any." A determined light shone in Vanda's eyes.

"All right, but I don't feel like much of a friend letting you wear that old thing."

"You're the best friend I've ever had, Eliza." Vanda turned away, peeling out of her wet dress.

Eliza laid some underclothes on the bed and reached to take the dress. "Here, I'll hang your clothes outside to dry." She opened the door and started through it when a large yellow and green bruise on Vanda's back caught her eye. Vanda's wet, tangled hair hung down, covering most of it.

She spoke before she thought. "What did you do to your back? It looks like someone took a stick to you."

Vanda looked over her shoulder at Eliza and laughed. "Don't be silly."

"There's a huge bruise on your back."

Vanda appeared to be puzzled. She tried to see her back by twisting around. "Maybe I fell on a rock in the creek."

"Maybe."

Eliza vaguely remembered seeing old bruises on Vanda's face and arms before, but she didn't pursue the subject; because at that moment the downstairs door slammed, and Lenny's voice called out, "I'm home now, and I hope you're satisfied. You just ruined a good afternoon for me."

"Whoa, fellow, I'd rephrase that if I were you."

Eliza's eyes grew wide as she recognized James's voice. "Your sister's not the one who took off without telling anyone where she was going."

Vanda grabbed up the undergarments and began pulling them on. "Oh dear. It must be getting late. I've got to get home before Poppa does."

Eliza barely heard her as she traced James's and Lenny's voices going into the kitchen. What was James doing here? Her heart rate increased as she closed the door and moved down the hall to the stairs.

Chapter 10

As Eliza carried Vanda's wet dress through the parlor, she saw Lenny curled up on the sofa, already engrossed in a book, munching a slice of bread. James straddled a chair in the kitchen. She didn't look at him, even though she could feel his eyes on her.

She pinned the garments to the clothesline, returned to the house, and walked back across the kitchen. James's voice, mocking, followed her into the parlor.

"Good afternoon, James. Thank you for closing up the shop while you looked for my little lost brother. You can't imagine how much I appreciate it."

Vanda ran down the stairs, her hair in wet ringlets down her back. "Eliza, thank you so much for the loan of this dress. I'll be especially careful with it." She pulled the front door open. "I've got to get home now. Cletis and Poppa will be wanting supper."

Eliza closed the door behind Vanda. She took a deep breath, then pushed the kitchen door open.

Eliza caught the twinkle in his eyes as James grinned at her. She turned away to hide her own smile. "Vanda's gone. She had to hurry home to fix supper for her father."

Kathrene dried her hands and hung the tea towel by the sink. "I guess she found some clothes to wear."

"Yes." Eliza nodded. "She took one of my oldest dresses. I couldn't get her to take a nicer one."

James cleared his throat noisily. Eliza turned to see a wide smile on his face. "Good afternoon, Eliza."

The corners of her mouth twitched. "Good afternoon, James. I've been so busy I haven't had time to tell you how much I appreciate the help you gave us in finding Lenny. I'm sure we couldn't have done it without you."

James stared at her. His smile faded and then came back with a laugh. He stood, shoving the chair under the table. "All right. Maybe I didn't find him, but I looked. When Mr. Leach said you still hadn't found him after dinner, I closed shop and looked everywhere I could think of. I just didn't think of the creek."

Eliza's conscience smote her as she listened to James's deep voice. "I'm sorry, James. I didn't realize. Really, I thank you for being concerned."

"That's all right." He stepped around Eliza to the door. "I'd better get back

195

to work. There are still a few hours left in this day."

He nodded toward Kathrene, his gaze returning to linger on Eliza. "I'll let myself out. Bye, Eliza. Kathrene."

❀

The day Father, Mary, and Nora were due home, Eliza left the dishes to Kathrene while she took the butter churn and a chair from the kitchen to the back porch. Lenny had behaved himself after the creek incident, but first one thing and then another had brought James to their door the last two weeks. First it was milk and now cream. He claimed his cow was giving more than they could use. And twice he had come about shop business. As if Eliza knew anything about making barrels. Mostly they'd just talked about nothing in particular before he went back to work. Eliza smiled, thinking how much she enjoyed his company.

She poured in the cream, dropped the wooden lid in place, and sat with her legs straddling the churn. As she worked, butter slowly emerged from the liquid while her arms grew tired. She lifted the lid to peer inside. Pale yellow clumps floated in the cream. Her butter was done.

She dropped the lid back into place at the sound of a wagon on the road. Her butter forgotten, she hurried from the porch and around the house. Father pulled back on the reins, bringing the wagon to a stop before jumping off to catch Eliza in a bear hug.

He pulled back and looked over her head. "I see the house is still standing."

She acted indignant. "Father, you know I'm quite capable of taking care of things."

He laughed as Kathrene and Lenny rushed from the house. "Why didn't you tell us they were back?" Kathrene admonished Eliza as she brushed past to give Father a quick hug. He then swept Lenny up and hugged him close.

Lenny's wide smile belied his protest. "Hey, I ain't no baby." His thin arms circled his father's neck and squeezed tight.

Mary, holding three-year-old Nora on her lap, watched her husband's homecoming with a smile before calling to him, "I'd like my share of hugs."

Father set Lenny down and reached up to circle her waist with his hands. "I was being selfish, wasn't I?"

"Just a little, but you're forgiven." She smiled down at him. "Why don't you take Nora first? I think Eliza is aching to get hold of her."

Nora was fine when Father handed her to Eliza, but the minute Mary's feet touched the ground, she began struggling to be free. "Mama. I want Mama." Her little arms reached toward Mary.

Eliza felt as if she'd been slapped. "Nora, don't you remember me?" She stroked the little girl's velvety face.

A wail mixed with cries for "Mama" was her answer. Nora's large brown eyes became puddles of distress, filling and overflowing down her cheeks. Nora strained against Eliza's hold, leaning her little body as far as she could toward Mary.

Mary reached for Nora. "I don't know what is the matter with her. It's really hard to tell what little ones are thinking."

Nora snuggled her head against Mary's shoulder and popped her thumb into her mouth.

Eliza saw the look of sympathy on Kathrene's face, and her heart hardened. This wouldn't have happened if she'd been allowed to go with Father.

Mary walked toward the house with Kathrene close beside her. They disappeared inside while Eliza stood watching.

Father patted Eliza's shoulder as he turned toward the wagon. "Don't worry about Nora. She'll come around. Remember, it's been a long time since she's seen you."

Eliza shrugged from his hand. She didn't want sympathy. She wanted her little sister. She went back to the butter she had left on the porch.

She soon had the butter wrapped and stored in the cellar and the buttermilk in a half-gallon jar ready to drink for breakfast. She was closing the cellar door when Father found her.

"So there you are. I've been looking for you." He grinned at her, slipping his arm around her shoulders. "I was beginning to think you'd disappeared."

She shook her head. "No, just working as usual. Mr. Hurley's cow is suddenly giving more than they can use. I made some butter."

Father laughed, giving her a quick hug. "That's my Eliza. One day you'll make some man a good wife. You're a lot like your mother, you know."

"I am?" Eliza looked up at her father. He couldn't have given her a nicer compliment.

"Yes, you are, more so than either Vickie or Cora." He sat on the back steps. "Here, sit beside me. I have some things to tell you."

Eliza's heart constricted at the serious look on his face. She sat beside him, turning so she could watch his expression as he talked.

His smile gentled, not lighting his face the way it usually did. "I've got letters from the girls for you."

"What's wrong?"

He sighed, looking off to the horizon before he answered. "It's Ben and Esther. On the first day of May, three months ago, they had a little girl. They named her Agnes Danielle. She died before the sun set that same day."

"Oh." The one word rushed out with the air Eliza had been holding. Her eyes filled with tears of sympathy for her brother and his wife. "How terrible."

"Ben and Esther are strong. Their faith in God will see them through."

As she thought of Ben and Esther's loss, her own problems seemed trivial.

If they could remain strong, so could she. She brushed at her eyes and stood. "I'm glad you told me. Maybe God will give them another baby."

"Yes, maybe so." Father stood and reached for the back door. "Come on inside, and I'll give you those letters. They wrote to Lenny and Kathrene, too."

Kathrene? Why would they write to her? She walked ahead of her father into the kitchen and took the letters from him. She smiled, holding them close to her heart. "I'll be in my room if you need me."

He grinned. "Don't worry. We won't bother you until you've finished reading."

"Thanks, Father." She reached up on her tiptoes to kiss him on the cheek. "I'm glad you're home." Then she turned and walked toward the parlor. She stopped, her hand on the door. "Father, what about the other two babies? Are they all right?"

"They're as fat and sassy as any two babies I've ever seen."

"And you're not proud of them?" She smiled at the obvious pride on his face.

"Of course I am. Now you get on upstairs and read your letters before I tell you everything that's in them."

Her smile faded when she caught sight of Kathrene on the sofa poring over the letters she had received. She looked up at Eliza, a wide smile on her lips. "You don't know how blessed you are to have sisters. All my life I wanted a sister, and now I have five."

Eliza forced a smile that she didn't feel and ran up the stairs to her room. She fell across her bed. She could hardly wait to read her letters. She placed them all in a neat stack to the side and reached for the first one.

As soon as Eliza opened her letter and saw the carefully printed script inside, she realized it was not from one of her sisters but from Grace Newkirk.

I miss our times together. I have no one to share my secrets with. My biggest news isn't much of a secret. Eliza, I'm going to be married. I wish you could stand with me at our wedding early next spring. I'll be Mrs. Jack Seymour. His family moved in this past spring. He's a wonderful Christian man. He's good, kind, and thoughtful. I know you'd love him, too, if you were here. (But not as much as I do!)

The ink on the page blurred as Eliza stared at it. So Grace was getting married. A gnawing pain pulled at her stomach.

She rolled over on her back, still clutching Grace's letter. Cora, Esther, and Ivy were all married, and now Grace had found the right man. Even Kathrene, who couldn't cook or keep a neat house, had two men clamoring for her attention.

A long, sad sigh escaped as she rolled back over. She read Esther's letter next. Like the woman who wrote it, it was filled with love and faith in God. Even her heartbreak over the loss of her baby was tempered by her faith.

A paragraph toward the end caught Eliza's eye.

Ben and I have been praying about God's will in our lives. We love it here in our cabin with most of our family around us. (You, Father, and Lenny would make our joy complete.) But it seems God is speaking to our hearts that He has work for us to do. Just as Father felt he must move on, so it seems, must we. We have talked to Brother Timothy, and Ben has written to the missionary alliance he recommended. Eliza, we are so excited that God has chosen us to be missionaries to the Indian people in Kansas Territory. We are preparing as much as we can now so we'll be ready to go next spring. From the way it looks now, we will be leaving here right after Grace's wedding. Isn't God good?

Eliza wiped tears from her eyes. Esther had just suffered the greatest loss a woman can have, yet there was no indication of self-pity in her letter. Instead it was filled with the wonder of God's love and of her desire to give herself to lost people. Eliza felt convicted of her own selfishness and lack of commitment.

She shrugged off the unwelcome mood and picked up Vickie's letter.

Hello, little sister, it seems forever since I've seen you. Can you imagine the surprise we all had when Father showed up with a wife? And what a wonderful woman! We fell in love with her immediately. Father said you introduced them. That must mean you love her as much as we do.

It didn't take long to see how much Father cares for her. I don't mean to say he has forgotten Mother. I'm sure he could never do that. But it's obvious this marriage is good for him. I remember how melancholy he was the first few months after Mother died. I worried when you moved to Springfield, not knowing if another location was what he needed. Maybe it wasn't, but Mary obviously is. I wanted to let you know that we all approve of your choice for a stepmother. If we can't have Mother, Mary is certainly our choice, too.

Eliza tossed her sister's letter aside and jumped to her feet. She paced the length of her room and back. How could her sisters welcome another woman into their mother's place? Was she the only one who missed Mother?

She sank to the bed and gathered up Vickie's letter. The rest was about her two rambunctious sons, Nicholas and Christopher. Then she told of her new baby daughter, Faith Victoria.

I was quite ill while I carried this baby. John and I prayed and claimed the promise in Mark 9:23. It says, "If thou canst believe, all things are possible to him that believeth." That's why, when our baby girl was born healthy and strong, we had to name her Faith.

Eliza was glad for the three children Vickie and John had but hoped they didn't have any more. As far as she was concerned, it was not worth the risk of her sister's life. She turned back to her letter.

Oh yes, I must tell you that both John and I have accepted Jesus as our Savior. Brother Timothy is a powerful speaker and very good at tending to the needs of his congregation. He is a young man without a wife, but he seems to have wisdom beyond his years. It was through his influence that we found our way.

Again, Eliza wiped away tears. Her oldest brother, Ben, had been first to accept Christ, and then their mother came to the Lord after Nora's birth. Cora was next. But it took their mother's death to bring Eliza and her father to the Lord. Now John and Vickie had joined their spiritual family. Eliza's heart sang.

Finally, she turned to the last letter—the one from Cora. She skimmed the part that told how much Cora liked Mary. Then Cora told of her new baby. Eliza read carefully.

Eliza, you don't know how much I've missed you. After my baby was born, I thought of you and was sad. My sadness is for both of you because you will not get to watch him grow, and he will not have the benefit of his aunt Eliza's guidance. After all, what better teacher could he have for arguing with his younger brothers and sisters? Could anyone have been better than the two of us, do you think? Truly, I would love to have one of our old verbal fights.

Eliza smiled at her sister's nonsense. She, too, missed the loving rivalry that had gone on between herself and Cora. She turned back to her letter to see what else she could learn about her new nephew.

Speaking of disagreements, Aaron and I had our first over our son's name. Can you believe that? For some reason, he wanted the name Jesse. I wanted Dane. Being the submissive wife that I am, I gave in to him. Our son's name is Jesse Dane. Of course, I call him Dane, and even Aaron is beginning to, as well.

Eliza laughed. She couldn't imagine Aaron disagreeing with Cora about anything. He doted on her and would give in to any whim she had. She sighed. If only she could find a man to love her half as much.

She gathered up her letters and put them in her dresser drawer. She knew in the coming months she would read them over and over, savoring each memory they brought of home and the ones she loved.

That night Nora slept in the downstairs bedroom with Father and Mary. Eliza kept silent about the situation, but inwardly she hurt. Nora treated her like a stranger. She ran to Kathrene and Mary with every need. By the end of the week, Eliza despaired of ever winning her confidence.

Then on Saturday evening after supper, the family relaxed together in the parlor. Father stood at the mantel, watching his wife sew by candlelight. "Why don't you put that down and see if you can win a game of checkers against me?"

Mary smiled up at him. "It's not likely I could do that."

"I'll go easy on you." Father picked up the set. "You'll be putting your eyes out, anyway, doing such close work in this dim light."

Mary lifted the garment and bit off a thread. "I've sewn in dim light for years."

"But you don't have to now." He moved a small table between Mary's chair and the end of the sofa. He opened the board on the table and started putting the pieces in place.

Mary laughed at his persistence. She laid the half-made garment aside. "I suppose Nora can wait for her dress."

Nora, who had been quietly playing on the floor with a doll, looked up at her name. She tossed her doll to the side and ran to Mary. "I can play, too."

"Of course, you may, darling." Mary held her hands out. "Would you like to sit on my lap?"

Nora's shoulder-length hair bounced as she nodded. Eliza bit her lower lip as she watched her little sister. She looked so happy with Mary.

Father leaned back in his chair and tried to look sternly at his little daughter. "All right, you may play, but you wait until Mama tells you what to do."

Nora's big, brown eyes were serious as she nodded. "Yes, Fauver."

They played one game with Nora moving Mary's pieces, and Father won easily.

"See, I told you I couldn't play this game." Mary laughed and gave Nora a hug. "Even with my little helper, I lost."

"You need practice. How about another game?"

Mary shook her head. "I've had all the checkers I want for one night."

Eliza stood. "I'll play with you, Father."

"All right." Father grinned at Mary, teasing her. "Now I'll have some competition."

"No, me play." Nora grabbed a red playing piece in each hand.

Eliza's heart sank, but Mary came to her rescue. "Nora, I know if you talk nice to your sister, she'll let you help, just like I did. Would you like to do that?"

Nora looked from the checkers to Eliza and nodded. Mary stood with her, letting Eliza take her place.

Eliza held her little sister close for a moment. It felt so good to finally hold Nora's warm little body without her squirming for freedom.

Once her sister was secure on her lap, Eliza kept Nora as long as she could. Father won the first game. She found it hard to concentrate with Nora moving the pieces. She lost the second game, but she had two pieces crowned king before Father's kings jumped them.

When she won the third game, Father yawned. "Well, I think we'd better call it a night. Lenny, why don't you hand me my Bible?"

"Are you quitting because you finally lost, Father?" Eliza smiled at him.

He grinned back. "Do you think I'm that childish? No, don't answer." He laughed and took the Bible Lenny handed him. "Let's see what God's Word has for us tonight."

Eliza kept Nora with her throughout family devotions and afterward. She helped her into her nightgown as the family got ready for bed. She even carried her outside to the outhouse.

The sun was just sinking below the western horizon when they returned to the house. Eliza's steps were slow, trying to delay the moment her sister would go back to Mary.

"Nora, how would you like to sleep in my room upstairs tonight?" She tried to keep her voice light, although she felt as if her life depended on the answer.

Nora looked at her older sister. "Where you room?"

"You haven't even seen my room, have you?" Eliza's steps quickened. "How about we go look at it, okay?"

Nora's small head nodded. "Okay."

Eliza carried Nora upstairs without confronting anyone. "It's right in here." She pushed open the door and tossed Nora on her bed so that she bounced.

Nora's happy laughter thrilled her. She scrambled to her feet, her arms lifted. "Do again."

Eliza picked her up and hugged her before positioning her over the bed. "Here goes." She pretended to drop her but didn't.

Nora squealed and grabbed for Eliza's arms. "Do again."

Eliza laughed, this time letting go. Nora fell on the soft bed with a shriek of laughter.

"What's going on in here?" At her father's voice, Eliza turned, lost her balance, and sat down beside Nora.

Nora scrambled up, standing on Eliza's lap, her arms wrapped around her neck. Her lower lip stuck out. "Liza mine."

Father laughed and then slipped his arm around Mary's waist as she came up beside her. He grinned down at her. "It would appear that we've lost a roommate."

Mary's smile widened. "I'm glad to see that you two girls have made up."

Eliza met her soft green eyes and for the moment felt no antagonism. "So am I."

She looked up at her father. "Does that mean Nora can sleep here now?" Her arms tightened around the little girl.

He nodded. "If that's what you want."

"It is." Eliza's smile lit her face. For the first time in a long time, she felt happy.

As if to make up for her earlier behavior, Nora became Eliza's shadow. She sat on her lap all through church the next morning. Eliza kept so busy trying to keep her quiet that she had no idea what the sermon was about.

However, she was well aware of James sitting on the other side of the church with his mother and sister. He added to her happiness when he stopped to talk to her and Nora after church. "I won't ask if you are all right this morning. That sparkle in your eyes tells me you are."

Eliza laughed. "Yes, I'm feeling much better now that my little sister is here."

"I'm glad." James smiled and stepped aside as a couple of young women joined them and exclaimed over Nora. He waved over their heads and said, "I'll see you later."

Chapter 11

Eliza was glad to see Vanda slip into the back pew Sunday evening jus before the minister opened his Bible.

" 'Except a man be born again, he cannot see the kingdom of God.' " He paused, stepped to the side of the pulpit, and pointed a finger at the congregation. "Where will you spend eternity?"

Eliza had never heard him talk so fast nor so loud as he paced from one side of the pulpit to the other. She bowed her head and prayed for any who were in need of salvation.

When the altar call was given, Vanda make her way with four others to the front. Mary, Father, and Kathrene went forward to pray with those seeking salvation. Mary knelt beside Vanda.

Eliza held Nora on her lap and made sure Lenny stayed by her side. She felt shaken. She could think of no time she had spoken to Vanda about her soul. She hadn't even considered that Vanda might be in need of salvation.

Tears of repentance for her own neglect trickled down Eliza's cheeks. She bowed her head and prayed, asking God to forgive her for being so selfish with all He had given her.

After church, she waited by the door while Vanda made her way toward her. A wide smile dominated her thin face. Her large brown eyes danced with happiness.

"Oh, Eliza, I'm so glad you waited." The two girls hugged. Vanda pulled back. "Do you know how wonderful I feel right now?"

A flush covered Eliza's face. Had Vanda not known she was a Christian? She nodded. "Yes, I do."

Vanda tugged on Eliza's arm. "Let's step outside. I want to ask you something."

Eliza allowed the other girl to lead her to a tree near the side of the church. It was dark there, away from the lantern light on the front steps.

"Will you pray with me for my father?"

"Your father?"

Vanda looked down with her head bowed. Eliza had to strain to hear her voice. "Poppa is a good man when he isn't drinking. He had so much in Germany, before he came to America. But he's a younger son, and there was no inheritance for him." She looked at Eliza. "He thought he would be successful in America, but every business he tried failed. Then he met my mother. She was young and beautiful, and her family had money. She was a Wingate."

"You mean you're related to Mr. Wingate?" Eliza couldn't keep the surprise from her voice.

Vanda nodded. "Yes, he's my uncle."

"I didn't know."

Vanda smiled. "Trennen works for them, but other than that we don't associate. Poppa's pride won't let us." She seemed impatient to continue as several people came outside. "My parents eloped. In Pennsylvania, Poppa was able to find enough work to keep us alive. Then Uncle Charles came here, and Mama got sick. Poppa would have done anything for her. When she wanted to be near her brother, he packed us up and moved. His heart broke when she died. He won't leave now because she's buried here."

"How sad." Eliza didn't know what to say.

"Eliza, I'm sure you already know the rest." Vanda looked down. "You've seen the bruises. Poppa's always sorry when he's sober, but the drink turns him mean."

Eliza's heart went out to her friend.

She nodded. "Of course, Vanda, I'll pray."

"Thank you, Eliza." She laughed. "I am so happy tonight."

Eliza looked around at the departing congregation. Her father stood on the steps. He shook the minister's hand, then took Mary's arm and stepped off the porch. Nora sat on Mary's other arm as if she belonged there. "Vanda, you aren't going to walk home in the dark, are you? Why don't you come with us? I'm sure Father won't mind taking you home."

"Thank you, but I have a ride." Vanda smiled and indicated some young men standing in a group several yards away.

As Eliza looked, James Hurley separated himself from the others and came toward them. "It won't be out of James's way to take me, but I do appreciate your offer."

"Good evening, Eliza." James smiled.

"Hello, James."

He nodded. "Well, Vanda, are you ready to go?"

"Yes." Vanda took his offered arm. Eliza watched them walk toward his wagon. Her heart wrenched at the sight, and she realized she cared for James more than she should.

❧

One day in late September, Kathrene came home with news of a taffy pull. "It's at Barbara Martin's house." Her eyes sparkled in excitement. "Charles asked me to go with him."

Mary looked up. "That's wonderful, dear. When is it?"

"This Saturday evening." Kathrene moved to stand next to Eliza. "Barbara said to tell you to come, too, Eliza. If you'd like, you may ride over with Charles and me. He said to be sure and ask you."

Eliza's rolling pin stopped in midstroke. She looked up at Kathrene, her brown eyes snapping. "Thank you, Kathrene, but if I go, I'll go by myself."

"Eliza," Kathrene spoke softly, pleading, "we really want you with us."

Eliza shook her head. "I don't think that would be wise." She lifted her pie dough and placed it carefully on the pan.

"Eliza, do we have any leavening?" Mary stood at the cabinet rummaging through the baking supplies.

"I thought there was some."

"Well, there isn't now." Mary turned and smiled. "Would you two girls mind running to the store?"

Eliza wondered if Mary asked them both to go in an effort to bring them together again. She felt the prick of her conscience as she realized that most of the problem was her fault. Walking to town with Kathrene was the least she could do to make amends.

They had just started down the road toward town when Eliza heard footsteps behind them.

"Hey, wait up, will you?"

"What do you want?" Eliza asked Lenny as he caught up with them.

"Ma, er. . ." He glanced quickly at Eliza. "Mary said I could go with you."

"All right." Eliza pointed her finger at him. "But you behave yourself. You either stay with us or go to Father's shop. Do you understand?"

He nodded. "I'm goin' to Father's."

After the girls left the store, they started across the square to Father's shops.

"Miss Kowski, wait a minute."

They both turned to see Stephen Doran hurrying toward them. Eliza stepped back, frowning at Kathrene's sharp intake of breath. Was she really so smitten by this penniless drifter?

"Miss Kowski." He smiled, and Eliza had to admit he was very good-looking. "I understand Miss Barbara Martin is having a taffy pull this Saturday evening. I would be honored if you would go with me."

"Oh, I can't."

Eliza smiled at the expression on Kathrene's face.

"If it's because I'm a stranger to your folks, I'd be glad to talk to your father. . . or mother." His expression was as woebegone as hers.

"No, it isn't that." Kathrene shook her head. "I've already promised someone else."

"Then you are going?"

"Yes, I'll be there."

"Well." He jammed his hands in his pockets. "I'll see you then." Again he smiled at her. "Until Saturday."

As soon as he left, Kathrene said, "Oh, I didn't think. Why didn't I suggest he take you?"

Eliza gasped. "Don't you dare! I don't need your charity. I'm going to see my father now. I'll come home later with Lenny."

How dare Kathrene patronize her just because she had two young men at her beck and call while Eliza had none? Tears stung her eyes, and she wiped at them as she neared the door to the chandler shop.

Father was alone in the shop when she entered. He looked up from the ledger he had been working on and smiled at her. "What a sight for sore eyes."

She smiled. "Is Lenny here? I thought I'd walk home with him."

"He's in the back. I thought he might as well do a little work before school starts again."

Eliza moved to a display of candles hanging from the ceiling and tapped at them, watching them swing back and forth.

"Why don't you tell me what the problem is?"

She tried to laugh, but it came out as a sob. "Can't I hide anything from you?"

He pulled her around to face him, his hands on her shoulders. "I know you haven't been happy. Please, tell me what it is."

"It's so silly." At her hiccupy laugh, he pulled her against his chest, and she couldn't hold the tears back.

While his shirt grew damp, she told him of the party. "Kathrene has two beaux. I don't have anyone. I'm almost twenty."

He patted her back. "Maybe it just isn't God's time yet, or maybe it is, and you haven't recognized it."

"What do you mean by that?" She looked up at him as he handed her his handkerchief.

A jingle at the door warned them that someone was coming. He pushed her gently toward the workroom. "You step in there just a minute until I take care of our customer."

Eliza stood in the workroom, trying to repair the damage to her face with her father's handkerchief. Two large vats sat in the middle of the room. Candle wax and rolls of wick waited on the floor. Finished candles lay in piles on a table. Lenny was nowhere to be seen.

After what seemed a long time, Eliza carefully opened the door to the shop a crack. She couldn't hear anyone talking. She pushed it open a little farther. She didn't see anyone. As she pushed the door all the way open and stepped into the shop, Father came in the front door.

He grinned. "Oops! I got caught, didn't I? Sorry to keep you waiting, but I had to take care of some business next door."

"That's all right, Father. I need to go home, anyway."

He lifted her chin and gave her a quick kiss on the forehead. "Don't look so sad. Maybe things aren't as bad as they seem."

She smiled for his benefit. "Maybe not."

She hadn't gotten more than a hundred yards from the shops on her way home when quick footsteps sounded behind her. Thinking it was Lenny, she stopped and turned around.

James came within an inch of running into her. "What'd you stop so quick for?"

"I thought you were my brother." She stepped back to put some distance between them.

"No, I'm not your brother." The look on his face and the inflection in his voice caused a flush to spread across her cheeks. "I was trying to catch up with you so I could ask you if you're going to the taffy pull Saturday night at the Martins'."

She looked down. "I planned to, but I don't see what business it is of yours."

He threw his hands out in a helpless gesture. "Eliza Jackson, you are the most aggravating woman I've ever dealt with."

"Oh, and I suppose you've dealt with a lot of women?" She turned a saucy face to him.

His gray eyes twinkled above a grin that set her pulse racing. "Not so many you need be concerned."

"And who says I'm concerned about what you do?"

"Eliza." He grew serious. "All I want is for you to go with me to the party. How about it? Can we call a truce and go as friends?"

She nodded, surprised that her voice sounded so normal. "I suppose it would be all right. I should ask my father first."

James smiled. "Good. I'll be at your house around six thirty." He turned and walked back toward town, whistling.

❦

The promise of winter brought crispness to the September air Saturday evening as Eliza left the house with James.

They walked down the steps toward the road. Eliza noticed the absence of any vehicle in front. She glanced up at James as he took her elbow to help her over a wagon rut.

"You realize, of course, that Kathrene left ten minutes ago in a shiny blue Victoria pulled by a matched set of horses."

"My, a blue one, even." Knowing James, she assumed he was making fun of her.

"Yes. Cobalt blue with matching Morocco upholstery."

"Now, I am impressed. First the horses and now the upholstery. Everything must match." He grinned down at her. "What did you do? Come out and inspect it?"

He was making fun of her. She fell into his mood. "Why not? I'm not so lucky as Kathrene. I suppose I shall always have to walk wherever I go, unless I can somehow take Charles from Kathrene. He's the only man I know who can afford such luxury."

"And what's wrong with walking?" A frown set on James's face. "The night is warm enough, there's a full moon overhead, and we're both young and able."

Eliza looked up at James. She had been joking, but by an instinct peculiar to women, she knew that in his mind the joke had turned to criticism.

"There's not a thing wrong with walking. Actually, I quite enjoy it."

She smiled at him and was glad to see his frown disappear.

The Martin house blazed with lights. Just before they went inside, James said, "Your father would have more business than he could handle if there were more parties like this one."

Eliza laughed. "I think you're right. They must have every candle in the house burning and a few lanterns as well."

Barbara opened the door at their knock. "Come on in. Make yourselves at home." She pointed toward a door off the parlor. "Pile your wraps on the bed in there."

James and Eliza shared a smile as she fluttered off to attend to someone's call. They tossed their outer garments on the bed and returned to the parlor just as Vanda came in, followed by her older brother.

Trennen nodded at James. When he turned to Eliza, a flush touched her cheeks at his scrutiny.

James's hand closed gently around her upper arm. "Come on, it sounds like they're starting the candy."

"Vanda." Eliza motioned toward her friend. "We don't want to miss out on the taffy pulling, do we?"

"We sure don't." Vanda smiled and joined them as they followed Trennen into the kitchen.

"Come on, everyone, it's just about ready." Barbara bustled about the large kitchen, setting out plates and butter for each of her guests. "This is going to be so much fun." She handed Eliza a plate.

"Hey, don't I get one?" James asked.

"Sorry, just one to a couple." Barbara turned to Vanda. "Here's your plate, but who's your partner? You don't want to pull with your brother. I know. Why don't you take mine?"

Before Vanda could answer, Barbara ran across the room and grabbed her brother's arm. He was talking to the Ross boys and resisted at first.

"I wish she wouldn't do that." Vanda looked embarrassed.

"Don't you like her brother?" Eliza asked.

"It isn't that. Joe's fine. But he doesn't look like he wants to come."

"I wouldn't be so sure about that." Eliza nudged her friend as Joe straightened and looked across the room. His frown of annoyance was replaced by a smile as he met Vanda's eyes. He nodded and followed his sister.

Joe Martin was at least six feet tall and thin. His hair, a dark brown, contrasted with his fair sister's. Eliza had never thought of him as anything more than Barbara's brother. Now she watched Vanda's face as he approached and wondered if the two of them might make a good couple.

She glanced across the room and caught Trennen's gaze on her. A slow, lazy smile crossed his face, and she looked quickly away.

She was glad when Barbara's mother lifted a large spoonful of candy from the pan and watched it sheet off. A sweet aroma filled the air. "The taffy's ready."

A chorus of cheers greeted her pronouncement. Eliza and James got into line with the other couples to get their plate of hot taffy. The atmosphere was festive and loud with everyone laughing and talking while they waited for the candy to cool enough to handle.

She avoided Kathrene and Charles as much as she could, but she noticed that Stephen Doran stayed close to them. He had come alone, and Barbara had agreed to be his partner, though Eliza knew she would have preferred David Ross.

Finally, someone decided the candy had cooled enough. James reached into the bowl and scooped off some butter. He inclined his head toward the only empty corner left at the moment. "Come on, Eliza, and bring the plate of candy."

"Yes, sir." She followed him, ignoring his raised eyebrows.

"Set the plate down and take my hands." He spread the butter over his own hands and then reached for hers.

"As you wish, sir." She set the plate down and started to stretch her hands toward his, but the look on his face stopped her.

"If you don't stop calling me *sir*. . ." If he had finished his sentence, she was sure she wouldn't have heard it for the pounding of her heart.

Her voice sounded small even to herself as she said, "James."

He grinned. "That's much better." He took her hands then and rubbed them between his own.

"There, that should be good enough." Their eyes met, and warmth radiated between them. James dropped her hands and reached for the plate.

As they pulled the candy between them, it stretched and hardened. Barbara told them to make some thin, ropelike strands for a game they would be playing.

"All right, everyone listen, and I'll explain the game to you." Barbara clapped her hands for attention.

She held up a large bowl. "Break off a piece of your rope candy about one to two inches long. Put it in this bowl, and then we'll pick someone to start the game."

"Aren't you going to tell us how to play first?" someone called.

Barbara's long blond ringlets swished across her back as she shook her head. "I won't have to. You'll know soon enough."

The bowl made the rounds of the room and came back almost full. Barbara giggled. "If we use all this, we may be here all night. Who wants to go first?"

"Why don't you go first and show us how?" Joe spoke from the corner. Several others voiced their agreement.

"All right, but I'll need a partner." Barbara turned to smile at David Ross. "I choose you, David."

David had brought a girl named Anna Johnson whom Eliza didn't know. He joined Barbara in the center of the room near the long trestle table. "Okay, what do I do?"

Barbara reached into the bowl and withdrew a piece of the short candy. "You remember this game, don't you, David? We played it before." She clamped one end of the candy with her teeth, her lips making an O around it. She then bent toward David with her hands clasped behind her back.

David grinned. "Sure, I remember." He put his hands behind his back and bent toward her. His mouth closed around the candy, and he bit it off, then straightened, chewing the piece in his mouth.

He grinned at the others and swept a bow amid laughter and hand clapping. As he straightened, he said, "All right, it's my turn now since I bit it in two." His eyes glanced about the room, settling on Anna. "Will you accept my challenge, Anna?"

Anna's face grew rosy, and she shook her head, a self-conscious smile on her lips.

"Come on, Anna, it's all in fun."

Anna allowed herself to be cajoled into playing. Her face was bright red by the time David again bit the candy off.

Since the same couple was not allowed to break the candy twice in a row, David chose Barbara next. When she broke the candy, she picked Stephen Doran. Eliza watched him bite the candy and then turn with a gleam in his eye toward Kathrene.

Kathrene's eyes sparkled as she placed her lips around the candy and they touched Stephen's. Eliza silently and slowly counted to five before she heard the snap of the candy in the quiet room. Kathrene picked Charles next, and on it went until it was Trennen's turn.

He turned slowly, his eyes taking in each girl until they rested on Eliza. He cocked his head to one side, his left eyebrow lifting slightly. "Well, come on."

Eliza's heart thudded in her chest. Trennen's good looks and confidence frightened and excited her. She leaned forward, taking the end of the candy in her teeth. Trennen's face was so close to her own. She looked down at the candy. Her vision blurred, and she became conscious of the many watchful eyes surrounding her.

Then Trennen's lips moved forward, across the fraction of an inch that separated them, and touched hers. She jerked back, and the candy broke off in her mouth.

Her face flamed as Trennen whispered, "That was nice. Let's try it again sometime."

"All right, Eliza. Pick another partner," Barbara called to her.

Eliza pointed at James. "I'll challenge you."

His grin showed his acceptance.

Again, Eliza's heart pounded. She picked the longest piece of candy that she could find and clamped the end in her teeth. With her hands clasped behind her back, she leaned toward him. The room grew quiet as he took the other end in his teeth.

Seconds ticked off as they stood, nose to nose, holding the candy. Then it snapped off in James's teeth. His eyes danced at her surprised expression. Their lips had not touched.

After a couple more games, Barbara stood up. "It's getting late, but I want to thank you all so much for coming. I don't know about you, but I've had lots of fun."

Kathrene caught Eliza and James as they put on their wraps. "Charles is bringing the buggy around. Would you like to ride home with us?"

James shrugged. "That's up to Eliza."

She thought of the plush Victoria and was tempted. But then she looked at James and shook her head. "We'll go home the same way we came."

Kathrene shrugged. "All right, if that's what you want."

"It is." James took Eliza's arm and guided her out the door.

They walked together, talking about the party, the town that was growing up around them, and James's plans for his life's work. Before she realized it, they had turned into her front yard.

"I like farming and hope to never live in town, but I also enjoy working with your father."

"So what are you going to do? Be a farmer or a cooper?"

"Both." James grinned down at her as they neared her house. "Unless your father runs me off for keeping you out too late. You know we'd have been here a lot sooner in that fancy blue Victoria."

She nodded as they stopped just short of the front porch. "I know, but it wouldn't have been as much fun."

"So you think walking is fun."

"Depending on the company."

He grinned and then became serious. "Eliza, I enjoyed this evening very much. So much that I hate to see it end." He searched her face. "Would you consider going with me next Saturday to see my farm? I'd really like to show it to you."

She smiled up at him. "Do I have to walk?"

He laughed. "I don't know. Do you think your father would loan me his buggy?"

"I don't imagine he'll say much against it. If he does, I might put in a good word for you."

James stepped closer, his hands on each of her elbows. "Does that mean you'll go?"

She nodded, unable to speak with him so near.

He leaned toward her. "Eliza, may I kiss you good night?"

Her heartbeat drummed in her ears. Without a word, she nodded.

As he pulled her into his arms and his lips lowered over hers, moisture came unbidden to her eyes. She had not expected such strong feelings to come with a simple kiss.

James smiled down at her. "You'd better go in before your father comes out."

Eliza walked into the house in a daze.

Chapter 12

The next morning at church, Eliza cast shy glances at James. He returned her smiles and after the service went out of his way to speak to her.

"I told my mother I was bringing you out next Saturday."

"I hope it's all right with her."

He smiled. "She's anxious to get acquainted with you. Now all I have to do is get your father's permission."

"Oh no, you don't." She gave him a saucy grin. "I already asked, and he said yes."

James laughed. "Great, now I know what his answer will be tomorrow when I ask for the use of his buggy."

Lenny ran by, yelling over his shoulder, "Come on, Eliza. Father and Mama are ready to go."

Eliza frowned after him. "I can't believe he calls her 'Mama.' He just does it because Nora does. But Nora doesn't remember Mother."

"Perhaps you shouldn't be so hard on him. He's young, too, you know."

"Maybe." Eliza turned back to him with a smile. "Well, I've got to be going. I'll see you later."

Monday evening Father told Eliza he'd been approached by James and had given him permission to borrow his buggy on Saturday. He grinned at her with a teasing light in his eyes. "I always heard tell a boy was getting serious when he took his best girl out to meet his mother."

Eliza's face flamed. "Don't get your hopes up yet, Father. I'm afraid James just wants to show off his farm. It looks like you're stuck with me for awhile."

Father laughed, but Mary said, "I can't imagine a nicer thing than to have you right here with us always."

Eliza turned toward the stairs without responding.

❧

On Saturday afternoon, the air felt cool while sunshine brought the trees alive with color as Eliza and James rode toward his farm.

They hadn't gone far when he pointed to the left. "This is the north boundary. I've only added twenty acres since my father died. Someday, I'd like to have at least two hundred."

"That would make a nice-sized farm for this part of the country," Eliza said.

"What do you raise? Cows, horses, pigs?"

He grinned at her. "Yes."

"Yes! You mean you have all of those?"

"All of those plus chickens, dogs, and cats."

"My, you do have quite a farm." Eliza laughed with him.

He pointed at a house sitting to the left of the road. "Here we are."

Someone had built onto the original log cabin, making a nice-sized house. It stood two stories tall with a fresh coat of whitewash. A dog curled up on the back steps wagged his tail as they walked toward him. He lifted his head, gave one sniff, and then settled back to complete his nap.

"He's not the best watchdog, but he's friendly." James patted the dog's head before opening the door for Eliza.

She laughed and stepped inside.

Mrs. Hurley took a pan of cookies from the oven. She smiled. "I thought you might like a warm treat. There's hot chocolate on the stove." She turned to her daughter. "Pour some out for each of us, Melissa. We'll sit here around the table and visit a spell."

"That sounds nice," Eliza said.

"How is your family, Eliza?" Mrs. Hurley placed the cookies on the table, then pulled a chair out.

James reached for another chair and pulled it from the table for Eliza. She smiled her thanks and then answered his mother. "They're just fine, thank you."

Eliza enjoyed the time she spent with James's mother and sister. Both made her feel at home as they talked about the weather, the town, and their farm. Eliza learned that the farm had been given to James at his father's death more than ten years ago. She was amazed that a boy so young would be trusted with such an undertaking. His mother assured her that he had proven himself worthy, getting up before light to care for the animals and do chores.

Pride set on her face as she smiled at her son. "He worked morning and night to make a living for us and still kept up with his studies. I worried that he couldn't do it with all the responsibilities he had, but James stayed in school until he knew as much as the schoolmaster." She smiled at him.

Eliza looked at James with shining eyes.

He laughed. "Don't let my mother fool you. I have a well-used fishing rod out in the barn to prove I didn't work all the time."

Mrs. Hurley laughed and patted James's hand. "Yes, all boys must play, or they don't make good men."

"Come on, Eliza." James set his mug down. "Let's go look around."

He grasped her hand, pulling her to her feet. She felt self-conscious when he kept her hand firmly in his as they went out the kitchen door.

Together they walked across his farm as he pointed out the various animals and crops. They were walking back toward the house when he pulled her behind a toolshed.

"What's the matter?" She grabbed her bonnet to keep it from slipping off her head.

He turned to face her. His eyes were dark as they looked deep into hers. "There's something I need to know."

She felt as if she couldn't breathe. "What is it?"

His hand touched her neck while his thumb stroked her cheek. "I want to know. . ." He paused a moment as his gaze dropped to her lips. "If I have to ask every time I want to kiss you."

Her heart thudded. She could not speak. All she could do was shake her head from side to side.

"Good." His hand cupped her chin, lifting it until their lips touched. Eliza responded as she hadn't the first time and experienced emotions beyond anything she had ever imagined.

When he pulled away, a grin set on his lips. "You know I plan to take advantage of this, don't you?"

"What do you mean?" Her breath came in short, quick spurts.

"I mean there's still that big tree between us and the house." He stepped around the corner of the toolshed, pointing to an old oak broad enough to hide the two of them from anyone looking out a window.

She walked past him, putting a little distance between them before she spoke. With her head tilted toward one side, she smiled. "That's true, but you'll have to catch me first."

Before the last word left her mouth, she was running as fast as she could toward the house. When she heard the pounding of his feet behind her, an unreasonable alarm gave her the impetus she needed to make it past the tree before he caught her.

He wrapped his arm around her and pulled her close to his side as they continued to the house. He grinned at her struggles to pull away. "If you think you're going to get away from me after that trick, you'd better think again."

"What will your mother think if she sees you holding me this way?"

"Probably that she raised her son to be as smart as she thinks he is." James laughed but removed his arm from her shoulders to hold her hand instead. He stopped at the back steps. "Your father may be worried about me keeping his horse and buggy out too late. I'd better get it back to him."

"What about his daughter?" Eliza pretended to be deeply hurt. "You men always put your possessions above us womenfolk."

"But, Eliza. . ." The twinkle in James's eyes gave away his serious expression. "Don't you know you womenfolk are our possessions, too?"

"You may consider your wife a possession, Mr. Hurley—if you ever find someone who will marry you—but I will never be any man's possession." Eliza lifted her chin defiantly.

James laughed. "That's one statement I can believe, Miss Jackson." He pulled her toward the door. "Come inside for just a minute; then I'll take you home."

Eliza sat close beside James on the way back to town. She scarcely knew what to think of the new emotions that he had awakened in her.

"You know, I just thought of something." James interrupted her thoughts. "We haven't had a good argument since before Barbara's party."

"It's rather nice, don't you think?"

He grinned at her. "Just being with you is nice."

Her face flushed, and she looked away. As she did, she saw a lone figure trudging toward town ahead of them.

"James, isn't that Vanda?" As they got closer, she gripped his arm. "It is. Please stop and let's give her a ride into town."

Vanda climbed into the back and leaned against the seat. "This is much better than walking."

"Where were you headed?" Eliza asked.

"I need to go to the general store, but my main reason for coming into town was to see you."

"Is something wrong?"

"I think so." Vanda looked to the countryside as it rolled by. "Before I was a Christian, I might have overlooked this, but now I realize how important it is that everyone comes to know the Lord in a personal way."

She looked at Eliza. "I'm concerned about Cletis and Lenny. They are young, but they're doing things they shouldn't, and I'm afraid it'll just get worse as they get older."

Eliza felt a sinking sensation in her middle. What had Lenny done now?

Vanda continued. "I thought you might tell your father that I caught Cletis and Lenny chewing tobacco the other day out behind our outhouse."

"Lenny was at your place?" Eliza was as shocked by that bit of news as she was at what he had been doing.

"Yes, he's been out several times. Cletis knows when Poppa isn't going to be there. The boys said it was all right with your folks."

Eliza sat in stunned silence. It seemed she had quite a bit to talk over with her brother when she got home.

❆

Eliza saw her opportunity to talk to Lenny the next day when he went to the outhouse right after the family returned home from church. She waited until he came out. "I had a talk with Vanda yesterday."

Lenny just looked at her.

"She says she caught you and Cletis with some tobacco. Is that true?"

"So what if it is?" He glared at her. "You ain't my boss."

"I may not be your boss, but I could sure tell Father that Cletis is a ba[d] influence on you. How would you like that?"

She saw fear come into his eyes and then change into something else. B[ut] she was unprepared for his next words.

"I guess you got reason to be jealous of me and my friends, 'cause Fath[er] don't have to get me no friends."

"What do you mean?"

"Father got you James, didn't he?" Lenny sneered. "I was in the cooper sho[p] when he told James to ask you to that party. James didn't want to, either. He sai[d] he didn't think you'd go with him. But Father said he'd sure appreciate it if he'[d] try, anyhow, so James said he would."

Lenny's voice pounded in Eliza's head as a drum that would not stop. Neve[r] in her life had she felt so humiliated and hurt.

Eliza spent the rest of the afternoon in her room. James had told her h[e] wanted to continue working as a cooper. Well, he had certainly earned tha[t] right. She reached for her pillow and buried her face in it as great sobs racke[d] her body.

✤

Before church that evening, Eliza crawled into bed and went to sleep. The grie[f] she suffered robbed her natural coloring, leaving her pale. It was not hard, when Kathrene came to wake her, to convince her and then Father that she would b[e] unable to attend the service with them.

As soon as the door closed, she looked to be sure everyone had left her room before she threw the covers back and sat up, clutching her knees to her chest.

Her pride had been deeply wounded, but she couldn't hide away forever while James laughed at her. She would show him and Father, too.

✤

Trennen came to church the following Sunday morning. Although he sat qui-etly in the pew behind her, Eliza was aware of his presence almost as much as she was aware of James sitting across the church beside his mother and sister.

Before James could reach her, she left the building, and Trennen fell into place behind her. Without touching her, he leaned forward slightly to speak close to her ear. "Good morning, Eliza."

She turned around with a smile. "Good morning, Trennen. It's nice seeing you in church."

She was not the only one glad to see him there. Several stopped to shake his hand. Eliza stayed with him. She saw James heading their way, so she tugged Trennen's sleeve. He went with her without question. James caught up with them before they'd gone far.

218

"Eliza, could I talk with you?"

"If you have a question about your work, my father is over there." She inclined her head, refusing to look at James. "Now, if you'll excuse me, I'll continue my conversation with Trennen."

She turned away, pulling Trennen with her. James did not follow. Trennen looked down at her, a lazy grin in place. "I might've come to church before now if I'd known everyone wanted me to."

"Of course, everyone wants you to come." Eliza turned to look up at him and saw James join his mother.

"I suppose that's why no one ever asked me."

Eliza looked up at Trennen. "Do you mean the Wingates never asked you?"

"Well, yeah, but they don't count. Vanda, too, but that doesn't mean anything."

"Why not?" Eliza suddenly realized his sister hadn't been at church. "Where is Vanda, anyway?"

"Probably home with Pop." Trennen shrugged. "I think he was supposed to come in this weekend."

Eliza's eyes widened as she remembered what Vanda had said about her father beating her and Cletis when he came home drunk. Was it possible that she was suffering at her father's hand right now?

Trennen touched her shoulder, bringing her attention back to him. "I'll walk you home."

"I'd have to ask my father first."

"I'll go with you." Trennen took her arm, and together they caught Father and Mary as they headed toward their buggy.

"Father, would it be all right if Trennen walked me home?" Eliza looked hopefully at her father.

He hesitated, looking first at Trennen and then at Eliza. "I suppose if you come straight home, it will be all right."

Trennen nodded. "Thank you, sir."

Trennen took her hand and placed it in the crook of his arm. Together they crossed the churchyard and started across the road just as James's wagon pulled out in front of them.

Eliza pushed James from her mind and tried to concentrate on the young man beside her. As they came up to the front porch, he stepped back.

"Why don't you come inside for awhile?"

He stuck his hands in his pockets. "Naw, I'd better not, but I'd like to see you again. How about tonight? Do you go to church at night, too?"

She smiled. "Yes, we usually do."

"Good. Then I'll see you there." With that, he turned and walked away.

From then on Trennen never missed a church service, and several times he walked Eliza home. She knew the people were pleased to see him. Many prayed for his salvation, hoping at each altar call that he would be the next to go forward. Eliza also prayed for him, but mostly she enjoyed having a young man interested in her because he liked her and not because he was afraid he'd lose his job.

James tried several times to talk to Eliza, but each time she managed to avoid him.

For awhile Eliza enjoyed Trennen's attention, but as the weeks went by she grew tired of his insincere compliments and chivalrous behavior. At first she pushed her discontent aside, but it would not leave. One Sunday morning she decided she would tell him she no longer wished to see him.

As usual, he sat in the row behind her. When church dismissed, he waited outside for her.

Lately, Father had not been as free with his permission for her to walk out with Trennen as he had at first. So she pulled her father aside. "Father, if Trennen asks to walk me home this morning, may I please? I'd really like to talk to him."

A frown creased Father's forehead. "I don't know, Eliza."

"Father, he's been a perfect gentleman."

"I'm sure that's true. But do you think his sudden interest in attending the house of God has anything to do with his concern for his soul, or is it the attraction he feels for one of God's children?"

Trennen had told Eliza that he started coming to church when he did because he enjoyed the kiss they had shared at the party so much. She flushed as she evaded her father's question. "I can't read his thoughts, Father."

Father sighed. "All right. Go ahead, but be careful."

"Don't worry. I'll be fine." She brushed off his concern. "We're just walking across town."

Before she made it to the back door, James blocked her path. "Eliza, could I talk to you?"

His eyes were dark gray as he looked down at her, his expression serious. She skirted around him. "I'm sorry, Mr. Hurley, but my *unpaid* escort is waiting for me. My father handles any problems with his businesses." She rushed past before he could stop her.

She waved at Trennen and walked toward him, wondering if James was watching.

Trennen smiled when he saw her. "May I walk you home?"

She nodded. "Yes, I've already asked Father, and he said it was all right. I wanted to talk to you."

When they were out of sight of the churchyard, he reached for her hand. She reluctantly curled her fingers around his.

Trennen squeezed her hand. "I thought you wanted to talk to me. You haven't said more than two words."

Eliza realized that they had already crossed the square downtown. If she were going to get this done, she'd have to do it now.

Her steps slowed. "Trennen, I'm flattered by the attention you've paid me. I enjoy our walks very much. But. . ."

His hand stiffened in hers.

"But I wonder if there isn't someone else you'd rather be with."

He laughed. "Are you jealous?"

"No." She looked quickly at him. "No, I didn't mean that."

His hand squeezed hers again. She winced at the pain, but he as quickly released her hand and, stopping in the road, turned to face her. "Are you wanting another man's attentions? Maybe Hurley?"

The anger in his voice and on his face surprised her. She shook her head. "No, that's not what I meant." How could she explain it to him? What could she say that wouldn't hurt him?

"Good. Then there's nothing to talk about." He took her hand again and continued walking.

They soon reached her front door, and she had accomplished nothing. Before he left, she tried again. "Trennen, I didn't mean to hurt your feelings."

As she hesitated, the front door opened, framing Kathrene. "Eliza, Mother says for you to invite Trennen in to eat with us. She says it's about time the family became acquainted with him."

Trennen's lazy smile softened his blue eyes as he looked down at Eliza. "Well, do I get to stay?"

Chapter 13

That night when Eliza went to bed, she pulled the covers up to her chin. Trennen had been the most gallant, attentive guest she had ever seen. He'd complimented Mary on her cooking so many times Eliza had felt like gagging. That was one of the problems with him. He said all the right things so often that she questioned his sincerity.

She sighed. How was she going to stop seeing Trennen? Even Father said that he seemed to be a nice young man.

Just thinking about it made her thirsty. She threw the covers back, climbed from bed, and went downstairs to the kitchen.

"Kathrene seemed quite pleased, didn't she?" The muffled voice of her father came from his bedroom.

With her ear near the door, she was able to hear Mary. "I hope we did the right thing."

Father said, "I've heard nothing but good about the boy. I know he's close-mouthed about his past, but I think he's everything he claims to be."

"I suppose."

Eliza realized they meant Stephen Doran.

Father said, "I wouldn't be surprised if this isn't the man Kathrene marries."

"You know, Orval, I love all our children. Yours and mine. Vickie and Cora are so sweet. And Ben. How could I help loving him? He's just like his father."

Mary paused for a moment. "Then there's Eliza. I think I began loving her when she walked into my house with that bundle of fabric that was almost as big as she is."

Eliza heard a muffled sob and Father say, "It's all right, Mary. Eliza's a good girl. She'll come around."

"I know." Mary cleared her throat.

"You're a good mother, Mary. You're good with Lenny, and Nora adores you. I'm proud of the way she took to you so quickly." He laughed softly. "And now God is blessing us with one that won't have to adjust to a new mother or a new father."

"Yes." Eliza could hear the smile in Mary's voice. "Our own little one to raise together. I know our baby won't be here until spring, but I get so anxious. I want to know what our child will look like."

Eliza's father spoke, but she didn't hear. How could this be? Surely Mary ıd Father were not expecting a baby. They couldn't be. Mary was supposed to ɔok and clean for him. She was not supposed to bear his children.

Eliza crept back to her room, her thirst forgotten.

❈

s November gave way to December, Eliza's worries grew. Mary's condition ecame more pronounced, and Trennen refused to leave her alone. Several ımes she tried to tell him that she didn't want his company anymore, but he ɛfused to listen. And James stopped trying to talk to her.

Eliza didn't feel the freedom to tell her father that she didn't want to go ıith Trennen. So he gave permission for her to ride to the Christmas play with 'rennen, just as he did for Kathrene to ride in Stephen Doran's well-worn uggy.

When the parts for the play were given out, Vanda was chosen to play ʌary, the mother of Jesus. Her eyes shone as she turned to Eliza. "Poppa's away ɔorking. He said he'd be gone all month, and I hope he is because he would be ɩngry if he knew what I'm doing."

"You mean he wouldn't want you in the play?" Eliza couldn't understand ⍳is problem.

Vanda nodded. "He doesn't want us going to church. Cletis comes out of ɛbellion, but I come because Jesus is my Lord. I can't turn my back on Him."

That evening when Trennen took Eliza home, he walked her to the door ɪhile Vanda and Cletis waited in the Wingates' buggy. In the two months they ɩad been keeping company, Trennen had never done more than hold her hand. ϒow he stepped up on the porch with her and pulled her into a shadowy corner ıway from prying eyes. Eliza's heart pounded.

"Trennen, please. . ."

"I love you, Eliza." He stopped her protest, pulling her close to him. "All ı want is one kiss."

When she resisted, he pleaded with her. "Don't you love me?"

All the time he talked, he held her close, his cheek against hers. Finally, his lips touched hers, and she felt she had no choice but to surrender. Maybe if she ıllowed him one kiss, he would let her go.

But Trennen's kiss deepened into something Eliza didn't understand. She shoved against him. "Trennen, no. . ."

"I love you, Eliza." He reached for her again.

"You can't do this, Trennen. It isn't right." Her heart pounded in fear.

She shoved him backward, making him stumble against the porch post. "I want you to leave, Trennen. And I don't want to ride home with you anymore."

He started toward her, a look of anger on his face. Then his expression changed, and his head bowed. "I'm sorry, Eliza. It's just that I love you so much.

Don't tell me I can't ever see you again."

Eliza's heart began a hard steady beat. Her head felt light. She watched him standing dejected, and sympathy replaced anger and fear.

"I have to go inside now, Trennen. I'll see you later." She turned and let herself into the house.

❧

A few weeks before the Christmas program, Trennen again asked her to let him take her home.

At first she said no.

"Are you afraid of me, Eliza?" Trennen looked sad.

She shook her head. "No, of course not. But I need to go. Father's waiting. He said they are working late on an order tonight so he needs to get back to the shop."

As she turned away, Trennen captured her arm in his hand. "Eliza, I need to talk to you. It's important." He pleaded with her. "I promise you, if you'll go with me tonight, I'll leave you alone from now on if that's what you really want."

She stood looking at him for several seconds, trying to decide what she should do. She didn't love Trennen, and she knew she never would. She loved only one man.

Pain seared her heart, burning the image of James Hurley in its depths. Hers was a lost love. Twice, she had been scorned, first by Ralph and then by James, but only once had she truly loved. She loved James and always would.

"Eliza, please say you'll go with me tonight." Trennen shook her gently, bringing her eyes to focus again on his face.

"Promise you'll leave me alone after tonight?"

His head drooped, but he nodded. "If that's what you want."

She shrugged. "All right. I'll tell my father."

Eliza's mood darkened like the clouds above when she climbed into the Wingates' buggy and sank into its plush cushions. Vanda squeezed her hand while Trennen settled into the front seat beside her.

"I'm glad you came tonight." Vanda smiled, oblivious to Eliza's unhappiness. "The play is coming along well, don't you think?"

Eliza nodded.

Vanda said, "I feel so unworthy playing the part of Mary. Can you imagine what it must have been like for her? She was just a young girl, but she became the mother of our Lord. Oh, how wonderful it would be to be used of God."

"You'd better not let Pop hear you talking that way." Trennen spoke across Eliza.

Vanda looked down at her hands. "I know. I keep praying for him, but. . . sometimes I get discouraged. I'm so afraid something will happen to him, and he won't know Jesus."

Trennen laughed. "You should worry about what happens to you if he finds out you're still coming here."

Vanda sighed. "I suppose." She was quiet as they dropped off three small children.

Eliza was glad the next stop would be hers, as she wanted desperately to close herself in her bedroom, climb in her bed, and have a good cry in her pillow.

But Trennen turned the horses south, away from her father's house. She looked at him in alarm. "Where are you going?"

He laughed. "Relax, Eliza. I have to take Vanda and Cletis home and then turn around and come back into town, anyway. You don't really mind, do you?"

Eliza did mind, but when she looked at Trennen's lazy grin and saw the determined light in his eyes, she knew it would do no good to protest. She shook her head and settled back.

They turned down the same road she had taken two months earlier with James. When the barn and the toolshed came into view, she remembered the kiss she had shared with James.

She turned her face away from the house as they drove past. James was in town, working with her father on a rush order, but she didn't want to be reminded of the wonderful day she had spent there.

Less than a mile farther down the road Trennen turned the buggy into a yard cluttered with various wagon parts and tools.

Vanda stiffened. "Poppa's home."

Cletis spoke from the backseat in a small voice. "Take us back to town with you, Trennen."

"Naw." He stepped down. "You wouldn't have anyplace to stay. Come on. I'll go in and talk to him."

Vanda lifted her chin as Trennen came around the buggy to help her down. "No, Trennen. You take Eliza home. We'll be fine."

"Vanda, why don't you come back to town?" Eliza caught her friend's hand as she climbed down. "You could stay with me. Lenny would love to have Cletis come."

Vanda shook her head. She gave Eliza a smile. "Thank you, but we can't. Someone has to take care of Poppa." She jumped to the ground. "Don't worry. We'll be fine."

As Cletis crawled from the buggy, Vanda turned to Trennen. "You go on and take Eliza home. It wouldn't do for Poppa to see you right now. You know he doesn't like you working for the Wingates. It'd just make things worse."

As Trennen guided the buggy back out onto the road and turned it toward town, Eliza looked over her shoulder to see the door close behind Vanda. "Are you sure she'll be all right?"

"Why wouldn't she be?" Trennen shrugged. "He probably won't lay a hand on her."

He turned and looked down at Eliza's worried expression. "Aw, don't worry about Vanda. What would your father do if you did something he didn't want you to?"

She spoke quietly. "When I was little, he spanked me. Mostly, he talks to me." She smiled. "I think the talks hurt the most."

His arm encircled her, drawing her close to his side. "Sit over here where it's warmer."

They were nearing the Hurley house. Eliza shrank against Trennen's side, turning her face away from the house.

He hugged her even closer, his hand rubbing her upper arm. His head lowered toward hers. They were in front of James's house. She turned away. "Trennen, we're in front of a house."

"You know who lives there, too, don't you?" His voice sounded angry.

She nodded. "But that doesn't—"

"Oh, it matters all right. I know all about you and Hurley. I've seen the way you look at him."

They were past the house now. Trennen's mouth covered hers in a rough kiss that frightened her. She pulled away. He let go of the reins, giving the horses their heads. They slowed to a leisurely stroll. "You are mine, Eliza. No one else is going to have you." He held her with both hands, his kisses now forceful and demanding.

She struggled for freedom. His voice sounded hoarse, his breathing ragged. "Don't fight me, Eliza. I love you."

She fought with everything she had. She screamed, but there was no one to hear. She beat at him, trying to push him back. He pinned her against the cushion. She kicked at him. He cursed.

The horses became skittish as the buggy bounced with their struggles.

Her head felt light and dizzy. She had to get away before she fainted. But Trennen pushed her into the corner of the seat. Fear rose within her.

Then as if a voice spoke within her head, she heard the words, *"Call upon Me in the day of trouble: I will deliver thee, and thou shalt glorify Me."*

"Lord Jesus, help me." Her cry came from the depths of her heart, and she knew her Lord would hear.

In the next instant she saw the buggy whip. She stopped struggling as her hand closed around it. She cracked the whip over the horses' backs, startling them. They reared and came down in a run, whinnying with fright.

Trennen fell off balance, landing on the floor with a cry of pain. Cool air rushed in where Trennen had been, and Eliza knew she was free. She scrambled to the side and, without thinking of the consequences, jumped from the racing buggy.

❀

ames stood outside on the street while Orval closed and locked the door of the cooperage.

"I sure appreciate you staying tonight," his boss said.

"That's all right. I'm glad to see it done."

The two men walked around the building to where James's horse and Orval's buggy waited.

James flexed his shoulders, then pulled his collar up around his neck before reaching for his horse's reins. A misty rain began to fall. "Think it might turn to snow before morning?"

"Could be," Orval said. "My girls always thought we should have snow for Christmas. Maybe they'll get their wish this year." He climbed into his buggy. "Take care going home. If this picks up before you get there, you'll be soaked."

James swung into the saddle and nodded. "I'll see you in the morning at church."

He rode at a brisk trot, glad that the cold mist fell against his back. He'd soon be home in the dry with a cup of hot coffee in his hands. His mind turned to the subject that had haunted him day and night for two months. What had he done to Eliza?

He shouldn't have taken the liberty of kissing her behind the toolshed, but she hadn't seemed to mind at the time. His heart quickened at the memory.

He'd tried time after time to talk to her, but she always cut him off. He frowned as he thought of Trennen. What did Eliza think she was doing, walking out with a fellow like that?

As he turned down the road to his house, he saw buggy lanterns coming toward him. It seemed odd that someone would be out so late on such a miserable night. The buggy came fast and then veered toward him as if trying to run him off the road.

James pulled his horse to the side, narrowly missing a collision. As it whipped past, he recognized the Wingate buggy. He was almost certain Trennen sat bent over in the driver's seat. He must be in an awfully big hurry.

James went on, hunching his shoulders against the rain while he watched for any more surprises. Then several yards before he reached his house, he heard a soft moan from the side of the road. He reined in and dismounted.

❀

Eliza lay in a crumpled heap. She heard the buggy go on without her and then a blackness, darker than night, closed in, taking her away from the terror she had just experienced.

"Eliza, what are you doing here? Are you hurt?" Gentle hands scooped her up, and she moaned in answer to the distant voice.

She tried to open her eyes, but her lids were so heavy. She laid her head on the man's shoulder, trying to burrow deeper into his arms.

He groaned. "Oh, Eliza, my love. If he's hurt you, as God is my witness, I'll make him pay."

She tried to respond, to tell him she wasn't hurt, but she was so sleepy. She couldn't keep her eyes open, and the words wouldn't come.

Then they were at his house.

❦

James struggled with the door, and his sister opened it. She looked at his burden with wide eyes. "What happened? What are you doing with. . . ?"

"I found her by the side of the road just outside," James interrupted as he brushed past. "Mother, can I put her on your bed?"

"Of course." She led the way and then pulled the covers back as James carefully laid Eliza down. He knelt by the bed to unlace Eliza's shoes and slip them from her feet. He pulled the covers up, pausing when he saw her torn dress. His gaze moved to her face where a new bruise marred one pale cheek just under her closed eyelashes. His eyes darkened and his jaw clenched as he gently tucked the covers under her chin.

"What happened, son?"

He turned toward his mother and shook his head. "I'm not sure. I'm going back into town for her father and the doctor."

"I'll take care of her." Mrs. Hurley followed him back into the kitchen. "There's hot coffee on the stove. Won't you have a cup before you go back out?"

"I can't take the time. If anything happens to her. . ." He didn't finish, but he knew his mother understood.

James couldn't push his horse fast enough. The mist had turned to a gentle drizzle, and it hit him full in the face, but he hardly noticed. All he could think of was the girl in his mother's bed. Would she be all right? He prayed every step of the way that she would.

Lights blazed from the front of the Jacksons' house. The door opened immediately on James's knock. Mr. Jackson stood framed in the doorway. "James, have you seen Eliza?" Worry lines etched around his eyes.

"Yes, she's at my house."

"Thank God. I was just getting ready to go look for her." Orval visibly relaxed.

"Sir, something's happened to her. I think you'd better come."

Orval's face went pale. "What do you mean? Is she hurt?"

"Right now she's asleep. I'd like to get the doctor to take a look at her, if you don't mind."

"I'm going with you, Orval." Mary crowded close to her husband's side.

"It's raining, Mary."

"Orval, she's my daughter, too. I'll get my heavy cloak." She turned back into the house.

"May I go after the doctor, sir?" James asked. He wanted to be on his way.

"I'd appreciate that, James." Orval nodded. "We'll be there as soon as we can."

When James reined his horse back into his own yard, the Jacksons had just arrived. He called to them before going to the barn. "Doc's on his way. Go on in."

James took care of his horse before he walked to the house. He stopped outside and looked in the direction of town. Right now Eliza was his primary concern, but tomorrow would find him at Trennen Von Hall's door.

She was still asleep. Mary sat beside the bed, holding her hand. Orval sat by his wife, his eyes never leaving his daughter's face.

The doctor came in a bustle of reassurance. He shooed all but Mary from the room. James paced the kitchen floor, finally throwing himself into a chair at the table when his mother pushed a cup of coffee into his hands.

He watched the closed door, willing it to open. How he longed for Eliza to look up at him again with her saucy little grin. He hadn't known how much he could miss her sharp tongue until now.

"James, I'm sure she'll be all right." His mother rested her hand on his shoulder.

"Trennen did this to her." He still watched the door.

Orval turned at his words. "I figured as much. He was supposed to bring her home. He must have decided to take his brother and sister home first."

"So he could get her alone." The words stuck in James's throat. "But he won't get away with it."

"There's the doctor now." Mrs. Hurley's hand tightened on James's shoulder as the door opened.

James tried to see past the doctor, but he pulled the door closed and crossed the room to the woodstove. He held his hands above it, warming them. "Before you go in, Mr. Jackson, I've a few words to say. She's awake now, but she's upset."

James's heart skipped a beat.

"The young man she was with suffered a broken arm when the horses got away from him. I set it just before James came to get me, although at the time I didn't know there was another casualty."

"Is she hurt in any way?" Orval asked.

The doctor shook his head. "Just a few bruises. She'll be fine. You take her home tonight and put her in her own bed. Let her take it easy a couple of days, and she'll be good as new."

Orval disappeared into the bedroom and closed the door behind him. As James sat there waiting, he knew without doubt that he loved Eliza Jackson. He determined that when she was well, if she would let him within shouting distance, he would tell her just how he felt about her.

Chapter 14

Eliza woke to a gentle kiss on her cheek. Mary straightened and smiled at her. "How are you feeling this morning?"

"All right." Eliza turned her face toward the wall. "Where's my father?"

Mary sat on the edge of the bed. "He's gone to church. Eliza. . ." Mary touched her shoulder. "Can you tell me what happened last night?"

Eliza pulled the covers close. "I have a headache. I'd like to sleep."

"All right, dear." Mary stood. "But you're going to have to face this sooner or later. Your father plans to visit with Trennen today. If he hurt you. . ."

"No." Eliza shook her head and then winced with the pain. Tears sprang to her eyes. She blotted them with the covers, keeping her face from Mary. "I jumped from the buggy."

Mary reached out and smoothed Eliza's hair. "We have a lot to thank God for."

Eliza tried to sleep, but she kept remembering. She knew Mary was right. It had taken a miracle for her to get away from Trennen and another to keep her from serious injury when she jumped.

She prayed, thanking God for His love and help. Although she felt better, heaviness remained in her heart—deadness to her soul that she didn't know what to do about. She prayed again, asking God to remove the heaviness, but still it remained. Something was keeping her from full favor with God.

At noon Father came into her room. He sat on the edge of her bed. "How are you feeling, Eliza?"

"I have a headache."

"I need to know what happened to you last night."

"What difference does it make?"

"It makes a lot of difference." Father frowned. "According to Mr. Wingate, Trennen didn't come home last night."

"He took the Wingates' buggy?"

"No, it's there, but Trennen is gone. Mr. Wingate is on his way to the Von Hall home." He shook his head. "I don't think he'd go far. According to the doctor, his arm was broken last night."

The hint of a smile broke Father's serious look. "What'd you do to him?"

Eliza looked at her father. "I prayed. Then I saw the buggy whip and cracked it across the horses. Trennen lost his balance and fell to the floor. That was when I jumped."

"And you got this bruise on your face." He tenderly touched the bruise with the back of his fingers.

Mary knocked on the door and entered, carrying a tray of food. Father stepped out of her way as she placed it across Eliza's lap. He grinned down at Eliza pushing herself upright. "So we're feeding this girl in bed, are we?"

"Don't bother Eliza." Mary straightened and playfully shoved her husband toward the door. "Your dinner's waiting downstairs."

Eliza watched them leave. She hadn't told him what Trennen had tried to do to her, but she thought her father knew, anyway.

What would Father do to Trennen? He said he planned to talk to him. At the moment she didn't care what happened to him as long as he never touched her again.

※

James went home from church with a heavy heart. He'd hoped to confront Trennen, but it seemed the scoundrel had disappeared. He ate dinner, then went outside to care for his animals. A light snow had fallen in the early morning hours. He'd have to fork some hay down and check on his stock.

On the way to the barn, he saw the Wingate buggy drive past. His heart quickened until he realized Mr. Wingate drove it. He waved and went on to the barn.

He'd just finished with the hay when he heard his name called. "James. James, I need your help."

Mr. Wingate hurried toward the barn as James ran out. "It's Vanda. She's been hurt bad. Come, help me." His sentences came out in gasps.

James told his mother where he was going before jumping into the buggy beside Mr. Wingate.

Vanda lay on a small cot in the front room of the cabin, her face a stark contrast to her dark hair spread out on the pillow. A thin blanket covered her, and the room felt like ice. Her face, with one eye swollen shut, was bruised almost beyond recognition. She appeared to be sleeping.

James looked at Mr. Wingate's ashen face. "Where's Cletis?"

"I don't know. He's not here."

James reached out and touched Vanda's neck. A faint pulse beat under his fingers. "She's still alive, but she won't be if we don't get help."

Vanda moaned as he picked her up, blanket and all. He tried to carry her as gently as he could. He laid her on the back seat of the buggy, then climbed in and put her head on his lap. He tried to cushion her as best he could to help smooth the ride.

James breathed a prayer of thanks when Mr. Wingate stopped in front of the doctor's house. They hurriedly carried Vanda into the doctor's examining room. As the doctor probed for broken bones and internal injuries, Mr. Wingate's plump face turned red with indignation. "It's that no-good father of hers, I'll wager. We tried to help the children, but he wouldn't hear of it."

The doctor nodded. "I know you did what you could. No one in this town can fault you there."

James felt cheated when the blame shifted from Trennen, but he shrugged off his personal feelings and asked the doctor, "Will she be all right?"

"There are some broken ribs, and as you can see, she's badly bruised." He shook his head. "Whoever did this to her did a thorough job."

"That no-good—" Mr. Wingate started.

"Yes, I've no doubt you're right about that." The doctor nodded. "But it may be tomorrow before she's able to tell us for sure."

James saw Vanda's eyelid flutter. He took a step forward. "She's coming to."

The three men crowded near. Mr. Wingate got down on one knee near her head. "Vanda, honey, who did this to you?"

Her good eye stared at him, but there was no answer. He tried again. "Did your father hit you?"

A tear ran out of her eye.

Mr. Wingate looked up. "There's your answer."

He turned back to her. "What happened to Cletis? Do you know if he took him?"

"Now you've gone and done it." The doctor frowned at Mr. Wingate. "If she didn't know he was gone, you've given her something to worry about."

"Look." James watched the slow up and down movement of her head. "She knows."

Mr. Wingate insisted that Vanda be moved to his house. After the doctor bandaged her and gave her some laudanum for pain, James carried her to the buggy and then into the Wingate home.

❦

Monday at noon, Eliza sat by her window to watch for her father. When she saw him, she pulled her dressing gown on and ran from her room. By the time she got to the kitchen door, she could hear Mary and Father talking. He said, "I suppose she's better than yesterday, but she's still in pitiful shape."

Eliza stopped, her hand on the door. She pressed close to listen.

"The poor girl." Mary sighed. "I can't understand how a father could do such a thing. Has she been able to talk yet?"

"As a matter of fact she has." A chair scraped across the floor.

Eliza pushed the door open a crack until she could see her father sitting by the table. Mary placed a buttered hot roll in front of him.

"M-m-m." He grinned his appreciation. "You're spoiling me."

Mary smiled before moving out of Eliza's sight. "What about Vanda being able to talk?"

Vanda had been hurt. Why hadn't they told her? Eliza pushed the door open and stormed into the room. "What's wrong with Vanda?"

"Should you be out of bed?" Father rushed to her side, taking her arm.

She jerked away. "I'm not sick. I want to know about Vanda. What's happened to her?"

Father told what he knew and that Vanda was now at the Wingates'.

"Father, I want to see her."

"I don't think so." He shook his head.

"Please, Father."

"Would it hurt for her to go just for a few minutes?" Mary intervened on Eliza's behalf.

He frowned. "She's been beaten, Eliza, almost to death. You won't recognize her."

Although Father argued, in the end, Eliza won.

She dressed with care in a blue dress made with thin balloon oversleeves. She selected the matching blue bonnet that looked like a hat with a wide rim framing her head. She tied the blue satin ribbons in a wide bow. She wanted to look her best for Vanda.

Yet when she saw her, she realized her father had been right. The purple, swollen face that turned toward her was unrecognizable.

"It's me, Eliza." The voice sounded like Vanda's, although slurred. "Sit here by me."

Eliza wiped tears away as she sat on the bed.

Vanda smiled and closed her hand around Eliza's. "It isn't as bad as it looks. I think he just hit me a couple of times in the face."

"Oh, Vanda, how can you joke about it?" Eliza wanted to cry.

"I'm not joking. I think that's what happened."

"But it looks like he ran your face through the sausage mill."

Eliza was surprised at Vanda's laugh. "Oh, that hurts." She quickly composed herself. "Here you sit, pretty as a picture, and tell me how ugly I am."

"I didn't mean that," Eliza quickly assured her and then saw the twinkle in the other girl's eye. "Oh. You're joking again. After what you've been through, I'd think you'd need to be cheered up instead of the other way around."

Vanda's eyes grew serious. "You have a bruise, too. I heard you went through a bad experience that same night."

Eliza's eyes widened. "How did you hear?"

Vanda's mouth twisted into a small, lopsided smile. "I'm learning to be quiet and listen." Her smile vanished. "At least Trennen won't bother you anymore."

Eliza's heartbeat increased. "What do you mean by that?"

"He left this morning on the stage."

Eliza frowned. "No one told me."

"They aren't telling me, either. I suppose they think I'm not strong enough Again she smiled. "They don't know that the Lord is my strength."

Eliza smiled tenderly at her friend. "Father said the entire church is prayin for your quick recovery."

"Then I will be out of this bed in time for the Christmas program. Vanda's eyes shone. "I want to see it even if I can't be Mary." Her hand move to touch her side. "I only have a couple of broken ribs. That won't keep m down long."

"I'm sure it won't." Eliza wondered how Vanda could possibly be up an around in two more weeks.

Vanda reached out and squeezed Eliza's hand. "Do you remember I aske you to pray for my father?"

Eliza nodded.

"I'd like for you to pray with me even harder now." A tear rolled from Vanda's eye. "I don't know where he is or what he's doing, but I'm afraid he wil die without knowing Jesus."

"Aren't you angry with him for what he did? You almost died. You woul have if they hadn't found you."

Vanda shook her head. "He didn't know what he was doing. Don't you see Eliza? My sins nailed Jesus to the cross. How can I help but forgive others when I have been forgiven so much?"

Eliza sat and stared at her friend. Vanda meant what she said. Eliza bowed her head. She nodded. "I'll join you in praying for your father."

Eliza didn't stay long after that. She needed the privacy of her room where she could think and pray. Vanda was a babe in Christ, but she had taught Eliza something that she would never forget as long as she lived.

For hours Eliza stayed shut away in her room, where the others thought she was resting. Instead she fell to her knees beside her bed, alternately reading God's Word and praying. At first unwilling to give up her own feelings, she finally saw herself honestly for the first time in many months as God revealed what she would have to do in order to be brought back to the right relationship with Him that she craved.

After a time, she arose and washed away the tears of her soul-searching. She glanced out the window and saw it was still too early for her father to be home from work. She needed to talk to Mary.

Mary sat at the table peeling potatoes for supper.

Eliza sat in a chair across the table, unsure of how to begin. How could she break down the wall she had built with a simple apology? But she knew she must try.

Mary turned to smile at her. "Did you have a nice rest, dear?"

Eliza shook her head. "I was praying about something that's been bothering me."

"Is it anything I can help with?"

Eliza smiled at Mary. "I think I already have my answer. Do you have a moment?"

"Of course."

Eliza looked into Mary's kind, green eyes. "Do you love my father? I mean, really love him?"

A tinge of pink touched Mary's cheeks. She smiled and nodded. "I love your father very much. I thank God every day that He led you to introduce us."

Eliza bowed her head as moisture clouded her vision. "I've been terrible."

Mary's hand stretched across the table to cover Eliza's with a sympathetic touch. "You've had a hard time adjusting, but God has assured us all along that you would come through this."

"You've been praying for me?"

"I pray for you every day, Eliza. I care about you. I loved you before I loved your father, you know. You were my friend, and then you were my daughter."

Eliza looked up at Mary, disbelief covering her face. Mary had forgiven her before she even asked.

But Mary misread Eliza's expression. "No, I don't mean I'm trying to take your mother's place. No one could do that, and I wouldn't want to. She will always have a special place in your heart and in your father's. That's only right. But don't you see? It's the same with me. I already have one daughter, yet I have plenty of room in my heart to love five more. That doesn't mean I love Kathrene less. It just means I love you as much."

Tears streamed down Eliza's face. All she could do was choke out the words, "I love you, too, Mary. I'm so sorry."

She didn't remember moving out of her chair, but she found herself kneeling on the floor with her head in Mary's lap.

Mary stroked her hair, crooning words of forgiveness as the healing tears fell.

Finally, Eliza pulled away, her face wet with tears, a smile on her lips. She reached out and took both of Mary's hands in hers. "I'm so glad I came to talk to you."

"I am, too." Mary smiled through her own tears. "You don't know how glad."

"What's going on here?" Neither had noticed Father come in. He stood looking from one to the other.

Eliza jumped up and grabbed him around the neck. "I love you, Father."

His arms slipped around her as he held her close. "I love you, too, Eliza." He looked over her head at Mary, his eyebrows lifted in question.

Mary stood. "Eliza and I have just come to a wonderful understanding." She stepped to her husband's side, and he put one arm around her. "We've decided there's room in our hearts for each other and for you, too."

Father let out a long breath. "That's the best news I've heard in a long time."

❧

The next day Eliza returned to visit Vanda. She went every day that week, each time noticing an improvement in Vanda's condition. Still, no word came about Cletis and his father. Eliza knew Vanda worried about them. On Friday, as Eliza left, Vanda caught her hand and held it. "Eliza, would you pray with me right now for Cletis and Poppa?"

Eliza nodded. Still holding Vanda's hand, she knelt beside the bed, and together the girls prayed that God would protect the two and bring them to salvation.

The following week when Eliza prayed with her friend again, Vanda kept her hand. "Wait, Eliza, please."

Eliza remained on her knees.

"I know what Trennen did to you. I know Uncle Charles sent him away because of it. And I wouldn't blame you if you don't want to, but I think he needs our prayers, too."

Eliza hesitated only a moment. "I'll pray with you for your brother."

As Vanda's physical strength returned, Eliza's spiritual strength grew. She spent more time in prayer and Bible reading during those weeks than she had in the past two years. Her relationship with Mary became a treasure. Kathrene, when she wasn't with Stephen, responded to Eliza's encouragement to become the sister she had always wanted to be.

But there was still one dark spot in Eliza's life. She could not forget James Hurley. Every time she thought of him, a dart driven by Lenny's words pierced her heart. *Father got you James, didn't he?* It hurt more every day.

A light snow began to fall Sunday afternoon. That evening, buggies and wagons arrived early for the Christmas program. The church shone with candles and lanterns and buzzed with the excited voices of parents and children alike. Both front corners of the church had been partitioned off with sheets and quilts to make two small rooms where the actors could get into costume. Eliza wound her way behind Lenny through the crowded church.

Someone jostled her, and she fell into James. His hands closed over her upper arms to steady her, and he did not let go. She found herself eye level with his mouth. Her gaze lifted to his dark gray eyes frowning down at her.

"Are you all right, Miss Jackson?"

At the formal use of her name, she stiffened and pulled back. "I'm just fine, thank you, Mr. Hurley. Now if you'll excuse me, I'm supposed to be an angel tonight."

A slow smile spread across his face. "That should be interesting."

"Oh!" She jerked away and moved as quickly as she could to the corner where the angels were dressing. She slipped through a space between two quilts, glad to be out of his sight. She knew her face flamed.

"Eliza, here's your costume." Kathrene tossed it to her, then slipped into her own. Eliza carefully wrapped the sheet around herself, and Kathrene tied it into place. The halo and wings were harder to keep on, but finally all three angels were ready.

"Who's going to play Mary now that Vanda isn't able to?" Barbara whispered.

"I don't know," Eliza whispered back. Yesterday afternoon at their last rehearsal, a replacement still hadn't been announced.

The program began with the small children. One gave a welcome that brought a round of applause. Then several others sang "What Child Is This?"

The angels peeked through narrow cracks between quilts. Eliza could see the front of the church where most of the activity took place.

"What's going on?" She whispered to the other angels as a hush fell over the congregation and several gasps were heard. Applause filled the church. The girls could only look at each other and wonder what was happening. Then as quickly as the applause began, it stopped.

As a hush fell on the congregation, Eliza saw a hooded Mary and Joseph cross the pulpit area. Mary turned and, with Joseph's help, sank to the floor behind the manger. It was Vanda. Her face, yellow and green with bruises and still distorted by the swelling, had never looked lovelier to Eliza. A glow seemed to emanate from her serene expression. She kept her eyelids lowered in reverence. Then she reached out and lifted a doll from the straw-filled manger and cradled it in her arms.

While the shepherds came from the opposite corner, Eliza followed Barbara to stand behind Mary and Joseph. Kathrene stepped forward and sang "Angels from the Realms of Glory."

When Eliza blended her voice with Barbara's on the chorus, she felt God's presence. She was so thankful that God had given His only Son to become the sacrifice for her sins. There was no love greater than that.

❄

James sat beside his mother and watched the Christmas program. He smiled at the small children and felt proud of his younger sister, but the one person he most wanted to see was hidden from his view in the front corner of the church. He brought to mind the snapping brown eyes that were becoming a regular visitor to his dreams. He remembered the feel of her satin cheek, the softness of her dark hair caught in his fingers.

He loved Eliza Jackson, but she wanted nothing to do with him. For the thousandth time he asked himself what he had done to turn her away.

And then she stepped from the curtains that hid her and stood behind Mary and Joseph. He had made fun of her being an angel, but as he stared at her, he knew he had never seen a more beautiful angel. Her eyes lifted above the heads of the congregation as if she looked into heaven. The yellowed bruise still covered her cheek, yet a soft smile touched her radiant face, making her appear beyond the reach of earth—and man.

The dull ache in his chest had become part of him. Because she was beyond his reach. He looked down at his clenched fists. He'd tried to talk to her, but she wouldn't listen. She went out of her way to avoid him. He had to find out what was wrong if he had to have a talk with her father to do it.

❋

Winter came with a vengeance after the Christmas program. One snowfall followed another until the drifts measured more than four feet deep. Father said Old Man Winter was making up for last year's mild weather.

Eliza was glad the weather kept her from seeing James. Maybe if she didn't see him, she could forget him. She spent most of her time in the house helping Mary and Kathrene or playing with Nora. She began to look forward to spring when she would have a new brother or sister.

Then, winter gave way to spring flowers and sunshine. A time of new growth. Kathrene accepted Stephen's marriage proposal, but Eliza's life seemed to stall as her heart refused to forget James. All winter she had tried to block him from her thoughts, yet the first day she went back to church, he was there. When their eyes met, she knew she would have to learn to live with the pain of her love for him.

One day Father came home from work at noon with some news. He came into the kitchen where the women were working, a large smile on his face. "You'll never guess who just arrived in town."

Lenny came into the kitchen from the parlor. Father reached out and ruffled his hair. "You'll be wanting to hear this, too."

"Tell us who before we burst with curiosity," Mary said.

"Cletis Von Hall."

"Cletis!" Eliza squealed before Lenny could react. "Was his father with him? Where had he been? Did he go see Vanda? Oh, she'll be so happy he's all right. Is he, Father?"

Father laughed. "Yes, Eliza, Cletis is fine. As soon as we told him where Vanda was, he went to see her." Then he grew serious. "His father wasn't with him."

Silence fell around the table as her father related the story told to him. "After Von Hall beat Vanda unconscious, he picked her up and put her on the cot in the main room of the cabin. He covered her with a blanket, but when she mained limp and unresponsive, he thought she was dead.

"Cletis said his father panicked and ran, taking him. By the time they got to town called Rolla, Mr. Von Hall was desperate for more whiskey, but he didn't ave the money. He shook like he had a chill, and then he broke down and cried. He was like that for hours until he slept. When he woke, he took Cletis into own. They stopped at the first church they came to. Cletis said he didn't know hat happened there except his father talked to the preacher, and he wasn't aking anymore. The preacher went with them to the sheriff."

"He turned himself in." Eliza frowned. "Why didn't we hear anything? Vouldn't they have checked to see if Vanda really died?"

"Yes, except before they could, the weather got bad. A fire broke out in a ouse next to the jail. The two prisoners were released to help fight it. Von Hall eard a little girl crying. He perished saving her life."

Eliza scarcely noticed the tears running down her face. God had granted anda's wish to be used by Him.

"Cletis stayed with the minister until the weather cleared enough to send im home."

❦

he next morning, Eliza put on her nicest visiting dress and went with Lenny o the Wingates' house. Mrs. Wingate took Lenny back to the kitchen to eat snack with Cletis, leaving the two girls alone in the parlor. They met in the niddle of the room and hugged. Eliza couldn't stop the tears.

As they pulled apart, she said, "I'm sorry, Vanda, about what's happened."

Vanda nodded. "Thank you. God knows what's best for us. I'll always emember my father died a hero. And I have Cletis back."

"Yes, how is he?"

Vanda smiled. "I don't think you'd recognize him. Oh, he looks about the ame, but he doesn't act it. He was so rebellious before, but now he's trying really hard to do right. He even asked me if I thought God loved him."

"That's wonderful, Vanda."

"Yes, and that's not all." Vanda sat on the edge of a chair. Her eyes shone. Cletis and I are going away. We have an aunt in Boston who wants us to come ive with her. She has no children. Uncle Charles says she and her husband are a wonderful Christian couple who will probably spoil us rotten."

"Oh, Vanda!" Eliza couldn't help the cry of dismay that leapt to her lips. You can't leave."

"I know, Eliza." Vanda crossed to the sofa and sat beside her, putting her arm around her shoulders. "I'll miss you, but I believe this is for the best. I want Cletis to grow up in a home where there is discipline and love. I think he will have that with our aunt and uncle."

"Why couldn't he get that here?"

"Uncle Charles and Aunt Martha do love us, but they are too close to all that's happened. And they aren't as young as our other aunt and uncle." Vanda smiled. "Besides, I have a feeling Cletis will need a father young enough to keep up with him."

Eliza knew in her heart that Vanda was right, yet she knew she would never forget her friend.

Chapter 15

Vanda left the first week of April. Eliza stood by the stagecoach with her. Vanda wore a soft blue dress of the latest fashion, and Eliza knew several more new dresses were packed in her trunk. Mrs. Wingate had made sure her niece and nephew would not be ashamed when they arrived at their new home. Eliza waited while the others told Vanda good-bye, and then she stepped forward.

"I don't know how I'll ever get along without you." She hugged Vanda with tears in her eyes.

"You promised to not cry." Vanda hugged Eliza tight. "I'll write to you as soon as I get there."

"You'd better." Eliza forced a smile. "Because I can't write to you until I get your address, and as soon as you're gone, I'll think of a million things to tell you."

"Eliza, you're the best friend I've ever had. If it hadn't been for you, I'd never have found Jesus as my Lord."

"I didn't do anything."

"Oh yes, you did. At first I only went to church because you were there. You were my friend, and I wanted to be with you. Then the message of God's salvation got through to me, and I went because I knew there was something missing in my life. If you hadn't been my friend, I'd have never heard that message."

Eliza could only say, "I'm glad."

"You're not going to leave without telling me good-bye, are you?" James's voice called from behind Eliza. Her heart began the hard quick pound that had become all too familiar in his presence.

"Of course not." Vanda extended her hand, and James shook it.

"This town will miss you two very much, you know." James smiled down at Vanda.

"Oh, I don't know about that." Vanda returned his smile. "But I do know we'll miss all of you."

"You take care." James turned as if to leave.

"I will." A twinkle entered Vanda's eyes. "And you take care of my friend."

James looked at Eliza. His eyes were serious as he said, "There's nothing I would like better." Then he turned and walked away.

"Better get aboard, miss," the driver called from the open door of the coach.

"I've got to go." Vanda gave Eliza another hug. She whispered near her ear,

"Be good to James." Then she and Cletis climbed on the stage.

Eliza stood by the side of the road, waving until Vanda disappeared in a cloud of dust.

❀

The next day, Kathrene came in from an outing with Stephen. Her eyes shone. "Eliza, do you want to hear something funny?"

Eliza sank into a nearby chair. "It would probably be more entertaining than what I've been doing."

Kathrene sat on the sofa. "Stephen has been keeping things from me, but today he confessed."

Eliza sat a little straighter.

"We went out to look at the house." Kathrene clasped her hands in front. "Eliza, he's building a mansion for me."

Eliza frowned. She was sure Kathrene would think anything Stephen built was perfect. But really! How could a penniless beggar. . . ?

"Remember how we all thought he was poor?"

Eliza nodded.

"He isn't poor at all." Kathrene laughed. "He just wanted me to think that because he wanted me to love him for himself and not for his money."

"What would make him do that?" Eliza was as puzzled by Stephen as she had been the first time she'd seen him.

Kathrene sobered. "He's from New York where his father owns some factories and several other businesses. His father wanted him, along with his younger brother, to take over the businesses." She paused. "Stephen was engaged to be married before."

Eliza's eyes widened. "What happened?"

"He found out she was marrying him for his money. He was deeply hurt and angry. So he sold his share of the businesses to his brother, reinvested a lot of it in some regional railroads, and came west."

"But, Kathrene, what if he wants to return to New York someday? Would you go with him?"

Kathrene shook her head. "I don't think I have to worry about that. Stephen has assured me that Missouri is where he wants to live and die. He knows I'm not marrying him for what he can give me. And he knows the people here like and respect him for himself, not because of his money."

She held up her hand. "Please, Eliza, don't ever tell anyone just how wealthy Stephen is. He loves it here, and he wants to make a home for us where we can be like our neighbors."

"Are you telling me that Stephen is even more wealthy than the Wingates?" Eliza could scarcely believe that.

Kathrene laughed. "I'm afraid so, but you'd never know it, would you?"

"What about your house? Is it really a mansion?"

"I might have exaggerated on that. It's a very nice two-story frame house." Kathrene smiled. "Eliza, I really love Stephen. I'd be content to live in a log cabin at the edge of town as long as I can be with him. I don't care about his money."

One morning in mid-April, about an hour before Father was due home for dinner, Mary called to Eliza, "Would you please run and get your father? Tell him I'm not feeling well."

As Eliza started to go, Mary called to her again, "If you see Kathrene, please tell her to come to my bedroom."

Eliza ran up the stairs as fast as she could and pounded on Kathrene's bedroom door before jerking it open. "Kathrene, your mother needs you right away in her bedroom. I think it's her time."

Eliza left the house in a run until she reached the business part of town.

With her breath coming in gasps, she passed the cooperage and stuck her head in the chandler shop. The front room was empty. She crossed to the back room. No one was there, either. As she turned around and started back across the showroom, James opened the door and came inside.

They stood for an eternity staring at each other. He spoke first. "I thought you were a customer."

How could she speak past her pounding heart? "It's Mary. Where's my father?"

Immediately he understood the problem. "He left just a minute ago to make a delivery. I'll catch him." He stopped at the door. "Do you want to wait here?"

She followed him as he went around the building where his horse stood grazing. She watched him saddle the horse, trying to decide what she should do. Kathrene was with Mary. Surely they wouldn't need her. Maybe she should stay and watch the shops until either Father or James returned.

"What about the doctor? Do you want me to leave word with him, too?" James swung into the saddle.

At her nod, he smiled. "Don't worry. I'll give your father my horse; then I'll make the delivery and come right back." He nudged his horse forward, calling over his shoulder. "If you decide to leave, be sure and put the closed signs in the doors."

She watched him spur his horse into a run before she turned back toward the chandler shop. She opened the door, stepped inside, and collapsed onto the stool behind Father's high counter. Her knees and hands trembled. She crossed her arms on the counter and laid her head on them, trying to still the tremors that passed through her body. She prayed for Mary, asking God to give her a safe delivery and a healthy child.

"Are you all right, Eliza?" Mrs. Johnson stood in the middle of the shop, a concerned expression on her face.

Eliza smiled at the elderly lady. "Yes, I'm fine. Is there anything I can help you with?"

By the time Mrs. Johnson had made her selections and gone, Eliza figured James had caught up to Father. Maybe he was on his way home. And that was exactly where she should be going. If she waited around the shops, James would come back, and she'd be alone with him. She didn't want to take that chance.

But before Eliza could close the shops, Mr. Morrison stopped with an order for barrels. He finally left, and she put the closed sign in the shop window. As she turned to leave, James pulled Father's wagon in and stopped. As usual her heart pounded when she saw him.

James jumped from the wagon and moved to her side. "I'm glad you're still here. I was afraid you'd go home."

He stood too close. "I'd really like to talk to you, Eliza."

"Whatever would we have to talk about?" She stepped back from his over-powering height. If she didn't get away, she might cave in and cry.

"Your father seems to think you're unhappy." He got no further.

Her head snapped up. She glared at him. "How dare you and my father discuss me! I am not your concern."

She pushed past him, then stopped long enough to fling one last remark at him, "I am also not a charity case, and I'll thank you to remember that."

❀

James watched Eliza disappear around the corner. What had she meant by her being a charity case? He shook his head. There was no understanding a woman when she was riled. But what had he done to make Eliza so angry with him?

He glanced at the wagon and smiled. Maybe there was one way to insure she stayed put long enough to find out what had got her back up. He'd have to wait a few days until the Jackson family settled down, but at the first opportunity, he'd enlist Mr. Jackson's help.

❀

The entire family crowded around the bed where Mary lay propped up, her face beaming with pride as she looked at Father. He sat on the side of the bed, a small bundle of blankets in his arms.

"Eliza, come see our new sister." Kathrene took her arm and pulled her to Father's side. "We've all been promised a chance to hold her, but Father's being a hog."

"You'll get your turn." Father looked up with a grin. He pulled a tiny hand from the blanket.

Nora squealed as the miniature fingers curled around Father's big one. "I hold my lovey."

She jumped on Mary's knees, and Father laughed. "Whoa, girl. You'll be hurting Mama doing that."

Immediately Nora stopped. "I sorry, Mama." She plopped down beside her father, her little legs stretched out. "I want my lovey."

"All right." Father passed the baby to Nora, keeping his hands under her head and back. "We'll start with the youngest and work our way back up to me."

"Be careful, Orval." Mary tried to see. "Don't let her drop her."

"Don't worry. I've got a good hold."

While Nora and Lenny got their turns with the baby, Eliza stepped to Mary's side. "Are you all right?" She clasped Mary's hand in both of hers.

Mary smiled. "I'm fine."

"Kathrene and I can take care of everything." Eliza remembered how tired her mother had been after Nora's birth. She had never regained her strength. She didn't want the same thing to happen to Mary.

Mary smiled and reached for Kathrene's hand with her other hand. "You don't know how much I appreciate both of you."

Eliza took her turn at holding the baby. The small bundle felt so light in her arms. She pulled the blanket back to see a tiny face framed by light brown hair with a hint of red in it. The little rosebud lips made a sucking motion and then grew quiet. The baby's eyes that had been closed in sleep opened and seemed to study her big sister's face. Love, as great as she had ever felt for Nora, swept through Eliza's heart. This baby was her sister.

She looked up at her father. "I wish Cora and Vickie and Ben could see her."

He nodded. "I know. I do, too."

"She's so perfect." Eliza was totally captivated. "What is her name?"

Kathrene reached for the baby. "Why don't you discuss a name with our parents while I hold my little sister?"

Eliza placed a kiss on the tiny forehead before relinquishing the baby to Kathrene. "Be careful with her."

"Eliza, I know how to hold a baby."

Father turned to Mary. "Have you picked a name?"

Mary shook her head. "Nothing I've thought of sounds right."

Eliza lifted Nora and sat with her on the bed. "How about you, Nora? Do you have any good ideas? What do you want us to call the baby?"

"Her's my lovey," Nora said.

Eliza squeezed her little sister. "Yes, she's a sweet little lovey just like you, but I don't think we want to name her that."

"Lovey, Lovelle, Lovena." Mary tried changing the word slightly. "Why can't we make our own name with some variation of that? I like the idea. It could mean sweet little loved one."

Father looked thoughtful. "What's wrong with Lovena?"

"Or we could spell it with a *u* so it's more like a name. How about Luvena?" Eliza suggested. "What about Luvena Anne or Luvena Marie?"

"Luvena Marie Jackson," Mary repeated and smiled. "I like it. What do you think, Orval?"

He nodded. "It sounds like our littlest girl has a name."

❈

Luvena, or Lovey, as Nora insisted on calling her, was a quiet baby. She slept most of the day, crying only when she had need of attention. And attention was one thing she had no lack of.

One day as Eliza rocked her little sister to sleep, she noticed Mary in the doorway of her bedroom watching them. A smile played around the corners of her mouth. "You are going to have that baby so spoiled no one can do anything with her."

"You don't really think love will spoil her, do you?" Eliza asked.

Mary reached down and took her baby. "No, and neither will rocking."

She stopped at the door, turning to say, "I'm going to put Luvena in her own bed, and then you and I are going to get your father's meal."

At dinner, Father looked across the table at Eliza. "How long has it been since you helped me with the shops?"

"Not counting the day Luvena was born?" At his nod, she thought back and couldn't remember the last time. She shrugged her shoulders. "I don't know. A long time, I guess."

He seemed interested in his food. "I've got a delivery needs to be made this afternoon. How'd you like to go along?"

"I'll go with you, Father." Lenny stopped chewing long enough to volunteer.

"No, this time I want Eliza to go. I'll tell you what, Lenny; you can go on the next delivery I have to make. How's that?" At Lenny's nod, Father looked back at Eliza. "How about it? There's a blue sky above and April flowers coming up all over the place. You couldn't pick a prettier day to go for a ride in the country."

She laughed. "All right. As soon as the dishes are done, I'll come."

"Eliza, I can do the dishes. Why don't you go on with Father now?" Kathrene urged her.

"Will we leave on the delivery right away?" Eliza didn't want to chance another encounter with James.

"Sure. The wagon's already loaded and sitting in back of the shops."

"All right, then." Eliza nodded. "I'll go." She knew Father had been concerned about her. If it'd make him feel better, she'd go with him. Besides, it was a beautiful day.

Her steps lagged as they approached her father's shops. Above all, she did not want to see James. She edged toward the side of the building. "I'll go around back and wait in the wagon."

Father nodded. "That's fine. I need to go inside for a moment." He waved her on as they parted. "This won't take long."

James was nowhere in sight. Eliza sighed with relief and climbed on the wagon. A bird scolded her from the branches of a nearby tree. She adjusted her skirts and tried to find the bird. The dense covering of green leaves hid it well. She tilted her head back and looked all the way to the top of the tree. The scolding went on, and still she couldn't see it. Slowly, her eyes searched for the bird, branch by branch. She became so engrossed in finding the bird she didn't realize her father had returned until she felt the wagon move as he climbed on.

A flicker of blue in the tree caught her attention then, and without turning to look at him, she pointed at it. "Look up there, Father. Do you see that bird? He's been making a racket ever since he saw me, but I've just now found him."

When Father didn't answer but flicked the reins over the horse instead, Eliza turned to see what was wrong.

James looked back at her.

"No," the cry tore from her throat. "I will not go with you. Where is my father?"

The wagon moved forward. James shrugged. "Your father's in the shop, and you are going with me."

"James, I assure you, if you do not stop this wagon now and let me off, I'll jump."

With the speed of lightning, James grabbed her arm and pulled her close to his side. "You're just the little spitfire who would do that, aren't you?"

They pulled out and turned north down the Booneville Road. James's arm slipped around her shoulders. "James, let go of me." Eliza spoke through clenched teeth. Her heart pounded hard in her chest. "This is not proper. People are looking at us."

He grinned at her. "If you promise to behave yourself, I'll let go."

She tried to sit as dignified as possible with her side pressed against James. "All right. Let me go, and I won't jump." At his triumphant look, she added, "I won't talk to you, either."

They were past the business part of town, where the houses spread out thin. James relaxed his hold on her, letting her scoot as far as she could get from him. He nodded. "I guess that's a pretty good bargain. With your mouth shut, I might be able to tell you a thing or two."

She turned to him with fire in her eyes. "Like how much my father's paying you for this little excursion."

He looked at her with a puzzled expression. "He doesn't pay me extra for deliveries. Besides, what's that got to do with anything?"

"It has everything to do with it, and you know it." She retreated back into silence.

James shook his head. "If you're ready to not talk now, I'd like to talk to you."

"I told you I wouldn't talk to you, didn't I?" She refused to look at him.

"Yes, but it doesn't sound like you're ready."

"I'm ready anytime. But I'll have to warn you. I don't plan to listen to anything you have to say."

James let a burst of air escape through his teeth. "Eliza, you are the most aggravating woman I have ever met." After a second, he added. "You're also the prettiest."

She swung around to look at him, but he stared ahead down the road. "In the last six months, I don't know how many times I've tried to talk to you. But every time I start to say something, you run away or do something to stop me."

"I don't see any reason for us to talk."

"Well, I do." James raised his voice as he turned to look into her eyes. "Were you in love with Trennen?"

Eliza gasped. How could he ask her such a stupid question? She glared at him and then shifted in her seat.

"Eliza! You either sit still, or you sit over here where I can keep hold of you." At his commanding tone she froze.

A smile curved her lips. "I wasn't going to jump, James."

"Then answer my question. Were you, or are you, in love with Trennen?"

"That's ridiculous." She looked out at the countryside they were passing through. "In the first place it's none of your business, and in the second place it's insulting to know that anyone would even think I possibly could be."

James let his breath out in a *whish*. Eliza looked at him and saw a wide grin on his face. For some reason his happiness just added fuel to her anger.

"For your information, James Hurley, I think Trennen Von Hall is an extremely handsome man." She felt victory as his grin disappeared. But she couldn't help adding, "At first I enjoyed his company, but it didn't take long for that to wear thin."

"Then why did you continue keeping company with him?"

"Because I couldn't get rid of him. I told him I didn't want to see him anymore, but he wouldn't listen. I was scared of him. I didn't know what to do."

"Why didn't you tell your father?" James's jaw clenched. He hadn't known the extent of Eliza's problems with Trennen.

"I didn't think of it," Eliza answered his question. "I kept thinking he would leave me alone if I asked him to."

"I would have been glad to take care of him for you."

"Thank you. But he promised to leave me alone if I went with him that one last time to take Vanda and Cletis home."

He pulled the wagon to the side of the road and stopped. He turned to her.

'Eliza, I don't know what you think of me or if you ever think about me at all. I'm not handsome, and I don't have much worldly goods, but I've loved you ever since the first time you put me in my place." He picked up the reins. "Now I've told you what I've been wanting to, so I guess the rest is up to you."

"Put those down." Eliza waited until he laid the reins back down. "I don't believe you."

He stared at her. "You don't believe me?"

"No, I don't." She crossed her arms. "I know my father paid you to take me to that taffy pull. You didn't want to. Why should I believe anything you say?"

"Because I don't lie."

"Oh, you don't?" Eliza's voice rose. "And what do you call being paid to take a girl out and then acting like you enjoyed it?" She looked at him with accusing eyes. "You kissed me."

James's voice rose in volume to match hers. "I kissed you because I wanted to. And I did enjoy it. Both times." His voice suddenly dropped, and he frowned at her. "What are you talking about being paid, anyway?"

"My father, James." She spoke to him as if he were a child. "Lenny overheard him tell you to take me to Barbara's taffy pull. I would assume that was part of your job."

"Well, it wasn't." He doubled up his fist and hit his knee. "How you and Lenny could have gotten such a fool idea is beyond me. It just so happens that your father knew of my feelings for you."

Eliza's eyes widened as she listened to him.

"I told you I've loved you for a long time. I guess I wasn't too good at hiding it—at least not from your father. When Barbara invited me to her taffy pull, he asked me if I was going and who I would take. I told him I probably wouldn't go because you were the only girl I wanted to take and I didn't think you'd go with me. That day Lenny eavesdropped, your father told me you were in the other shop and would be leaving soon and I should ask you. Again, I told him I didn't think you'd go, but he was insistent that I'd never have a better chance."

He grinned at her then. "I decided it wouldn't hurt to ask. You couldn't do much more than bite my head off, and you'd already done that so many times I was getting used to it."

Eliza sat in stunned silence staring at him. Then she found her voice. "You mean you really wanted to take me? My father didn't talk you into it?"

He nodded, his eyes sparkling with amusement. "I mean I really wanted to take you."

"What about today? Whose idea was it to trick me into going with you?"

He grinned. "That was mine. Your father thought it was a good idea. Who knows? I may get a raise because of it."

"Oh, you." She halfheartedly hit at him, but he caught her hand in his.

They sat, turned toward each other, holding hands. Finally, he said, "I've told you I love you, Eliza. I need to know how you feel about me."

Her eyelids lowered, hiding her eyes. A spot of pink tinged each cheek. "I love you, James."

He moved across the seat closer to her. His forefinger cupped her chin, raising it until she had to look at him. "Please, say that again."

A smile played around the corners of her mouth as she obeyed. "I love you, James."

"Eliza, will you marry me?" James held his breath as he waited for her answer.

She nodded and uttered the one word he wanted to hear. "Yes."

His lips closed on hers in a long, sweet kiss. But when he lifted his head, Eliza's saucy little grin came back. "How much did my father pay you to ask me that?"

He groaned. His tone threatened. "Eliza. . ." But then he stopped and laughed. "I can see right now it'll take a heavy hand to keep you in line."

"And you're just the man for the job?"

He nodded. "That's right, and don't you forget it."

Her eyes widened as James leaned slowly and deliberately toward her. His right arm slipped around her while his left hand touched her cheek, then slid to the back of her head, taking her bonnet with it. When his mouth claimed hers, she felt as if she were floating, and she never wanted to come back to reality.

When the kiss ended, she saw that James was just as shaken as she was. He pulled her close, looking down at her with the light of love still shining in his eyes. "How soon can we get married?"

She pulled her bonnet back up and then leaned back against his shoulder with a sigh. "My birthday is in October. How about then?"

"October!" He pulled forward to see her face better. "I think my birthday would be a better time. It's in June."

"But Kathrene's getting married in June. I don't know if I can get ready that soon."

"Of course you can. What's there to do? We just stand up in front of the church and the preacher talks a little."

Eliza giggled. "Someone had better tell Kathrene she's doing it all wrong, then."

James let out a long breath. "Eliza, we won't need a bunch of stuff. We'll have to live with my mother."

When Eliza didn't say anything, James looked at her. "You don't want that, do you?"

She smiled, shaking her head. "We need to talk."

"What we need is our own cabin. How long would it take to put together a one-room cabin? A week or two at the most. That's all we'll need, and then after we're married, we'll build on to it. I know the folks around here would help us." He grinned. "We could get married the first of May."

Eliza laughed, then gave him a quick kiss. "You are wonderful, James Hurley. But you're going to lose your job if you don't get these barrels delivered, and then where will we be?"

"You don't have to worry about that." He laughed. "After all, I'm marrying the boss's daughter."

He picked up the reins and flicked them over the horse's back. This time, as the wagon rolled down the country road, there was no distance between its two occupants.

DEBORAH

Dedication

To those who read and enjoy my books.
Without you, there would be no reason to write.
May God's blessings always be yours.
Also to my son, Jonathan, who once upon a time
was an adorable two-year-old much like Tommy Stark.
Now he's a man with his own family.
Always walk with God, Jon.

Chapter 1

St. Louis, 1865

Deborah Asberry stood by the open grave between her mother and younger brother. Her husband's body rested in a pine casket next to the gaping hole, waiting to be lowered into the earth.

Tears ran down her cheeks as her father's voice, often choked by grief, expounded the bravery and sacrifice of his much loved son-in-law who had given his life in service to his country.

"Struck down by a rebel bullet in the prime of life, Jamison Lee Asberry fought with valor to reunite this great land. We will not forget Jamison or will our love for him wane as we look forward to seeing him again in that Holy City one day where we shall ever be with the Lord."

You loved Jamison, Father, but I didn't. I shall grieve for the loss of a young life, but I cannot grieve for lost love when there was none. Deborah knew her thoughts would have shocked everyone there. Everyone except her brother, Caleb. He knew she had been forced to marry Jamison. He alone knew how much she had hated the very idea.

She mopped at the tears and felt Caleb's arm slip around her shoulders. At sixteen, and four years younger than Deborah, he still stood a head above her. She leaned into his comforting embrace.

"It'll be all right, sis." His whispered words brought little assurance. "At least you don't have to live with him anymore."

"Father says I must move back home." Just the thought brought a fresh surge of tears. She knew they shouldn't be whispering during the service, so she forced a smile for her brother. "I'm sure you are right, though. Everything will work out."

"Shall we pray?" Jacob Smith, Deborah's father and pastor of the country church that sat beside the cemetery, bowed his head. "Father, into Your hands we commit the spirit of this beloved son, husband, and friend. He was Your child, born again of the Spirit of God. Truly a man of God, he served You in all his ways."

Her father's voice droned on as Deborah determined to make the most of her situation. She wiped the remaining tears from her face, knowing that she had no choices in her life. If her father said she must move back home, that's what she would do. Already her belongings had been taken to her father's house.

Her married life, though quite short, had taken her out from under her father's rule for almost a month. She and Jamison were married in a simple ceremony conducted in the church by her father. For two weeks they had lived together in the small cottage three blocks from her childhood home. In those two weeks she had learned that life under her husband's rule differed little from life under her father's rule. Then Jamison returned to his unit, and Deborah became mistress of her own home. For twelve days she had lived the life of freedom in a land torn by war.

Deborah let out a ragged sigh. What difference did it make? Married or single, her life was not her own and never would be.

Jacob no sooner had closed his prayer than a yell of triumph broke the muted sounds of weeping. A rider on horseback galloped hard toward the cemetery. With scarcely a pause in step, he called as he rode past, "The war's over! The South has surrendered!"

As if caught by an invisible net held by the rider, men and women ran to their buggies and horses. Soon the road leading into town became alive in a race for truth.

"No–o–o." The word became a wail as Jamison's mother fell to her knees before the closed casket. Her sobs and keening touched Deborah's heart. To lose her only son within days of the surrender no doubt was more than she could bear.

Deborah knelt beside the older woman and placed her arm around her shoulders. Her husband knelt on the other side, tears streaming down his face.

"I'm so sorry." Deborah tried to lend comfort only to have her mother-in-law pull away.

"Come, Deborah." Her father grasped her arm. "We must be going."

She watched Jamison's father lead his grieving wife away. Neither spoke to Deborah. By the time she and her father climbed into their buggy, the workers had lowered the casket and began covering it with dirt. Deborah watched until her father drove the buggy out of the churchyard, and then she turned her back on her married life and her in-laws.

Her father stopped at the parsonage long enough for Deborah and her mother to climb down. Then he and Caleb joined the throng seeking confirmation of the word that had already spread like wildfire across St. Louis, Missouri, that the War Between the States had at last ended.

Taking advantage of the reprieve her father's absence gave, Deborah went upstairs to her room. She closed the door and sank to her old bed. One glance around her bedroom revealed the few pieces of furniture she had taken with her into marriage. Her wardrobe stood against the wall again with all her clothing in it, and her trunk sat at the end of her bed.

She had been glad to leave Jamison's clothing and all his belongings to his mother. What the woman might do with them, Deborah neither knew nor cared. She looked down at her left hand where her wedding ring still remained. The plain gold band gleamed in the light from her window. She moved to the window seat and leaned back against the inside wall.

Slipping the ring from her finger, she looked inside where the initials D.R.S. and J.L.A. had been engraved with a heart between. A tear slipped from her eye and another followed.

Why couldn't she have found someone to love who would love her as much? She closed her eyes and leaned her head back, letting her fingers curl around the ring.

"Lord, why? Does love between husband and wife exist? Now that the war is over the men will be coming home. Am I asking too much? Please forgive me if I am. But if there is love left in this world, could You please send someone to me who will love me and treat me and our children with gentleness and care?"

Deborah allowed the pain of her lost dreams to wash over her as she leaned against the wall. After several minutes, she lifted her spirit before her Lord in praise and submission. "I am sorry, Lord, that I have questioned Your will for my life. For surely You know all things. You know my coming in and my going out forever. I give my will to You. Please help me submit to my father's direction."

With renewed peace in her heart, Deborah stood and crossed to her dresser. She opened the top drawer and took out a small box that held special treasures from her girlhood. Dropping in her wedding ring to nestle with a broken necklace and her grandmother's cameo brooch, Deborah closed the lid, placed the box back in the drawer, and went downstairs.

She found her mother in the kitchen. "Have Father and Caleb returned?"

"I heard the buggy just before you came down." Her mother crossed the kitchen and placed a hand on each of Deborah's shoulders as she searched her face. "Are you all right, dear?"

Deborah felt tears spring to her eyes at her mother's sympathy. She gave a short laugh that sounded more like a sob. "Oh Mother, I'm fine. I will grieve for Jamison because he died so young and so near the end of the war, but I will be fine."

The young widow brushed at the tears that would not stop. "But what will I do? I can't live in my father's house forever. I'm no longer a child."

" 'Take. . .no thought for the morrow.' " Her mother quoted the words of Christ, and Deborah knew she had been reprimanded in her mother's own gentle way. "Let's get through the next few days before we think of packing you off again, shall we?"

Deborah nodded, and the women separated to set out dishes of food that had been brought in by members of their church congregation.

Within a few short days, Deborah realized she had already fallen into the old habits of her childhood. So short had her marriage been that she felt as if it were nothing more than a figment of her imagination. Then almost one week after Jamison's funeral, the world rocked with the shocking news that President Abraham Lincoln had been shot down while attending a theater with his wife. Deborah had yet to recover from the national tragedy when her father called the family into the parlor after church the following Sunday evening.

Deborah sensed tension between her parents as she sat perched on the edge of her chair. She had no doubt this meeting concerned her.

Jacob Smith sat in the center of the sofa, leaning forward with his elbows on his knees, his head bowed as if in prayer. His wife, like Deborah, sat forward in her chair, her back rigid and her face expressionless except for the worry in her eyes.

Caleb stood behind Deborah's chair as if he, too, knew the news would not be good.

Jacob lifted his head and spoke. "I have received a letter from a small country church in the southwest part of the state. They've asked me to conduct a revival meeting. Mrs. Cora Stark, the lady who wrote, is an old family friend. Years ago, when we were children here in St. Louis, we all played together—I with her younger brother and she and her sister with your Aunt Margaret."

Deborah watched her father, wondering what this had to do with her.

"Mrs. Stark moved with her family to that sparsely settled part of Missouri back in the thirties and met her husband there. I understand her husband, Mr. Aaron Stark, is a good Christian man, and together they have raised seven fine boys." Jacob cleared his throat before going on.

"In her letter, Mrs. Stark wrote of her oldest son, Dane." He looked down at his hands. "He recently lost his wife in childbirth and is bearing the burden of raising his two small children alone. Mrs. Stark has tried to get him to allow another member of the family to take the children until they are older, but he refuses."

Jacob met Deborah's puzzled gaze with a stern look. "It is quite admirable that this young man desires to keep his children with him as they, too, have suffered greatly in the loss of their mother."

Deborah felt an icy tremor of premonition move through her body. She anticipated her father's next words before he spoke.

"Your mother and I have discussed this, and after much prayer I have decided that, considering your own recent loss, it would be prudent to accept this offer."

"Offer?" Deborah had not expected this so soon. "I don't understand what you mean, Father."

Jacob's steel-gray eyes fixed on her as he answered. "Next week, Deborah, you and I are going to southern Missouri, where we will meet Mr. Dane Stark and determine if it is indeed God's will that you and he marry. If all seems well, you will become the wife of a fine Christian young man and a mother to his child and baby."

By whose standard will we determine if all is well, Father? Deborah didn't bother voicing her concern because she already knew the answer. For the second time in half a year, she would be forced to marry a man she didn't love and who did not love her. Only this time she would be torn from her mother and brother and might never see them again.

She turned to her mother for support but realized none would be coming as her mother sat with her head bowed, looking at neither husband nor daughter.

Deborah tried to reason with him. "But, Father, Jamison is scarcely cold in his grave. It isn't proper that I marry again so soon."

Jacob brushed her concern aside. "Recent events have brought many changes to our land, Deborah. The country is ripe for revival. Now is the time to go. Besides, you will be far from Jamison's family and friends. No one in southern Missouri will think ill of you."

"Father, what if Deborah doesn't want to go?" Caleb asked. His hand touched her shoulder.

"We will not discuss that. Certainly Deborah does not want to be remiss in her Christian duty to help a brother in need. She will benefit from this union as well, if this young man is indeed a born-again believer as his mother says. My telegram should have reached the Starks by now so all is settled."

Deborah's heart sank at her father's words. There would be no room for discussion. He had made up his mind. She barely listened as he talked about his plans. All she heard was that they would be leaving in two days which would give her scarcely enough time to pack her trunk.

Before she went to bed that night, Deborah sat on the window seat in her room and looked out at the stars shining in the black sky above. She had been born again at a young age. As long as she could remember, she had tried to live her life to please her father.

At his insistence, she had married Jamison, who was so much like her father he could have been his own son. She had hated the war, but when Jamison left she had secretly rejoiced. For the first time in her life she thought she would have a home of her own where no one berated her or told her what to do.

Now she would be forced to again marry against her will. She thought of the infant her father had mentioned and wondered if it was a girl or a boy. She had never held or cared for a baby and knew so little about them that the thought of motherhood frightened her. What if she did something wrong? Jamison had struck her only once in their short married life and not so very hard then. But what of this other man? Would he take his anger out on her with blows?

What had her mother said the day of Jamison's funeral? " 'Take. . .no thought for the morrow.' " Deborah quoted the words from Matthew 6:34 in her darkened room, bringing a measure of comfort. " 'Sufficient unto the day is the evil thereof,' " she added.

She slipped into bed to pray, turning her fears over to her heavenly Father.

Chapter 2

Deborah clutched her handbag close against the sudden hiss and jerk of the train. She looked through the smoke-hazed window and wished her mother and brother could have come with them. But Father had barely given them time to say their good-byes at the house before he rushed her off to the train station. He didn't seem to care that she might never see her family again.

Stores and office buildings moved past the window slowly at first, then gathered speed as the train gained momentum. First residences and then farms and open fields replaced the city. Deborah watched the fields of grain become a blur in her vision.

She turned just enough to see her father. He did not pay her any mind, which suited Deborah. She preferred her own company.

As the morning wore away, Deborah longed to stand and stretch. They had passed through several villages, stopping only once for water. The passengers had been allowed a fifteen-minute break, which gave barely enough time to take a turn in the outhouse behind the way station and stretch a bit. That had been two hours ago.

Deborah's stomach rumbled. She placed her hand over the emptiness to will away the pangs of hunger. A loud whistle and a huge puff of black smoke announced their arrival in the town of Rolla. Deborah straightened, trying to see out her window that was now covered with smoke and soot. By the time the smoke cleared, the train had come to a shuddering stop.

"Come, Deborah." Her father stood, waiting for her to join him before leading her down the long aisle toward the door. "This is where we get off."

Deborah stiffened as she followed her father. She would marry this man from the backwoods of southern Missouri, and she would make a home for herself where no man ruled her life. How she intended to do that by marrying another man of her father's choosing, she had no idea. But somehow, she promised herself, this time would be different. This time, far removed from her father's influence, she would stand up for herself and make a home she could call her own. She had to, because she would not get another chance.

"We'll take a stagecoach directly from here to Lebanon." Her father's words confirmed that her hunger would not be appeased anytime soon.

"How far will that be, Father?" she asked, dreading the answer.

"Why, not more than a sixty-mile distance. From there it will be almost straight west to our destination." He smiled down at her in a rare moment of consideration. "Take courage, child; your mother has prepared a bite to tide us over until we reach a station that serves hot meals."

Dusk covered the village of Lebanon by the time they rolled to a stop at the relay station. Deborah accepted her father's helping hand before climbing down from the stagecoach. Every bone in her body ached, every muscle screamed for rest. Never had she spent such a day. She had done nothing but sit, yet she felt as if she had worked long hours scrubbing on the washboard.

For the second time that day, her father smiled at her as they entered the inn where they would eat and rent rooms for the night. "Let's see what the cook has prepared for our supper. We scarcely ate at noon, and I daresay I'm quite hungry. How about you, Deborah?"

She looked at her father's smile then turned away and nodded. "Yes, I'm hungry, too."

Deborah sat at the table and smiled at a girl near her own age who placed filled plates in front of them. "Thank you."

"You are most welcome." The girl curtsied a quick dip and left. Turnips smothered with butter and baked beans in molasses covered one side of her plate. Thin slices of beef on thick slabs of bread covered the other side. Deborah wondered if she could eat it all. She could still feel the sway and jolt of the coach and felt little interest in the food in front of her despite her hunger. She lifted a fork loaded with baked beans to her mouth and almost sighed as the flavor aroused her appetite. By the time her father finished his supper her plate was also empty.

Several minutes later, Deborah slipped into her long, flannel nightgown and crawled into bed. As soon as her head touched the pillow she slept.

"Deborah!" Loud pounding on her door awakened her, and she jumped from bed confused. She could scarcely see in the dark room.

"Yes, Father, I'm awake." She opened the door just enough to see her father standing in the hall.

He seemed to be in a pleasant mood. "The Lord has graciously granted us transportation for the last leg of our journey. I've hired a hack that delivers mail three times a week. We'll have to change conveyances at each stop, but we must praise God for His provisions."

"Yes, Father," Deborah agreed, as she knew he would expect.

Jacob smiled. "Hurry now with your morning preparations. We cannot keep the mail service waiting."

Deborah turned from the door and lit the lamp sitting on a table by the bed. Soft light radiated from it, touching the bed as an invitation to climb back under the covers.

They left Lebanon in a buggy. After that they rode in the back of a farm wagon for twelve miles wedged between wooden boxes of freight. Deborah's resentment toward her father mounted the closer they came to the end of their journey. Each stop she hoped was the last, but another day and a half of hard travel passed before they pulled up on the north side of the square in the town of Stockton late Saturday afternoon.

"Reverend Smith?"

Deborah and her father both turned at the voice. Jacob nodded. "Yes, and you must be Aaron Stark's son. The resemblance is amazing."

Deborah looked into eyes bluer than she could have ever imagined. The fact that the man stood staring at her didn't at once occur to her as she stared back. This must be Dane Stark, the man she would be marrying. He was tall, a few years older than her, with unruly black hair curling in wild abandon on top of his head. His build was lean and muscular, his jaw strong, his features extremely handsome. But the haunted look in his sky-blue eyes drew her attention from the rest. Surely, this man had suffered greatly in recent days.

Without speaking to her, he turned and shook her father's hand. "I'm proud to meet you. I'm Dane Stark. My parents sent me to fetch you and your belongings to take to their house."

"Wonderful," Deborah's father said. "I look forward to seeing them again." He nodded toward Deborah. "This is my daughter, Deborah Renee, of whom we wrote."

As Dane's gaze fixed on hers again, Deborah felt a flush warm her face. He nodded and turned away. "I'll bring my wagon 'round and get your things loaded."

Deborah watched him cross the thick, green grass until he disappeared behind the courthouse, which sat on a patch of lawn in the center of the square.

Jacob stepped close to her side as he, too, watched Dane. "His mother says he is a dedicated Christian man, and like many in Cedar County, his sympathies lie with the preservation of our nation. I believe that is most admirable."

Deborah wondered why her father would try to convince her of Mr. Stark's attributes. Surely it made no difference to him whether she approved of her future husband. She hadn't approved of the first one, so why should this time be any different? A helpless feeling washed over her as she stood at the edge of the street watching the men load her heavy trunk into Mr. Stark's wagon.

Within minutes Deborah found a spot in the back of the wagon, leaving her father to sit in front with Dane as they rumbled west out of Stockton. She watched the gently rolling hills and longed for her mother and home. Even remaining under the strict dominion of her father for the rest of her life would be better than marrying a stranger and subjecting herself to an unknown future.

When the wagon turned north, Deborah turned her attention to the front seat where her father sat deep in conversation with Mr. Stark.

"Did you see much action during the war?"

Dane shook his head. "No major battles, thank God. We had our share of skirmishes, though. And with Kansas so close we were always on the lookout for Jayhawkers and bushwhackers alike."

"I understand your sympathies are with the North." Jacob looked at the younger man. "Does that hold true for the rest of your family?"

"All but one." Dane stared straight ahead. "Wesley, my brother just younger, has always had a mind of his own. Mother says he's the spittin' image of our uncle Ralph." His laugh held no mirth. "I'd reckon he's not the only one. I've got a cousin she says the same thing about."

"Ralph Stark," Jacob said. "Yes, I remember meeting him. Didn't your mother write about his passing several years back?"

"Probably." Dane nodded. "He died before the war started."

"This brother you mentioned," Jacob said, picking up the thread of their conversation. "Did he fight with the South?"

"Yep. He left to join the rebels more'n two years ago. We haven't heard from him but once in all that time. He still hasn't come home."

"I'm sorry to hear that. Your other brothers—what are they doing?"

"Ash and Levi fought together with the regulars. Joshua, too, just not with the twins. They've all been home several days now. Then I've got two baby brothers still at home."

Jacob nodded. "Where did you serve?"

"I served with the militia here in Stockton since the war started. Felt like I could do more good stayin' home defendin' my own land."

"That's quite admirable. A man must take care of what is rightfully his."

Deborah wondered at her father's eager acceptance of this young man. He seemed quite impressed with him. Just as he had been with Jamison, she recalled. Did he want to be rid of her so much that he would shove her off on anyone?

The two men talked of other things then. The countryside, crops, and the little church where they would be holding revival meetings. Deborah looked past Dane's broad shoulders to his strong jaw. From her vantage point behind and to the side of him, no one was paying attention to her, so she took time to study his profile.

His clean-shaven face revealed strong, regular features. She wished she could see his eyes. She knew they were blue, but she wanted to see past the color into his soul. Only then would she know if Dane Stark would be a good father to his children and a kind husband to her.

As Deborah listened to the men talk, the wagon rattled and jounced its way over the narrow dirt road to the Stark farm. They entered a plush meadow covered in thick, green, waist-high grass. Deborah sat straighter and looked about.

Dane followed the faint wheel tracks through the waving grass until it gave way to a log and frame house that looked as if it had grown from the meadow.

Behind the house a small hill rose, leading the way into a large stand of trees.

The wagon jerked to a stop in front of the house. A woman who stood framed in the doorway stepped out into the sunshine. Deborah saw that although her step was light and quick, her light brown hair held highlights of gray. Laugh lines near the corners of her dark eyes and around her mouth added character to her still attractive face. Her smile included them all.

"Welcome to our home." She shook hands with Deborah's father as he stepped down from the wagon. "It's been a long time, hasn't it, Jacob, since we played as children on the streets of St. Louis?"

"That it has, Cora," Jacob agreed. "A long time, indeed."

"How is your sister Margaret? It's been more than a year since I've heard from her."

"She's well, but busy with her new grandson. I'm sure she'll write soon and tell you all about him."

Cora laughed. "So Margaret is a grandmother now? We are getting old, Jacob. I have two grandchildren myself." Her gaze shifted as Dane helped Deborah from the wagon. "This must be your daughter."

"Yes, Deborah Asberry." Jacob drew her forward. "Deborah, this is Mrs. Cora Stark, Dane's mother. I'm sure she will want to discuss the wedding arrangements with you later."

Deborah's heart sank. Surely this meant that Father approved of Dane. She looked into the woman's soft, brown-eyed gaze that seemed to envelop her in understanding and love. In spite of her natural reserve, Deborah smiled and offered her hand. "I'm pleased to meet you, ma'am."

Cora took Deborah's hand in hers and drew her close for a quick hug. "I'm so glad you agreed to come, Deborah. What you are doing means so much to us."

She stepped back and, still holding Deborah's hand, smiled. "Right now I need to get dinner on the table so we can eat. I imagine you're starved and worn out from the trip. In a day or two, after you've had a chance to look us over real good, we'll have us a talk. Just you and me."

Deborah hadn't expected to like anyone here, but she already knew she liked Mrs. Stark. She looked forward to the promised talk.

As she moved beside Mrs. Stark to the house, she glanced over her shoulder at Dane who had moved the wagon to the barn where he'd started unhitching the horses. He had ignored her for the most part. She wondered if he were also being forced into this marriage. No doubt, because of circumstances, he was.

❦

Deborah dried the last dish from their evening meal and placed it in the cupboard. Cora gave her a quick hug. "Thank you so much, Deborah. It's a real treat for me to have female help and company. What with a house full of boys, there's always been more dirtying than cleaning around here."

Deborah smiled. "I don't mind helping."

She glanced toward the front room of the house, wishing that the men would go outside. But the Starks' two younger sons were the only ones who hadn't stayed indoors. After they'd finished eating, Cora's husband suggested the men, all six of them, sit down and chew the fat while their dinner settled. Deborah assumed that meant talk since that's all they had been doing for the last half hour.

A quick rap at the door caught her attention. A pretty young woman stuck her head inside, a wide smile brightening her face. "Hi, is anyone home?"

"Lenore, come on in." Cora pulled the door open wider.

Deborah noticed Dane's eyes come alive when Lenore stepped into the room. She wondered at that until she saw the small bundle in Lenore's arms.

Dane stood and reached for the blanket-covered infant. "I sure do appreciate you keepin' an eye on my young'uns today."

Lenore smiled up at him. "It was my pleasure, I assure you."

Deborah watched as Dane took the baby and cradled it against his strong, muscular chest. He looked like he'd done the same thing many times, yet somehow his masculine presence dwarfed the tiny baby. Then a small boy burst through the open door and flung himself against Dane's legs.

"Daddy, I miss you whole bunch." He tilted his head back as far as he could to see his father's face.

Dane bent to scoop him up with his right arm while he held the sleeping baby in his left. Cora took a step forward. "Dane, be careful."

A fleeting grin broke the somber expression on his face for a moment. "Don't worry, Mom. I'm getting used to it."

The little boy's dark, curly hair, so like his father's, brushed Dane's neck as he snuggled close. His thumb found his mouth and his eyes closed in contentment.

Cora's eyebrows lifted. "How long has that been going on?" She nodded at the little boy sucking his thumb.

"Been doin' it off and on all day, I'd reckon." A young man stepped through the still-open door and slipped his arm around Lenore.

Dane nodded toward the man. "Evenin', Billy. Thanks for bringin' Tommy and Beth over. I appreciate y'all keepin' 'em today."

"It was no trouble, Dane." Lenore spoke for her husband. "They are both little angels."

"Speakin' of angels, who's that you got hidin' in the kitchen?"

Deborah looked up to meet the bright blue eyes of the young man. A slow grin spread across his handsome face as his arm dropped from around his wife and he took a step toward her.

Cora moved forward, effectively stopping his progress. "Deborah, please xcuse our manners. I'd like for you to meet Dane's cousin and his wife, Billy and Lenore Reid." She slipped her arm around Deborah's waist. "This is Deborah Asberry. She's come all the way from St. Louis to marry Dane and become a mother to his children."

Deborah watched shock register on Billy's and Lenore's faces as Mrs. Stark turned toward the men watching from the sitting room. "As you know, our church will be in revival this next week. Deborah's father, Reverend Jacob Smith, will be doing the preaching. I'll expect you two to be there every night."

Jacob stood and crossed the room to shake hands with the young couple. As he extended a second invitation for them to attend the revival meetings, Cora nudged Deborah.

"Why don't you go rest for a spell? I imagine you're worn-out after such a long journey."

Thankful for the older woman's understanding and kindness, Deborah slipped into the upstairs bedroom Cora pointed out and closed the door. Dane's cousins had obviously not been told about her. Probably no one had been. She didn't suppose an arranged marriage was something one would spread around until they were sure of the outcome.

Deborah lay across the bed and closed her eyes. How she wished she could go someplace far away where no one would bother her. She almost laughed aloud at her foolishness.

For years their country had been ravaged by war. The past few days, as Deborah and her father journeyed across Missouri, they had seen evidence of destruction on every side in the abandoned farms and burned-out hulls of once fine homes. There was no place for a young woman alone to run. Deborah knew without doubt that she must now depend on a man whom she knew little about except that he didn't want this marriage any more than she did.

Chapter 3

Revival services began the following morning after Sunday school in the little one-room country church just a couple of miles from the Starks house. The pastor, Brother Timothy Donovan, stepped back and gave Jacob freedom to conduct the services. Deborah sat beside Mrs. Stark on the second pew from the front and breathed a sigh of relief that she didn't have to sit with Dane since he had yet to arrive with his children.

She hadn't seen him since the day before when she hid from his cousin in the Starks' bedroom. After taking a much needed nap, she had returned to the other room to find that Billy and Lenore had gone home as had Dane and his children. She wasn't sorry to have missed them. If she never saw Dane or his cousins again, she wouldn't mind.

After the congregation sang several songs, Deborah stood and made her way to the front. She'd tried to get out of singing, but her father had been adamant. He insisted that God had given her a gift, and she would sin if she didn't use it for His glory. She gave in as she always did.

Deborah stood beside the pulpit with her hand resting on the edge. As the organist played the introduction, she scanned the congregation. There were few empty seats. She skimmed over the front rows until her gaze rested on the back pew where Dane sat alone with his two children. She assumed he had slipped in after the service started.

While she watched, his young son used Dane as a step-ladder so he could see out the open doorway behind them. Something must have caught the little boy's attention. She tried to see and almost missed her cue. As she began to sing "Come Ye Sinners, Poor and Needy," she saw a large, brown dog scarcely ten feet from the door lift its shaggy head and smile inside at the little boy, its tongue hanging out one side of its mouth.

Then, as always happened when she sang, her mind and heart became lost in the beauty of the music and she forgot all else. She lifted her focus to a spot high on the back wall while she felt herself swept along on a rising crescendo of emotion that became her praise and worship to her Savior.

❀

Dane cradled his tiny baby daughter in one arm while he kept a firm grip on the shoulder strap of his small son's overalls. He'd missed Sunday school because Tommy kept getting into something and smearing it down the front of his shirt.

After changing the little boy's clothing and washing his hands and face twice, he gave up on dressing the baby until he figured out how to keep Tommy clean.

Standing just inside the bedroom where he could peer around the doorframe at his son, he waited. Tommy, oblivious to his father, raced across the large room that served as both parlor and kitchen. Dane watched him climb on a chair he had pulled from the table to the pie safe and then he knew. The custard pie his mother had insisted he bring home the night before was the problem.

With long strides Dane raced across the floor and grabbed his son just as one chubby hand dipped into the destroyed pie.

Dane smiled now as he remembered Tommy's howl of frustration when he tried to insert his sweet-coated hand into his mouth and couldn't.

But now, as Deborah's song filled the church, Dane tightened his hold on Tommy and forgot all else but the beauty of her voice. Rich and vibrant, it caressed his soul, soothing the turmoil that had been his since Anne's death. When the song ended and she returned to her place beside his mother, he realized he had never heard a sweeter voice. Nor had he been touched so deeply by a song.

❊

After service that morning Deborah knew she would have to sing each evening of the revival as she accepted praise from one person after another. For as always happened, after the congregation heard her once, they would not let her rest until she sang again. Her father always said that Deborah's voice drew the crowds who must then listen to him preach.

She sighed as she made her way to the wagon past small clusters of men and women visiting. She dodged children running and playing, their childish voices calling out to one another as her mind returned to her problem. It wasn't that she didn't like to sing. She loved losing herself in the beauty of music and praise. But she had never been given a choice. For as long as she could remember, she had been told that she would sing. Just as now she had no choice in marriage.

As Deborah placed a toe on the wheel hub and grasped the rough wood of the wagon to hoist herself up, a hand closed around her arm.

"Here, let me help you." Dane's deep voice startled her so that she lost her balance and fell back against his chest.

"Oh, I'm so sorry." Her face flamed. She jerked away, turning to look up at him. He stood much too close.

His blue eyes crinkled at the corners as he smiled down at her. He was quite good-looking when he smiled. "It's my fault. I shouldn't have come up behind you like that without lettin' you know."

He looked from her to the big farm wagon. "I thought you might need some help gettin' up there."

"That's all right. I've climbed into wagons before all by myself." His presence brought a strange feeling in her chest. She didn't want his help. She looked away, glad to see his mother coming toward them with his baby in her arms.

"Dane, where are your manners? Aren't you going to help this girl into the wagon?" Cora smiled at them, and Deborah knew she would have to accept his assistance now.

Amusement lightened Dane's face as he looked down at Deborah. His eyebrows lifted and his bright blue eyes twinkled. "I was just gettin' to that, Mom, before you showed up."

Then, before Deborah could object further, he reached down to span her waist with his hands. As if she weighed nothing, he lifted her above his head and set her on the seat of the wagon.

Warmth that had nothing to do with the noonday sun beating down on her spread throughout Deborah's body. She had expected a helping hand. She certainly hadn't expected to feel like a sack of potatoes—or maybe like a young lady who had caught the eye of the most appealing man she had ever seen. She glanced at Cora and saw the smile of approval on her face. Sure that her cheeks were a brilliant red, Deborah stared at her hands that were clenched into balls in her lap. Unable to resist longer than a few seconds, she lifted her gaze to meet Dane's blue eyes, now cool with the spark of humor gone. Then Cora stepped between them.

"Deborah, would you mind holding the baby while I climb on board?"

Deborah looked at the tiny scrap of humanity that Cora lifted toward her. The encounter with Dane all but forgotten, she reached down, placing one hand under the baby's neck and shoulders, the other cradling her backside. She could not tear her eyes from the miniature face that slept so peacefully. Soft fuzz of blond—almost white—hair peeked out from around the pristine white bonnet that framed the baby's perfect features.

Deborah barely noticed scooting over to make room for Cora as she brought the infant close and cuddled her in her arms. She watched the tiny rosebud lips purse and suckle for a moment as if seeking comfort from the disruptions in her short life. A wave of pity broke over Deborah's heart, and she gently tightened her hold as if to assure the tiny child that all would be well.

Although she heard Dane and Cora talking, Deborah didn't listen, for at that moment a tiny, perfectly formed hand came free of the white lacy blanket and jerked in the air. Deborah placed her forefinger against the tips of the baby's fingers. Each finger couldn't have been bigger around than the crochet hook that had been used to make the blanket, yet when she gently pried them open they closed around her finger with surprising strength.

"She's a beautiful child, isn't she?" Deborah looked up at Cora's softly spoken words.

"I've never been around babies much."

"Why don't you hold her on the way home?" Cora suggested as her younger sons came running to the wagon, followed at a slower pace by Deborah's father and Aaron Stark.

The men climbed into the back while one of the boys squeezed in beside Deborah. He slapped the reins over the horse's back and they were off. As they pulled away, Deborah watched Dane scoop his small son up and head toward his own wagon.

Deborah held her precious charge close, reveling in the little, warm body that fit so well in the crook of her arm. A wave of maternal love surprised and frightened her as the baby's eyes opened and stared up at her in solemn scrutiny.

When they reached the Starks' house, she placed the baby on a downstairs bed and joined Cora in the kitchen to help with dinner preparations. Deborah was thankful that the men remained outdoors until Cora called them in to eat.

After a dinner lightened by laughter and conversation, Deborah helped Cora clean up the well-picked-over table. Several minutes later, she hung the damp tea towel on a nail and followed Cora from the kitchen.

Dane now held his infant daughter. His eyes, cold and brooding, seemed to follow Deborah's every movement. Not knowing what else to do, Deborah stood behind her father's chair, wishing she would wake and find that the last several weeks were a horrible nightmare.

She listened to the men talk, although their conversation meant little to her. She imagined she felt Dane's gaze on her, but she refused to look.

"Daddy, go see kitties?" Tommy's childish voice stood out from the lower rumble of the adult voices.

Deborah glanced toward Dane. His son tugged on his sleeve. As she watched, Dane looked up and met her gaze. He handed the baby to his mother.

"All right, Tommy. Maybe we should show Mrs. Asberry the kitties, too. Why don't you go ask her?"

When the toddler turned his confident grin on her, Deborah wondered if he knew who she was. He ran across the room, stopped in front of her, and craned his neck to look into her face. One chubby little hand reached out and took her fingers.

"Wanna see my kitties, Miss 'Berry? Wiff me and mine daddy. Kitties in barn."

Deborah looked down at the little boy who continued to hold her hand and tug as if he would take her to his father. She shook her head. "No, thank you. Maybe another time."

As she tried to free her hand, her father turned in his chair and frowned at her. "Nonsense, Deborah. Run along with the boy and enjoy yourself. This will be a good opportunity for you young people to become better acquainted."

Deborah clenched her free hand, buried in the folds of her wide skirt, into a fist. She should have known better than to think she had a choice on even such a trivial matter. Without a word, she followed the little boy to the door, grabbing her bonnet as she went.

Deborah preceded Dane and Tommy into the bright sunshine. A strained silence hung between them as they walked across the yard until Deborah's steps lagged behind as much as Tommy's ran ahead.

"C'mon," Tommy called back to the adults. He waited at the barn door, bouncing first on one foot and then the other. "See kitties."

"We're comin'. Just hold your horses," Dane called to him before looking back at Deborah. "You makin' it okay?"

"Yes, I'm fine." She quickened her pace, even as her teeth gritted in frustration. As she hurried toward the barn, she breathed a prayer of petition. *Dear Lord, please help me accept my lot in life as is in keeping with Your will.*

Dane opened the heavy log door and Tommy ran inside. Dane stepped back and waited as Deborah brushed past before following her into the dim barn.

Specks of dust danced in long slanting rays of sunlight that entered through cracks in the walls. The musty scent of hay and animals created a strange combination to Deborah's city-bred senses. The huge barn felt cooler than outdoors and much more frightening. She glanced into the shadowy recesses of the stalls and wondered what might be hidden from view behind the walls. Then a rustle in the straw startled her, and she jumped with a tiny squeal.

"Don't worry. It won't hurt you. It's probably a rat or maybe just a tiny mouse." Dane stood several feet away. "That's what the kittens are good for. At least they will be when they get big."

At the first mention of rodents, a shiver chased down Deborah's spine. She instinctively stepped closer to Dane, her only thought to get away from the danger she couldn't see.

He grinned. "Honest, they won't bother you. They're just after the grain we put out for the horses."

When she cast him a disbelieving look, he laughed. "Come on. There's one place in this barn you can be sure there are no mice. Meow-meow won't let one within sight before she's got it caught."

"Meow-meow?" Deborah looked up at him. He seemed to be serious.

When he laughed again, she decided she enjoyed the sound. She supposed that was because he so seldom even smiled.

"My son named her. I reckon it fits since that's about the only thing she ever says." Dane looked down at her and grinned.

Deborah's heart froze. Did he have to be so handsome? Did he have to be so nice? Jamison wasn't as handsome, but he had been nice—until they were married. Then he had treated her as one might treat a child who didn't know her own mind. Dane would be the same. Deep in her heart she knew it, just as she knew there was not one thing she could do about it.

"You ready to see the kittens?" Dane took Deborah's arm, and she allowed him to lead her to the back of the barn where she could hear childish laughter. They found Tommy lying in a pile of straw with a kitten on his tummy, one batting at his hair, and another standing with its front paws against his side. A gray-and-white striped cat that Deborah assumed was Meow-meow lay nearby watching.

"Kitties like me, Daddy." Tommy grinned.

Dane squatted beside his son and picked up the one at his side. He held the kitten out to Deborah. "Would you like to hold it?"

She took the tiny ball of gray fur and felt the vibration of its purr against her hand. As Dane turned back to his son and she watched father and son play, a feeling she didn't understand welled up within her heart. She couldn't remember her father ever playing with either her or her brother.

She thought of the sweet baby sleeping in the house and of the little boy who seemed ready to accept her presence. Maybe marriage to Mr. Stark wouldn't be so bad. The children needed a mother and she needed a home. For the first time since her father had told her she would be moving to southern Missouri to marry a widower with two children, she felt ready to accept her lot in life. She would marry Dane Stark and, with God's help, she would make a home for herself and be a mother to his two adorable children. Then, if God allowed, maybe soon she would have children of her own.

Chapter 4

Monday morning Deborah descended the stairs from the tiny bedroom in which she had been sleeping. She crossed the living room and stopped outside the kitchen door. Cora sat at the table with her tiny granddaughter in her arms. Dane stood across from her holding his son.

Cora cuddled the baby as she smiled at Dane. "I'm going to miss this, but I believe you are doing the right thing. Deborah seems to be a wonderful girl."

"I reckon so." Dane didn't sound convinced. "I don't have a lot of choice in the matter."

"I guess not." Cora's smile never wavered. "But remember, son, good marriages have been made with less reason."

Deborah stepped back before either noticed her presence. As she stood in the middle of the floor wondering what she should do, Dane walked into the room. Surprise widened his eyes for a moment when he glanced her way. She tried to appear as if she had just come downstairs.

Expecting him to speak, she gave him a smile, getting a curt nod in response as he went outside.

She moved to the window and peeked out to see her father and Aaron Stark approach Dane. He seemed to have no trouble talking to them. Deborah didn't know whether she felt angry or amused at his actions. Mr. Dane Stark obviously didn't want to marry her any more than she wanted to marry him. What a plight they both were in!

"Miss 'Berry?" Deborah felt a tug on her skirt. She turned from the window as Tommy tugged her skirt again. "Me comed to see you."

Cora stood several feet away with the baby. A smile hovered around her lips. Deborah's face flamed. What must she be thinking? "I heard voices and. . ." Her voice trailed away.

Cora's smile spread. "Tommy and I thought you might be awake. Dane usually brings the little ones before the sun comes up. Farmers are notoriously early risers. It took me awhile to get used to crawling out of bed in the dark, but now I don't think I could sleep in if I tried."

Thankful that the older woman had graciously ignored her confusion, Deborah smiled. "I guess our city ways are quite different, but I'm sure I can adjust."

"You will do fine." Cora crossed into her bedroom just off the living room.

"Baby Beth fell asleep in my arms. I'll put her on my bed, and then I'd better get breakfast on the table. If you heard the men outside, they will be underfoot before I'm ready for them."

"Miss 'Berry, I comed to see you," Tommy repeated with another tug on her skirt.

Deborah knelt beside the little boy and put her arm around him. At only two years of age, he seemed small to her, yet his shoulders felt sturdy under her touch. She smiled at him. "I'm glad you did. We'll have lots of fun today, won't we?"

"Yes." He nodded. "Daddy come get me."

"That's right." Deborah wondered if he worried that his daddy might leave as his mother had. Her heart softened toward this tiny replica of Dane Stark. No wonder Dane felt such a need to provide a mother for his children.

Cora was stirring the gravy when the men came in from outdoors. Deborah didn't think she would ever get used to the noise of so many men and boys as the Stark family boasted. Her father seemed to enjoy their constant talk and rough-housing. Deborah wondered at that since he insisted that she and her brother always behave with the utmost decorum at home as befitted the children of a minister of God.

Dane's five younger brothers ranged in age from twelve to twenty-five. Deborah had heard them talk about another brother a year younger than Dane. The black sheep of the family, as his brothers sometimes called him, Wesley left home at the beginning of the war to join the Confederate Army. As the first year rolled into another, he sent one letter, but not once had he made an appearance. Deborah could see the worry in Cora's and Aaron's eyes when anyone mentioned Wesley's name. Not one spoken prayer ended without a plea for his safe return.

Cora poured the gravy into a bowl and set it on the table then sat in the chair held for her by her youngest son, Benjamin. As soon as Benjamin sat down, Aaron bowed his head and asked the blessing on their breakfast.

After the men left, Deborah helped Cora clean while Tommy finished his breakfast. He then climbed from the table and announced that he was going outside.

Cora smiled at her grandson and turned to Deborah. "Would you like to keep an eye on him? There's a spring over by the woods that is beautiful this time of year. I made the mistake of taking Tommy there, and he's tried to go alone more than once."

"Are you sure you don't mind? I expected to help with the housework." Deborah looked out the open kitchen door into the sun-brightened yard beyond. What would her father think if she neglected the household duties to go outside and play?

"You've already helped more than enough. Besides, you will find that watching Tommy is no picnic. Don't worry about little Beth. I'll be right in the house where I can hear her when she wakes."

A flush moved through Deborah's body. She had forgotten the baby. What kind of mother would she be to forget a child in her care? She managed a weak smile and a murmur of agreement before following Tommy outdoors.

"See kitties," Tommy announced as his sturdy little legs carried him toward the barn.

Rats and mice lived in the barn. Deborah shuddered. She watched Tommy trudging ahead and realized he wouldn't turn back without a fuss. With a resigned sigh, she followed, catching up with the little boy at the barn door.

"Hey, Tommy, what are you doin' out here?" One of Dane's brothers stepped into the sunshine from the interior of the barn. He nodded toward Deborah with a quick grin.

"Unca Levi, me comed to see kitties." The little boy seemed to forget Deborah as he ran through the wide, open space in the middle of the barn and disappeared in its depths. Levi laughed.

"He sure likes those kittens."

Deborah smiled. Twins Levi and Ashton looked no more alike than any of the other brothers. Levi had light brown eyes like his mother. His hair wasn't as dark as Dane's, and he wasn't as good-looking.

Heat crept into her cheeks as soon as she realized where her thoughts had gone. She looked away toward the back of the barn where she could hear Tommy's laughter.

She gestured toward the sound. "I'd better keep an eye on him."

"Sure. See ya 'round." Levi moved on out the door and walked away, whistling as he went. He carried some sort of long-handled tool with a sharp blade that Deborah couldn't have named if she'd tried.

She turned back to the interior of the barn and cringed. Only one path led to Tommy, with furry scavengers lurking on either side. She took a deep breath and stepped forward.

"Tommy." Maybe the sound of her voice would send the rodents running in the opposite direction. She called again halfway through the barn. "Tommy."

A sound to her right sent her running the rest of the way with a sharp squeal. "Tommy!"

Tommy stood and looked up at Deborah with wide, blue eyes. "Want mine mommy."

Deborah didn't know how to answer. "Grandma's in the house."

Tommy stared at her a moment and then ran toward the front of the barn. She threw out her hands in frustration. She wouldn't have taken the chance of running into a mouse if she'd known she would have to run the gauntlet a second time so soon.

Leaving the safety of Meow-meow's presence, Deborah ran as fast as she could after Tommy. Again she called his name hoping to scare away any rodent brave enough to make an appearance.

Deborah burst through the doorway into the outdoors and breathed a sigh of relief until she wondered if Tommy might be deaf—she had called his name at least three times and he hadn't even slowed. Already he was halfway to the house. How could such a small person cover ground so quickly? She ran to catch up.

Tommy reached the house as Deborah reached Tommy. "Are you running away from me, Tommy?"

Without sparing her a glance, he jerked the front door open and ran through. "Gamma. Gamma, me want you."

"Slow down, Tommy." Cora stepped around the table as the little boy launched himself at her. "What's your hurry?"

"Want you."

Cora lifted her grandson and settled him on her hip. He gave her a hug and then squirmed to get down. Deborah watched Cora laugh and set him on the floor. She wondered if this was normal behavior for a two-year-old. Since Cora didn't seem to be concerned, she assumed it was.

"So have you already tired of playing outside?" Tommy ran into the parlor ignoring his grandmother. Cora shook her head with an indulgent smile as he disappeared into the other room.

"I'm so sorry." Deborah felt as if she had failed her first attempt at making friends with her future stepson. What kind of mother would she be? She couldn't remember the baby, and she couldn't keep up with the little boy.

Cora gave her a puzzled look. "What do you have to be sorry for?"

"I was supposed to keep Tommy occupied outside." Deborah was glad her father hadn't seen her pitiful attempts at motherhood. He would have scolded her if he had, and she felt bad enough already.

"You've done nothing to be sorry about." Cora washed her hands and dried them on a towel hanging on the end of the table that held the washbasin. "Tommy doesn't stay anyplace long. You'll get used to him."

She pulled a large ball of bread dough from the mixing bowl on the table. Placing it on a pile of flour on a cloth-covered board, she began kneading.

Deborah wasn't sure she wanted to get used to Tommy, or Beth either, for that matter. She knew nothing about small children and babies. She stepped near the door leading into the living room and watched Tommy play with a horse carved from wood with deep red streaks running through it. The craftsmanship intrigued her. The horse looked so real as Tommy made it gallop across the floor.

She had noticed the chairs in the kitchen, too, had intricate designs carved in the backs. Eight chairs sat around the Starks' long table and each had a different

variety of flower that seemed to have been taken from its natural surroundings and placed on each chair by a master carver. When she had commented
on them, Cora said Aaron had carved them. Such works of beauty would have
brought top price in St. Louis.

"Go outside."

Deborah looked down into Tommy's upturned face. She smiled at the little
boy. "Okay, let's go out and play."

For the rest of the morning, Deborah spent her time running after Dane's
young son. By noon she realized Mrs. Stark was right. Watching young Thomas
Wayne Stark and keeping him out of trouble was no picnic. Spring housecleaning, even with her mother's high standards, had been an easier job.

She helped Tommy wash his hands at the washbasin and then got him settled into a chair at the table. Cora gave her a smile as she passed by with a steaming bowl of corn. "Thanks, Deborah. You've done so much already this morning,
I hate to ask, but I hear little Beth crying. Would you mind getting her?"

"Of course not." Deborah noticed her father's nod of approval as she gladly
left the noisy confusion of the male-dominated kitchen for the relative quiet
of Cora's bedroom. As she opened the door, the baby's cries became louder.
How had Mrs. Stark heard her over the scraping chairs and voices of her sons
when Deborah had heard nothing until the baby's crying was brought to her
attention?

She felt a measure of satisfaction for her morning's work. She had chased
Tommy all over the meadow, visited the kittens in the barn three times, popped
back into the house twice—mostly she suspected so Tommy could reassure himself that his grandmother was still there—and even managed to play some games
with the little boy. She didn't know how Tommy felt about her, but she suspected
she could easily lose her heart to the adorable toddler.

Beth was another matter, however. At barely two months of age, she was
so tiny and helpless. Deborah closed the bedroom door and crossed the room
to sit on the bed beside the baby. She had held her once on the ride home from
church and felt she could love her as if she were her own baby if only she knew
what to do with her.

Right now for instance. One touch told Deborah that she was about to learn
how to change a diaper. If she didn't do it right away, Mrs. Stark would be coming to see why the baby still cried.

"Shh, little Beth. It's all right. Let's not cry now." Deborah gingerly slid
one hand under the infant's soggy diaper and another under her back and neck,
lifting until she held her against her chest. She patted the tiny back, pleased that
the crying had stopped. Now to find a clean diaper and figure out what to do
with it.

Finding a stack of folded diapers on the corner of the dresser wasn't hard.

Mrs. Stark probably kept a supply on hand since she had been watching the children for Dane. With one hand supporting the baby, Deborah took a diaper from the stack. She turned and lowered Beth to the bed.

"Everything all right in here?" Mrs. Stark slipped in the door.

"Oh." Deborah looked up with a tremulous smile. "I was just going to try changing her diaper. She's pretty wet."

Cora laughed. "That doesn't surprise me. Do you need help?"

"I've never changed a diaper before. I don't know if I know how."

"Not a thing to it." Cora brushed her concerns aside as she sat on the opposite side of the bed. "If this one's just wet, it'll be perfect to practice on."

Deborah's heart sank. She hadn't thought that the diaper might be more than just wet. Her concerns must have shown on her face, because Cora laughed again.

"You'll get the hang of it all soon enough."

Cora talked Deborah through the simple steps of changing the diaper. When she finished, Deborah picked Beth up and held her close in her arms. Beth watched her with bright blue eyes, bringing a smile to Deborah's lips and chastisement to her heart. How could she have forgotten such a precious baby this morning?

"I want you to know how much all of us appreciate your willingness to marry Dane and become a mother to his children." Cora patted Deborah's arm. "It can't be easy. Leaving everything you know to come to a backwoods place like this. I know how it was for me, and I had my entire family around me. I missed St. Louis so much back then. Little did I know this place would become more home to me than St. Louis ever was. I hope you feel the same way in time. If it's all right with you, we can have the ceremony on Sunday before your father returns to St. Louis."

Deborah didn't know what to say. Cora surely didn't know that she had no choice—that if she went against her father's wishes she might very well have no home to go back to. She simply nodded her agreement and was almost glad when the baby began fussing.

"She's probably hungry. I have a bottle fixed for her in the kitchen." Cora stood. "Would you like to feed her?"

"If you don't mind."

"Not at all. There's a rocking chair in the living room. I imagine you are ready for a rest after chasing after Tommy all morning." Cora smiled before going out the door. "He takes a long nap in the afternoon."

By the time Dane returned for his children, Deborah was ready for a good night's sleep. Not that his children were especially hard to care for. They were just so busy when they weren't sleeping. During Tommy's nap, Beth stayed awake. Deborah soon learned that tiny babies demand attention every bit as much as toddlers do.

Dane stayed for supper, sitting at the table across from Deborah, yet ignoring her as if she didn't exist. She wished she could do the same. Although she managed to keep her gaze averted, she could think of little else. She was glad when they finished eating and Dane left with his children.

That evening at church, as Deborah went forward to sing, her gaze moved to the back where Dane sat with his little ones. Then, as she allowed her heart and soul to lift in praise to the Savior, she forgot about Dane, his children, her father, and everything except for the words she sang and the beauty of the music.

❧

Two more days slipped by without Dane making a move to speak to Deborah about the wedding. Not that Deborah minded. The less she had to do with him the better she liked it. But she knew he would not ignore her forever, especially after they were married. On Thursday evening after church, Dane asked if he could escort her home, and she turned to her father for permission.

"Yes, that's a fine idea. This young man can serve as your chaperone." He placed his hand on Tommy's head and smiled down at him.

Deborah had expected her father to accompany them. To assign the duties of chaperone to a two-year-old showed how little he cared for her. She turned away to meet Cora's smile.

"It will be fine, Deborah. Dane is honorable, and Tommy is probably a better chaperone than most adults would be. Go on and see if you can't get my son to talk to you. You need to become better acquainted."

Dane helped Deborah climb onto the wagon seat before lifting Tommy to sit beside her. Deborah scooted over so that Dane would have room to sit beside his son.

"I thought you might like to see my place first before it's too dark." Dane spoke as they started off. "We'll drive by."

"Yes, I would like that." Deborah hadn't thought about the house she would be living in. She had resigned herself to this marriage with little more enthusiasm than one might give a life sentence.

"Mine house." Tommy nodded.

"Yeah, we're going to show the pretty lady your house."

Deborah caught her breath. Dane didn't say more, and she wondered if he had intended to call her pretty. Probably not. Tommy chattered endlessly about his house, the horses, and everything they saw between the church and the house. Deborah understood why Cora thought Tommy would make a good chaperone. If they had tried, they couldn't have gotten a word in edgewise.

Dane pulled into the yard and stopped in front of the house. "We won't go inside, but this is home. My mother lived here with her parents when they first came to the country."

Deborah looked at the log cabin and smiled. It had a homey appearance to it as if just waiting for a family to move in.

"My uncle Ben and aunt Esther lived here after my grandmother died and my grandfather moved to Springfield. Uncle Ben is a missionary to the Indians in the West now. My mother's youngest brother lived here for a few years before he and his wife joined Uncle Ben on the missionary field. The house set empty after that until I moved in four years ago."

When Dane fell silent, Deborah wondered if she should say something. But what? *I'm looking forward to living here with you?* That would not be the truth.

Then he spoke again, rescuing her. "I have no idea why you agreed to marry me and take on these kids. I know your husband recently died and I'm sorry for that. I think you need to know that I will never love you as a husband should love his wife."

Deborah looked over Tommy's head into Dane's serious gaze. What did he mean by that? She shook her head. "I don't understand why you are telling me this."

Dane looked away and Tommy remained silent. "My wife died when Beth was born. I will never again put another woman in that danger."

"Are you saying—"

"Yes." He looked back at her. "That's exactly what I'm saying. This is where we will live as husband and wife in name only. We will live together in this house, but we will not share a bed. If that isn't all right with you, now's the time to speak up."

Chapter 5

Deborah sat in stunned silence, staring at Dane. She had never thought much about children until this past week. Caring for Dane's two little ones had brought out a maternal side to her that she hadn't known existed. She knew that if Jamison had lived, they would likely have had children. But now she would never have any. Must she be content to raise someone else's children?

"Do you have any objections?" Dane broke into her thoughts.

She focused on his face then looked away. "My father says I must marry you as it is my Christian duty to help a brother in need. I have never gone contrary to my father's demands and will not now. You seem to be a reasonable man, and I already adore your children. If you wish a marriage of convenience, I have no objections."

Then why did she feel as if he had rejected her? And why did it hurt so much? She should be glad that he would leave her alone. She had found Jamison's attentions undesirable; why would Dane's be any different? She stole a glance at him and saw the set line of his jaw.

"Fine. I'll get you back to my folks' then." He flicked the reins, and the wagon moved out.

They rode in silence for several minutes before Dane spoke. "There is one thing. I'd appreciate you keeping this between the two of us. It's no one else's business."

What did he think she would do? Tell everyone she met that her husband's only interest in her was as housekeeper and mother to his children? She noticed that Tommy had fallen asleep against his father's leg. No wonder he'd been so quiet.

"I assure you that I will tell no one. Furthermore, I will do my best to keep all appearances as if we have a normal relationship." She thought of her father and would have smiled if she hadn't been so hurt by Dane's rejection. Father would be surprised if he knew why Dane had asked to take her on this drive.

"Thank you." Dane stopped the wagon in front of his parents' house. He scooped Tommy up and twisted on the seat. A wooden box behind the seat held straw covered by a blanket. He lowered the little boy to the makeshift bed and met Deborah's curious gaze. "I can't drive the wagon and hold two babies. Beth is safe in the box, and Tommy does pretty well up here with me when he's awake."

"I see." Deborah's heart softened toward this young father who tried to be everything to his two motherless babies. She thought of her prayer the day Jamison was buried. She had asked God to help her submit to her father's rule even before she knew of Dane and his children. How could she let pride stand between her and the work God had set before her? She turned to climb down from the wagon.

"Just a minute." Dane stopped her. "I haven't officially asked you to marry me, and I'd like to do that. Now that you understand how I feel about things, will you, Deborah Asberry, agree to be my wife in name only?"

Deborah glanced down at the little boy sleeping behind them and back at Dane's steady gaze. "Yes, I will."

"I think they are planning the wedding for Sunday after church. Is that all right with you?"

Her smile held a touch of bitterness. *As if either of us has much choice.* She nodded. "That will be fine."

"Did Mom tell you about the party Saturday night after service? I imagine she invited the entire community."

Deborah nodded. "Yes, she mentioned it."

"Can you. . ." He looked away, then back to search her face. "Can you act like you're happy about all of this and stand beside me to greet our neighbors? I've known these people all my life."

Deborah understood that he thought she might embarrass him in front of his friends and family. He wanted everyone to think they would have a normal marriage. She wanted the same thing, didn't she? Then why did she feel so empty when she thought of living in Dane Stark's house day after day, always knowing that he didn't care for her?

"I'll do the best I can."

He smiled his approval, and Deborah lowered her gaze. Dane was the best-looking man she had ever met. She had recognized that at their first meeting, but she had assumed he would be like Jamison—overbearing and even cruel at times. Maybe that would come later after he became accustomed to her presence. She could only hope not.

He jumped from the wagon and came around to her side. As he helped her climb down, she looked back and asked, "Will Tommy be all right out here?"

"I'll just walk you to the door and get Beth. He'll be fine no longer than that."

At the door he stopped before opening it and looked at her. "Thank you."

Deborah knew that Dane felt gratitude for her sacrifice. For surely their marriage would be a sacrifice to her. In less than three days she would be bound to a man who cared nothing for her and refused to give her children of her own. She would be forever giving up the chance for a real marriage with a man who loved her. But was there such a man, anyway? Jamison had never loved her although he had used her, just as Dane intended to do in a different way. Why, then, did Dane's rejection hurt so much, while she had felt nothing but repulsion for Jamison's attentions?

❦

On Saturday evening, Deborah dressed with care. During the week of the revival meetings she had met most of the people who would converge on the Starks' cabin to express their congratulations and best wishes to Dane. She knew that he wanted his friends to accept her. She hoped to make the best possible impression on both Dane and his friends and family.

At the close of the service, Deborah again found herself riding to the Starks' with Dane and Tommy. Beth lay cuddled close in Deborah's arms. Dane drove past the house to stop the wagon out by the barn. "I hope you don't mind the walk," he said as if he had just realized she was with him. "The yard will be full, and I wanted to leave room for the others near the house."

"No, this is fine." She smiled down at the baby in her arms. Already the tiny girl had captured her heart. Tommy, too. Even if she could back out of this marriage now, she wouldn't. At first she had thought her father asked too much of her. Now, as she allowed her love to reach out to the two small children, she knew that God was giving her so much more in return.

Deborah waited while Dane took care of the horses and then together they walked to the house. Dane carried Tommy while Deborah carried Beth. Already she felt a part of his family, although she knew that position would never really be hers.

A festive atmosphere had overtaken the cabin. As Dane had predicted, wagons filled the yard and barn lot. The Starks' roomy cabin became crowded within minutes. Dane held the door for Deborah as she entered the parlor.

"Here're the lovebirds now." Billy Reid's voice carried over the others.

Deborah would have liked to hide her burning face when half the gathering turned to stare at her and Dane. Then Cora moved forward with a warm smile. She stepped between Deborah and most of the guests as she reached for her granddaughter.

In a low voice, she said, "Don't mind Billy. He likes to stir things up, but he doesn't mean anything by it."

Cora held the baby against her shoulder and patted her back. "Why don't you two move around the room and visit with your guests? I'll watch Beth and Tommy."

At that moment, Cora's husband joined them. "Hey, how's my favorite grandson?"

Tommy lunged for his grandfather and the two went off together. Cora laughed. "I guess that takes care of that. Now go on, both of you. And don't let Billy bother you."

"Thanks, Mom." Dane took Deborah's arm and spoke close to her ear. "If Billy gets out of line, I'll take care of him."

They moved through the room, speaking to each guest. Deborah could place a few names with faces but didn't remember everyone. The pastor of the church, Timothy Donovan, and his wife, Grace, were there. Deborah recognized several members of the large Newkirk family. Dane introduced her to the Seymours, the Sinclairs, the Jordans, and so many more that she couldn't keep track.

Everyone seemed to welcome her with smiles and best wishes as if she and Dane had made a love match. If they knew, how would they act then? Deborah wondered.

A woman stepped to Deborah's side and gave her a warm hug. "Hi. I've never been in the right place at the right time to meet you, Deborah, but I enjoyed your singing in the revival. You have a beautiful voice. How wonderful that you are using your talent for the Lord."

"Thank you." Deborah looked into bright blue eyes. The woman's hair, as black as a moonless night, shimmered with highlights of gray, which added to her beauty.

Dane stood close to Deborah. "This is my aunt Ivy, my father's sister. She is Billy Reid's mother."

"I'm pleased to meet you." Deborah smiled at the older woman, realizing now that she must be close to fifty although she looked much younger.

Ivy smiled. "I'm glad to meet you, too, Deborah. I will be praying for both of you that as the years pass, your marriage will grow to be as filled with love and mutual understanding as mine was."

"Thank you, Aunt Ivy."

Deborah remained silent.

The older woman patted Deborah's arm and laughed softly. "There was a time when I did not serve the Lord. I made life miserable for everyone around me, but all I wanted was love and acceptance. I thought I'd found that when I married Bill and he took me to that big, fancy house of his." She laughed again. "The house soon became common, and I found that my husband didn't always understand me." She paused. "It wasn't until I turned my life over to Jesus Christ and accepted His forgiveness that I found the love I really needed. From that point on, I had the best life possible."

A faint smile crossed Deborah's lips. "I have already learned that Jesus' love is all I need, Mrs. Reid."

Deborah sensed Dane stiffen beside her. She didn't look at him, but she knew he understood that she meant she didn't need his love.

Ivy laughed and touched Dane's arm while she kept her other hand on Deborah's arm. "That is true, Deborah, but don't turn from the extra crumbs that the Master may throw under His table. Bill and I did not marry for love, either, yet we loved each other very much." She looked from one to the other. "I will be praying for you both that this marriage of convenience turns into a marriage of love."

With that, Ivy released them and turned away. Deborah watched her walk across the room to visit with another woman as if she had not just opened a wound that could not be healed.

Dane cleared his throat. "My aunt is outspoken. Like Billy, only in a nicer way."

Deborah looked up at him and saw his half-smile of apology. She shrugged. "That's all right. I'm sure she doesn't understand the situation."

"Deborah. Dane. There you are." Cora motioned for them to join her.

Cakes and pies had been brought in for the reception. The ladies cut and handed out pieces until they were gone. Then someone cleaned off the table and piled gifts on it for the bride and groom. Again they were called forward to acknowledge the thoughtfulness of everyone there. They received hand-sewn linens, embroidered pillowcases, dresser scarves, and a tablecloth. A Single Wedding Ring quilt came from Billy and Lenore Reid.

Deborah wondered at the lavish gift. Surely Lenore had made this quilt for another purpose and decided to give it to her husband's cousin when she had nothing else ready.

She smiled at Lenore. "Thank you for such a lovely gift. I'm sure we will treasure it always."

Lenore lifted her eyebrows with a half smile. "You are quite welcome. I wanted to give something you could both use."

Deborah knew that all of the gifts had been gathered from the meager possessions of people who had gone through four years of war with both outlaws and soldiers taking whatever caught their eye. She appreciated the generosity of Dane's family and neighbors and, as she had said, would treasure each gift. Most had given from their hearts. She wondered about Lenore. Something didn't seem right. Almost as if she knew their marriage would not be real.

Dane waited until everyone else had gone; then he asked Deborah to step outside where they could speak privately. She walked a short distance from the house with him.

"I want to thank you for what you did tonight."

She looked up at him in confusion. "I didn't do anything."

His smile seemed sad. "Yeah, you did. You acted like everything was okay even when Lenore and Billy said things. They can be a trial, but you didn't let them ruffle your feathers."

Dane's approval meant more to Deborah than she wanted to admit. She smiled at him. "They didn't bother me too much."

He gave her a nod and walked her back to the house. Just when he seemed to be warming up to her, he grew cold again. She sighed. If they couldn't truly be husband and wife, couldn't they at least be friends? After all, they would be living in the same house, working together, and making a home for his children. It would seem the Lord had more work for her to do than first met the eye.

A few minutes later, as Deborah prepared for bed, her father knocked on her door. "Deborah, may I speak to you?"

She slipped into her robe and opened the door. "Come in, Father."

Deborah sat on the edge of the bed and was surprised when her father sat beside her and took her hands in his. "Tomorrow you will be married."

"For the second time, Father." She couldn't help reminding him and wished she had enough courage to mention the fact that both were his choice.

"Yes." He nodded. "You have been blessed to find two such wonderful Christian men. May God's blessing be on this union that you may have a long, happy marriage, fruitful in the work of the Lord."

Deborah almost choked at her father's words. She wondered what he would say if he knew that her second marriage would not be the fruitful union he thought. Would he call it off? Did she even want him to? She thought of Beth and Tommy and knew that she didn't. She wanted to be their mother. She could live with Dane as friends if she could get past the wall he had erected between them. This was the work God had given her to do—to banish the sorrow from Dane's eyes and to mother his children. Not an easy task, she knew, but one that she could do with God's help.

"I'll be leaving early Monday morning, and before I go, I want you to know that I'm proud of you, Deborah. God will bless you as you work for Him."

Deborah looked at her father while conflicting emotions of love and anger warred in her heart. Could she ever find the grace she needed to forgive her father for taking her so far from her mother and brother and for forcing her into two loveless marriages?

Chapter 6

Deborah awoke on Sunday morning to the noise of Dane's two youngest brothers scuffling in the next room. The scent of frying bacon drifted up the stairs into her room, causing her stomach to turn. She threw the covers back. No doubt hunger stirred her stomach, but she knew that some of the turmoil she felt came from anxiety over the coming ceremony—and afterward.

Today was her wedding day. Never had she missed her mother more! She swung her feet to the floor and sat up, putting self-pity away. She had learned long ago that feeling sorry for herself never helped. The wedding would go on no matter how she felt. Her father would see to that. She might as well make the best of things.

She looked around the tiny bedroom, its sloped ceiling making it seem more of a hideout than an actual room. Her wedding dress hung on the wall beside the door. The dress she had worn when she and Jamison were married was safely stored at her parents' house. Her mother had helped her choose this dress as one they both believed would be appropriate for a second wedding. Cut in simple lines, lace covered the cream-colored silk underbodice. The full skirt attached to the bodice just below her natural waistline emphasized her slender figure. She would put on her wedding dress at the church after services.

❀

Dane stood back and watched Deborah. She had dutifully stayed by his side throughout most of the meal but was now standing alone on the edge of the crowd. For the first time he thought beyond the needs of his children to what this marriage might mean to Deborah. Who was he to force her this way? To make her marry him when she'd rather head back home with her father in the morning. Why would she want to tie herself to him when he couldn't even offer her a real marriage?

Of course he had given her a chance to back out when he asked her to marry him Thursday night. She'd said yes. He could tell that she liked his little ones. Her father seemed to think the marriage was a good idea. Maybe Deborah wanted this. She'd been married before. Maybe she'd loved her husband so much she figured she'd never fall in love again.

"Why ain't ya over there with her instead of standin' here lookin'? Shame to see a pretty girl like that go to waste gettin' married to you."

"Well, if it isn't Billy Reid." Dane turned toward his cousin. "Seems I could say the same about you and Lenore. Where's your wife?"

Billy raised one dark eyebrow. "What's it to you?"

"Nothing." Dane sighed. "I was just making polite conversation."

"Yeah? Seems to me you always were too interested in Lenore."

"Where would you get an idea like that? I had a wife I loved very much."

"Yeah, and now you're about to get another one that you don't care a fig about."

Dane stared at his cousin. "Whether I do or don't care about my wife is none of your concern."

"Jist see that you don't care too much about mine."

Billy spoke low, but Dane heard as he walked away. He had never cared for Lenore the way Billy seemed to think, but he wasn't so sure about his feelings toward Deborah. His wife? Deborah would never be his wife for real. Why should that make him feel as if he were missing something just outside his grasp? A marriage in name only was what he wanted, wasn't it?

He stopped beside Deborah. "Hi. Are you all right?"

She smiled at him. "Of course. A little nervous, maybe, but otherwise I'm fine."

He cleared his throat. "Are you sure you want to go through with this?"

When she looked at him as if she didn't understand, he said, "The wedding. Marrying me. Being a mother to my kids."

"I already love Beth and Tommy. I just hope they can care for me a little."

"I doubt there's any problem with that."

She laughed. "I don't know. I've never been around children before. I have no idea how to care for them."

He grinned. "Most parents don't when they first start."

"I suppose not."

"Dane. Deborah. There you are." Deborah's father joined them, a wide smile on his face. "Dane, if you will go into the church, we'll be along shortly."

Dane noticed that most of the people were already heading toward the church door and realized that if Deborah was going to back out it had better be now. He caught her gaze and asked, "Are you sure?"

She nodded, giving him a sweet smile. "Yes, I'm sure. Go on."

Dane gave a quick nod and turned toward the church. Inside, he headed for the front and stood to one side. Deborah had requested that they have no attendants, so Dane stood alone with Pastor Donovan in front of a full church and watched the back door. The organist began playing a song he scarcely listened to. He wiped his hands on his trousers, and then Deborah and her father stepped through the open doorway. Dane watched his bride walk with her back straight, her head held high. Each step she took seemed to declare her determination to get through the ordeal before her with as much dignity as possible. His heart hurt for her.

Dane stepped forward to accept Deborah's hand from her father, then turned to face the minister. He promised himself at that moment that even though their marriage could never be real, he would see that Deborah's life with him was as pleasant as he could make it.

"Dearly beloved, we are gathered together. . . ." The traditional ceremony continued to the end as they promised to care for each other in sickness and in health. "I now pronounce you husband and wife."

Pastor Donovan looked at Dane. "You may now kiss the bride."

Dane stared at the older man he had known all his life as the words penetrated his brain. Kiss Deborah? How could he have forgotten this part of the ceremony? He turned to his bride. She looked frightened. He couldn't very well announce to the waiting congregation that he didn't want to kiss his wife, could he?

He gave her what he hoped was a reassuring smile and took her into his arms. She felt so tiny—and soft—and warm. Her hands touched his chest. As he leaned closer, they slid up to circle his neck. His lips touched hers, and he became lost in the sweetest kiss of his life. Emotions threatened to choke him when he finally pulled away. He couldn't care for Deborah. Not after only one week of barely seeing or talking to her. How could this be?

He stepped back and her hands slid away. He couldn't think right now, but soon after they were at home, he would sort out these feelings and figure out what to do. Somehow he had to keep his distance from Deborah. He could not break the vow he'd made the night Anne died. He could not place a second wife in danger of death just because of his own unbridled emotions.

He took a slow breath to quiet his racing heart and faced the congregation with Deborah by his side as Pastor Donovan said, "May I present to you, Mr. and Mrs. Dane Stark."

❅

Deborah stood beside the wagon and gave her father a parting hug. "You've made me proud today, Deborah. Mrs. Stark says someone goes into Stockton occasionally where letters can be mailed, so you be sure to write and let us know how you are doing. I'll tell your mother about the wedding as I know she will want the details."

"Please tell Mother and Caleb both that I love them and I will write as soon as I can." Deborah still felt anger toward her father. He seemed happy to leave her here among strangers. How did he know Dane would not be cruel to her? All that mattered was getting rid of her. Well, he had done that so now he could leave, and if she never saw him again she wouldn't care. Yet, deep in her heart she knew she did care and that made the pain so much harder to bear.

Dane appeared by her side and shook hands with her father. "Thank you, sir."

Deborah stepped back as they talked. She swiped at the moisture in her eyes and crossed the yard to Cora and the children. Cora gave her a warm hug while she held Beth in her other arm. "Are you all right?"

Deborah nodded. "I'm fine. I was just telling my father good-bye. May I hold the baby?"

As Cora handed Beth to her, Deborah knew that she needed the warmth and love that only a baby snuggled in her arms could give. She held little Beth close and marveled that she fit so perfectly with her head resting in the hollow of her shoulder. Deborah could feel tiny puffs of breath on her neck. She rested her cheek against the downy softness of the baby's hair and patted her back, taking in the sweet smell of powder and baby.

"You look natural holding her," Cora said.

Deborah smiled. "I must confess, I didn't expect to feel natural, but I think I'm getting the hang of holding her, at least."

"Are you ready to go?" Dane asked.

She turned to look at him, unsure if he meant her. But of course he did. They were married now whether she felt like his wife or not. Whether she would ever feel like his wife. She nodded. "Yes. Any time you are."

Tommy grabbed Dane's leg. "Me go, too."

Dane scooped him up and set him on his shoulders to Tommy's delight. "I guess that's everyone, then."

"Deborah—" Cora lay a detaining hand on Dane's arm. "Just a minute. I had the leftovers from the dinner put in the back of your wagon. There should be enough for several meals. Most of it should keep a day or two, but you can put any perishables in the cellar. Just be sure to wrap it good."

Deborah didn't know the condition of Dane's kitchen. He had been taking his evening meals at the older Starks' each day this past week. Could it be that he had no foodstuff for her to cook? Is that why the women had fixed enough to last a few days? As she thanked his mother, she wondered what she might be walking into. She hadn't even seen the inside of the house.

Twenty minutes later she stepped into Dane's house and tripped over a boot that had fallen beside the door.

"Are you all right?" Dane steadied her, then just as quickly pulled his hand away and stepped back.

"Yes, I'm fine."

She no sooner spoke than Dane picked up his boots and threw them up the stairs that led to the floor above. "Sorry about that. I usually take them off by the door, but I don't have to."

Deborah stepped away from the dried mud lying in clumps on the floor where the boots had been. With one hand she lifted her cream-colored silk skirt a couple of inches and hoped there were no more piles of dirt. She looked around. Although the floor looked as if it needed to be swept, the dirt was at least spread thin over the rest of the large room that appeared to be parlor, kitchen, and dining room all in one.

An open door to her left revealed a bedroom. The stairway in the back of the big room led upstairs where she assumed there were more bedrooms. She saw an outside door in the back wall of the kitchen.

Letting her gaze return to the parlor, Deborah's heart sank at the job before her. A couch held various articles of clothing. Deborah assumed that was Dane's clean laundry since dirty clothing littered the floor from the bedroom door into the kitchen.

Dane set Tommy down and said, "I'll carry in the food from the wagon before a stray animal decides to have supper."

Before Deborah could answer, he slipped out the door with Tommy toddling after him. She let them go and, clutching Beth close, stepped over dirty clothing, tools, and even a saddle on her way to the kitchen. A closer look there showed dirty dishes that would have to be washed before they could eat supper.

No wonder he'd been eager to run outside while she looked around. She sighed. She couldn't do it overnight, but in a few days she would have a clean house to live in. Dane didn't seem to be overbearing like her father and Jamison had been. His main concern seemed to be for his children. As long as she kept the house and took care of the children, he would likely leave her alone just as he had suggested. She would be free for the first time in her life.

Why, then, did she feel a sense of something missing? Why did she keep remembering the kiss Dane had given her at the close of their wedding ceremony? Why did she want another?

She picked her way across the floor to the door at the other end. She would do well to forget Dane and his kisses and concentrate on the opportunity that had been handed to her. As Dane's wife she would have the children she longed for without the danger and discomfort of giving birth. She would have a home of her own to care for without an overbearing man criticizing her every move—at least she hoped Dane would not turn out to be like Jamison.

She stepped into the bedroom and laid the sleeping baby in the crib that stood beside the four-poster double bed. She gave her a pat and backed out of the room as Dane and Tommy came in from outdoors.

Dane carried a large box. "Where do you want this? Looks like there's everything from meat dishes to desserts in here."

Deborah closed the door and stepped around and over the littered floor to the kitchen table. She marveled that Dane didn't trip on anything as he followed her. "I'll clear a space for it."

Dane waited without a word until she had the corner clean enough for him to set the box down. At the very least, Jamison would have complained about the heavy box. She mentally reprimanded herself for thinking ill of the dead.

"I'll go take care of the horses now." Dane picked up his son. "You want to go with me, Tommy?"

"Yes." The little boy nodded.

"I'll have supper ready by the time you get back." Deborah watched them go back out the front door, then turned toward the dirty dishes.

She was glad to find some warm water on the cookstove and soon had a dishpan of soapy water. She couldn't wash them all, but she determined to make a dent in the pile before she set out their food.

❄

Dane unhitched the team and took care of their needs while his little boy watched, chattering endlessly about one thing and another. He didn't listen and didn't figure Tommy cared as long as he nodded and said "Uh-huh" at the right times. His mind was on the woman in his house.

Deborah hadn't liked the mess she found when she stepped through the door. He should have thought and cleaned it up. After Anne died he'd let things go. There never seemed to be time for everything, and the house kept getting dirty, anyway.

He wandered around in the barn, finding things to do that didn't need to be done until he figured he'd run out of time. He milked the cow and picked up the full pail. Might as well go in and face the disappointment he'd already seen in her eyes. As he and Tommy walked past the corner of the barn, Dane saw a couple of tiny white flowers with yellow centers growing just off the path. He stopped on impulse and picked them. Holding them out of sight, he opened the door to the house and let Tommy go in first.

While Tommy held Deborah's attention, Dane poured water in a glass as if he were going to take a drink but slipped the flowers in instead. He set the tiny bouquet on the table that he noticed was now cleaned off and shining.

He stepped back to watch while Deborah set a dish of potato salad on the table. He knew when she saw the flowers by the way she stopped and her eyes widened.

She turned with a smile. He liked the way her dark eyes lit up when she smiled. "How pretty and thoughtful. Thank you."

He shrugged, but her praise warmed his heart. After Dane prayed, Tommy kept the conversation going as he told of helping his daddy with the horses. Which was just as well. Dane couldn't have thought of anything to say if he'd tried. He found that he liked Deborah's smile, though, and wished he could bring another to her face.

When they finished eating, he leaned back in his chair and patted his stomach. "That was mighty good for a change."

293

Deborah looked up at him. "I can't take credit since the food was already cooked."

Dane grinned. "Maybe not, but you didn't burn anything heating it up either. This is the first meal we've had at this table for ages that didn't have a charcoal taste."

His reward was a bubble of laugher from Deborah.

Chapter 7

Deborah slipped into the big bed alone and smiled. How wondrously different from her first wedding night. Dane had taken Tommy to the outhouse, and then he'd locked the door while Tommy scampered up the stairs to the floor above. With no more than a gruff good night, her new husband had left her standing alone in the sitting room and climbed upstairs after his son.

She blew the light out and lay back to stare into the blackness of her strange, new bedroom. Hers and Beth's. As she thought of the baby, her smile widened. Tommy might remember his mother, but Beth would have no memories of any mother but Deborah. Now, away from Mrs. Stark, she could begin being the mother to Beth and Tommy that she wanted to be. Cora Stark was a wonderful woman, but Deborah hadn't felt free under her watchful eye to act as more than a sitter for the children. She felt strangely content with her new life and, at the same time, felt angry and hurt by her father for his high-handed ways of forcing her to marry a man she didn't know. She closed her eyes as sleep claimed her body.

Deborah felt as if she had no sooner lay down than the baby's wail brought her to a groggy awareness. She had never heard Beth cry so—as if she were in terrible pain. Deborah stumbled from bed and with fumbling fingers lit the lamp. In the soft light she saw the baby's arms and legs waving while the high-pitched crying continued. She scooped her new daughter up and wrapped the blanket around her to hold her close.

"Poor baby," she crooned while she patted Beth's back. "You are freezing. No wonder you are crying."

Deborah walked the floor patting the baby while she held her close, hoping her body heat would warm her. But Beth was not so easily consoled. She continued crying, her tiny body tense, her arms and legs thrashing.

Deborah didn't understand. The night was not that cold. She held one miniature arm in her hand and realized that she was no longer cold. What then could be the matter?

When she heard the stairs to the floor above creak, she knew that Dane had been awakened. Maybe he would know what to do. She opened the door and stepped out into the larger room. Dane didn't even glance her way as he carried a lamp to the kitchen table and set it down. He lifted a damp cloth from a crock sitting near the back door, dipped milk out, and poured it into bottle. Then he fitted a rubber nipple over the end and set it in a pan of wate already warming on the stove.

Deborah watched him and felt heat course through her body. No one ha told her that Beth needed to eat at night. Dane acted so sure as if he knew how t stop the crying. Deborah took the bottle he handed her and offered the nipple t Beth. She latched on and sucked as if she were starving.

Deborah looked up and found Dane watching her. She sank into a rockin, chair in the sitting room, holding the baby against her as a shield when she real ized she wore only her flannel nightgown. Although it covered her completely she still felt undressed before him. That and her incompetence unnerved her.

"She gets hungry in the middle of the night." Dane spoke as his gaze shifte from his daughter.

Deborah met his gaze, knowing he would think her totally stupid. "I'n sorry. I didn't know that. I've never been around babies before."

He grinned, the whiteness of his teeth flashing in the dim light. "Yeah, think you mentioned something about that earlier today. If you're all right with her, I'll head on back to bed."

"Yes, we're fine." She stood and walked toward the bedroom door.

"Good." He went to the kitchen table and picked up his lamp before start-ing upstairs. His voice stopped her at the door. "The bottles are in that cabinet there over the milk. She'll want another one early in the morning."

She turned around and saw him standing at the foot of the stairs. He had pulled his clothes on before coming downstairs, but had not buttoned his shirt. The intimacy of the situation set her pulse racing. She stepped into the bed-room. "Thank you."

Deborah could not get Dane out of her mind and lay awake long after Beth slept. The early morning sun had just touched her window when Beth's cry woke her. Knowing what caused the screams this time, she smoothed the baby's blan-kets in passing and went into the kitchen to fix a bottle. With almost every other dish dirty, Deborah was amazed to find a clean bottle. Obviously Dane realized the importance of keeping a supply handy.

Just as she headed back to the bedroom with the warmed bottle, Tommy started down the stairs. Deborah hesitated. Beth screamed as if she were in ter-rible pain. "Tommy, do you need help on the stairs?"

"No."

That was plain enough, but what if he fell? He was only two years old, and he had on some sort of a nightshirt. What if he stepped on the tail and tripped? She started up the stairs.

"No." Tommy backed away from her, and Beth's screams sounded even louder.

Deborah was sure Tommy would fall, but she needed to feed Beth. Where was Dane?

"Stay right there, Tommy. Don't come down yet." Deborah hurried into the bedroom, hoping Tommy would obey. She picked up the baby, blanket and all, trying to ignore the soaked diaper, and went back into the big room.

Tommy had descended several more steps. Deborah stuck the nipple in Beth's mouth, but the baby didn't seem to realize it was there. She continued screaming, and Tommy went down another step. His hand barely touched the railing. He teetered before regaining his balance. Deborah had both hands full with the baby and didn't know what to do. She ran up the stairs to stand in front of Tommy.

"No." He pushed at her. "Me do."

Deborah backed down a couple of steps. All right, she'd let him do it himself, but she'd stand ready to block his fall. She brushed the nipple against Beth's lips, moving it back and forth until the baby latched on. The silence almost deafened her. She continued down the stairs a step ahead of Tommy and breathed again when he reached the ground floor.

Why had she thought she could be a mother to two babies? She knew nothing about them. She lowered herself and Beth into the rocker as she relaxed her trembling limbs. Where was Dane, anyway?

Tommy bounced in front of her and then ran through the room to the back door. He probably thought his father had gone outside. She would gladly let Dane take over the responsibility of his son, but she couldn't let him out when she didn't know where Dane was, and she couldn't go looking for him until Beth finished her bottle.

"No, Tommy, we have to stay inside now."

Tommy ran back and straddled the saddle that still sat on the floor. He played while Beth finished eating. Deborah stood and went back into the bedroom. She needed to get dressed before Dane showed up. Beth's bright blue eyes looked up at her as if trying to recognize her. Deborah smiled and after a quick kiss on the baby's forehead, laid her in the middle of her bed.

Tommy pushed the door open as Deborah slipped her dress over her head. For just a moment she thought Dane had come in and her heart pounded. Then her head came through, and she saw Tommy looking up at her as if he wondered what she might be doing in his house.

She smiled at the little boy and buttoned the bodice of her dress. "Hey, are you going to help me with breakfast?"

He pranced around her saying, "Me go. . . ."

She couldn't understand the last word. "You go where?"

He ran through the house with her following. Again he went to the back door and tried to open it. "Tommy, I don't understand, but if you are looking for your father—"

The front door opened and Dane walked in. "He isn't looking for me. He needs to go to the outhouse."

Deborah felt as if she had shrunk two feet. In a tiny voice she squeaked, "I didn't know."

Dane ignored her as he grabbed his son and went out the back door. Deborah watched the door block them from sight. How many more times would she be saying "I didn't know"? A hundred? A thousand? How long before Dane realized he had made a mistake in marrying her?

As the baby let out a piercing cry, Deborah's heart jumped into her throat. She had left her on the bed alone. "Please, Lord, don't let her have fallen off the bed."

She ran, jumping over the objects on the floor and burst through the door into the bedroom to find Beth still lying on her back, her arms and legs jerking as she cried. Deborah picked her up and remembered the wet diaper that now gave off a pungent odor. "Oh, baby, I'm sorry. I forgot about your little problem, which is just as well, I suppose, since it seems to have grown into a big problem."

Beth stopped crying and looked into Deborah's eyes as if trying to understand. Deborah smiled and continued talking to the baby. "Let's get you cleaned up. At least that's something I've done before. Maybe I can do something right for a change."

Deborah found a supply of diapers by the crib. She wet a washcloth to clean the baby and soon had her smiling again. She carried the clean, sweet-smelling baby into the other room just as Dane and Tommy came inside. When Dane glanced at the table, she realized he had probably expected breakfast.

"I'm sorry, I haven't had time to cook anything yet. I need to get Tommy dressed and then I can start some oatmeal. That shouldn't take long."

"No, want mine mommy." Tommy stuck his thumb in his mouth and sidled closer to his father.

Deborah looked up at Dane in surprise. Tommy had not mentioned his mother since that first time in the barn. She stood holding Beth, not sure what she should do. She looked for a safe place to put the baby.

Dane stepped forward. "Here, let me take her. I'll get Tommy dressed while you see about something for us to eat."

Deborah relinquished the baby while she fought against the burning in her eyes. She would not give in and cry in front of either Dane or his children. Her emotions seemed so close to the surface, and she didn't know why. Dane had not spoken even one harsh word to her in spite of her ineptitude in caring for his children. Jamison had struck her for less and she hadn't cried. Now here she was, wanting to cry because her husband hadn't yelled at her. Nothing made any sense.

Deborah soon had oatmeal bubbling and bacon frying. At least she knew her way around a kitchen. Dane and Tommy would eat well if nothing else. But what of Beth? Did she eat real food? She couldn't remember Cora giving her anything other than milk. She set the table with dishes she had washed the night before and called Dane and Tommy.

Deborah took Beth so Dane could eat. She sat across the table from him and bowed her head while he prayed. With Beth balanced in one arm, Deborah picked up her spoon. Eating with one hand was not easy, but she managed.

"You could lay her down," Dane suggested.

And have her start crying again? Deborah gave him a tight smile. "This is fine."

Both babies were quiet. While Tommy ate, Beth sat propped against Deborah and watched the others. Dane didn't speak again until he finished eating.

He stood and Tommy scrambled to get down from his chair. "I need to get some plowing done today. I'll be back in about noon."

"Me go wiff you." Tommy ran to the door.

"No, Tommy, you stay here with your new mama." Dane caught the little boy up and set him down well away from the door.

Tommy's face puckered and he wailed. "Mommy. Want mine mommy."

"Oh, great." Dane looked as if he'd like to bolt for the door.

Deborah pushed Dane's clean clothing to the end of the sofa, then laid Beth toward the back and hoped she wouldn't roll off. To make sure, she pulled a handful of the clothing into a pile in front of the baby. Then she turned toward Tommy.

"Hey, Tommy, we'll have fun today while Daddy works. Okay?"

"No." He grabbed his father's hand and held on as if Deborah might pull him away. "Want mine mommy."

Beth added her tearful voice to Tommy's loud cries. Deborah didn't know which child to go to as their cries reached a deafening level. She feared what might happen if she tried to console either of them. Whatever she tried would probably just make matters worse.

The front door opened and Lenore stepped in. "Hi. Guess I don't have to ask if anyone is home." She squatted down and held her hands out to Tommy with a wide smile. "Hey, fella, come see Auntie Lenore."

Tommy released his father and ran across the room to Lenore, his tears forgotten. Deborah watched her pick him up and give him a hug before she went to the sofa.

"Well, no wonder you're crying, precious." She sat on the edge of the sofa and, with Tommy on her lap, picked up Beth and patted her back, all the time crooning nonsense to her about the cruelty of being stuffed into the corner and left. Deborah felt that each word she spoke was meant as criticism toward her, but she ignored Lenore and met Dane's gaze.

In the sudden quiet, his voice sounded loud. "I'll go milk the cow while you get the kids settled down, and then I've got to get to work."

As he went out the back door, Lenore looked up from the little ones and made a sound of disgust. "Anne milked the cow and gave birth to the children, too."

Deborah wondered what she had done to deserve Lenore's scorn. This morning had been rough, and she hadn't known what to do. That was true. But she would learn and the little ones would adjust to her in time. Although if she did what she wanted to do at the moment, she would be out the door and on her way back home to her mother before Dane ever missed her. She didn't know whether to laugh or cry as she remembered the look on Dane's face. Too many more mornings like this one and he would be taking her all the way back to St. Louis himself.

Chapter 8

Deborah turned away from the door and her longing to walk through it. Tommy sat at Lenore's feet playing with something he'd picked up off the floor. Lenore sat in the rocking chair with the baby held close. She didn't act like she planned to leave anytime soon, but maybe it wouldn't hurt to ask.

"I'm sorry things were in such an uproar when you stopped." Deborah tried to smile. "Did you need something, or were you just passing by and heard the racket?"

"Oh no." Lenore laughed. "I started out to my mother's. She lives a couple of miles up the creek. When I saw Dane's house, I thought it would be the neighborly thing to stop in and see if I could help with anything. Seein' as you're new, you know."

No, she didn't know. She had a week's worth of cleaning staring her in the face. She didn't have time to entertain company now. Besides, she had hoped to spend some time alone with Dane's children. How could they ever look to her as their mother if someone else always took care of them?

"That's very nice of you." Deborah picked her words carefully, trying to sound gracious. "As you can see, I've got my work cut out for me, though. I can't think of a thing I need right now more than time and elbow grease."

Lenore laughed again. "Don't let me stop you. If you want to clean Dane's mess up, you go right ahead. I'll play with Tommy and Beth for a while. We always have so much fun when we're together. Don't we, little angel?"

Lenore turned her attention to the baby, playing with her hands, talking nonsense and laughing at Beth's facial expressions. Deborah stared at her and then shrugged. Beth seemed happy enough. Tommy, too. She should be thankful to have a few minutes without the children underfoot. Maybe she could get some cleaning done if she ignored the trio in her sitting room. It was worth a try. She headed toward the kitchen with resolute steps.

By the time the dishes were washed, Deborah knew she wouldn't have the luxury of ignoring Lenore. Already she had heard more than she wanted to know about how Dane and Anne had met.

"We all grew up here together. Dane, Billy, Anne, me—and Wesley. That's Dane's brother. You haven't met him yet. We're all terribly worried about him since he hasn't come home from the war yet." Lenore walked with the baby into the kitchen while Deborah tackled the sitting room floor. She found a large basket in the corner and started filling it with dirty clothing.

"Billy and Dane, of course, are cousins. We went to school together. You can't imagine how ornery Dane was."

Deborah straightened and stared at Lenore. She tried to picture Dane dipping Lenore's dark braids in the inkwell or stealing a kiss behind the schoolhouse and couldn't. Surely Lenore was making up most of the stories she told. Otherwise Dane must have been in love with Lenore when he married Anne. The walk home from school, the parties, running off to go fishing together, even her first kiss had come from Dane. Maybe she had Dane and Wesley confused.

Deborah went back to work when Lenore took Beth into the bedroom to change her diaper. Tommy trailed after her, saying he had to go to the outhouse. Deborah understood him perfectly that time, but she ignored him, letting Lenore handle the problem. She stuffed the last article of clothing in the basket and set it to the side. Already the place looked better. She went into the kitchen to check on the bread that she had set out to rise earlier.

A glance out the window showed that the sun had already moved past midmorning. Dane would want his noon meal soon. She punched the dough down and shaped it into loaves. She still had enough leftover dishes from their wedding for lunch, so she didn't have to worry about cooking anything except bread. She went back into the sitting room and started sorting the clean clothing on the sofa while Lenore took Tommy outside.

She could hear the baby cooing in the crib. She laid the shirt she had just picked up on Dane's pile and went to check on her. She tiptoed into the bedroom, feeling as if she were trespassing and might be caught at any moment. But that was ridiculous. This was her house now—certainly not Lenore's. The two children were her stepchildren, not Lenore's.

Her heart softened at the sight of little Beth lying on her back, her hands held up in front of her face. As Deborah watched, the baby's eyes drifted closed and her arms slowly relaxed until they rested at either side of her head.

Deborah jumped and turned back to the sitting room when the back door opened. She faced Lenore and, in spite of herself, explained, "I was just checking on Beth. She's asleep."

"Yes, I knew she would be." Lenore's superior attitude grated on Deborah's nerves.

The thought of shoving her visitor back out the door and locking it flitted through Deborah's mind. Of course, she would never try such a thing. But the fantasy made her feel a little better.

"Where do you live, Lenore?" She tried polite conversation instead.

"Ours is the next house to the west. We live just across the creek from Billy's mother. Most folks built along Cedar Creek at first to be near water before they lug wells. Dane's folks had their own supply with that spring there at the edge of the woods. Did Dane take you down to see it?"

Deborah shook her head. "No, I've only been here a week and kept pretty busy then."

A smile spread Lenore's lips. "He took me a few times." A soft giggle escaped. "It's mighty pretty there. Romantic, if you know what I mean."

No, but she had a good idea. Deborah turned her back toward Lenore to set out the food she needed to warm for lunch. She made a face and wished she had the nerve to tell Lenore to go home. Maybe their marriage wasn't real, but she'd still like to spend some time with Dane so that they could become friends. And the children—how could she become a mother to them if she couldn't get near them?

Deborah set three plates on the table, hoping Lenore would get the message. She should have known better. Lenore didn't seem to notice, and when Dane came through the back door, Billy Reid followed him inside.

"Figured I'd find you here." He frowned at his wife.

Deborah waited, hoping he would take Lenore and go home.

"I've been helping Deborah get settled in." Lenore swept a hand out to show the much neater room, as if she had done the work herself.

"That's real nice of you, Lenore. Are you and Billy stayin' for dinner?" Dane turned to Deborah then, as if just remembering her. "There's plenty left over from the dinner yesterday, isn't there?"

"Sure, we'll stay." Billy stepped to the table all the time keeping his gaze on Deborah. A slow grin settled across his handsome face. "If the food's as good as the cook looks, then we can't go wrong."

"Oh, Billy." Lenore smacked his arm. "She's just warming it up. She didn't cook anything."

Deborah opened the oven door and slid a pan of golden-brown bread out. She turned the loaf upside down on a platter and then righted it to spread butter over the top.

"Don't reckon that came from the leftovers." Billy winked at Deborah. "Looks real good, angel."

"Her name's Deborah." Lenore turned to smile at Dane. "So your wife said you were plowing. Are you getting ready to plant corn?"

Deborah listened to Dane and Lenore talk about the crops he would be putting in. She knew little about farming and didn't understand everything they said. Or maybe her mind wasn't on the conversation. Billy kept looking at her and grinning as if they had a secret. Dane didn't seem to notice. Or if he did, he didn't care. She was glad when they finished eating. Maybe now Billy and Lenore would leave.

"Guess I'd better get back to the field. I'll be plowing all week and need to put in as much time as I can while it's light." Dane pushed back from the table.

He looked directly at Deborah for the first time since he'd come in. "You might want to go ahead and fix supper for Tommy and yourself at the usual time. Just leave some out for me, if you don't mind. I probably won't be in until dark."

"All right." She nodded and couldn't help wondering if he planned to stay outside to avoid her.

When Dane stood and headed toward the door, Tommy scrambled out of his chair and followed him. "Me go, too. Me go wiff you, Daddy."

"Tommy, I can't take you out in the field." Dane looked across the room at Deborah in a silent plea for help.

She stepped forward. "Tommy—"

"I'll take him out for a while." Lenore stepped in front of Deborah. "We were so busy inside that he didn't get to go out and play."

"Thanks, Lenore." Dane didn't look at Deborah again as he went out the door.

"I'll get your jacket, Tommy, and then we'll go outside," Lenore promised as she hurried across the floor.

Deborah didn't realize where she was going until she started up the stairs. Her heart sank. She hadn't had time to clean upstairs yet. Lenore had already been in her bedroom. If she had looked, she'd seen all of Deborah's things in there and none of Dane's. Now she would see Dane's and Tommy's clothing and know where each of them had slept.

Her face flushed as she turned away to clear the table. There was nothing she could do now except hope that Lenore didn't snoop. Billy followed her around the table before he pulled out a chair and sat in it.

"Lenore's in love with Dane, you know."

"What?" Deborah swung around, almost dropping the glasses she clutched in her hands.

"Always has been. Dane, too." Billy shrugged but looked none too happy. "Don't know why Dane married Anne. But, soon as he did, Lenore said she'd marry me. I thought she'd get over him. Never has, though. Nor him her. Guess you saw how cozy they were, talkin' about puttin' in the crops."

She'd seen but hadn't thought anything about it. Then Lenore's stories of her and Dane walking out and meeting behind the school and at the spring came back to her. But it didn't matter. None of it did. Because she and Dane didn't have a normal marriage. She couldn't feel threatened when she had nothing to lose. So what if Dane loved Lenore? He would never love her anyway.

She smiled at Billy around the hurt that didn't make sense. "Even if what you say is true, it doesn't matter. Maybe something did go on between them, but that was a long time ago. Lenore married you, and I'm sure she has come to love you very much."

Billy grinned, his good nature seemingly in place again. "You're a catch, you know that? Poor ol' Dane probably didn't have any idea what he got when he married you."

Deborah stared at Billy and wondered what trouble he was trying to stir up. She was almost glad for the interruption when Lenore clambered down the stairs, Tommy's jacket in her hand.

She laughed as she helped Tommy put his jacket on. "Did you get scared all by yourself last night, Tommy, so Daddy had to stay with you?"

Tommy didn't seem to understand, or he didn't hear as he chattered about going outside. But Deborah did, and if the gleam in Lenore's eyes and the smirk on her face was any indication, she knew that Deborah understood.

❀

Deborah breathed a sigh of relief when Lenore and Billy left an hour later. Lenore had insisted on putting Tommy down for his nap, and Deborah didn't argue. Now, with Beth lying on a folded quilt on the floor playing with her hands, she headed to the kitchen.

Dane probably thought Lenore had helped clean the house. Deborah turned and looked at the large room that served as both sitting room and kitchen. She hadn't had time to sweep and mop the floor like she wanted to, but she had picked up most of the clutter and she'd folded and put away the clean clothes. The house looked much better, although there was still plenty to do.

She turned back to her next project. She wanted to bake something special for Dane. Thanks to Lenore and Billy the dishes from their wedding dinner were empty. She stirred up the fire and set the teakettle of water on the stove to warm then rummaged in Dane's supplies until she pulled out a container of dried apple slices.

A tendril of hair fell across her face as she readied the pan to wash dishes, and she brushed it back. The kitchen was too warm, but she needed the fire if she was going to bake an apple pie with the dried apples. With summer just around the corner, she wondered how she would be able to cook then. She thought of her mother's summer kitchen and realized what a luxury it had been.

By the time Tommy woke from his nap, Deborah had the dishes washed and the pie sitting on the pie safe cooling. She ran upstairs when she heard Tommy moving around.

"Hi. Are you ready to get up?"

Tommy sat in the middle of the bed, rubbing his eyes. When he lifted his head, Deborah saw the pucker and knew what was coming. A wail erupted with the barely distinguishable words, "Want mine mommy."

"Oh, Tommy." Deborah sat on the edge of the bed and took the little boy in her arms. He resisted at first, but she held him close, patting his back as if he were Beth. "It's all right, baby. I'm sorry I'm not your real mama. But I'm here and I'll do the best I can to fill in for her."

About the time Deborah's own lashes grew moist, Tommy stopped crying and pulled away. He climbed from her lap and headed to the stairs, dragging a small quilt behind him. Deborah followed.

Tommy didn't mention his mother again that afternoon, but he stayed as far from Deborah as he could, ignoring her overtures of friendship. He lay on his tummy and played with Beth, keeping her occupied while Deborah fixed their supper of sweet potatoes and peas with a couple of slices of side meat. She cut thin slices from the second loaf of bread she had baked that morning and set a place for Tommy at the table. She decided she would wait for Dane. Maybe their marriage wasn't real, but they still needed to function like a family, and she was getting tired of being ignored by both Tommy and Dane.

While Tommy ate, Deborah fed Beth and wondered about the vegetables in Dane's pantry. Did he have a garden? She had helped her mother with their small garden plot and had always enjoyed watching the plants grow. Surely tomorrow Lenore would stay away, and she could get outside to see what she could find.

When the house grew dark, Deborah lit the lamp in the sitting room. Tommy and Beth were both asleep in their beds when Dane came in the back door. His gaze swept the room, and Deborah thought he stiffened for a moment when he saw her sitting on the end of the sofa.

"Your supper is ready." Deborah stood and went to the kitchen where she set a plate for each of them on the table.

"Thanks." Dane washed his hands and dried them on the towel hanging above the basin. "You didn't have to wait up."

Don't you mean to say "I wish you hadn't waited up"? Deborah smiled. "I didn't mind. The children have already eaten and are asleep. This will give us time to get acquainted."

"Yeah, I guess so."

Deborah bowed her head while Dane prayed. She knew he felt as strange as she did, sitting across from her. This was the first time they had been alone since they had met. They ate in silence for a few minutes. Then Deborah asked, "Did you get a lot done?"

He looked up at her as if he had forgotten she was there. "More than usual. It helps not having to make the trip to get the kids." The hint of a smile touched his face. "Pretty nice to not have to wrestle them to bed, too."

"I imagine." Tommy had wanted to stay up, but he'd gone to his bed easily enough when Deborah had suggested she rock him to sleep. It still hurt that he'd rather go off alone to his bedroom than let her hold him.

They talked while they ate. Not a real conversation, but Deborah was content. All she wanted was to be friends with Dane. Yet, after he locked the house and went upstairs, Deborah stopped by the mirror in her room, and before she could control her thoughts, she wondered if Dane found her pretty.

Chapter 9

One month later in June, Dane asked Deborah, "Would you like to go to Ivy?"

When she just stared at him, he grinned. "It's a little settlement named after my aunt Ivy. We could drop the kids off with Lenore on the way."

He watched a frown touch her face. She probably didn't care for Lenore any more than he did, but Tommy seemed to think a lot of Lenore. That meant she treated the kids well, and she always seemed to like watching them.

"I thought you might like to mail a letter to your folks. Ivy's got a post office."

Deborah smiled then. "Yes, I would like to write to my mother. How soon do you plan to leave?"

He shrugged and picked up Tommy. "Soon as you get a letter written, I reckon. We'll be outside. Just let me know when you're ready."

He headed toward the barn. Might as well hitch up the team. The corn was planted, and he figured Deborah deserved an outing and a break from taking care of the kids. She'd done wonders with the house. Seemed almost like a home again. After Anne died, he'd gone through each day doing only what had to be done. Was Beth only three months old? Seemed like a lot longer since Anne died.

He hadn't said much about the house being clean and having three good meals on the table each day, but he appreciated Deborah's efforts. Beth already cried for her when anyone else tried to take her, just like she was Beth's own mother. Tommy hadn't been so quick to take to her, but he had started letting her do things for him. Wouldn't be long before she won him over, too.

"Hey, you wanna go for a ride?"

Tommy nodded. "Yes."

Dane set his small son up on Old Dobbin's wide back and grinned at his "Gettyup!"

Holding Tommy steady with one hand, Dane led the big horse to the buckboard. He moved Tommy to the back of the wagon while he hitched up the horse, then drove to the house, stopping near the front door. He set the brake and secured the reins then reached for his son.

"Let's go see if Mama's ready."

He'd been afraid to call Deborah "Mama" at first, using "your new mama" instead. But the last few days, he'd started referring to her as "Mama" and Tommy hadn't seemed to mind. Tommy was little, but Dane knew he remembered Anne. His prayer was for Deborah to fill the void left in Anne's absence but not take her memory completely from Tommy. Yet Dane wondered how long it would be before Tommy's memory of his mother would be centered on the one tintype of her that they had.

Deborah had Beth dressed and was finishing her letter when Dane and Tommy went back inside. She stood with a smile. "Looks like you two are ready to go and so are we."

Dane couldn't tear his gaze from her face. She seemed prettier now than she had the first time he'd seen her. The difference, he thought, was in her eyes. They'd shown fear before. Fear and maybe anger. He understood that. From what she'd said, her father had pretty much forced her into marrying him. Maybe he should have put a stop to the whole thing, but he hadn't known what else to do. His kids needed a mother. And from what he'd seen in the last month, he couldn't have made a better choice if he'd had a whole bevy of girls to choose from.

Besides, there wasn't any fear or anger in her eyes this morning. They sparkled with excitement. He grinned. She probably thought Ivy was something worth seeing.

"Yeah, we're ready, but we didn't intend to hurry you."

She picked Beth up. "You didn't. I finished my letter. Can I get a stamp there?"

He nodded. "Should be able to at the post office."

He took Beth and held her in one arm while he helped Deborah climb onto the buckboard seat. As soon as she straightened her skirts around her, she took the baby. Dane swung Tommy up to sit beside her and then he climbed on and took up the reins.

It didn't take long to get to Billy and Lenore's house. Dane took the kids in while Deborah waited outside. Lenore seemed eager to watch the kids, and Tommy ran through the house with no more than a wave and a good-bye. Dane gave Beth a quick kiss, handed her to Lenore, and hurried back out to the buckboard.

"That didn't take long." Deborah seemed to hesitate before she allowed a smile to curve her lips.

Dane snapped the reins and they moved out. "Tommy went running off to get into who-knows-what, so I handed Beth to Lenore and left before she changed her mind."

Deborah's soft laughter touched a cord in Dane's heart. He felt comfortable with her sitting beside him—as if she should be there—and hoped she felt the same way. They didn't talk much on the drive to Ivy, but the silence rested him. He glanced at her as they approached the tiny town.

"There she is. I told you it wasn't much."

Deborah looked from side to side as they drove down the only street. A scattering of homes sandwiched the businesses that lined the street on either side. Dane pulled to a stop in front of Ivy's general store. Deborah turned to him with a smile. "It may not be much, but besides the store you have a blacksmith and a feed store. And no saloon. That's good."

Dane grinned. "Nope. Some have tried, but Aunt Ivy won't stand for it. Since she still holds the deed to this land, she has the say in what goes in here."

"Imagine owning a town."

Dane laughed. "Imagine anyone in my family owning a town. Aunt Ivy's about the only one who has the ambition to do more than farm. Billy sure didn't inherit her drive."

Dane climbed down and walked around to help Deborah. In the store, the proprietor, Tom Jordan, stood behind the high counter talking to a local farmer and the area doctor. Dane spoke to them and handed the list of needed supplies to Tom. "Here's what we need, and we want to check on any mail. My wife's got a letter to mail out to her folks, too."

"Yeah, I heard ya got married again." Tom turned to Deborah. "Glad to meet you, ma'am. If you'll come back here, we'll check on that mail for you first."

Dane started to follow Deborah, but Harley Sinclair stopped him. "Hey, Dane, you had any trouble out your way?"

"Trouble?" He looked from one man to the other.

Doc Lewis nodded. "Yeah, seems the area's been visited by bushwhackers here lately."

"I thought the war was over." Dane glanced at Deborah in the back of the store. She looked up and met his gaze with a hesitant smile. He didn't want her worrying about something like this.

Harley shrugged. "You know well as I do that an outlaw don't clean up his act just because his excuse for raidin' other people's property is gone. Word is that a couple of farms west of here lost some tools and some food. Neither family was home when it happened."

"Might be a good idea to lock up whatever you can if you're going to be gone, especially after dark." Doc Lewis shook his head. "The war brought a lot of changes to our country, didn't it? And not all of them good."

"Yeah, I reckon so. Thanks for letting me know about this." Dane watched Deborah turn and browse through the store. As she headed their way, a strong desire to protect her rose in his heart. He decided a change of topic was in order. "I just finished puttin' in my corn. If the weather holds out, I should have a good crop."

As he had hoped, the other two launched into a discussion of farming and the weather. As Deborah drew close he stepped to her side. "Did you find anything you'd like to have?"

Deborah looked up at him as if she didn't understand. "The shopkeeper has the list."

"I mean something for you. Maybe some cloth for a new dress?" He pointed at the bolts of fabric where she had been looking.

"I don't have to have anything."

Anne had never turned down a gift. Dane wondered at Deborah's hesitation. "You've been doing a great job with the kids and the house. I'd like to give you something special as a sort of wedding present. Why don't you go see if any of that cloth catches your fancy?"

A shy smile relaxed her lips. "If you're sure it's all right."

"I'm sure." He placed a hand on each of her shoulders and turned her in the right direction, then gave a gentle push.

She giggled as she walked away. Dane liked her giggle. As a matter of fact, he liked Deborah. Maybe too much. They'd been married only a month, and he found it harder each day to keep his mind, and his hands, off her. How could he continue to keep his distance with her slowly but surely making a place for herself in his home and in his heart? When Anne died he'd retreated into a protective shell where there was no feeling. No laughter or happiness. In the past month he'd found his way to the edge of that shell where he could peek out once in a while and laugh with Deborah. He turned back to the front counter to check over his purchases while Tom helped Deborah cut a length of cloth from the bolt she had selected.

❊

Deborah stood to the side while Dane paid for their supplies; then she walked ahead of him outside to the buckboard. She hadn't expected to get fabric for a new dress. Jamison had never bought her a gift during their courtship or during their marriage. She'd been married to Dane now almost as long as she and Jamison were married. Funny how the two weeks she'd spent with Jamison had seemed like a year. This past month had flown by. Maybe that was because of the little ones. She already loved them as if they were her own.

She held Dane's hand as he helped her climb to the high seat. Dane was such a gentleman even when they were alone. Jamison had been a gentleman in public. Deborah closed her eyes a moment. Why was she comparing the two men? She already knew that Jamison would come up short.

"Is there anything else you want to see while we're here?" Dane picked up the reins and waited for her answer.

Deborah glanced from one end of the street to the other and laughed. Dane's laughter blended with hers. "In that case, why don't we go have our picnic lunch?"

"Yes, I'd like that." Deborah checked to see if the covered basket she had placed under the seat was still there.

Dane drove just outside of town before pulling over to stop under the sheltering branch of an ancient oak tree growing near the side of the road. The dense foliage above provided ample shade to cool and protect them from the warm sun.

"Do you want to get out and spread a quilt on the ground, or would you rather sit in the back of the wagon?" Dane left the decision to Deborah.

Deborah thought of the insects that would soon cover their food on the ground and said, "Is it all right if we stay in the wagon?"

"Sure is." Dane jumped down. "Let me get Old Dobbin's lunch and I'll be right with you."

While Dane fed his horse, Deborah moved some things out of the way and spread the quilt on the floor of the wagon. She dug the basket from under the seat and set it in the middle of the quilt. Feeling like a young girl on an outing with her best beau, she sat cross-legged on the quilt and watched Dane climb aboard.

He sat across from her while she pulled the cover from the basket and took out cold fried potatoes and bacon, a bowl of leftover brown beans, and an apple pie. When she set the pie to the side, she noticed that his eyes lit up, and she smiled. Dane didn't often comment on her cooking, but he always ate his share. She handed him a plate and fork.

After Dane prayed, Deborah waited for him to fill his plate, and then she dipped out her own food.

"Wonder how Lenore's getting along with the kids," Dane said.

"Probably just fine." Deborah hadn't intended to sound so unconcerned and spiteful. The truth was, she had been missing the little ones ever since Dane came out of Lenore's house without them. But she knew they were all right because of the way Tommy always ran to Lenore when he saw her. Lenore would be a good mother. Deborah wondered why the Reids didn't have children then decided it was none of her business.

"I'm sorry," she apologized for her hateful tone of voice. "I just hope she isn't getting along so well with them that they don't want to come home."

Dane looked at Deborah as if trying to see inside her mind. "You don't think Tommy still has a problem, do you? I know he didn't take to you right off, but I thought he'd got used to you by now."

"He cried for his mother at first, but he hasn't done that for a week or so." She smiled at Dane. "I think he likes me all right. I'm just not his mother."

Dane seemed to concentrate on his food for several bites before he looked at her again. "I know you didn't want to marry me and take on my kids. I guess if I'd known what else to do, I'd have put a stop to it before you got all tangled up in my problems."

"Wait." Deborah lay a hand on his arm. "Don't apologize. You are right that I didn't have much choice in the matter, but you must understand that I chose to marry you. That first week at your folks' house, I could see that you were hurting and you needed help, but I saw something even more important than that."

When he just looked at her, a question in his eyes, she continued. "I saw that you were different from either my father or my late husband. I didn't want to go back home and live under my father's roof. He's a good man, but I've always felt bound by his firm rule. I've never been able to live in the freedom I have found here with your family."

"What about your husband?"

Deborah lowered her gaze to her hand still resting on Dane's arm. She jerked her hand back while warmth flooded her cheeks. How could she have sat there touching him, and why had he let her?

"Deborah, how am I different from your first husband?" Dane repeated the question.

She met his gaze. "Jamison ruled with an iron hand."

"Did he ever hit you?" Suspicion glittered in Dane's blue eyes.

Deborah shrugged. "Only once."

"How long were you together?"

"Two weeks."

Dane made an indistinguishable sound of disgust. "A man who hits a woman, or in any way hurts her, should be horsewhipped."

"Thank you, Dane," Deborah whispered as she fought the tears that threatened at his gentleness. He would be so easy to fall in love with. But she couldn't. She just couldn't fall in love with a man who didn't want her.

"I reckon we'd better be getting back." Dane started picking up and putting the food away.

Deborah couldn't stop the giggle that came partly from his actions and partly from her own raw emotions. "That's exactly what I mean. Jamison and my father would never have cleaned up after a meal."

Dane grinned. "I think we need to forget Jamison."

Deborah sobered as she helped him with the bowls and dishes. "I agree. So why don't you tell me instead about the bushwhackers."

"Bushwhackers?" His hands froze in place.

She nodded. "I heard part of what those men were telling you. Are we in some kind of danger?"

Chapter 10

Dane's sigh spoke of the seriousness of the problem. "I didn't intend for you to hear. There's no need to worry. I'll take care of you and the little ones."

"Dane." Deborah again placed her hand on his arm. "I need to know if I should be careful when I go outside or when you aren't near the house."

"Yeah, I guess you're right." Dane put his hand over hers and held it in place. Then he told her all he knew about the reports of roving outlaws taking what they could get from outlying farms in the area. "Just be careful and I think we'll be all right."

She nodded, glad he had trusted her enough to tell her of the danger. When they stopped at Billy and Lenore's, Deborah went with Dane to get the babies.

Billy met them at the door. "Hey, come on in."

Deborah stepped ahead of Dane into the small cabin. Tommy, sitting on the floor near the rocking chair where Lenore sat holding the baby, jumped up and ran to his father. "Daddy, I miss you."

Dane lifted him and gave him a hug. "I missed you, too."

Deborah looked longingly at the little boy. She loved him already and was thankful that he had warmed up to her as much as he had, but she could only dream of the day he would run to her saying he missed her.

"Are you going to give Mama a kiss, too?" At Dane's voice, Deborah held her breath and smiled at the little boy.

He leaned forward with one arm circling her neck and kissed her on the cheek. When he pulled back, he gave her a smile and said, "I miss you."

She moved close to Dane so she could give Tommy a kiss. In just that brief contact with man and boy, Deborah closed her eyes and absorbed the warmth of their presence. She pulled back, knowing she should not open her heart to any more hurt but seemed unable to stop.

Lenore stood to bring Beth to them. As Deborah took the baby, Lenore said, "She's been an angel, as usual. They both have. They are always so good for me."

Deborah cuddled the baby close, ignoring Lenore's insinuations. The children were good for her, too, now that they'd gotten used to her. She smiled at little Beth, getting a sweet baby smile in return.

"We'd better be going." Dane opened the door. "Billy, you gonna walk us out?"

Billy shrugged. "What's up?"

Without answering his cousin, Dane said, "We sure do appreciate you all watching the little ones for us."

"You know we like having them here." Lenore handed Dane a cloth bundle. "I wrapped the soiled diapers in this. The clean ones are still in the satchel you brought."

"Thanks." When Dane took the bundles, Deborah went out to the buckboard. She waited while Dane set Tommy and the bundles in the back of the wagon. He took Beth, then helped Deborah climb aboard. After she took the baby, Dane stepped to the side to speak with Billy. Although he kept his voice low, she could still hear.

Billy's voice carried to her. "The war's over in case you haven't heard."

"Doesn't matter. Some men don't know when to quit. They're outlaws. They don't have a living so they take where they can get it. All I'm saying is that you keep a good lookout and don't let Lenore go out alone."

"So this is about Lenore, is it?"

"What do you mean by that?" Dane's voice rose and Deborah heard each word.

"You always wanted Lenore. Do you think I didn't know that? Ever'body knows it."

"Billy, I have a wife. I'm not interested in yours."

"Hah! You have a housekeeper and that's all." Billy's laugh held no mirth. "So stay away from Lenore."

Deborah's face burned. She turned her attention to the baby in her lap, ignoring the men as Dane spoke in low, serious tones to Billy. How could Billy say those things about her? And how could he think Dane wanted Lenore? She had seen no indication. But what did she know? A small seed of doubt crept into her heart.

Dane climbed onto the seat, taking the reins in his hands. Billy stood watching them leave, but Dane kept his gaze ahead on the short drive home. Deborah didn't know what to expect from her husband because she had never seen him angry before. More than once Jamison had taken his anger out on her, but she sensed that Dane would not. He stopped near the door of the house and climbed down.

At her side, he reached for the baby. "I'll get you in the house, then I'm going to hide our meat. We had to do that during the war sometimes."

"It won't be safe in the smokehouse?"

"No, that's the first place they'll look."

Deborah started a fire in the stove to cook supper while Tommy ran through the house as if making sure everything was still there. She smiled as she watched him run from one thing to another and at last settle on the floor to play with some wooden animals that Dane said his father had carved. Dane didn't come inside until supper was on the table, and then he was quieter than usual.

After supper they put the children to bed, and as if they had agreed, both went back to the kitchen. Deborah filled the coffeepot while Dane sat at the table. "Would you like a slice of cake and some coffee?"

He lifted his head and smiled at her. "That sounds good if you'll have some with me."

Deborah had long been aware of Dane's attractive features, but at that moment when he smiled at her, a melting took place deep in her heart. She turned away on the pretext of putting the coffee on to heat, afraid that her feelings would show in her expression. When she had her flighty emotions under control, she flashed a smile at him. "I was planning to."

"Good."

Deborah cut two slices of cake and set one in front of Dane and the other across the table from him. She set two cups next to the plates, poured their coffee, then sat down.

"Thanks," Dane said. "This is good."

"I'm glad you like it." Deborah hadn't felt so shy around Dane before. In spite of her determination to keep an emotional distance, she felt a special drawing toward him that she had never felt for any other man. Perhaps their outing today without the children had brought them closer together. She hoped so.

"What was your childhood like?" Dane's voice and question surprised her.

Deborah tried to think how to answer his question honestly without sounding as if she were complaining. "My father has always been very strict. When he was home, my brother and I were not allowed to run through the house and play as Tommy does." She smiled, remembering. "However, our mother often let us break the rules when Father was gone. We could not speak at the table. Father's word was law."

"So you married the first time to get away from the restrictions?"

Deborah shook her head. "No. I married because Father told me to."

Dane's eyes widened. "Are you saying—do you mean. . . ?"

She looked down at her coffee. Dane couldn't seem to form the question. She nodded, lifting her gaze to meet his. "I'm saying that this is the second time my father has told me who to marry." She gave a short, bitter laugh. "I'm beginning to think he wanted to get rid of me."

Dane covered her hand with his. She looked into blue eyes soft with compassion. "I'm sorry. I promise you that I didn't know."

"Don't be." She blinked against tears and didn't know why his gentleness upset her more than Jamison's anger had. "I'm glad now that he decided I should marry you and help raise your children. I miss my mother and Caleb, but for the first time in my life, I feel as if I've found a place I can call home. I love Tommy and Beth very much. I hope that's all right."

Dane smiled and lifted her hand to his lips in a soft kiss. "Of course it's all right." He let her hand go as if regretting what he had done. Sadness filled his eyes as he looked across the table at her. "I'm sorry you had to marry me. I can't give you the marriage you deserve, but I promise I'll do everything in my power to make your life easy."

A tear slid down Deborah's cheek before she could stop it. She swiped at it with her hand and tried to smile. Not knowing how to express herself, she stood and picked up their dirty dishes. She rinsed them off and heard Dane scoot his chair back. When she turned around he was gone.

❧

On the Fourth of July, Deborah rose early, anticipating a fun day ahead. Dane's parents had invited them to spend the day visiting and celebrating the holiday. With the war just past, the celebration seemed especially important to Deborah. She left the baby sleeping and went to the kitchen to cook before the sun came up and made the heat unbearable. By the time she had two pies in the oven, Dane came in the back door and went upstairs with no more than a nod in her direction.

Deborah watched him disappear into the bedroom he shared with Tommy. She could hear the low rumble of his voice and Tommy's higher answers. At least he could speak to his son. She turned back to her work, wondering if she had done something to anger him. He had been so gentle and kind the day they'd gone to Ivy. But since then he had seemed to withdraw from her.

They pulled into Cora and Aaron's drive a couple of hours before noon. Deborah allowed Dane to help her climb from the high seat; then she took Beth into the house in search of Cora.

As she went through the front door, Cora called out, "I'm in the kitchen, Deborah."

Dane followed her into the house with the basket of food she had prepared. Cora turned from the stove and smiled at them. "Bless you. Looks like you've brought enough so I can stop cooking right now."

They laughed with her, and Dane set the basket on the table before going back outside where the men were.

Cora watched him leave, then turned to Deborah with a searching gaze. "Dane has looked happier this last month than I've seen him in a long time. I hope that means you two are getting along all right."

Deborah kept her gaze on the dishes she lifted from the basket. "We get along just fine. You can be proud of your son, Mrs. Stark. He's a true gentleman."

"Gentleman?" Cora's eyebrows lifted. Her voice grew solemn. "Deborah, are you happy here?"

This time Deborah had no problem meeting the older woman's gaze. "Yes,

I'm very happy here. I miss my family, but I wouldn't want to go back to St. Louis."

Cora smiled. "Good. Because we certainly wouldn't want you to. You've been my daughter-in-law for two months now. Do you think you could call me something besides Mrs. Stark?"

Deborah had liked Cora from their first meeting. To please her mother-in-law, she would call her whatever she wanted. "What would you like for me to call you?"

"Dane calls me Mom. What do you call your mother?"

"I've always called her Mother."

"Then I would not be taking her name if you called me Mom. Do you think you could do that?"

As tears burned her eyes, Deborah nodded. Her emotions seemed to be on edge all the time anymore. Besides wanting to cry at the least provocation, she had been feeling so tired by the end of the day. She hadn't realized the extent of upheaval moving away from home and marrying a stranger had caused until just the past week when she realized that her monthly hadn't shown up on schedule. Actually, she couldn't remember the last time what with Jamison's death, the war ending, the assassination of President Lincoln, and leaving home to marry Dane. So much had gone on in her life, no wonder her body was reacting.

She smiled at her mother-in-law. "Mom. I think I can do that."

Cora wrapped her in a warm hug, and Deborah blinked to keep the tears at bay. When they pulled back, Cora said, "Let's go outside and see what the men are doing. We need to relax today, too."

Aaron and his sons were playing a game of horseshoes, so Cora and Deborah sat on the porch in the shade and watched. Tommy ran from one uncle to another, soaking up attention while Beth watched with wide-eyed interest from the protection of her grandmother's lap.

Deborah heard several of the family mention Dane's brother, Wesley, who had still not returned from the South where he had fought as a Confederate soldier. Aaron's telegram asking for information had returned saying he was not listed with the casualties, but no one seemed to know where he had disappeared. Without a doubt the family missed him and longed to have him at home.

Dane seemed to enjoy the time with his family. Deborah watched him as they played and teased each other. He laughed, giving as good as he got from his younger brothers. They ate lunch and played again in the afternoon while the babies slept. As Deborah helped Cora set out the warmed leftovers for supper, she felt as if she'd put in a full day's work.

By the time the men had fired a couple of rounds with their rifles to—as Cora said—make as much noise as they could, Deborah could barely keep her eyes open. She was glad when Dane said it was time to go home.

❋

July and August brought no relief from Dane's busy schedule. Deborah felt the heat more than she ever remembered in St. Louis and wondered if they were really that much farther south. When her time of the month again failed to appear, she became concerned. When frying bacon sent her outside to heave up the contents of her stomach, she wondered.

Her marriage to Jamison had been short, but it had been real. In late August, she stood in the kitchen cleaning up the breakfast dishes. She had managed to keep her sickness each morning from Dane simply because bacon seemed to be the worst offender. Most other odors caused nausea, but not vomiting. And if Dane missed his usual bacon with his eggs, he never mentioned it.

She touched her still-flat stomach and hoped with all her heart that her suspicions were right. If she could not have a real marriage with Dane, she would never have a child of her own. Although she loved Beth and Tommy as if they were hers, she wanted this child very much. But if she was right and there was a child growing inside her womb, she could not tell Dane—at least not yet.

Chapter 11

September brought cooler temperatures as Deborah settled into her life as a farm wife. Dane had never indicated that she should do the milking, and she had no intention of volunteering. From a distance the cows seemed like large, lumbering but gentle animals. Up close, she wasn't so sure how gentle they might be.

The chickens were different. They threw a fit when she stole their eggs, but she didn't mind their hysterics as they flapped their wings and did their funny little running fly across the henhouse while squawking at her. If she took eggs out from under them, they pecked her, but she soon learned to entice them away from the nests with their morning ration of grain first.

Most of her evenings after supper were spent sewing and mending in front of the fireplace. She made a dress to wear to church with the fabric Dane had bought during their trip to Ivy. From the scraps she made a matching dress for Beth and started a rag doll. She worked on the doll after the children had been tucked in bed since it would be a Christmas gift for Beth.

With each passing week, Deborah noticed changes in her body that confirmed her earlier suspicions that she would soon have her own baby. She longed to confide in someone, to ask the multitude of questions that bounced through her mind when she had time to think, but her mother was too far away and she could not go to Cora. She knew she must keep her secret as long as she could because Dane had made it clear that he did not want his wife going through the danger of childbirth. She could only imagine what his reaction would be when he found out she had been with child before they married.

One afternoon in early October, Deborah asked Tommy if he would like to take his nap on a pallet in the sitting room.

"Why?"

She smiled at his usual response to anything new. "It's warmer down here than it is upstairs. Besides, I thought you might like to do something different."

Just that morning, Tommy had tried to follow his father outside. Dane didn't see him, and Deborah had to tell him that he couldn't go. Tommy had been just as determined to go with his daddy. When he opened the door, refusing to listen to her, Deborah threatened him with a spanking. She didn't know if she could have carried out her threat, but Tommy believed her and moved away from the door.

He had behaved without a murmur the rest of the morning, and now Deborah wanted to keep him close. She wanted to watch him sleep and know that he was all right. She spread a folded blanket on the floor a short distance from the fireplace where the warmth of the fire would reach him.

"How's this?" She knelt by the pallet and patted the pillow into place then looked at Tommy.

He stood watching her. As soon as she sat back on her heels, he ran to the makeshift bed and lay down with a little boy giggle. "Me seep here."

"Would you like for me to tell you a story?"

At his nod, she sat on the floor, getting as comfortable as she could. "One day a long time ago, a little boy decided to go hear the new preacher who was coming through his country. His mother didn't want him to go hungry, so she packed him a lunch."

Tommy patted her on the hand. "Are you mine mama?"

Deborah looked down into his large, questioning eyes, and her heart filled with love. She bent forward and kissed the little guy on the temple, brushing his curly dark hair back from his face. She smiled. "Yes, I guess I am your mama. Is that all right with you?"

Tommy nodded with his own sweet smile.

When he didn't say any more, she continued her story of the five loaves and three fishes that Jesus blessed and multiplied. Before she finished, Tommy's long, dark lashes lay on his cheeks. She tucked the cover around him and pulled herself up from the floor.

When Beth went to sleep in the bedroom, Deborah decided she would lie down and rest before she started preparing supper. Taking a quilt and a pillow from her bed, she went back into the sitting room and snuggled down on the sofa.

She thought of Tommy and his determination to follow his father that morning. He was too young to understand the danger of a little boy, not quite three years old, going off alone across the field. Besides the usual dangers, there was always the chance that the bushwhackers Dane had told her about might be nearby. She didn't think an outlaw would bother a little boy, but she'd rather not find out the hard way. Five months ago she had known so little about children. She thought of her own parents and wondered if they had ever been unsure of the right thing to do in raising her and her brother. They always seemed to know just what to say and exactly the right thing to do. At least her father did. She couldn't remember him ever wavering on a decision. Did he make mistakes? Yes. Forcing her to marry Jamison had been a mistake.

Maybe Dane was a mistake, too. Deborah was happier now than she ever remembered being. But she wanted more. She wanted a real marriage with Dane. She wanted his love because, in spite of her resolve to keep her heart out of this marriage, she had fallen in love with her make-believe husband.

She closed her eyes and brought Dane's features to her mind. Surely her father should not have forced her into a loveless marriage. Certainly not with Jamison. But not with Dane, either. Why had he? The answer that had eluded her before became clear as she remembered how firm she'd had to be with Tommy that morning.

Just as she had known what was best for Tommy, so had her father believed he had known what was best for her. He wanted her to marry a Christian, who would care for her and treat her well, so he chose for her.

She thought of her two husbands. Jamison had professed to be a Christian, and her father still believed that he had been. Dane was a true Christian, and maybe in time he would learn to love her. For the first time, she understood that her father's concern for her had prompted his actions. She whispered a prayer for forgiveness of the anger she had carried toward him for so long.

As Deborah relaxed, she felt herself drifting toward sleep when a flutter in her womb brought her eyes wide open. She placed her hand against the small bulge of her stomach and waited. Again the baby moved and she laughed.

※

Several hours later, Dane led Old Dobbin into the barn. He lit the lantern hanging just inside the door and hung it on the nail by the stall so he could see. Then he closed the door against the cold north wind. Barely October and already winter had nudged the warm weather away. He stripped the saddle from his horse and began brushing him down. The barn felt warm after the damp wind had cut across his face and through his coat on the ride in.

While he worked he thought of his warm house and the woman waiting there who had made a home for him and his little ones. She'd probably have Tommy and Beth fed, bathed, and tucked in for the night by now. His own supper would be waiting on the table when he walked through the door. Each night she waited to eat with him when he came in late. He hadn't expected Deborah to seem so much like a wife. In the five months of their marriage, he'd grown used to her, yet he wasn't used to her at all. So many times he caught himself longing to make her truly his wife. When he watched her with the children. When she rocked Beth to sleep and smiled down at the baby with a mother's love shining from her eyes. When she read to Tommy or told him stories then tucked him into bed with a hug and kiss. But most of all, when he remembered their wedding kiss. The thought of her soft lips that were responsive under his haunted him now just as it had since the day of their wedding.

He threw the brush to the side, breaking his train of thought, and reached for the lantern. After checking to be sure everything was secure for the night, he blew out the light and hung it back beside the door, then went to the house.

As he expected, Deborah sat across the table from him as they ate and asked him about his day. She seemed more beautiful tonight than usual. Her eyes shone in the lantern light, and a smile played around the corners of her mouth. He would like nothing better than to take her into his arms and let her know how much he cared for her. He frowned as he realized where his thoughts were leading.

Dane stood, pushing his chair back. "I'll check the doors and head on up to bed, if you don't mind."

He hated the look of confusion on her face. She probably thought he was as bad as her first husband had been.

"That's fine. I imagine you are tired after putting in such a long day." She smiled and started gathering their dirty dishes.

He felt lower than a snake's belly, but he didn't know how to make things right. He couldn't have a real marriage with her. Especially not now. Not now that he cared so much. If she died, he didn't know what he would do. He nodded and without another word turned to go upstairs. At the bottom of the steps he stopped.

"Deborah."

"Yes?" She turned with an expectant light in her eyes, making him feel even worse.

"I thought I'd go to Stockton tomorrow. We still haven't heard from Wesley, and I'd like to send another telegram to see if anything has changed."

She nodded. "I understand. Do you want me to go with you?"

He started to say no but stopped. Just last week he'd heard about a farm that had been raided while the people were gone. He didn't know if the outlaws would bother a woman, but he didn't want to take a chance. He nodded. "You can either go with me or stay with Mom for the day."

A hesitant smile touched her lips as she looked across the room at him, setting Dane's pulse racing. "If you don't mind, may I go with you?"

He nodded, trying to appear as if he didn't care. "Suit yourself. Mom will probably keep the kids so they don't have to make the trip in the cold."

"Yes, I know." Deborah's smile widened. "She asked me Sunday when she could have them for the day. I think she misses them."

"Probably." Dane turned back toward the stairs. "I'll see you in the morning then."

❧

Deborah glanced across at Dane. He sat beside her on the buckboard seat, his eyes straight ahead. He'd been quiet all morning. When they dropped the kids off with their grandmother, he had scarcely spoken to anyone. Deborah had hurried to kiss the little ones and tell them to be good before he ushered her back outside.

A brisk breeze lifted the rim of Deborah's bonnet, and she huddled closer into the blanket she had pulled around her shoulders.

"Are you too cold?" Dane's voice startled her.

"No, I'm fine." She smiled at him. "Even my toes are warm."

"Those bricks will be cold on the return trip."

Deborah looked up at the leaden sky that seemed to be pressing close around them and hoped they would not get wet before the day was over. "Maybe the sun will come out and chase the cold away."

Dane smiled for the first time that morning. "Yeah, maybe so. Stranger things have been known to happen."

Deborah laughed. "You don't believe it will, do you?"

"Nope." The twinkle in his eyes when he slanted a glance at her let her know that his mood had lifted.

"All right, then. I'll have to pretend all by myself." She looked ahead and saw the village in the distance. "We're almost there, aren't we?"

"Just about. I want to go by the telegraph office, and then we can do some window shopping if you'd like."

"Window shopping?" Deborah couldn't believe he had suggested such a thing. She hadn't known there was a man alive who would offer to let her browse through a store. Did he know how much she missed living near a large city with more stores than she could visit?

"Sure, that means you can look, but you can't buy."

When he laughed at the shocked look on her face, she knew he was teasing, and she punched his arm. "Oh, you! Just for that, I may buy the store out."

"Oh yeah? I'll be keeping a close eye on you today, then." Dane's chuckle warmed her heart. He didn't laugh nearly enough. She'd like to see him truly happy and wished she could be the one who brought him out of the grief and sadness that seemed to be so much a part of his life.

They rode into town and parked near the courthouse. Deborah went with Dane and waited while he sent his telegram. As he had promised, he took her to a couple of stores and let her look to her heart's content. He even walked through the stores with her, pointing out things that he thought might interest her. He picked out a comb and brush set and against her protests that it cost too much, paid for it, then presented it to her before they left the store. By the time they headed home, Deborah knew that much more of this treatment would send her headover heels in love with her husband.

On the way home, Deborah sat as close to Dane as she could without touching him. The cold, damp air made her long for the warmth of their little house. Before they were halfway home the first snow of the season began to fall.

Dane held one hand out and caught a snowflake on his glove. He held it in front of Deborah and watched it melt before looking at her with a serious expression on his face. "I reckon that was some of that sunshine you were talking about on the way to town. Only I never saw white sunshine before, did you?"

"Oh, you!" Deborah shoved her shoulder into his side, and he swung his arm around her in what she assumed was a reflex movement. But he kept his arm there and pulled her close.

Their playful mood dissolved as quickly as the snowflake had disappeared from his glove. He looked down into her eyes. She watched his gaze move across her face and lower to her lips. Without conscious thought she lifted her face toward his as her lashes lowered. When his lips touched hers, they were cold, but warmed within seconds as they lingered, taking and giving from emotions that had been building for the past five months.

Deborah felt as if she had just received her first kiss when Dane pulled back and looked at her with a dazed expression. Never before had she experienced such warmth and love. Then Dane's face grew hard and cold, and she realized she had never before felt so lost and alone when a kiss ended. Dane removed his arm to take up the reins again without a word spoken. He sat, staring straight ahead as if she did not exist. How could he shut her out so completely after sharing such a moment with her?

Snowflakes fell in a silent curtain around them. Deborah pulled the blanket close about her shoulders and watched the cold, white flakes melt on her dark woolen skirt. She knew why Dane had pulled away from her, but knowing didn't stop the hurt. Why was he so afraid of childbirth? Women had babies all the time, some many times. There were several large families who attended the little country church with them. Even his own mother had given birth to seven healthy babies. Why did he think that she would die just because his first wife had? More important, what would he do when he found out she would be giving birth in another four months anyway?

She spread her hand over her rounded abdomen and knew she could not continue much longer to hide her condition. Soon the baby would grow so much that even a cloak would not cover her condition. She was surprised that Cora or one of the women at church hadn't already noticed.

Dane's father came out of the house as soon as they pulled up. "Thought we might be gettin' a snow. Looks like it's stopped now."

"Yeah." Dane started to get down, but Aaron stopped him.

"Mom thought you might as soon leave the little ones here for the night. She's been hankering to have 'em over for a spell now."

Dane looked toward the west. "It's an hour before dark."

"Don't matter to her." Aaron looked from Dane to Deborah and back. "Might jist as well take her up on it. Give ya some time to yourselves."

Deborah felt Dane stiffen, but she didn't look toward him. She couldn't. If his father only knew how things were, he wouldn't suggest they spend any time alone. After a few moments of silence, she knew Dane had given in when he picked up the reins.

"All right. Tell her I'll be after them in the morning."

Aaron nodded and headed back toward the house as they drove off.

Neither spoke the rest of the way home. Deborah knew what Dane was thinking. He didn't want to go home with her without the children to act as a chaperone. His kiss that afternoon had told her that he was attracted to her. But he was afraid. Well, he didn't need to worry. She would keep her distance.

The snow had stopped some time ago, and now the sun made a feeble effort to show itself through the gray blanket of clouds low in the west. Dane stopped the buckboard near the house and helped Deborah climb down.

"I'll be in as soon as I put the buckboard away and take care of Old Dobbin."

"All right." She took the package of candy for the kids and her new comb and brush set. Then, without a backward glance, headed toward the house.

As soon as she stepped inside, she knew something was wrong. Stifling the scream that filled her throat, Deborah turned to run back outside and felt a man's hand close around her arm.

"Not so fast, ma'am." The low voice came from behind her. "Where's your man?"

"What are you doing in my house?" Deborah tried to see the man who held her pulled back against him by both of her arms.

"I asked you where's your man."

"Maybe this will help her talk." A second man stepped out of her bedroom. He pointed a long gun at her. She didn't know what kind it was but thought it looked like the ones the soldiers had carried. Were these men the bushwhackers they'd been hearing about?

The blood drained from her head leaving her dizzy as if she might faint, which was something she had never done before in her life. She fought against the fear that crept over her mind and heart. She couldn't panic now. Dane didn't know anyone was in their house. She had to do something to save him.

Chapter 12

Dane drove the buckboard to the barn. He knew his mother thought she had done them a favor, giving the two of them time to be alone. If she only knew. He thought of Deborah. He should never have given in to the temptation of her sweet lips earlier, but he hadn't been able to stop when she looked up at him. They'd been having fun together, just as if they really were sweethearts. And he'd ruined their day by kissing her. And wanting to kiss her again. If only he could, but he knew that once he got started, he wouldn't be able to stop with a few kisses.

His mind churned with thoughts of Deborah and what they could have if there were no danger of her becoming pregnant. He longed to have a true marriage with her. One where he felt free to love her as a husband should love his wife. Not only physically but emotionally as well. If he had known how hard it would be to keep his emotions in check, he would have never gotten married again.

He stopped in front of the barn and got down to open the doors and saw footprints, not quite covered by snow, in the damp ground. The doors were not latched the way he always left them. He looked at the footprints again. Two men had gone into the barn and then walked toward the house. His heart stopped in his chest. Deborah could be in danger.

How stupid could he be? He knew outlaws had been raiding nearby, and he'd let his wife go into the house alone after they'd been gone all day. Berating himself for his lack of forethought and for becoming so caught up with his own churning emotions, he grabbed his rifle and crept toward the house.

As he rounded the corner, he saw the front door standing open. Keeping to the side where he wouldn't be seen, he moved toward the door, his rifle ready. At the edge of the door he peered in. A man stood with his back to him. His heart froze when he saw that the rifle in the man's hand was trained on Deborah while a second man shoved her into the rocking chair. That was the break Dane needed.

Without waiting to think about Deborah's fear or his anger at the rough treatment she had just received, he took quick aim and fired. With the loud boom from his gun ringing in his ears, he watched the man fall to the floor, clutching his leg. A string of curses flew from his mouth, disgusting Dane. He saw the man with the gun move and reacted by falling back against the cabin's rough log siding just as a ball zinged past his head.

Dane rushed through the open door, his rifle held ready. The other man came at him, and Dane stepped to the side at the last second, bringing the butt of his rifle down hard against the back of the man's head. Momentarily stunned, the outlaw shook his head and turned to fight. Dane again used the hard wood of his rifle in a sharp blow to the man's head, knocking him to the floor. The outlaw's rifle slid out of his reach as he slumped, unconscious near the door. Dane turned, ready to give the injured man some of the same treatment and saw that he still sat on the floor holding his leg while he rocked back and forth, moaning.

"Deborah, are you all right?" Dane kicked the outlaw's rifle toward the center of the room while he reloaded his own rifle.

"Yes, I'm fine. Do you need something to tie them up?"

"You wouldn't happen to have some rope on you?" His attempt at levity met with a wide-eyed look from Deborah. He knew she was frightened, and he didn't know how to reassure her.

"No, but I started to braid a rug from some old woolen material. Would it work?" Deborah got up and went to the corner where she kept her sewing projects.

"Probably, but I'd hate to cut up your rug." He kept his rifle on the injured man who sat against the wall, scowling at him.

"That's all right. It really isn't very long yet." She handed him a length of braid. He saw her hands tremble at the same time he heard a sound outside.

"Hey, what's going on here?" Billy stuck his head in the door. He came in followed by Lenore.

"We heard shots clear over at our place." Lenore looked from one man to the other. "This one's coming around. What did you do, catch the outlaws everyone's been worrying about?"

"Yeah, I think so." Dane tossed the braid to Billy. "Here, help me get 'em tied up. We'll turn them in tomorrow in Stockton."

Billy held up the woolen braid. "Fancy rope. Okay to cut this?"

"Yes, go ahead." Deborah sat in the rocking chair with her hands clutched in her lap.

Dane felt sorry for her—and proud of her. She'd walked into a nightmare and hadn't fallen apart. Most women would have been hysterical by now.

After they had the men tied and the flesh wound taken care of on the one Dane had shot, they locked them in the empty smokehouse. Dane asked Billy if he'd like to go with him the next morning to the sheriff in Stockton.

"Wouldn't miss it. I'll be over at daylight."

"I'm glad the babies weren't here," Lenore said.

Dane agreed. "God must have put it in Mom's heart to keep them. They'd have been with Deborah when she went in the house."

He stood outside the smokehouse talking with Billy and Lenore, but he wanted to be in the house with Deborah. He knew she had been frightened, and he needed to see that she was all right.

As soon as his cousins left, he went inside and found Deborah huddled in the rocking chair. Tears ran down her cheeks in silent testimony of her fear.

He knelt in front of her. "Hey, it's all right now. We've got those two tied and locked in so tight they'll never get loose."

A strangled sob escaped her lips, and she leaned forward wrapping her arms around Dane's neck. He held her close, murmuring assuring words while a strong desire to protect and keep her close overwhelmed him, banishing his carefully planned reserve.

He slipped one arm under her knees and, cradling her close, stood to lift her from the chair. She melted against him, her arms wrapping around his neck, her sweetness wrapping around his heart.

She must have surprised the outlaws before they could ransack her bedroom. Both the other rooms had been gone through, as evidenced by the food he'd seen piled on the kitchen table and the clutter of things pulled out. Deborah's house was always neat and clean just as her bedroom was now. He laid her on the bed and took off her shoes. She sat up.

"Do you want me to help you change into your nightgown?"

She shook her head. "I can do it."

When he would have walked out of the room, she reached toward him. "Dane, will you stay for a while?"

Without answering, he moved to the other side of the bed and sat down, keeping his gaze away from her while she changed. He felt the bed dip when she climbed under the covers. He turned to look at her, and she pulled the covers back. "I'm so cold. Can you hold me just until I stop shaking?"

Dane took his shoes off then slipped beneath the covers and stretched his arm under Deborah's head. She scooted close enough for him to feel the trembling in her body. He rubbed tiny circles on her shoulder.

"I don't think you are cold so much as in shock. You'll be fine as soon as you've had a good night's sleep. I'm proud of you, Deborah. You know that?"

She shook her head, and he kissed her forehead. "I am. You stood up to those men just fine. Most women would have screamed or swooned, but you kept your head and even thought of using the braid for a rope."

"I don't know what I'd have done if they'd hurt you. I was so scared. I knew they would kill you if you walked through that door."

"You were scared for me?" Dane had trouble accepting that thought.

She nodded. "Yes, very."

Dane fell silent, marveling at the woman beside him. She was one in a million and he knew it. He did not deserve the sacrifice she had made by marrying him. She deserved so much better than he could ever be. He held her for a long time until the trembling stopped and she fell asleep. He could have eased away from her and gone upstairs to bed, but he couldn't seem to make his muscles obey. Instead he sent a silent prayer heavenward. He thanked God for keeping Deborah safe and for allowing him to hold her now, even if for only one night.

Then he closed his eyes and went to sleep, waking early the next morning to find Deborah snuggled close beside him. Dane lay for a moment absorbing the fact that he had slept next to Deborah for the first time in their five months of marriage. How he wished that things were different so he could make a habit of waking every morning to Deborah's beautiful face. But nothing had changed.

He eased his arm from under her neck, taking care to not wake her. When he was free he picked up his shoes and stood watching her sleep. He hadn't planned to fall in love with Deborah. He'd thought he could marry a woman he didn't know and keep his distance, emotionally and physically. He couldn't imagine life without her.

He thought of Anne and knew he hadn't stopped loving her. But something had changed there, too. In less than a year, the pain of losing Anne had dimmed. Deborah had brought healing to his soul, to the grief he thought would never leave. She had brought life and laughter and even love back into his life. Deborah had found her own place in his heart. He loved her. An overwhelming tide of love swept through him, and he bent across the bed to kiss her on the cheek and on her forehead. He had never before felt so much love for anyone, but with his love came sadness. Deborah could never be fully his.

Dane slipped from the room and closed the door without a sound. He put his shoes on in the kitchen then put the food still on the table back where it belonged. With as little noise as possible, he straightened up the house before going outside to meet Billy.

❦

When Deborah woke she reached for Dane and found he'd gone. As she came fully awake she sat up and looked at the pillow beside hers. A smile touched her lips when she saw the indention where his head had been. She spread her hand out on the bed where Dane had slept. The covers were still warm. A smile touched her lips. Dane had stayed through the night.

She thought of his gentleness when he held her. He said he was proud of her. She wondered if he might love her a little. After last night, she knew she loved him. Then she remembered the men who had grabbed her, and a shiver coursed down her back. She threw the covers off and ran from her room, hugging herself against the cold chill that would not leave. No one was in the sitting room or the kitchen. She opened the door and looked outside but saw no one in the early morning light.

She turned back to find a square of paper on the kitchen table. Her hand trembled as she picked up the note from Dane and read, "I've gone with Billy to take the outlaws to Stockton. I'll go by and get the kids on my way back. Don't worry about breakfast for us. Just take it easy. You've earned a rest, Dane."

She read the note twice before laying it back down. For a reason she didn't understand, she felt disappointed. She was thankful that those awful men were gone. With no one to cook for, she could laze away the morning. But she felt so alone. The house felt empty and cold even with the stove radiating heat from the fire Dane had built before he left. The warmth she craved was that of Tommy's childish prattle and Beth's baby sounds. But mostly she had wanted to see Dane before he left. To reassure herself that he was all right and that he would still treat her with the tender concern that he had the night before. Would he sleep in her bed again? Had last night marked a change in their relationship, or would he force them back to being strangers living in the same house?

Deborah went to her bedroom and dressed. After she gathered the eggs from the few hens still laying, she spent the rest of the morning cleaning the house and preparing the noon meal for Dane and Tommy.

She took the pan of potatoes off the stove just as she heard the wagon turn in toward the house. She almost dropped the pan on the table in her hurry to get to the door. Grabbing a shawl from the back of a chair, Deborah threw it over her shoulders and ran outside.

Dane drew to a stop when he saw her. His wide smile gave her the assurance she needed that he did care for her. "We got them delivered. Sheriff was mighty happy to take 'em off our hands."

"I'm glad. Did you have any trouble with them on the way?"

Dane shook his head. "No. Billy rode behind with his shotgun trained on them the whole way. They were afraid to move."

"Maybe we can rest easy now with no outlaws taking what isn't nailed down." Deborah leaned over the side of the wagon bed to see Beth. Dane had her so bundled against the cold in her little bed that all Deborah saw was a mound of quilts.

"You want to take Beth? Tommy's going to help me give Old Dobbin oats."

Deborah smiled at Tommy who sat close to his father on the wagon seat. "So you're a big boy, are you?"

Tommy's big blue eyes, so like his father's, looked seriously at her as he nodded. "Me help."

Dane handed Beth, quilts and all, to Deborah. She smiled at the tiny face of her little daughter that peeked out. "I'll unwrap this package and then you two need to come in for dinner. It's on the table."

As she turned away, a thought occurred to her. "You haven't already eaten, have you?"

Dane grinned. "Nope. Mom tried to get me to, but I figured you'd have something ready."

Deborah smiled. Didn't that prove he cared? She turned away and went inside. As she discarded the covers that had kept Beth warm, she talked and played with the baby and felt as if she and Tommy had been gone forever instead of only twenty-four hours. Beth had grown so much in the last five months. She'd been crawling for some time and had recently started pulling up to the furniture. Soon she'd be walking. Her baby was growing up.

At that moment Deborah felt movement that reminded her of another baby that would soon make an appearance. She placed her hand on the small mound of her stomach and marveled at the new life within. How much longer could she keep her secret from Dane? How much longer did she want to?

She set Beth on the floor to play while she finished setting out their dinner. She put Beth in the high chair and pulled it up to the table just as Dane and Tommy came in the back door.

"Something smells good in here." Dane stopped at the washbasin to wash his and Tommy's hands.

"Probably the bread. I always like the smell of fresh-baked bread."

"Oh boy, Tommy." Dane picked the little boy up and set him in a chair at the table. "Looks like Mama went all out."

Deborah blushed at his praise. His smile held a tenderness she hadn't noticed before. His voice was low with concern. "Are you all right?"

"Yes, I'm fine now."

Dane reached for Tommy's hand and took Beth's little hand in his. Deborah did the same on the other side of the table as Dane bowed his head and offered a brief prayer of thanks for their food.

Before they finished eating, someone pounded on their door. Dane shoved his chair back as Lenore burst into the room. Her eyes were wide, her face splotched from crying, her hair straggling from the bun in back. Mud spotted her dress. She ran across the room and grabbed Dane's arm, pulling him with her. "Dane, come quick. It's Billy. He fell and I can't get him up."

Without a backward glance, Dane and Lenore ran from the house.

Chapter 13

A cold autumn wind dried the ground and left frost on the brown grass in the early morning of Billy Reid's funeral. By midmorning, the sun came out, promising warmth to the shivering mourners that gathered around the open grave in the little cemetery beside the church.

Deborah stood close to Dane. She felt his hurt, knowing that although he hadn't always agreed with Billy, he had loved him. But the worst was Billy' relationship with God. She knew Dane had tried to get Billy and Lenore to go to church with them, but they had always found an excuse. Neither would they listen when he spoke of salvation. Now she could only assume that Billy had not been ready for death, and she felt the weight of that knowledge.

Lenore stood with her parents. Tears ran down her cheeks as great racking sobs shook her body. She held a handkerchief to her eyes and then tore it in her anguish. Deborah had never felt so sorry for anyone in her life as she did Lenore. Surely she must have loved Billy. How terrible that he hadn't known.

Dane had told Deborah that after delivering the outlaws to the sheriff, Billy had taken off across the country alone. They didn't know where he had gone, but when he didn't come home as expected, Lenore had gone looking and found him not far from the house facedown on the ground. His horse had apparently slipped in the mud when he'd tried to jump the creek at its narrowest point. Billy's neck broke when he landed.

Poor Lenore. To have found her husband that way. Deborah wiped her own tears when Billy's mother hugged Lenore, and they clung to each other crying.

Dane and Deborah left as soon as they could get away. Although the children were bundled against the north wind, they didn't want them exposed to the cold too long. Beth, as usual, took their outing without a fuss, but Tommy had been ready to leave long before the service ended. Deborah looked forward to his nap time.

Dane stopped the wagon at the house and helped Deborah carry the little ones inside. He stoked the fire in the cookstove, adding a couple of sticks of wood, then went back outside to care for his horse.

Deborah busied herself with the children and in putting a meal on the table. She fried potatoes and onions with thin-cut strips of cured ham. Reheated beans and cornbread completed their meal. As she filled glasses of milk, Dane came in and helped Tommy wash his hands.

Deborah watched him as she lifted Beth into the high chair. She didn't know what to do to ease his pain. How could she say everything would be all right? How could she bring comfort to him when his cousin might be lost not only to him but to the Lord as well? She said nothing.

After Dane's prayer, Deborah dished out small portions for Beth and Tommy before taking food for herself. She handed Beth a spoon to keep her hands busy while she fed her. She smiled at the baby's attempt to scoop beans up in her spoon. She looked across the table at Dane and shared a smile that didn't reach his eyes.

"She thinks she's all grown up." Deborah slipped a bite of potato into Beth's mouth.

"We spend the first twenty years of our lives trying to be older than we are and the rest wishing we were younger." Dane's voice broke on the last word.

"Yes, I guess that's true."

Dane pushed his chair back, his plate still half full. "I've got work needing done in the barn. If I don't come inside in time for supper, don't wait for me."

"All right." Deborah agreed, although she knew she would set back a plate for him.

She watched Dane put his coat on and go out the back door. Did he want to get away by himself because he grieved for Billy? Or did he want to get away from her? Deborah knew he hurt for Billy and he would for some time to come. But since the night he held her after they caught the outlaws in the house, he had kept his distance, denying the special bonding that had begun between them.

She had so hoped he would continue to share her bed after that one night, but that had not happened. The next day Billy had died, and Dane retreated into the polite stranger he had been before. Maybe she had dreamed the closeness they'd shared. Maybe Dane didn't care for her as she had hoped. But she hadn't dreamed her own feelings. She loved Dane Stark as she had never loved another man. She would love him until she drew her last breath.

When Beth turned away from the spoon and Deborah noticed Tommy's eyelids drooping, she cleaned Beth's hands and face and put her to bed, glad that she was such a docile child. She washed Tommy's face and hands next and went upstairs with him.

"Would you like for me to tell you a story?" She tucked the covers around him and sat on the edge of his bed.

At his nod, she began the story of Jesus's birth but stopped when she saw that he had fallen asleep. She kissed him on the forehead and went downstairs.

By the time Dane came in for supper, the children were again in bed sleeping for the night. Deborah set his plate on the table and poured a glass of milk.

"I ate with the children, but I'd be glad to sit with you while you eat. If you'd like, that is."

"You don't have to." Dane bowed his head in silent prayer then picked up his fork. "Thanks for saving some back for me."

Deborah sat across the table from him and forced a smile. "You are welcome. I know I don't have to sit with you, but I want to. If you don't want me here, you can tell me to leave."

The corners of his lips twitched. "You know I won't do that."

This time she gave him a real smile. "I was hoping you wouldn't."

When he'd eaten in silence for a few minutes, she asked, "So how was your day in the barn?"

He chuckled and she loved the sound. "That makes me sound like an animal."

She laughed softly. "It does, doesn't it? I didn't mean it that way. I just wondered if you got a lot accomplished."

His expression hardened. "Not much. I spent most of the time asking God why He took Billy when he wasn't ready to go. The rest of the time I asked Him why He doesn't send Wesley home."

"Did you get an answer?"

He shook his head. "No."

"I've often heard my father say that God's ways are above our ways. We cannot begin to understand the mind of God. But He is a just and righteous God. We need never fear for He has our best interests in mind."

Dane stared at Deborah until a faint smile touched his lips. "I would argue with that, but I'd be in the wrong. Billy was almost a year older than me. We played together all our lives. And fought. Seems like we always competed for the same things. Trying to outdo the other."

He seemed to be looking into the past. Deborah waited. When he spoke again, moisture filled his eyes.

"But Billy wouldn't ever come to the Lord. Aunt Ivy prayed for him and taught him the right way all his life. He laughed at everything I said. Maybe he would have come later if he'd lived."

Deborah reached across the table to lay her hand on Dane's. "Maybe he wouldn't have. Sounds to me that he knew what was right. You and his mother and probably everyone else did what you could. Don't you see, Dane? It was his choice in the end. Everyone has to decide for themselves whether they will serve the Lord or not."

"I've been racking my brain all afternoon trying to figure out what I could have done—what I could have said that would have made a difference."

"Nothing." Deborah shook her head. "You couldn't have done anything more than you did. God gave us each the will to decide. We can't save people. Only God can do that and then only if they will let Him."

Dane smiled his first real smile that evening. "Thank you. I do feel better, but would you mind praying with me? I'd like to pray for Lenore and Aunt Ivy. I know they are hurting tonight. This hit them pretty hard."

Deborah came around the table and sat in the chair next to Dane. She took his hands in hers and bowed her head. She led in prayer, asking for comfort and peace to each person who loved Billy. She prayed for Dane that he would receive God's assurance and peace in his heart. Then Dane prayed and cried.

Deborah felt tears running down her own cheeks as she heard her husband sob. He held her hands tight so that she could do nothing but sit and pray for him. Finally he grew quiet and released her hands to fumble in his pocket for a handkerchief.

"Again, thank you. I don't think I could have gotten through tonight without you."

Deborah stood. "I'm glad I could help, but I'm sure you would have come to the same conclusion."

"It's late, isn't it?" Dane shoved his chair back and kissed her on the forehead. "Why don't you go on to bed? I'll lock up and bank the fires."

Deborah's heart soared as she turned to her bedroom. Would he come to her bed tonight? She wanted desperately to have a real marriage with Dane. She loved him as she had never believed possible.

She changed into her nightgown and opened the door to receive warmth from the fire. She climbed into bed, pulling the covers up to her chin in the chilly room. She could hear Dane moving about; then she heard his footsteps on the stairs leading to the rooms above, and she knew he would not be coming to her that night. Tears filled her eyes and she dashed them away. Oh, well. If he got too close, he would discover her secret before she was ready.

She spread her hand over her rounded belly and wondered how much longer she could hide her baby. What good would keeping her secret do, anyway? Soon Dane would know, and what would he do when he found out? Would he send her home to St. Louis before she became too big? Would his gentle, caring manner with her turn to anger? She fell asleep with the determination that she would hide her baby as long as she possibly could.

❈

Sunday evening had been set aside as a special service with singing only. When they pulled into the churchyard, Dane asked Deborah, "You are singing tonight, aren't you?"

She laughed. "I've been asked to."

"Then that means you are." He grinned. "Nobody sings as good as my wife."

Deborah felt a blush cover her face. She had never heard him refer to her as his wife before. "Oh, Dane."

"No, I mean it. When you sing, there's not another sound in the church.

Nobody wants to miss a single note. I wouldn't be surprised if the angels stopped to listen."

"I think we'd better go in before you have me so nervous I can't sing."

Dane laughed as he came around to help her and the kids.

Another wagon pulled to a stop beside theirs. A family that lived across the creek climbed down. The two sons ran toward the churchyard where other children were gathering.

"You boys better not get dirty," their mother called to them, then turned to Deborah. "You will be singing tonight, won't you?"

Deborah heard Dane's soft chuckle as she nodded. "Yes, Brother Donovan asked me to prepare a song."

"Only one?"

"Maybe two, but that depends on how many others will be singing."

"I'll be hoping for two, then."

Dane carried Tommy while Deborah took Beth, and they followed the other couple to the church. As they greeted others, almost all assured Deborah that they were looking forward to her singing. She sang a special song almost every week. The people were used to hearing her, but they never seemed to get tired of listening to her voice.

She realized as she sat midway in the church beside Dane that she didn't mind being asked to sing anymore. Before, in St. Louis, she had resented having to sing in each service. Was that because her father had given her no choice? Or had she simply been rebellious? Most of her life she had resented the high-handed way her father ruled over her. She had not wanted to marry Dane any more than she had wanted to marry Jamison.

Now she thanked God every day for allowing her to marry Dane. Even with a make-believe marriage, she couldn't imagine her life without Dane and the children. She loved all three as if they had always been her real family.

Brother Donovan opened the service with prayer and a congregational song before the special singing began. Deborah sang near the middle of the service and again toward the end. Although the crowded church felt warm, Deborah kept her long, flowing cloak on when she stood in front of everyone. Her full skirt hid her baby well, but she didn't want to take the chance that someone would notice before she had a chance to tell Dane. And how to tell Dane was a problem she hadn't figured the answer to yet.

At the close of the service, Brother Donovan asked Deborah to sing an invitational song while he called the people forward for prayer. She stood to the side in the front as she sang "Just a Closer Walk with Thee." By the time the song ended, many had come forward to pray. As their voices were raised in prayer, she started again at the beginning and when the song ended the second time, slipped to the back of the church where Cora stood holding Beth.

As soon as she got close, Beth lunged for her, calling, "Mama."

Cora smiled. "I'd say she knows who loves her."

Deborah took her daughter and smiled at her mother-in-law. "I do love her just as if she were my very own. And Tommy, too."

Cora slipped her arm around Deborah and hugged her close. She pulled back with a wide smile. "Oh, my. Is there something you and Dane should be telling us?"

Deborah felt as if the temperature in the building had risen twenty degrees. She looked Cora in the eyes and said, "No, because Dane doesn't know."

Confusion showed in Cora's eyes. "How could he not notice? When do you plan to tell him?"

"I don't know." Deborah put her hand on Cora's arm as if to keep her from running to Dane. "Please don't mention it to anyone until I can tell him."

Cora shook her head. "Deborah, what's going on?"

Deborah looked around and knew that they couldn't talk in confidence for long. "The baby isn't Dane's. It's my first husband's. I didn't know when we got married, but I'm afraid to tell him now."

"Oh." Cora also looked around the church at her friends and neighbors who would soon be filing out past them. "Why?"

Deborah kept her voice as low as she could. "He's afraid of childbirth because of Anne. He doesn't want me to have a baby, and I don't know what he will do when he finds out."

"Oh, Deborah, I'm so sorry." As the import of Deborah's confession hit Cora, her eyes widened and she put a comforting hand on the younger woman's arm. "I had no idea. But you must know that you can't keep a baby hidden under a full skirt and an apron for much longer."

"Yes, I do know. I'll tell him soon. I promise."

"When will it be?"

"I think near Christmas."

Cora nodded and whispered as Brother Donovan prayed a dismissal prayer. "You have remained small so far, but babies blossom in the last three months. The sooner you tell him, the better."

Chapter 14

With Thanksgiving barely two weeks away, Deborah decided she needed to inventory her supplies. Dane's parents would be providing the turkey, one they had raised especially for this meal, but she wanted to make some pies and contribute a dish or two.

Tommy played quietly on the floor, so Deborah set Beth in her high chair with some spoons to bang while she sorted through the jars of canned goods she had put up through the summer as well as some Anne had left. She pulled green beans and pumpkin out and set them on the table just as Dane burst through the door.

"Wesley's back!" A wide smile lit his face. "Mom sent Benjamin to tell me."

Deborah knew Dane, as well as the rest of his family, had been worried about Wesley. The war had been over since April, and they'd had no word from him in all that time. To have him return now before the holiday season was a special miracle for the entire family.

Dane crossed the room and caught Deborah's shoulders in his hands. His eyes sparkled with happiness, and he drew her ever closer. Deborah's heart caught in her throat. Not only did he intend to kiss her, but also in his excitement, he planned to hold her close. He would without doubt feel the baby who at that moment decided to wake and stretch.

Just as his hands slid across her shoulders to encircle her, there was a quick tap on the door and it opened a second time. Dane stepped back, turning to see who had come in. Lenore closed the door and turned to face them. Deborah didn't know whether to be glad for the interruption or resent the intrusion.

"Have you heard that Wesley's back?" Dane's smile had not dimmed.

"Wesley's back! That's great news." Lenore seemed as pleased with the news as Dane had been. In fact, she crossed the room to give Dane a hug. "I am so glad to hear that."

Deborah stood to the side and watched Lenore get the hug that should have been hers. *Billy isn't cold in his grave yet, and already she's after my husband.* The thought had no sooner taken form in Deborah's mind than she felt ashamed. Of course Lenore wasn't trying to take Dane from her. Just because Billy thought Dane and Lenore were in love, that didn't make it so. No doubt she missed her husband very much.

"Deborah." Dane brought her attention to him. "I'd like to run over and see Wesley for a few minutes. Then tonight we can all go and spend some time with him and the rest of the family. Mom wants us there for supper. Is that all right with you?"

"Of course. You should go see him." Deborah smiled, pleased he had asked her. "I'll look forward to meeting him tonight."

Dane did something then that surprised her. Right in front of Lenore, he gave her a quick kiss on the lips. She tried to act natural, as if he did such things all the time. Lenore's eyes narrowed as if she suspected Dane was putting on a show for her benefit.

"Me wanna go, too, Daddy." Tommy tugged on Dane's pant leg.

"Grab your coat. It's cold outside." Dane helped his son bundle up with mittens and woolen hat and carried him out.

As the door closed behind them, Lenore took Beth from the high chair then pulled a chair out from the table and sat down with her. She ignored Deborah while she talked and played with the baby. "How's my angel girl?"

Beth's mouth spread in a wide smile as she soaked up the attention. Lenore looked up at Deborah "So what are you doing today?"

Wishing her visitor would go home, Deborah answered, "I thought I would see what I have to cook for Thanksgiving dinner."

"I suppose you'll be eating with the Starks."

"Yes, we will."

"Why do you bother pretending?"

Deborah stared at Lenore. "Pretending what?"

Lenore shrugged. "You and Dane. It's so obvious, everyone knows."

Deborah's hand rested on her stomach. Had she been fooling herself? Cora had noticed, but surely no one else had. Dane still didn't know about the baby.

When she didn't respond, Lenore shook her head. "That kiss. Your marriage. It's all a big deception, isn't it? You can't honestly believe anyone thinks you have a real marriage. You don't even sleep in the same room."

The hot flush of anger swept over Deborah. "What business is it of yours whether our marriage is real or not?"

Lenore shifted Beth to the side. "Because Dane loves me."

Lenore's words were like a cold dash of water, leaving Deborah without breath. She groped for a chair and sank to it before her knees gave way.

"Oh, come now. Don't act so surprised. Dane and I have been in love for years. I got mad at him and married Billy so he married Anne to get even with me."

"Why are you telling me this?" Deborah could barely choke out the words past the pain in her heart.

Lenore leaned forward. "You don't even have to get a divorce. You've never shared his bed, so you can get an annulment and go back to St. Louis where you belong. Maybe you can find a real husband there. Then Dane will be free to marry me. Anne and Billy are both gone. This is the chance we've longed for all these years."

"How dare you!" Deborah jumped up, shoving her chair back. "You can't come into my house making such claims. If my husband wants a divorce, he will have to ask me himself. And I'm—I'm with child."

As soon as the words were out of her mouth, Deborah wished she could call them back. Everything she had said was true, if misleading. She knew better. Her father had told her often enough to make sure her speech was honest in meaning as well as in words. But before she could make amends, Lenore shoved Beth at her and ran to the bedroom.

"Wait!" Deborah called to her. "You have no right to go into my bedroom."

Lenore ignored her and pushed the door open. She looked around, then headed toward the stairs.

Deborah ran to the foot of the stairs. "Lenore, stop. It's none of your business."

She might as well be speaking a foreign language for all the attention she got. Lenore shoved her way into Tommy and Dane's room.

Deborah could feel her blood boil. "This is not your house or your business." Deborah could hear the words echoing off the walls as she raised her voice at Lenore. How could Lenore do this? What did she think she was going to prove?

Within seconds Lenore came back down the stairs, a triumphant smile on her lips.

"So, you share his bed, do you? I suppose that's why his things are in one room and yours are in the other. Looks to me like Dane sleeps with Tommy and you sleep with Beth."

Deborah heard the wagon go by the house to the barn. Dane was home and from the way Lenore's eyes lit up she knew it, too. She smiled at Deborah. "You can get the annulment at the courthouse in Stockton. I'll be glad to go with you. How about Thursday?"

"Get out of my house." Deborah jerked the door open and glared at Lenore. She held Beth close in her arms. "Get out and from now on stay away from Dane and our family."

Lenore pulled her coat on as she stepped through the door. "Think about what I said, Deborah. You're too young to be stuck in a pretend marriage with a man who doesn't want you."

Deborah slammed the door and moved to the window as Lenore ran past toward the barn and Dane. She could follow Lenore to the barn and create another scene in front of Dane, but what good would that do? If Dane didn't want her, he wouldn't listen to anything she had to say.

She sat down and rocked Beth, who had been upset by the confrontation with Lenore, until Dane came in with Tommy, barely stepping inside the door before he went back out. Deborah heard him chopping wood just outside the back door and assumed that meant Lenore had gone home.

As the day wore on, her imagination supplied more information about what had gone on in the barn that morning than she wanted to know. She tried to convince herself that Dane would never be unfaithful even if he didn't love her. Dane was an exceptional man. A Christian man. He treated her with respect and kindness. She had never met a gentler man who cared for his children more than Dane did.

Lenore said she and Dane had been in love for many years, even before either of them had married. If so, Dane could still be in love with Lenore.

Deborah wrestled with her thoughts all day. She withdrew, saying little when Dane came inside for the noon meal. He didn't seem to notice as he talked about Wesley. When the war ended, he said, Wesley had decided to go west to see what lay beyond the plains. Dane said he'd gone all the way to California before turning around and coming back home. Deborah thought Dane's brother inconsiderate for causing his family so much worry while he was gallivanting all over the country and beyond, but she kept her opinion to herself since Dane seemed so happy to have him home.

When the children took their naps, she laid down, too, since she wouldn't have to get supper that night. Just before falling asleep, with tears pooling in her eyes, she prayed for wisdom that she would know what to do about Dane and Lenore. Then she prayed for strength to leave Dane and return to her father's house if that should be God's will.

Later, after Dane helped her to the wagon seat and climbed up beside her, he picked up the reins and they started the drive to his folks' house. Neither spoke for the first few minutes, then Dane said, "Are you feeling well, Deborah?"

She swung around to look at him. "Yes, I'm fine."

His gentle smile made her want to cry. "You're awfully quiet. More so than usual. Anything bothering you?"

"Nothing important." When had she taken up lying? Even without meaning to, it seemed she said things that were not completely true. "I mean it wouldn't be important to anyone but me."

"Then it is important." He touched her cheek with his gloved finger, sending waves of love straight to her heart. "Please tell me what it is."

Deborah hesitated. He would think her jealous and he wouldn't be wrong. She decided it didn't matter. If he didn't want her, he could think whatever he wanted. "I saw Lenore go to the barn before she went home."

"Yes, she did. She wants me to go over sometime this week to do some chores for her. With Billy gone, everything has fallen on her shoulders. Her father has been doing what he can, but he's got his own work."

"That's all she wanted?" Deborah searched Dane's eyes, trying to see beyond his words to the truth.

He looked back at her with an open, honest expression and the hint of a smile that warmed her all the way to her heart. "Yep, that was it. You don't mind if I help her out, do you?"

How could she say that she did mind when that would make her look even worse than she felt? She shook her head. "No, that's fine. I'm sure she does need help."

She might want help with chores, but mostly Lenore wanted Dane. This plea for help was a ploy to get him where she could flirt and win his heart again. Deborah could see in Dane's bright blue eyes that he did not know of Lenore's plan. Still, she knew that a man could be easily persuaded to agree with the woman he loved. Soon he would know and then he would be offering to drive Deborah to Stockton himself. Especially when he found out about the coming baby.

At the Starks', Cora took Tommy from Dane and gave her grandson a kiss on the cheek. She took his coat and set him on the floor. As he ran off, she took Dane's coat. "Go visit with your brother."

Levi stepped to Deborah and took Beth, creating a scramble of uncles vying for her attention. "Hey, how's my baby girl?"

"You don't want him. Come see Uncle Ashton." Beth's baby words, coos, and giggles blended with the young men's voices as they settled in the sitting room to play with her.

"Help me carry the wraps into the bedroom, will you, Deborah?" Cora started through the sitting room and Deborah followed.

Cora threw the load she carried on the bed before turning to close the door. "Are you all right? Are you getting enough rest and plenty to eat?"

Deborah smiled and, tossing her coat to the bed, gave Cora a quick hug. "Thank you for being concerned. The answer to both is yes. I take a nap with the children almost every day." She patted her tummy. "And, from the looks of this, I'm getting plenty to eat."

"Have you told Dane?"

Deborah's smile disappeared. "No."

Cora's gaze rested on the barely discernable mound under Deborah's full, flowing skirt. "I will admit you are hiding it well, but you must know that he will take the news better if you tell him."

"I promise I will."

Cora smiled. "Come and meet Wesley. All seven of my boys are home tonight. We have much to be thankful for." She slipped an arm around Deborah's shoulders. "We have a full house of sons, a daughter, and two—almost three grandchildren. God is so good to us."

When Deborah met Wesley, she felt as if Billy had come back to life. Beyond the physical resemblance, he had the same cocky grin and lazy assurance of a son much loved. When Lenore showed up at the door without escort, Deborah's heart sank. She didn't feel up to facing her adversary, but Lenore paid little attention to either her or Dane.

She threw her arms around Wesley and the two embraced almost as if they were lovers.

"I heard about Billy." Wesley pulled back and looked at Lenore. "If there's anything I can do, jist give a holler."

Still cuddled in his embrace, Lenore looked up at him from under her lashes. "Well, since you mentioned it—I could use a big, strong man to help me finish bringing in wood for the winter. Billy never did get around to getting it all done."

"Sounds like fun, long as you're there, too." Wesley released her and sat back in his chair. Lenore plopped to the floor beside him.

Deborah realized there weren't enough seats for everyone without bringing chairs from the kitchen, but she felt embarrassed by the way Lenore clung to Wesley and the way he soaked up her attention. Maybe he felt sorry for her. Maybe she was glad to see him. And maybe she didn't care as much for Dane as she let on. Dane didn't seem to notice, but he could be hiding his feelings. Deborah didn't know what to think and was glad when Dane said it was time to go home.

"Lenore, would you like to ride home with us since we're going your way?"

Wesley took Lenore's arm. "No way, big brother. I'm taking her home. Right, Lenore?"

Lenore looked from Dane to Wesley with a flirtatious expression. "Right, Wesley." She turned back to Dane, but her gaze shifted to Deborah. "You don't mind, do you, Dane?"

Dane shook his head. "No, of course not."

Deborah looked at Dane to see if he really did care, but he was helping Tommy with his coat. He either didn't care or he was doing a good job of covering his feelings. She felt so confused inside. She didn't know what to believe.

Chapter 15

The following Sunday morning after church Deborah stopped to speak to the preacher's wife, and when she turned around, Dane had gone outside. A rare warm day in late November, everyone soaked up the sun while they could. Children played tag, running among and around the adults. Deborah stood on the porch steps with Beth wrapped in a warm blanket. She shaded her eyes against the bright sun as she looked from one group to another trying to see Dane.

Then she saw him. With Lenore. They stood to the side alone. Their heads were together as in a deep discussion. Deborah's heart sank. She had hoped that Lenore would turn her attentions to Wesley, but that didn't seem to be happening.

Deborah turned her back on her husband and joined Cora who had Tommy's hand securely in hers.

※

Dane had let Tommy pull him outside when Deborah stopped to talk to Sister Donovan. Then Lenore had latched on to his arm, and Tommy ran across the yard to his grandmother. When he saw that Tommy was all right, he turned to see what Lenore wanted.

"I need to talk to you." She pulled him away from the others.

"What's the matter?"

"There's something I think you need to know." Lenore looked around as if afraid someone might overhear. "Has Deborah told you about the baby?"

"Beth?" His heart missed a beat. "What about her?"

"No, not Beth. I'm talking about Deborah's baby."

Dane frowned. "What are you talking about?"

A satisfied smile set on Lenore's face. "I see she hasn't told you. Open your eyes, Dane. Deborah is with child. Probably by her first husband. Don't worry; I know the baby isn't yours."

Dane stared at Lenore. Surely she was wrong. She laughed, and he knew she had just made him confess that he and Deborah had not lived together as husband and wife. They had been married over six months. A real husband would know if his wife were with child in all that time. How had she hidden a baby from him for so long?

He looked across the yard at Deborah. All the women wore fluffed-out skirts that would hide anything, he supposed, even a baby. But six months? Or would she be seven months along now? He intended to have some answers. Without another word, he turned away and met Wesley coming to take possession of Lenore.

"Hey, Dane," Wesley greeted him.

Dane gave him a curt nod, never taking his eyes from Deborah.

"What's the matter with him?" he heard Wesley ask then Lenore's laughing response as Dane walked away.

"Oh, just a domestic problem. Don't worry about Dane. I'd rather talk about Wesley. Why don't you tell me some more about your exciting trip into the wild West?"

Dane touched Deborah's elbow. "Are you ready to go home?"

She smiled up at him and his heart melted. She was so beautiful. So pure and innocent. Lenore had to be wrong. Surely, Deborah wouldn't have deceived him. She knew how he felt about childbirth. But, of course, that was the problem, wasn't it? She knew and—and what? Was afraid to tell him? Thought she could keep it a secret? Hardly. A woman could not keep the birth of her child a secret from her husband. To keep the unborn child a secret for six months was feat enough.

Dane did not speak on the trip home. He stopped near the house and helped Deborah take the children inside, and then he went to the barn. He took care of Old Dobbin and the buckboard. He paced from one end of the barn to the other, picking up a harness and hanging it, moving tools, and doing nothing worthwhile.

With each minute that passed he thought of Deborah. He remembered their wedding day when she walked down the church aisle toward him. That was when he had really seen her for the first time. When he'd realized how lovely she was both inside and out. He should have called off the wedding. But he couldn't. He hadn't wanted to.

He sank to the milking stool and buried his face in his hands. That was when he'd started falling in love with Deborah. And each day for the last six months she had taken a small piece of his heart until now she had it all.

Lifting his face to the rafters and beyond, he cried out, "Lord, help me. I can't lose Deborah, too."

He stood then and went inside to the warm meal Deborah had waiting on the table.

After they ate, Dane took Tommy upstairs for his nap. He read a story to him, tucked him in, and gave him a kiss. Then he went downstairs to confront Deborah.

She stepped out of her bedroom as he reached the lower floor. "Deborah, could we go into the kitchen?"

"Of course." Her eyes were large and questioning, but she followed him.

He held her chair and sat across the table from her. Deciding the direct approach would be best, he looked at her and asked, "Are you with child?"

Her hands moved to caress her stomach, but she held his gaze. "Yes, I am."

"When will the baby be born?"

"Near Christmas."

"Did you honestly think you could hide it from me forever?"

She shook her head, her eyes closing for a moment before she looked back at him. "No, but I was afraid to tell you."

"Why?"

Instead of answering, she asked, "Will you send me away?"

"Of course not." He towered over her. "Is that why you married me? Because of the baby?"

She shrank against the chair. "No. Honest, Dane, I didn't know about the baby until after we were married." Tears glistened in her eyes. "I'm sorry. I really didn't know."

He glared at her, angry and hurt. One tear slid down her cheek and another followed. She didn't move, but sat with her hands protectively hiding her child and watched him while she cried. He wasn't angry with her. In his mind he knew she hadn't done anything wrong. But deep within he felt as if she had tricked him somehow. He had kept himself from her. No matter how much he had wanted a normal relationship with her, he had been strong so that this wouldn't happen. Yet, it had happened in spite of his sacrifice.

He couldn't watch his wife go through childbirth. He couldn't stand by while she screamed until she could scream no more. He couldn't kiss her cold, pale lips for the last time and hear the echo of dirt hitting her casket for the rest of his life. He just couldn't. Not again.

He stumbled toward the back door and jerked it open. He heard her call his name just before he closed the door.

❀

Fresh tears blurred Deborah's eyes. He hated her. He said he wouldn't send her away, but he might as well. He would never love her. Not after she had hurt him so much. She turned and buried her face in her arms on the table, letting the tears flow as she prayed for Dane and for God's direction.

After a long time, Deborah rose and moved to the couch in the sitting room where she lay down, letting the hurt in her heart settle into a dull ache. She closed her eyes and slept, waking to the stirring of the children. Her head ached and her eyes felt swollen. Her body seemed big and heavy and her lower back hurt, but she got up and spent the rest of the day with Tommy and Beth.

She fixed supper, but Dane didn't return to the house so she fed the children and let them play until bedtime. After the house grew quiet, she stood at the window looking out into the dark night. Where had Dane gone? To Lenore? No, she didn't think he would do that. Their marriage wasn't real, but she knew he would be faithful even to a pretend marriage.

She tried to think where he might have gone, but she couldn't imagine him taking their problems to anyone else. She turned the lamp down low and stayed up to wait for him. The room grew cold, so she added wood to the fire, then curled up on the couch under a quilt.

※

When Deborah opened her eyes, sunshine streamed across the couch. She sat up as the previous night's vigil returned to her mind. She threw the covers off and went upstairs. Tommy lay asleep on his bed. Dane's covers were rumpled, but he was gone.

Deborah let her breath out and realized she had been afraid that he hadn't come in at all. She went back downstairs to fix breakfast. Surely he would come in to eat.

Dane did come in. He spoke to Deborah as if nothing had happened. Then after they ate, he ignored her. He rough-housed with Tommy and tickled Beth until both children begged him to stay and play with them. Beth had progressed to walking as long as she could touch something solid. If Dane moved out of her reach, she dropped to the floor and crawled to him.

He picked her up and held her high above his head, bringing baby giggles and squeals. Deborah smiled as she watched them. Dane was a wonderful father. His children loved him without fear. That was something she had never known and desperately wanted for her own unborn child. If only Dane could love her as much as she loved him. If only he could accept her child as his, just as she had accepted his children.

But Dane didn't love her. He pulled some hard candy from his pocket and handed one to each child, kissed them, and told them he had to go to work. Then he turned to Deborah.

"Don't worry about lunch for me. I've got a lot to do today."

In November? Deborah didn't ask what he would be doing. She wondered if he even knew. Obviously he planned to keep his distance.

The weather turned cold, and still Dane found so much outside work that he spent little time in the house with Deborah. On Thanksgiving Day, she wondered if he would find something else to do so that they wouldn't have to pretend at his folks' house. But he became a polite stranger just as he had been when they were first married.

He carried her offerings of two pumpkin pies and a couple of vegetable dishes out to the wagon. He helped bundle the children against the cold and helped her climb into the wagon.

They hadn't been with his family long before Cora took Deborah aside. "What's wrong, Deborah? Did you tell Dane?"

"Lenore told him."

Cora's eyes widened, but she didn't comment on that. "He's just worried then."

"Maybe."

"Of course that's it. What else could it be?"

Yes, what else, indeed? *Unless Lenore is right that he is in love with her. He'd probably like for our marriage to be annulled.* Deborah knew Dane would never ask. She almost wished he would. She didn't know how much longer she could stand being ignored by the man she had grown to love so much.

Deborah woke Friday morning with another headache. Her lower back ached constantly, and she could find no comfortable position for sleep. She had spent most of the night thinking of Dane and Lenore. Billy and Lenore had both said that Dane was in love with Lenore. She had known Dane such a short time. She hadn't expected to fall in love with him, but she had. She loved him so much that she would sacrifice her own life for his if necessary. It would be such a small thing to give him the annulment he wanted.

She knew her decision was as selfish as it was sacrificial. Dane didn't love her and he never would. He thought she had deceived him by marrying him while she carried a child he did not want. She could not continue to live in the same house with a man who despised her. And she would not subject her child to a lifetime of neglect by a father who doted on his own children. She was sure Dane would never abuse her child, but neither would he treat an unwanted child the same as his own children.

Deborah dressed and fixed breakfast. When Dane came in to eat, she asked him to hitch the wagon for her. "I'd like to go to your mother's."

"We were there just yesterday."

"I know. I didn't get a chance to really talk with her, though."

"Deborah, you can't drive a wagon in your condition."

"I'm fine."

"No, I'll take you later this afternoon and you can visit all you want. You can wait."

Deborah watched Dane go to the barn. He came out a few minutes later, leading his saddle horse. That meant Old Dobbin was still in the barn. Deborah went into her bedroom and packed a bag. She'd like to take everything but knew she could never lift a trunk into the wagon. She straightened the house, working as quickly as she could.

The last few weeks she had been feeling the burden of her body, as the baby seemed to be growing all at once to make up for staying so small the first few months. She had awakened that morning with a strange feeling and knew if she didn't go to Stockton today, she might not have time before the baby was born. When she was sure Dane was gone, she wrapped the children against the cold and carried Beth while Tommy walked.

With the children sitting in the back of the wagon, Deborah got the harness for Old Dobbin. She had been so confident that she could hitch the horse to the wagon without a problem. But that was not to be. Dane made the job look easy, when in reality, the harness weighed almost more than Deborah could lift.

By the time Old Dobbin stood in place, she felt as if she had done three days' worth of laundry all rolled into one. Sweat poured from her face and body. Her breath came in quick puffs of vapor that drifted away in the cold air. A pain moved through her body so that she gasped and bent double. When it went away she straightened. She climbed onto the wagon, feeling awkward and heavy. Her head pounded until she wished she could go back inside and rest. Instead she settled Tommy and Beth in the little bed with covers tucked around them.

She picked up the reins and shook them as she'd seen Dane do. Old Dobbin stepped out and they were on their way. Halfway to the Starks', another pain ripped through Deborah's body, bending her forward with her hands pressed against her rounded stomach. She took short, quick breaths until the pain eased.

What had she done? Dane said she couldn't drive the wagon in her condition. He had been afraid she would hurt herself. Fear for her baby's life crept through her heart. She should have listened to Dane. By hitching the horse to the wagon she had killed her baby.

"Haw!" she called to Old Dobbin to hurry. He picked up his pace and she felt the warmth of her water break. Tears ran down her cheeks as she realized the foolishness of her actions. Dane would be so angry with her. If her baby died she wanted to die, too. She sagged with relief when she saw the Starks' cabin appear.

Old Dobbin stopped in front of the house, and Cora came outside as if she had been expecting them. She rushed to the wagon. "Deborah, what's wrong?"

"My baby." Deborah burst into tears. She heard Cora issuing orders as another pain ripped through her body, and then strong arms lifted her from the wagon seat and carried her into the warmth of Cora's house.

Chapter 16

Dane rode across the pasture, his mind on Deborah while he searched for the missing cow and calf. He'd been so worried about his problems at home that he hadn't realized he had a cow ready to give birth. If he'd had his mind on his job, he'd have brought her in to the barn so he could keep an eye on things and make sure they were all right. But he'd let it go and now she was off hiding someplace in a vain attempt to protect her young. Oh well, cows generally went through the birthing without a problem. On the other hand, humans didn't always fair so well.

He rode on looking behind every tree and in every clump of brush he passed, determined to spend the day away from the house and the fear he felt every time he looked at Deborah. The fear that he would lose her. He loved her more than he'd ever dreamed possible. He couldn't imagine living without her.

He thought of the child she carried—of the fact that her child was not his. Could he raise another man's child? The jealousy he had denied from the time he knew of the baby's existence surrounded him like an ugly fog. If his wife must go through childbirth, he wanted the baby to be his. And he wanted them both to live. He lifted his eyes to the gray-covered sky and prayed for Deborah and her baby.

The soft cry of a baby calf caught his attention, and he swerved toward the sound. He found mother and baby without a hitch and soon had the calf across the saddle in front of him with his mama trailing behind. They made it to the barn before Dane saw his father walking toward him.

His lifted his hand in greeting. "Hey, what's up?"

"Deborah's at our house."

Dane swung from the saddle then carried the newborn calf into the barn where he established mother and baby in a stall. He called over his shoulder, "How'd you all know she wanted to go to your place? I told her I'd take her this afternoon."

Aaron hurried after his son. "Dane, you'd best listen. She hitched the wagon and come on her own."

Dane swung around and stared at his father. "She what? Is she all right?"

Aaron shook his head, his expression guarded. "Your mom says the baby was comin' anyhow, but I don't reckon hitchin' a wagon helped none."

"Dad, please." Dane grabbed his father's arms. "Is Deborah alive?"

Aaron nodded. "She was. Now are you comin'?"

"Of course." Dane left his father to close the barn as he ran to his waiting mount and set out in a run to Deborah, his heart racing faster than the horse.

He left his horse with Levi and ran inside. The door to the bedroom just off the sitting room was closed. Benjamin sat at the kitchen table. No one else was around. Dane headed toward his younger brother.

"What's going on? Is she—" He couldn't get the rest of his sentence out past the tightening in his throat.

"Naw, she's all right. Mom says the baby's just comin' early. Mrs. Newkirk's in there with them. I'm supposed to wait out here in case they need something." He looked up at Dane with a hopeful expression. "Since you're here now, can I go?"

Dane scarcely registered what his brother had said except that Deborah was all right. He nodded. "Sure, go on."

As soon as the door closed on Benjamin, Dane started praying. He prayed while he paced across the floor from the kitchen to the door that shielded him from Deborah and back to the kitchen. Over and over he made the trip alone until his father came inside.

"Anything happen yet?" Aaron pulled a chair out from the kitchen table and sat down.

Dane sat next to him and shook his head. "I don't know what's going on. I'm afraid I'll lose her, Dad, and I don't know if I could go through that again."

"They say birthin' babies is natural. But every time your mom went through it I vowed that'd be the last one. 'Specially with the twins. I couldn't handle the worry and the fear no more."

"But you did. Six times."

Aaron nodded. "She wanted you, ever' one. Anne always was frail. Deborah's like your mom. She'll do fine."

"She's early, though. Anne went until her time and still didn't make it. I don't know what I'd do if. . ." He looked away, closing his eyes against the thought.

"You love this girl?"

Dane turned and met his father's concerned gaze. "It's different than it was with Anne. I thought I loved Anne, but I don't know anymore. Deborah is so vital, so much a part of my life in so short a time. When I get near her I want to touch her, to make sure she's really there and that's she's mine. I never felt that way with Anne."

"What about the baby?"

Dane knew what his father was asking, but he didn't have the answer. "I don't know. I haven't had time to get used to the idea. I don't know if I can be a father to someone else's child."

Aaron stayed with Dane until Cora came out and prepared lunch. The rest of the family ate, but Dane mostly pushed his food around. He realized Tommy and Beth were there, and then Cora took them upstairs for their naps. The house grew quiet, and his mother went back into the bedroom. After what seemed like hours, he heard Deborah cry out and he heard the tiny cry of a baby; then he didn't hear anything more. He sank to the kitchen table and prayed.

"Dane, you can go in and see Deborah." He hadn't heard his mother come out of the bedroom.

"Is Deborah. . . ?"

"She's fine. Go on and let her know you're here."

Dane stood on shaky legs and crossed the sitting room to the open door. He stepped inside the room and stood staring down at Deborah. She lay in the bed with her eyes closed. She didn't look fine to him. As he watched, Mrs. Newkirk took the blanket bundle from Deborah's arms and she didn't move.

"Would you like to see the baby?" The midwife stepped to him. "She's early so we've got to keep her warm, but she's strong. I'll put her in a box on the oven door."

"The oven?" Dane looked at the tiny face framed by the blanket. The baby's eyes were closed, too. Would either of them live?

"Yes, the oven will keep her warm until she adjusts to the air in the house. I'll stay at least until tomorrow so we can make sure she's all right." She pulled the blanket back over the baby's face. "You have a fine daughter here, Dane. Why don't you sit with Deborah awhile? She's tired, but she'll wake up if you talk to her."

Dane looked back at Deborah as Mrs. Newkirk went out the door. She hadn't moved. He couldn't see her breathe. They would both die—Deborah and her baby. He turned away as panic rose in his chest, choking him. He couldn't stay and watch her die.

As he ran out the front door, Cora came from the kitchen. "Dane, what's the matter?"

She called to him, but he didn't stop. He heard her behind him. "Dane, wait. Deborah's all right."

He stopped. "She's going to die, Mom. Just like Anne did. I tried to keep this from happening. Why? Why did God do this to me? Why did He give me a woman to love then jerk her away from me in the very same way He took Anne? I know it was my fault Anne died, but not Deborah. I stayed away from her, Mom. That baby isn't mine." A sob shook his frame. "I was afraid I'd lose her, so I kept away and it didn't matter."

Tears ran down his cheeks and sobs shook his shoulders as he turned from Cora and hugged his arms in front of his chest. Grief, even more intense than what he had felt for Anne, held him in its powerful grip.

Cora's arms went around her son, and she held him close. He clung to her and cried until he could cry no more. He pulled away first. "I'm going home, but I'll come back for the kids."

"Dane, look at me." Cora touched his cheek, forcing him to meet her gaze. "Deborah is not dying. She's tired, that's all. Let her sleep and build back her strength. When she's well, take her home and love her. Don't be afraid to make her your wife in every way. I can't promise you that Deborah will live to be old any more than you can promise Deborah that you will. We didn't expect Billy to die, did we? Death is part of life. But you can't let your fears take the joy out of living. Please promise me you will love Deborah and you will treat her baby just as if she were your very own."

Dane looked away. "I don't know if—"

"Dane, there's one thing more." Cora waited until he looked at her. "I know you blame yourself for Anne's death. You don't have to answer me, but think about this. What did Anne have to say about Beth? She knew the risk after she had such a hard time with Tommy. Did you force her to have another baby, or did she want to?"

Dane looked at the ground so he didn't have to see the compassion in his mother's eyes. "I'll think about what you've said. Please take good care of Deborah. I love her, Mom. Even more than I loved Anne. I know that now. Anne will always be a part of my past, and I did love her. But if Deborah dies, I don't think I can go on."

Cora smiled. "I understand more than you know. I feel the same way about your father. But the older we get, the more I realize it's going to happen someday whether I want it to or not. One of us will go first. So I've decided to live each day as the gift that it is from God. Enjoy Deborah's love while you have her with you. Don't ask for trouble, Dane."

Dane didn't make any promises as he turned toward the barn. He'd find his horse and go home where he could spend some time in prayer. He felt as if he'd been hit with a boulder and he wasn't sure where he might fall.

That evening when Dane returned for his wagon and his children, Cora pushed him into the bedroom. "Deborah's awake and she wants to see you."

He hadn't been sure what to expect, so when he saw Deborah propped up in bed with color in her cheeks and a shy smile for him, he felt a heavy burden roll from his shoulders. He stood by the door. "How're you doin'?"

"I'm fine." Her smile disappeared as she clutched the quilts in front of her. "I wanted to tell you that I'm sorry I took the wagon."

"Yeah, it wasn't too good an idea. You could have killed yourself." He realized he was still a little sore at her for taking such a risk.

"Your mother and Mrs. Newkirk both said the baby was coming, anyway. I just hurried things along."

He shrugged. "Yeah, well I came by to get the kids. I'll take 'em home and put 'em to bed."

He wanted to leave. He felt as if he wouldn't be able to breathe if he stood there looking at her another minute. He turned toward the door. "I'll get out of here and let you rest."

Dane was at home and had the little ones in bed sound asleep before he realized he hadn't seen Deborah's baby that night. For the next week Dane fell into his former pattern of dropping the children off each morning with his mother and picking them up at night. He ate breakfast and supper with his folks so he didn't have to cook except at noon. He stopped in for a minute or two each evening to see how Deborah was and saw the baby a couple of times, but he kept his distance for the most part.

During the day he worked hard. Every night after Tommy and Beth went to sleep, he knelt in front of the couch in the sitting room with his Bible and tried to make sense of his life.

Midway through the first week that Deborah was gone, Lenore stopped by at noon to see Dane. "I heard that Deborah had her baby."

He nodded.

"How's she doing?"

"You could go see her."

Lenore shrugged. "Maybe I will. So how are you getting along with her gone?"

"I'm fine, Lenore." He didn't have time to visit with anyone and especially not Lenore. When they were kids she'd followed him around getting on his nerves. She hadn't changed much as an adult.

"Is she going through with the annulment?" Lenore took off her scarf and twirled it through her fingers.

Dane turned from the stove to stare at her, the taste of fear in his mouth. "Annulment? What are you talking about?"

Chapter 17

Lenore smiled. "I see she didn't have time to tell you. I imagine she was heading to Stockton the day she had the baby. You'll have to ask her if you want to know for sure. All I know is that she was talking about getting your marriage annulled so she could go back to St. Louis and find someone she could have a real marriage with."

Dane staggered under the pain of Lenore's revelation. Had Deborah confided in her? Told her things that she couldn't tell him? He hadn't considered that Deborah might want to leave—hadn't thought beyond his own desire to keep her with him always.

"I had thought about offering to step in and take her place." Lenore walked close and placed a hand on Dane's arm. She smiled up at him. "I don't like living alone."

When he cringed from her touch and stepped back, she laughed and turned toward the door. With her hand on the knob, she looked back at him. "Don't worry, Dane. That was before Wesley showed up. Your little brother can be a lot of fun, you know." With that she swept out, letting the door close on her laughter.

Dane closed his eyes against the hurt Lenore's words had inflicted. He loved Deborah. Why would she want to leave him? Yet, why would she want to stay? He offered her nothing more than a home to clean, children to care for, meals to prepare, and laundry to keep up. What woman would enter a loveless marriage willingly? What woman would stay with a man who withheld his love from her? Obviously Deborah didn't plan to stay.

Not wanting to confront the continual turmoil that churned through his mind, he shoved the leftover stew to the pie safe and grabbed his coat. He had work to do.

❈

For two weeks Deborah stayed with her in-laws while her body healed and her baby filled out, losing the shrunken, wrinkled skin and look of an early baby. She thanked God that little Clara Elizabeth had survived. Dane had scarcely looked at the baby and he spoke to Deborah only when he had to, so she hadn't asked his opinion on Clara's name. She decided she didn't care whether he liked it or not. Just as she had feared, he seemed determined to ignore both her and the baby.

"Mama, is her mine baby?" Tommy pressed against her side while she sat in the rocking chair. He held a finger out to Clara's tiny hand and laughed when she jerked in response.

Deborah held the baby in one arm while she hugged Tommy. She didn't know how to answer his question. Was the baby going to be his sister, or would his father send her away? She decided no answer would be best.

"She's precious, isn't she?"

"Yes." Tommy nodded. "I like babies."

"Let's take her home, then." Dane's voice startled Deborah. She hadn't heard anyone come in.

"Dada." Beth stepped away from the chair she had pulled up to and stopped. She looked up at Dane with her special baby smile.

Deborah held her breath and watched as Dane squatted with his hands outstretched toward his daughter encouraging her. "Come on, Beth. You can do it."

Beth took another step and teetered. She took another, more sure this time. Two more steps and she landed safely in her father's arms. He laughed and picked her up high above his head. She chortled and drooled, barely missing his face.

Deborah laughed. "I think she's cutting teeth."

"I'd say you are right." Dane brought Beth back for a hug. "Were those her first steps?"

"Yes, that was her first without holding on."

"Good girl." Dane hugged her again. "What say we take Mama and go home? Where's Grandma?"

Deborah bit back disappointment that he still ignored Clara. When they got home, she would ask him for the annulment. She knew he wanted a house-keeper and a mother for his children, but surely he wouldn't want her now that he could have Lenore. The children loved Lenore and wouldn't miss Deborah, no matter how much she would miss them.

She forced her thoughts to the present. "She's in the kitchen, I think."

Dane took Beth into the next room. Tommy followed so Deborah took Clara into the bedroom she had been using and packed her few belongings. She had missed her home and even if she couldn't stay long, she was eager to see how Dane had kept the house. When Dane and Cora came back to the sitting room, Deborah was ready to go.

"There's no need for Tommy and Beth to go home tonight, is there?" Cora held her hands out, and Beth fell into her embrace. "Dane, I think Deborah needs your attention her first night back at home. We can keep this big boy and girl one night, can't we?"

Tommy grinned up at his grandma. "Me big boy."

"Yes, you are. Would you like to stay with Grandma and Grandpa tonight?"

He nodded and Deborah held her breath. She loved Tommy and Beth, but she'd very much like to talk to Dane without worrying about them interrupting.

When Dane looked at her and nodded, she released her breath. He turned to his mother. "If you're sure it isn't too much trouble."

"No trouble at all. Get your things and get out of here. Deborah needs her rest."

Deborah laughed. "I'm fine, really. All I've been doing for the past two weeks is rest. Now it's time I made myself useful."

Before Deborah knew what he had in mind, Dane bent, hooked an arm behind her knees, and picked her up. She clutched Clara close and looked at him with wide eyes.

"What do you think you are doing?"

He grinned at her. "What's it look like? I'm carrying you and your baby out to the wagon. I'll come back and get your things."

"Bye-bye, Mama." Tommy watched them with a solemn expression.

"Bye, sweetheart," Deborah answered. "I'll see you in the morning, all right?"

He nodded and Beth puckered, squirming in her grandmother's arms. "Mama."

"I think now would be a good time for you to get Deborah out of here." Cora turned toward the kitchen, trying to distract Beth.

Deborah heard the little girl's wails as Dane carried her outside. "Maybe we should just take Beth."

"She'll be fine."

Deborah sensed a change in Dane as soon as they were alone. Gone were the grins and light tone to his voice. He set her on the wagon seat and stepped back. "I'll just be a minute."

Dane couldn't have picked a better day for her homecoming. Although the air felt cold against her face, the sun shone down on her head, giving her a feeling of warmth. She had wrapped Clara so that no breeze could touch her; still she held her close, shielding her with her coat.

"Was that everything? Just what you had sitting by the door?" Dane lifted her bag into the back and climbed on.

"Yes, that was it."

They didn't speak again until they got home. Dane stopped by the front door and carried Deborah into the house.

"Dane, I can walk."

"Maybe so, but you don't have to." He took her to the couch and set her in a reclining position against a pillow.

"I'm not an invalid." Deborah didn't know whether to laugh or be angry.

"Sit still. I'm going to get you a hot cup of cocoa." He went into the kitchen and since she sat with her back to him, she kept quiet.

Why was he waiting on her, treating her as if she were a delicate piece of china that might break? She slipped her arms free of her coat and took the outer blanket from her baby. Clara stretched and her eyebrows lifted, but she did not awaken. Deborah looked down at her, amazed at the perfection of each miniature feature. She gently pressed her finger into the tiny open hand and smiled as Clara's fingers tightened around hers. She brought Clara's hand to her lips, then kissed her daughter's forehead. As always when she looked at the miracle in her arms, maternal love overwhelmed her. God had been so good to her.

"What did you name her?" Dane knelt beside Deborah with a steaming cup of cocoa in his hand.

"Clara Elizabeth."

"What about her last name?"

Deborah didn't know how to answer. So much depended on Dane. If she offered him an annulment, would he grab the chance to be rid of her and Clara? She had wanted to talk to him, but now that the opportunity presented itself, she didn't know how to begin. As she tried to form the correct words, she saw a piece of fabric that she didn't recognize draped across the back of the sofa.

"What is that?" She pointed and Dane reached for the fabric.

As he pulled it toward him a strange look crossed his face. The pain of betrayal and jealousy ripped through Deborah's heart. Lenore had been there while she was gone. How could Dane do such a thing to her?

"It belongs to Lenore, doesn't it?"

"Yes." He tossed the scarf to the end of the sofa. "She came by to ask about you. To see how you were doing."

"Why didn't she come to see me? I'd have been glad to tell her myself." Deborah fought against tears that threatened to show Dane how much he had hurt her.

"She said she might. I thought maybe she did."

Deborah looked down at the baby who still slept, unaware of the tension surrounding them. She hated the thought of leaving Dane and the children, but she didn't know what else to do. She loved him so much. She would not—she could not stay here while he loved another woman. It wasn't as if their marriage was real. Dane obviously didn't care.

She looked up and met Dane's gaze. "Lenore didn't come to see me. Several women from the church came at different times. The pastor and his wife came. Everyone thinks Clara is a beautiful little girl."

"Deborah, you didn't tell me about her last name."

"I don't know. That depends. I thought maybe you would want to go with me to Stockton and have our marriage annulled. I don't guess there's much reason to give her your name if we aren't married."

Dane pulled back. "No, I guess not."

He stood, his expression guarded as he looked down at the baby. When he finally spoke there was a sneer in his voice. "Well, Clara Elizabeth Asberry, it's been nice meeting you. I hope you have a life filled with love and get a new father who will spoil you just as much as you deserve."

Deborah sat watching him, not understanding. She had thought he would be relieved to have her step out of the way. Instead he acted as if she had hurt his feelings.

"Does that mean you want the annulment?" She hoped with all her heart he would say no.

He shrugged. "Why not? That's where you were heading when she was born, isn't it?"

Deborah nodded and watched with a broken heart as Dane turned and walked through the kitchen and out the back door.

Chapter 18

Dane couldn't stay in the house another minute. He felt as if he might explode if he heard the word annulment one more time. He headed for refuge in the barn. The setting sun sent a rosy glow over the sky, and Dane wondered how God's creation could continue in so much beauty while his life had turned to ashes. He stepped into the warmth of the barn and closed the door. He lit the lantern and hung it on the wall out of the way. He paced from one end of the barn to the other, ignoring the curious stares of the animals.

Lenore had been right. Deborah did want out. She wanted freedom to return to St. Louis where she could find love with a man who wasn't afraid to take her as his wife. And why wouldn't she want that? He couldn't blame her. No normal woman would take on the job he had offered Deborah.

Why had he thought she would be content to serve as housekeeper and substitute mother when all he offered in return was room and board? Not that he believed for a minute that she loved him and wanted his love. No, the missing piece to the puzzle of their lives was the one thing he had taken out of their marriage. The one thing he knew that Deborah wanted: family. She wanted a home of her own. A place where she could love and be loved and know that she belonged. By making their marriage a business arrangement he had denied Deborah the family she craved. And now he had lost her.

The thought of his life without her sent him to his knees in the straw-littered floor. "Lord, please help me. I can't lose Deborah, too."

He prayed while sobs shook his strong shoulders. He asked God to show him what to do—to help him keep Deborah. He thought of Anne and of her death. He couldn't go through that again. Maybe it would be better to let Deborah go than to keep her and eventually kill her in childbirth.

His mother's words came back to his mind. *"What did Anne say about having Beth? Did you force her to have another baby, or did she want to?"*

He remembered the day Anne came to him, telling him that she was going to have another baby. He'd told her then that he didn't want her to go through childbirth again. He was afraid for her life because she'd had such a hard time with Tommy.

Anne had just smiled at him. "I want this baby, Dane. I know you are afraid, but this is a precious life, given by God. I'm not afraid of death. Please don't worry about me. If God calls me home, I will have at least given life to our precious child. God holds my life in His hands. He alone appoints the time when He will take me home. Always remember I wanted another baby. Whatever happens will be all right."

Anne's faith had been strong even though her body was weak. She never could have hitched Old Dobbin to the wagon and driven it the way Deborah had. For the first time Dane compared the two women he had loved and found that they were very different. Anne's strength had been in her spirit. Her will. She had been sickly as a child and had been raised by doting parents to expect everyone to give in to her.

Deborah, on the other hand, had been raised by a domineering father who expected her immediate obedience. No matter how difficult the task, Deborah knew she must bow her own wishes to another. Yet she was strong in body and in spirit. Hadn't she proved that in the hard work she performed every day? She had stood up to the outlaws in her house without a single scream, staying strong until the danger passed. And she had given birth after hitching a wagon and had brought forth a beautiful little girl.

Dane didn't know what to think about Deborah's request for an annulment. Did she really want it, or did she think he wanted it? He bowed again, praying for forgiveness. He prayed that God would help him forgive himself for his part in Anne's death. He asked for a chance to show Deborah how much he loved her. He asked for forgiveness for not trusting God to take care of Deborah. He prayed while tears of regret and repentance wet his cheeks.

❧

Deborah stared at the back door after Dane left while her heart broke. Lenore was right. Dane wanted his freedom so he could marry the woman he loved.

She carried Clara in to Beth's bed and laid her on her back. While she covered her, tucking her in securely, her mind stayed on Dane. She thought of his reaction to her suggestion that they get an annulment. Letting the scene go through her mind again, she remembered the lack of expression on his face when she first mentioned going to Stockton. Why hadn't he seemed happy about her offer of freedom? Why had he taken so long to answer?

Deborah bowed her head. "Lord, help me. Show me the truth. I love him, Lord. I don't want to lose Dane. If there's any hope, if there's any chance that he wants me for his wife, I want to stay."

She returned to the sitting room and kitchen. The house had grown dark. It felt cold and empty with Dane not there just as her heart felt cold and empty without his love.

Deep inside she knew Dane was not happy about the annulment. He didn't want it any more than she did. She stood with her arms crossed staring out the back window toward the barn. He was out there, she knew. He hid in the barn when he didn't want to face her. Well, he couldn't hide from her tonight. With determination she hadn't known she possessed, she grabbed her coat and looked in on Clara.

"Be good, little girl, while I go get your daddy. It's about time he and I have a long talk. I've decided if I have to fight Lenore for Dane's love, I will. If we're going to be a family, we need to start doing things the right way."

With more bravado than she felt, Deborah hurried out to the barn. She slipped inside, letting the door close behind her without a sound. Dane knelt on the floor to the side and didn't seem to know she was there as he prayed and cried. She couldn't understand what he said, but she knew he hurt and she hurt for him.

She knelt beside him and, placing her hand in the center of his back, leaned against him. He turned toward her and enclosed her in his strong arms. Without saying anything, he clung to her and held her close while sobs shook his body. They stayed on their knees, holding each other and crying until he all at once jerked away.

"Deborah, what are you doing out here? You are supposed to be lying down."

She laughed. "No, I'm not. How can I convince you that I'm perfectly all right? Certainly well able to walk."

He brushed her hair back from her face while his thumb dried the tears on her cheek. "I don't want anything to happen to you. I thought I had lost you when Dad said you hitched the horse up to the wagon and drove yourself to their house. Don't ever do anything like that again. When I saw you lying there in the bed, you looked—"

"I know." She smiled. "I'd just had a busy day. I was tired."

His smile looked so tender. So full of love. "Let's get you back inside."

He stood and picked her up as if she weighed nothing. With long strides he carried her to the lantern. "Could I get you to blow that out?"

She did and hung it back on the hook. He carried her out the door and across the yard then through the kitchen door and back to the couch. "Where's the baby?"

"In Beth's bed." She caught his hand when he started to step away. "Please sit beside me."

When he did, she curled up against him, and he put his arm around her. She turned to look up into his face. "Dane, I want you to understand that I really am all right."

He smiled. "I know that you are."

Deborah felt the wonder of his words sweep through her soul. Dane was no longer afraid. She looked deep into his bright blue eyes and saw what she had longed to see for so long. Dane wanted their marriage to be real, too, because he loved her just as she loved him. She moved closer, and he claimed her lips for his own.

When they pulled apart, Deborah took the crumpled scarf from the end of the couch where Dane had tossed it earlier. She held it up and looked at it. "Lenore told me that you loved her. She said you had loved her for years, but you'd had a fight so she married Billy. She said you married Anne to get even with her."

Dane snorted. "And you believed her."

She looked at him and nodded. "Yes, I had no reason not to."

He shook his head. "She lied. I never loved her. Besides, Anne and I were married first."

"I'm sorry. I had forgotten that both you and Billy told me that. Lenore said I should do the right thing and get an annulment so the two of you could get married. Tommy and Beth love her. I knew they would be all right with her, so what else could I do?"

"I love you, Deborah. I think I started to lose my heart right after Brother Donovan pronounced us husband and wife."

"That was the first time you kissed me."

Dane grinned. "Yeah. I didn't expect to enjoy kissing you so much."

Deborah felt heat rise in her face. "I liked it, too."

"Can we start over, Deborah? Will you be my wife for real?"

"That depends." Deborah held up Lenore's scarf. "What are we going to do about this?"

Dane looked across the room at the fireplace. "Let's burn it as a symbol that we will never let anyone come between us again."

"An excellent idea." Deborah scrambled from the sofa. "Let's do that now."

Before Dane caught up to her, a knock sounded on the front door and it opened. Lenore stepped inside followed by Wesley. Dane slipped his arm around Deborah's waist.

She glanced up at him and smiled, then turned to Lenore as Dane asked, "What brings you out tonight?"

Lenore smiled at him, ignoring Deborah. "We wanted to tell you our news. And, of course, make sure Deborah got home all right."

Deborah spread her skirt out to each side and curtsied. "As you can see, I'm quite fine. I appreciate your concern, Lenore, especially since I didn't realize you cared so much." She held the scarf out. "Oh, by the way, I believe you left this here one day while I was gone."

Dane snickered behind her, and Lenore's face turned red as she snatched the scarf. Wesley laughed. "You got a live one this time, big brother."

Dane pulled Deborah back against his side and smiled down at her. "Yeah, and I hope she never changes." He looked at his brother. "Now what's this news you have to tell us?"

"Reckon I'm gonna try my hand at the married life. Lenore's agreed to go out West with me." He draped an arm around Lenore's shoulders.

Deborah was not overly surprised at Wesley's news, but she was pleased. With Lenore married, she wouldn't have to worry about her trying to steal Dane away. She was so thrilled with the idea of Lenore and Wesley getting married that the full import of Wesley's news didn't hit her until Dane asked, "What do you mean by out West? You aren't heading away again, are you?"

Wesley grinned. "Reckon so. There're great opportunities out in the territories. Land free for the taking. Kind of like our grandpas did here thirty years ago."

"In the Indian territories, you mean."

Wesley shrugged. "There's bound to be some Indians around. Uncle Ben and Uncle Lenny live with the Indians and have for years. I reckon I can get along with 'em, too."

"Our uncles are missionaries to the Indians. What's Mom and Dad say about your plans?"

"Haven't told them yet." Wesley grinned. "Hey, we'll stay until after Christmas and break it to them then. Lenore thought you'd want to know."

"I'm glad you told us and I wish you the best with your marriage, but I wish you'd stay around here, Wesley."

"The war changed us all, Dane. You know that. I can't stay here anymore, but I'll do my best to come back from time to time for visits. Lenore will want to see her folks, too." Wesley eased Lenore toward the door. "Reckon we'll head on out. We'll let you know when the wedding is so you can get us a gift. How's that?"

Dane chuckled. "You haven't changed as much as you think, Wesley."

Lenore stopped at the door and turned to face Deborah. "I hope there's no hard feelings."

"None at all." Deborah smiled at Lenore. "Without your help, Lenore, I'm not sure Dane and I would have ever found out how much we love each other."

Lenore looked at Dane, her expression sad. "Yes, I think you would have."

Dane closed the door behind Wesley and Lenore then turned toward Deborah as a tiny cry came from the bedroom. Dane grinned. "Our youngest is calling."

Deborah stared at him and then smiled. "Yes, she is. I'll go get her."

"No, you don't. Sit down and rest. I'll bring her to you."

Deborah sat on the sofa, leaving room for Dane. He came back carrying the small baby who had stopped crying as soon as he picked her up. He dwarfed the tiny baby, yet held her with such tenderness in his expression that tears sprang to Deborah's eyes. She had never known such joy existed.

He sat beside Deborah but did not relinquish the baby. He smiled at her wide-eyed inspection of him. "Hey, little Clara. I didn't know you had such pretty eyes. Just like your mama's."

"Mrs. Newkirk said she would sleep most of the time for the first few weeks until she catches up with herself. She was early, after all."

"Yeah, it can't be easy for her." Dane lifted Clara's tiny hand with one finger that seemed huge by comparison. "I've forgotten how little a newborn is."

Deborah smiled. "She's even smaller than most. According to the women I've talked to, we are blessed that she's alive. Most early babies don't make it."

"What about that last name now?" Dane's grin held a touch of uncertainty. "Clara Elizabeth Stark sounds awfully nice to me."

Deborah leaned her head against his shoulder. She loved him so much. She no longer feared that he would ignore Clara. Something special had happened earlier that night. God had touched Dane in the barn, taking his intense fear away. She'd sensed it when he carried her back inside. Yet she needed to hear the words.

"I think so, too, but before I make it official, I need to know how you feel about a little sister or brother for our three older children."

A ragged sigh left Dane's lungs. "There must have been some prayers going up for me this last year. God met my need, Deborah. I don't guess I'll ever be real comfortable with the idea of childbirth, but more than anything, I'd like for us to have a baby that belongs to both of us."

Clara's face scrunched moments before she let out a tiny wail. Dane handed her to her mother and laughed. "I wasn't asking you, little Miss Stark. I'd rather have your mother's opinion."

Deborah took her baby and slanted a mischievous smile toward Dane. "I think at least two or three more should be about right."

She laughed at his dubious expression then sobered. "But Tommy and Beth already feel like mine."

Dane's gaze shifted to Clara, who was busy making her demands known. He smiled. "Yeah, now I understand that. I think our daughter is hungry. How about you feed her while I fix some supper for us?"

Dane took time to kiss Deborah thoroughly then drop a light kiss on Clara's head before going to the kitchen. While Clara nursed, Deborah watched the love of her life cook—a task she had thought no man would ever do in her presence. But Dane Stark was no ordinary man. She bowed her head for a quick prayer of thanksgiving. God had turned her tears into laughter with a promise of more joy to come.

A Letter to Our Readers

Dear Readers:

In order that we might better contribute to your reading enjoyment, we would appreciate your taking a few minutes to respond to the following questions. When completed, please return to the following: Fiction Editor, Barbour Publishing, Inc., P.O. Box 719, Uhrichsville, OH 44683.

1. Did you enjoy reading *Missouri Brides* by Mildred Colvin?
   ❑ Very much—I would like to see more books like this.
   ❑ Moderately—I would have enjoyed it more if _____

   _____

   _____

2. What influenced your decision to purchase this book?
   (Check those that apply.)
   ❑ Cover   ❑ Back cover copy   ❑ Title   ❑ Price
   ❑ Friends   ❑ Publicity   ❑ Other

3. Which story was your favorite?
   ❑ *Cora*   ❑ *Deborah*
   ❑ *Eliza*

4. Please check your age range:
   ❑ Under 18   ❑ 18–24   ❑ 25–34
   ❑ 35–45   ❑ 46–55   ❑ Over 55

5. How many hours per week do you read? _____

Name _____

Occupation _____

Address _____

City _____ State _____ Zip _____

E-mail _____